PRAISE FOR WORLD OF FIRE

"The story zooms along at a rip-roaring pace,
told in an irreverent tone that perfectly matches
the character of our hero. Planet Alighieri is
rendered in such believable detail that I almost
got a sweat on when Harmer got into trouble on
the surface. Lovegrove has got things off
to a brilliant start here."
– *SF Crow's Nest*

"I read this on holiday and it was perfect for
kicking back, a throwback to the likes of
Dumarest and James Bond. ★★★★"
– *Theaker's Quarterly*

"Lovegrove nails the tone: the technology, the
atmosphere, all of it was vivid and real."
– *Adventures in Sci Fi Publishing*

"Sarcastic and funny, Dev Harmer's the
kind of guy who can keep you reading
about his antics."
– *Fresh Fiction*

"A combination of *Quantum Leap* and
James Bond starring Bruce Campbell; a great
concept, very well executed right out of the gate.
If you like your heroes smarmy, your villains
inscrutable, and your action crunchy, the new
Dev Harmer Missions are for you."
– *Strange Currencies*

WORLD OF WATER

A DEV HARMER MISSION

JAMES LOVEGROVE

First published 2016 by Solaris
an imprint of Rebellion Publishing Ltd,
Riverside House, Osney Mead,
Oxford, OX2 0ES, UK

www.solarisbooks.com

ISBN: 978 1 78108 304 8

10 9 8 7 6 5 4 3 2 1

A CIP catalogue record for this book is available from the
British Library.

Designed & typeset by Rebellion Publishing

Printed in the UK

In the century after it cast off all religion, humankind flourished and prospered, spreading out beyond Earth, beyond the solar system, to colonise far-flung planets.

This expansion, the Diaspora, continued until it reached the territory of the race of artificial intelligence zealots known as Polis+.

There followed a gruelling, decade-long war that ended eventually in an uneasy truce.

In the years since, along the notional Border Wall between the two empires, a body of men and women – the officers of Interstellar Security Solutions and similar companies – have stood guard against enemy sabotage, sedition and subversion.

One of these agents is Dev Harmer...

1

111101010100010101011010100101000101010101101
010100011111101010001101010101010101111100110
1 troublemaker like you won't amount to anything in this
world, Harmer 10101010101001010101010010101010
000101 1010101010110101010101001010101101100 10
1010111110101001100110111100010101011110110101
0110001111110001

01 make yourself available for military service 010010
1001011110100101101010100001101011110   Ninth
Extrasolar Engineers 10101110000101010101111101
111000101010110111101011111010111101100111111
Leather Hill veteran 110010101010001010101001001010
0100100110101100001010100000000010 extreme courage
under fire 1011010010101111101010001010 Interstellar
Security Solutions 010010101010011110000111111010101
01 the war against the digimentalists is not over 1110000
100101111100001111110111100101 data 'porting into
genetically modified host forms 10110110111000110111
11100101010001101010111110010 11 Alighieri 0110111
11111010010100100101010001100 take the bait 11101110
100010100000111000111101010101110000000000111

010001010 Trundle? Where's that – ? 101010010111110 01010010110101010101011111110011011 a little closer to your thousand 11110010111101001011010101010100101 00111111111010001111100001100000001100 good things 01011001 good things 01101 good things 01

Dev awoke to patterns of rippling, multifaceted light. Sunshine bouncing off water, broken into a million pieces.

His first thoughts were of a slightly awkward but tender farewell with Astrid Kahlo at the ISS outpost before he clamped the transcription matrix over his head and set it for automatic upload.

The dazzle of the reflected light made him wince, but suggested he no longer had enhanced Aligherian night vision.

He sat up on the mediplinth, feeling awful as usual after a data 'port. No, he decided. More than usually awful. It wasn't so much like a hangover this time, more like a persistent migraine.

Facing him was a slim, prim-looking man with an oddly distended neck. His epidermis had a slickness to it, as though he was encased in resin. Webbing stretched between his fingers.

Dev's own fingers, too.

The man blinked, white nictitating membranes shuttering across his eyes.

"Mr Harmer?" he said. "Welcome to Robinson D in the Ophiuchus constellation, also known as Triton. I'm your liaison, Xavier Handler. Do you want the good news or the bad news?"

"Good news first," croaked Dev. "Always start with good news."

"The good news is the installation has been entirely successful," said Handler. "No transcription errors occurred during download. Brain imprint and host form are fully integrated."

"So what's the bad news?"

A flap flared on either side of Handler's neck, exposing an underside of raw red flesh.

Gills.

It was an embarrassed gesture. Like a sharp intake of breath.

"The bad news is: the host form itself has been compromised."

"I'm sorry, what? Compromised?"

"Yes." Webbed fingers fluttered. "A problem with the growth vat. Something went wrong during the assembly process. Something small but crucial. I'm afraid it means your host form has sustainability issues."

"Cut the crap. Sustainability issues? What is that jargon-speak for?"

Xavier Handler shifted his feet. "Your host form is breaking down at a cellular level. It's already begun. At best guess, you have seventy-two hours. Seventy-two hours before your body becomes irredeemably damaged and no longer functional."

"Three days..." said Dev.

"Three days," Handler confirmed with a brief, despairing nod. "And there's so much for you to do. So very much..."

2

DEV DRESSED UNSTEADILY in a booth. The clothes – tunic and leggings – were form-fitting, made from a fabric with a glossy texture and an iridescent gleam. The lining was soft and porous.

There was a mirror. With the usual trepidation, Dev studied his face.

His new face.

It was not dissimilar to Xavier Handler's. High cheekbones, narrow jaw, pronounced lips. That waxy skin, which Handler had told him was less permeable than Terratypical skin and provided insulation against cold.

He tugged at the corner of one eyelid to expose a sliver of the membrane beneath. He tried to close the under-lids but they did not seem to respond to conscious command. It must work autonomically, responding to reflex rather than demand.

Next he examined the gills. Triple grooves, scored into either side of his neck. He probed one with a tentative finger, gingerly, as you might a wound.

His fingertip slid inside the flap. It was painless but odd, a bit creepy, a more intimate action than sticking a finger in your ear, say, or your mouth. The gill was a tight, fleshy, *personal* orifice.

He tried to flare the gills as Handler had done. Again, he couldn't seem to do it. No matter how he tensed the musculature of his neck, they remained stubbornly shut.

This form was going to take more getting used to than most. Dev recalled telling the xeno-entomologist Trundell on Alighieri that he had yet to experience amphibiousness, but it was surely only a matter of time.

Looked as if the moment had finally come.

A knock at the door. "Mr Harmer? You decent?"

"Never." As always, the voice issuing from Dev's throat was unfamiliar: higher-pitched than any he'd had before, something of an oboe in its tone.

He exited the booth.

"Fabric coated with hydrophobic nano particles, right?" he said. "With a unidirectional absorbent lining to wick out stray moisture."

"What the well-dressed ISS operative is wearing this season," said Handler. "A drysuit that doubles as fashionable daywear."

"It really rides up under the crotch."

"It'll loosen up with use."

"Ugh." A sudden wave of nauseating pain, worse than the normal post-installation hangover. Much worse. Dev clutched his head. "Got anything I can take for this? Feels like my skull's full of lava."

Handler fetched a sachet of edible analgesic gel, which Dev squirted gratefully down his throat. Relief was almost instantaneous.

"I'm used to a bit of grogginess and discomfort when I 'port in," he said. "Goes with the territory. But this is something else."

"I'm afraid it's going to keep hurting," the ISS liaison said, "and it's not going to get any better. As the cellular breakdown continues, it'll accelerate and become exponential. A snowball effect."

"Joy."

"Pain management is relatively easy, and I think I can also do something to retard the deterioration. Regular shots of stabilising nucleotides should hold the damage at bay."

"Giving me longer than three days?"

"Unfortunately not. My estimate factored that in. Without the nucleotide shots, you'd be looking at more like two to three hours. A very messy two to three hours, at that."

"So three days is a best-case scenario."

"I'd say so."

"Dose me up, then."

Handler produced a microneedle-array patch with a sac containing 20 millilitres of a clear serum and applied it to Dev's arm. A painless procedure – nanites bonded to the serum molecules, then perfused the liquid down through his skin into his bloodstream.

"Any idea how this happened?" Dev asked.

Handler's shrug was apologetic. "Best guess? The hybridisation of two types of DNA isn't an easy trick to pull off. Especially when we're talking about genes from vastly differing species."

"So I'm half human, half... fish?"

"Not quite. Triton has an indigenous, non-terrestrial population. Like me, you're mostly human but with chromosomal attributes drawn from the native Tritonians."

"Great. So I'm part alien."

"If that's how you choose to regard it. Before I submitted to alteration myself, I was told there was a chance the procedure might not 'take.' The odds were fifty-fifty. In my case it worked."

"But in my case, it failed. I didn't develop properly in the growth vat."

"So the vat readout told me. You sound remarkably sanguine about it."

"Hey, it's Interstellar Security Solutions. Shit goes wrong all the time. I'm kind of used to it. Resigned, at any rate."

Handler laughed. "It's a huge corporation. Huge corporations aren't known for the loving treatment of their employees."

"Yeah, it's almost as if they don't care about us."

Dev's headache had almost entirely receded. He felt human again. Or rather, to be accurate, human and the other species that was mixed into his host form's genome.

"Okay," he said. "Let's get down to business. Robinson D, Triton, whatever it's called. Where's that again?"

"Ophiuchus constellation, as seen from Earth."

"I know. You said. Care to be a little more specific?"

"Well, it's right on the edge of the Border Wall. In fact…"

Handler held up a hand, fingers rigid and pointing straight ahead, to represent a wall.

"On this side," he said, canting his head to the left, "Diasporan territory. On *this* side" – he bent to the right – "Polis Plus territory. Triton sits here."

He lodged the forefinger of his other hand a fraction to the right of the hand he was holding out.

Dev let out a low whistle. "We're over the wall?"

"Debatable. TerCon doesn't think so."

"I bet Polis Plus disagrees."

"It's on their back fence, that's for sure. Maybe even in their back yard."

"And it's an ocean planet, yeah?"

"Originally an ice giant with a negligible atmosphere, until a slight shift in axial rotation – probably a reversal of the magnetic poles – triggered a warming, melting the ice. Now it's water all over, hundreds of kilometres deep in places, and the atmosphere's breathable."

"I know how ocean planets are formed. Well, I do *now*. What kind of Diasporan presence is there?"

"Not significant. Forty thousand colonists, give or take. Also a couple of military bases."

"Which the Plussers are no doubt delighted about. Oh, I'm going to have fun here."

"It's started well, hasn't it?" said Handler wryly.

Dev had the feeling that this was someone he could bear to work with.

It was an opinion he would consider revising five minutes later, as they stood outdoors and Handler prepared to give him a crash course in amphibianism.

3

"THERE'S ONLY ONE way to learn how to breathe underwater," Handler told Dev. "The hard way."

"And how does that go?"

"I drag you under and you figure out how not to drown."

They were on a platform jutting out from the dome-shaped floating habitat. Waves lapped and slapped at the platform's edge. Rolling, sun-brilliant sea stretched all the way to the horizon.

The habitat was one of a cluster of domes, all bobbing sedately on pontoons. The smallest of them, on the outskirts, were single-family dwellings. The nearer you got to the heart of the settlement, the larger the domes. The main central dome was a communal zone some 300 metres in radius, its surface a lattice of clear geodesic plates.

Footbridges linked the domes, constructed from hinged platforms that flexed with the rise and fall of the ocean swell. A couple of residents were walking across one now, negotiating motion with practised finesse.

Areas between the domes were filled with maricultural units – fish ranches, algae farms, phytoplankton cultivators. There was also a desalination plant, a tidal power barrage, and a marina where a variety of seagoing vessels were moored.

It was called Tangaroa, according to Handler. A mid-sized, modular-built township, one of several dozen Diasporan settlements distributed across Triton. Tangaroa was the Maori god of the oceans; Triton, a son of Poseidon in the Ancient Greek myths. Deity-derived place names were common all across the planet – something that was exceptionally rare in the Post-Enlightenment era. The first settlers of Robinson D had had an ironic and truculent sense of humour. They had known what a backwoods, boondocks world they were colonising, and had chosen their lexicon accordingly.

"So I can't just dunk my head in the water and it'll happen naturally?" Dev said.

"It might," Handler replied, "but probably won't. This is how my predecessor taught me. Sink or swim. Are you ready?"

"No."

"Neither was I."

Handler gave Dev a hefty shove between the shoulderblades, and Dev flew headlong off the platform, hitting the water with a spectacular bellyflop. He surfaced, spluttering, just as Handler executed an arrowing swan dive, entering the sea beside him with barely a splash.

Handler vanished beneath the waves. Dev, treading water, peered but couldn't see him anymore.

A minute passed. Two.

Dev waited, braced for Handler's reappearance. *Sink or swim.* Any moment, he expected to feel the ISS liaison's hands fastening on his ankles, tugging him down. He took deep breaths in anticipation. He knew that he shouldn't have to, but he wasn't going to leave anything to chance.

There had been a problem with the host form's assembly, after all. Those sustainability issues. What if the gills failed to function?

Handler burst up from the water right behind him, breaking at such speed that he almost completely cleared the waves.

As he fell back, he brought his hands down on Dev's shoulders and plunged him under, amid a welter of bubbles.

Far under.

Metre after metre, Dev went down, Handler pushing him mercilessly.

Dev resisted. Couldn't help it. He thrashed with arms and legs, struggling towards the surface.

But Handler had all the advantages. He was above him, pushing down with powerful frog kicks. He was in his element; Dev was not.

The rippling sunlight patterns above rapidly receded. The further away it got, the more desirable it seemed to Dev – and the more unattainable.

Panic set in. He fought it, but failed.

Ten metres down. Fifteen.

He needed to breathe. He needed to be free.

He punched at Handler's wrists, but the ISS liaison's grip was firm, inexorable.

The water darkened. The daylight dimmed.

Dev was convinced he was about to drown.

4

THEN SOMETHING INSIDE him clicked. Some insight. Some instinct. As though a door was opening in his mind.

Relax, it seemed to say. *Go with it. It's all right.*

These weren't the feelings of a dying man accepting his fate. Dev inhaled.

It went against common sense, against everything the human part of his host form knew was safe behaviour.

He sucked in seawater. A great, cold, brackish draught of it rushed down his throat...

...and out through his neck.

A surge of respite as oxygen suffused his bloodstream. A sensation of rightness, of wellbeing.

His panic subsided. He drew a second liquid breath. There was a knot in his trachea. He could feel it. Some sort of valve or sphincter which clenched automatically, preventing the water from flooding his lungs.

A third breath, and he was almost no longer aware how unnatural it was to be gulping in water and pumping it out through gills.

Handler, sensing that Dev was calming down and had got the hang of aquatic respiration, let go of him.

Dev floated freely amid slanting beams of amber sunlight. He looked up at the underside of Tangaroa. Silhouetted against the sky, it resembled a schematic of a solar system, worlds of assorted sizes orbiting a sun. Massive anchor columns descended from several of the domes' bases, stabilising the town like a yacht's keel. Directional vents in the columns drove water through the waves to counteract the ocean currents and keep the township from drifting out of position.

His vision was sharp. He touched his eyes, to discover that the membranes had snapped into position. Although they'd looked milky in the mirror, they gave him perfect sight in the water.

He began experimenting with swimming. Normally he would have to battle to keep from rising, but his host form had no problem maintaining depth.

Some kind of swim bladder, he assumed. A gas-filled sac which expanded or contracted according to the ambient pressure, standard in most fish.

His feet were webbed as well as his hands. Even the gentlest of kicks thrust him along faster than he would have expected. Hard kicks, coupled with arm-strokes, propelled him through the water like a torpedo.

Somersault. Barrel roll. Pirouette. He was immensely agile in three dimensions.

Dev the fish-man. Freaky, but he liked it. The bonuses outweighed the essential weirdness.

Handler swam up beside him. Dev accessed the host form's commplant in order to talk to him.

Offline. No signal.

He tried again but got the same error message.

The commplant didn't work underwater. It couldn't get through to any of Triton's telecommunications satellites or insites.

So instead Dev shot Handler a big cheesy grin and gave him a thumbs-up.

In response, a pulse of light rippled across Handler's face, starting at the jawline and ending at the hairline. It was blue-green in colour, with hints of yellow at the edges.

Bioluminescent display.

Wonders would never cease.

What surprised Dev most, however, was that he understood what it signified. It wasn't simply a show of light; it had meaning.

It was saying: See? Nothing to worry about.

Dev nodded, then looked quizzically at Handler and gestured to his own face. The implication was obvious. *Can I do that too?*

Colour swirled across Handler's brow, more blue than green this time, stippled patterns interleaving.

Of course you can, the ISS liaison was saying.

Dev made an exaggerated shrug. *How?*

Don't think, just feel, was Handler's bioluminescent reply.

Dev frowned. It seemed easier said than done.

There. Handler pointed to Dev's face.

Dev had been conscious of a slight tingle accompanying the frown, a sensation akin to blushing.

Result, Handler said.

Success made Dev exultant, and his face tingled again, more intensely now. He saw the glow of his own bioluminescence reflected in Handler's eyes. It had a pinkish tinge.

The lights were as much an expression of an inner state as a method of communication. Tap into whatever you were feeling and it would show on your face. Combine feelings and you could generate concepts, phrases, sentences, the subtleties of which were fleshed out by their context.

It was a foreign language, but the easiest foreign language to learn, ever. You could translate it without effort, because the vocabulary was universal: emotions.

Dev conveyed to Handler that he was pleased to have mastered his host form's planet-specific adaptations, but now he was eager to head back to the surface and get on with his mission, whatever it might be.

Handler's answer was an incongruous flare of bright red with purple streaks.

Alarm. Fear. Horror.

The ISS liaison gesticulated.

Something behind Dev.

Dev spun round.

A dark shape was moving through the water, ascending from below. With purpose.

It was large, with a streamlined profile. A creature built for speed. For attack.

An apex predator.

And it was heading straight at them.

5

DEV FELT THE buffeting turbulence of frantic activity at his back. Handler, beating a hasty retreat.

He followed suit, hardly needing to think about it. If Handler was scramming, so should he.

They thrashed towards Tangaroa. Handler was the more adept swimmer, by far the quicker. He scooped his way through the water as though boring a tunnel for himself. Dev was lagging behind.

He darted a glance over his shoulder. The predator was still in pursuit.

He made out a tapered head, questing back and forth. Twin ridges of erect dorsal plates. Crocodile-like limbs. A mighty, sinuous tail.

The beast seemed ancient, a reptilian thing from some long-gone geological epoch. Unchanged by evolution because it was fit for purpose already and could not be bettered. Perfectly suited for the catching and killing of prey.

Teeth glinted like rows of ivory daggers.

And it was even bigger than it had first appeared. Seven metres from end to end, he estimated. Its head alone was two metres long.

Tangaroa still seemed far away, too far to reach in time, an impossible goal. The creature was gaining on Dev. He could feel it displacing water as it hurtled towards him.

Redoubling his efforts to escape was the only option.

Or was it?

However hard he swam, the creature would still overhaul him. It was inevitable.

What he could do was turn and meet it head-on. He doubted it would be expecting *that*. How many of its victims actually charged *at* it rather than away? None. None would be so insane.

Dev flipped around and made a beeline for the oncoming sea beast.

This was suicide. He didn't even have any weapons on him.

But he would be dead for sure if he continued trying to flee. This way he stood a chance, if a slim one. At the very least he might be able to inflict some pain on the creature before he became its dinner. Hardly a victory, but it was perhaps the most he could hope for.

They barrelled towards each other, Dev and the monster, like knights in a joust. A maw gaped. It looked big enough to swallow a person whole.

The creature was probably thinking it had never been presented with such an easy meal. Its prey was volunteering to be eaten, practically swimming down its gullet.

At the very last instant, Dev diverted. He jinked sideways and the reptilian monster shot past. Darting out a hand, Dev managed to latch onto one of its dorsal plates.

All at once he was being dragged along, at startling speed. He clung on for dear life. The dorsal plate was as thick as a roof tile, with a finely serrated edge that cut into his palm. He ignored the pain, refused to let go.

The creature could not figure out where its prey had gone. It was lethal but not terribly smart. What need did you have for quick wits when you were so huge and powerful?

It careered on, oblivious to the fact that it had picked up a passenger. The other swimming human was ahead, so the creature wasn't too bothered that the first had somehow disappeared. Plenty more fish in the sea, as it were.

Handler was by now close to Tangaroa. Thirty more metres, just a few strokes, and he would gain safety.

But the predator was swiftly narrowing the gap. Dev estimated it would catch up with seconds to spare. Handler wasn't going to make it.

Not unless Dev did something to waylay the creature.

Something even more rash and foolish than playing chicken with it.

He let go of the dorsal plate and watched the bulk of the creature rush by below him until he was level with its tail. Then he grabbed hold again, with both hands this time, right at the tail's very tip.

The creature might not have noticed a hitchhiker riding on its back, but it couldn't fail to miss one dangling off the end of its tail.

Especially if that hitchhiker began to work against the tail's lashing motion, using himself as a counterweight. When the tail swung one way, Dev hurled himself the other.

The sea beast soon realised its propulsion was being inhibited. It twisted round to see what the problem was. A baleful eye the size of a bowling ball fixed on Dev. Dragon fangs were bared.

The creature lunged for him, but once more its limited intelligence worked against it and in Dev's favour. Its head couldn't quite reach the end of its tail. It began to go in circles, chasing after the prey that was attached to it but tantalisingly untouchable. Its mouth snapped repeatedly at Dev but missed each time, sometimes by only a few centimetres.

Round and round they went, at a dizzying rate, like a living centrifuge. As long as Dev kept his grip, the creature would not get him.

The trouble was, he could not hold on forever. And he was starting to feel sick. He was trapped on the worst carousel imaginable, and the moment he got off, he would be dead meat.

Oh, for a gun. A knife. A nano-frag mine, why not? Since he was wishing for the impossible...

He glimpsed two shapes looming from the depths. He couldn't be sure he had seen them at all, whirling helplessly as he was. Might have been some trick of the eye.

No, they were there. Closer now.

More of the creatures? Allies of this one? Family? Coming to see what the commotion was about?

They would have no trouble snatching Dev off the creature's tail. The only question was which of them would get there first and win the privilege of consuming him. Maybe they'd share him. Grab a leg each. Split him like a wishbone.

Mission fucked before it had even started. Ten minutes from host form installation to termination. Must be some kind of ISS record.

On the next pass, Dev got his first clear view of the new arrivals.

They weren't the same creatures after all. They were something else.

Humanoid. Scaly. Finned.

Tritonians.

Both of them were carrying what looked like weapons.

Both of them were zeroing in on Dev and the creature with grim, deadly intent.

6

ONE OF THE Tritonians seized Dev's wrists and plucked his hands off the creature's tail with almost indecent ease. Dev was swept away from the monster, which immediately lunged after him in a rapacious fury.

The other Tritonian swam in above the creature, matching its course and speed. It raised a weapon – a kind of spear with a knobbly, striated texture, reminding Dev of a narwhal tusk.

The spear slammed down, piercing the creature in the back of the neck, just behind the head. The blow was a perfectly judged, aimed at what must be a weak point, a chink in the armour.

The creature spasmed, its legs splaying out in all directions and its maw going slack.

The Tritonian withdrew the spear and shimmied out of range as the creature went into paroxysms. Death throes. It coiled and whipped, while blood billowed from the wound, enveloping it in a dark cloud.

The Tritonian who had wrenched Dev free now let go of him. Dev paddled a couple of metres away, then turned to face his rescuer.

The indigene was taller than him by a couple of handspans, and slender, with delicate, elongated proportions. There were no obvious sexual characteristics, but the narrow shoulders and pointed chin told him this was a female. Some instinct, a gut feeling from the Tritonian half of him.

She wore a tunic like a one-piece swimsuit made from a sort of leathery hide stitched together with cord and held in place by shell clasps. The scales that covered her skin were small, fine and pale pink, with a silvery sheen. Thin, wafting fins of the same colour ran down from the nape of her neck to the top of her spine and along the backs of her limbs.

At her breastbone was a raised design etched in her skin, a cutaway of a nautilus shell showing its logarithmic spiral and the chambers within. The keloid scarring was precise but pronounced. The detail of the design was exquisite. The pain it must have caused in the carving would have been exquisite too.

The weapon she bore was not a spear like the other's. It looked more sophisticated, like a cross between a lance and a rifle, manufactured from a blend of organic materials. Coral for the handle and firing mechanism, something rigid yet pulpy for the rest.

She brandished it at Dev defensively, its tip level with his belly. Dev floated inert, wary, careful not to make any sudden movements. She seemed angry and he had no wish to antagonise her.

The other Tritonian swam over to join her. He was clad similarly but broader-shouldered, thicker-jawed – male. Slung over his shoulder was a sack made from strands of some sort of seaweed, plaited into a web. It held several dead fish.

Together, side by side, the pair of them surveyed Dev. Their eyes were round, black, lidless and inscrutable.

Dev did his best to thank them for saving him from the creature. After his brush with death his thoughts were in turmoil, his heart racing, but he tuned in to the gratitude he was feeling beneath it all. The emotion was sincere and he embraced it.

His face tingled, his cheeks especially. He wondered what colours were dancing across his skin. He hoped they meant what he thought they meant.

The Tritonians remained blank-faced, their eerie dark stares unwavering. It occurred to Dev that he had made an error of judgement. They might not communicate using bioluminescence. That or he had expressed himself incorrectly. Could be he had even insulted them by mistake. *Your mother's a walrus*, something like that.

He resorted to dumb show, pointing downward to indicate the slain beast, then to himself, and finally patting his chest as though in relief and heartfelt appreciation.

Still no response from the Tritonians, and Dev felt like a prize chump.

They continued to face one another, Dev and the two indigenes, for another half-minute or so.

Then the Tritonians turned and slowly, solemnly, swam away. Dev watched them go until they became indistinct blurs, lost in the marine murk.

It was, he realised, his second ever encounter with a sentient alien species. At least, unlike every Plusser he had met, these two hadn't been trying to kill him. Standoffish they might have been, but compared with Polis+ they were downright friendly.

7

"I'M SORRY, I'm sorry, I'm sorry."

This from Handler as he helped Dev out of the water and back onto the platform of the ISS outpost at Tangaroa.

"A thalassoraptor," he went on. "Only the most dangerous animal on the entire planet."

"You don't say."

"Yes. The theory is it was one of the dominant land species back when Triton was a big ball of ice. It managed to adapt as the ice thawed over millennia, and became a sea dweller."

"Fascinating."

"Thalassoraptors rarely come this near the surface. Their usual haunt is the mesopelagic zone, about a thousand metres down. We were incredibly unlucky to bump into one."

"We both survived the experience, that's the main thing." Dev slumped on the platform, glad to feel the warmth of the sun on his face and a solid structure beneath him. Glad also to revert to breathing the traditional way.

"By the skin of our teeth," said Handler. "Last I saw of you, you were right behind me. When you didn't emerge, I had no idea what had happened. I was terrified the thalassoraptor had got you."

"It was a close-run thing."

"I should have thought to take a repellent with us. A sonar pulser, an electric prod, something. Just in case. I'm so stupid."

"Stop beating yourself up over it. We're alive, aren't we? And intact."

"How did you get away from the thing? How on earth did you manage that?"

"I'd like to claim I scared it off with my aura of sheer hard-bastard-ness," said Dev, "but in fact I had help."

He explained about catching the thalassoraptor by the tail and about the Tritonians.

"That was a stroke of good fortune," Handler said. "They must have been a hunting party. Doubtless there's a drift cluster – one of their nomadic communities – within a few kilometres of here."

"They were tooled up, that's for sure. And the one who killed the thalassoraptor looked like he knew exactly what he was doing."

"They're a hardy, indomitable bunch, the Tritonians. They live every day surrounded by a thousand different marine species that would like to bite them or sting them or maul them to death, and they're tough enough to cope. You mess with them at your peril."

"I got that impression," Dev said.

"They don't like humans much, either. I wouldn't have been surprised if they'd killed you as well."

"I got that impression too. Seemed like they were trying to make up their minds about me and finally decided to let me off with a caution. I gave them the old flasheroo." Dev waved a hand over his face. "But no dice."

"It should have worked. That's why I have that capability."

"Yeah, I thought it was worth a shot. You're some kind of diplomatic envoy, right? In addition to being an ISS liaison."

Handler nodded. "That's my main role here. I'm a go-between, employed to keep Diasporan–Tritonian relations amicable. ISS have me on retainer, but that's a sideline. Most of the time I'm doing what I can to resolve disputes and convince everyone to play nice. Hence the amphibian adaptations and the subcutaneous photophores."

"Photophores?"

"Light-emitting cells. Tritonians have them, of course. If the two you met didn't answer back when you 'spoke' to them, it's most likely because they didn't want to."

"I was getting the cold shoulder. The silent treatment."

"Just so. It would be fair to say that the Tritonians have no great fondness for us."

"Colonists land from outer space and occupy your world without your consent – what's not to love?"

"Well, quite. The issues are pretty complex, actually, but there's always been a general resentment from them towards us, right from the start, and it's getting worse."

"But those two saved me all the same. They could have just left me to become thalassoraptor chow."

"Maybe you found a couple of compassionate ones," said Handler. "How are you doing, anyway?"

Dev sat up. His clothes were already bone-dry. His headache, however, was returning.

"I could do with some grub," he said, "and maybe some more painkillers. Otherwise, I'm fit as a fiddle and raring to go."

"Good," said Handler. "We're on the clock, remember?"

"As if I could forget."

"And we've some travelling ahead of us. Places to go, people to meet."

"More Tritonians?"

"No. Humans."

"That's a relief. Simpler to deal with."

"Not these ones."

8

THE *RECKLESS ABANDON* skimmed across the wavetops at 150 knots.

Driven by twin thousand-horsepower super-charged turbine impellers, the jetboat went so fast and ploughed such a furrow in the water that the froth didn't begin to subside until it was over the horizon. To Dev, standing at the aft rail looking back, the boat's wake was a permanent, indelible white scar.

Handler was stationed up on the flybridge, keeping an eye on the autopilot. The *Reckless Abandon* was more or less sailing itself, but he was clearly the sort of person who liked to stay busy and be useful, or at least to make a show of it.

The journey from Tangaroa to Station Ares, the principal Diasporan military base on Triton, was scheduled to take five hours. Dev whiled some of that time trawling local insites and the ISS central office hub for facts about the planet.

Triton, it turned out, was one of the less-well-documented places in the known universe, if not the least. There was infinitely more information available about Neptune's largest moon – also Triton – than there was about the planet. It was eclipsed in significance by its uninhabitable, uncolonised namesake.

Even its strategic value was downplayed, as though the presence here of Diasporan settlers and troops was a dirty secret, something no one really wanted to mention. Dev found a couple of blogs by radical peace activists campaigning for all humans to be withdrawn from Triton and relocated elsewhere, so as not to tweak the Plussers' noses. Conversely, there were online interviews with hawkish politicians who demanded that the colonisation of the planet be stepped up, so as to keep the Plussers on their toes.

Aside from these fairly niche opinions, no one had much to say about it. Triton was in every sense a backwater. Gulf cruisers docked here almost never. The settlers were self-sufficient and left pretty much to their own devices.

Having done as much astropolitical homework as he was able to, Dev resorted to researching fauna. Triton's boundless, all-covering ocean hosted an abundance of life, but only a tiny fraction of it could be seen from the deck of a boat. There were gigantic cinnamon-coloured cetaceans that rolled through the depths, breaching the surface just once an hour to breathe. There was the indigo bubble, a type of jellyfish that gathered in such vast numbers during their spawning periods that they formed temporary islands with circumferences of anything up to eight kilometres. There were tentacled squid-like things the size of tree trunks which jetted along just beneath the waves, raiding the sunlight zone for small fry – easy pickings – before returning with their bellies full to the abysses that were their home. Dev peered for them all, but in vain. Not even a glimpse.

This was not least because the *Reckless Abandon* made course corrections whenever its sonar picked up larger examples of the creatures, so as to avoid a collision. The jetboat itself was not small – some thirty metres from stem to stern, with a full load displacement of fifty tonnes – but the cetaceans, for instance, dwarfed it. An adult male of the species, which had been dubbed the redback whale, was half as long again as the boat and twice as heavy, and could be very aggressive towards anything he perceived as a competitor trying to horn in on his harem of females. In a contest, the *Reckless Abandon* would definitely come off worse.

Soon the sun – Beta Ophiuchi, to give it its proper designation – had begun to set. Two moons glimmered into view overhead as it sank. One was perfectly round, but the other had had a jagged-edged gouge eaten out of it and bore a halo of debris, evidence of some primordial cosmic impact.

According to one local insite, the two moons could play havoc with Triton's tides and weather:

> Sometimes, when they're in close conjunction, their gravity differential fields conspire together and you can get a tidal range of up to ten metres. This is almost invariably accompanied by atmospheric disruption leading to powerful climate events. On the occasions when all three bodies are aligned, Triton and both moons, the phenomenon of the "syzygy storm" is not uncommon. That's like a Terran hurricane, but magnified by a factor of ten. When one of those sets in you really have to batten down the hatches!

Dev doubted he would be here long enough to have to worry about any so-called syzygy storm. In just under seventy hours, succeed or fail, he would be zipping through ultraspace to his next host form, since the current one would have broken down catastrophically and be dissolving back into the protoplasmic goo it was conjured out of.

His mission.

Earlier, just after they had put out to sea from Tangaroa,

Handler had given Dev a mission briefing, sketching out the details.

In certain regions of the planet, the Tritonians were in open revolt. There had been clashes between them and settlers, and some bloodshed.

At first it had been sporadic, random skirmishes, one here, another there. Sabotage, mostly. A boat hull holed while it was in dock. A fish ranch fence broken. A desalination plant vandalised. A trawler's net split open at the bottom so that its catch spilled out. Regrettable but understandable, the sort of friction that tended to occur when two very different cultures butted up against each other. The settlers had adopted the sensible tactic of turning a blind eye and waiting for the Tritonians to get bored and give up.

But the attacks had increased in frequency and ferocity. There had been abductions, and the drowned bodies of the abductees had turned up shortly afterwards, sometimes gruesomely mutilated. A xeno-ichthyologist had vanished while out on a solo specimen-gathering expedition, never to be seen again. The pontoons on a private habitat had been destroyed, causing the whole unit to sink, with the loss of a dozen lives, an entire extended family.

It was a pattern of escalation and mounting aggression, with the settlers responding in kind. Someone had dropped a homemade depth charge on a Tritonian drift cluster. A posse of scuba-diving humans armed with spearguns had ambushed an indigene hunting party, killing two and badly injuring three others. And those were just the incidents that were public knowledge. There were surely countless others that had never got reported.

You didn't need to be a genius to foresee where all this was headed. The mutual hostility would keep on growing, the violence spiralling, until settler and Tritonian were engaged in full-scale, widespread war.

Was Polis+ responsible for the unrest? Was there a Plusser agitator working behind the scenes, stoking the fires of grievance among the Tritonians, prompting this previously passive race to rise up and fight? Was it all a cunning plot to oust the Diaspora from a world which was too close to their territory for comfort?

Handler didn't know, and neither did Dev. Someone in TerCon must think so, though, since ISS had been contracted to send in an operative.

Dev and Handler's primary goal was securing a military escort from Station Ares. Then they would need firepower, Handler insisted, and reinforcements. Because they were headed right into the thick of the unrest.

Dev reflected on the nature of the task ahead. It was the usual mishmash of nebulous intel and impending disaster. He wondered if this was how ISS treated all its operatives, bunging them out into the field to fumble their way to a solution, or if it was a policy they reserved specially for him.

Probably not. He was nothing special. He had been selected for this particular mission since he was available and in closest proximity, that was all. Luck of the draw. The short straw.

But then every straw was short when you were an indentured employee of Interstellar Security Solutions.

Dev was working for the company because he had no choice. Technically he did not exist. He had no body to call his own. He was an itinerant consciousness, a being of pure data that ISS could transmit wherever they liked, wherever they decreed he should go.

His true body had been all but destroyed on the battlefield during the Frontier War. ISS had promised to build him another one, good as new. The condition was that he would first serve as one of their agents. An entire human body, grown from scratch, was not cheap. He could never normally have afforded one; only the fabulously wealthy could. ISS had offered him the option of earning one.

All he had to do was hit his quota of a thousand points.

It was a system of payment by instalments, a scheme based on notional credits which ISS could dole out or take away as they saw fit. Dev was awarded points according to the outcome of his missions. The more resounding the success, the greater the number of points he would receive. Failures and excessive collateral damage incurred deductions.

Once he hit the magic one thousand mark, his debt to ISS would be discharged. A pristine new body, an exact copy of the original Dev Harmer, would be his. Dev would be free to be himself again – literally.

Until then, he was just so much space flotsam, fetching up in trouble spots and flashpoints, fighting fires before they could burn out of control.

Beta Ophiuchi was making its last gasp, melting into the horizon. It was an aged star, past the hydrogen fusion phase of its life, now burning helium to carbon at its core. The name the ancient Arabic astronomers had given it was Cebalrai, meaning 'sheepdog.' Dev imagined a tired old hound, worn out from years of hard labour, lapsing into a rickety, arthritic senescence.

He could empathise.

Onward the *Reckless Abandon* went, beating a path through unending sea. Though it was a well-designed vessel, with a plethora of active stabilisation technologies such as gyroscopically-controlled hull fins and self-regulating smartfluid internal anti-roll ballast tanks, the continual sine wave motion of its passage took its toll on Dev. His host form, it seemed, was a swimmer but no sailor; good *under* the water but not *on* it. The perpetual nagging headache didn't help, nor the buzz in his ears that now accompanied it.

He went below decks, slapped on a seasickness patch from the first aid cabinet, and found a cabin to lie down in. He drifted halfway between sleep and wakefulness until a commplant call from Handler roused him.

We're approaching Station Ares. Ten klicks out.

Be right there.

"I've messaged ahead," Handler said as Dev scaled the ladder to the flybridge. "They should be expecting us."

It was fully dark now. The sonar scope indicated a sizeable bulk, due west. It was getting nearer, but Dev could see nothing through the windscreen except tar-black ocean and a myriad of constellations.

"Haven't they heard of lights?" he said.

"Station Ares is a low-profile structure. No part of it rises more than four metres above sea level. You won't be able to see it with the naked eye until we're virtually on top of it."

There was a sudden, low *whump*, like a huge, distant door slamming.

"What was that?" Handler said.

Dev knew. He recognised, all too well, the sound of an artillery shell being fired.

"Get down!" he cried, and when Handler, startled, didn't budge, he grabbed him in a bearhug and fell with him to the deck.

The air shrieked.

The sea exploded.

9

THE DETONATION OF the shell, just a few metres off the bow, sent a spray of water over the entire boat. The *Reckless Abandon* rocked and wallowed crazily.

Dev, his ears ringing, reached up to the control console and groped for the button to disengage the autopilot, then hauled back on the throttle. The boat slowed.

"What are you doing?" Handler demanded. "We'll be dead in the water. A sitting duck."

"And if we keep going, they'll take us for hostiles and hit us."

"They're already trying to hit us."

"No, they're not. If they'd wanted us sunk, we'd be sinking already. That was a warning shot."

"So we're not going to take evasive action?"

"No. You're going to boot up your commplant and tell whoever's in charge here that we're ISS and we come in peace."

The fog of panic on Handler's face cleared. Unlike Dev, he had never come under fire before. It was a new and terrifying experience for him. Dev's words cut through the fear.

"Yes. All right. Of course."

His eyes lost focus as he accessed his commplant. Dev,

meanwhile, scanned ahead, looking out for the telltale flash of a shell exiting a barrel. He hoped he was right about the warning shot. If not, then by now the artillery piece's targeting guidance system would have a solid fix on the boat. The first shell might have been a near-miss. The next would be a dead cert.

"Through yet?"

Handler shook his head. "Connections are slow on Triton. We have about half the number of communications relay satellites a planet this size needs." He raised a finger. "Hold on. I think I'm... Yes."

There followed a conversation between Handler and someone at Station Ares which Dev was not privy to. His only clue to its content was Handler's face, which ran the gamut of expressions from anxious to indignant to relieved. At the end of it, the ISS liaison looked up and gave a broad smile.

"Phew," he said.

"I like 'phew.'"

"It was all a misunderstanding, apparently."

"*That* was a misunderstanding? I'd hate to see what they do when they're really confused."

"The base is on high alert. Someone on watch got over-keen. We're safe to go in and dock now."

Handler piloted the boat cautiously for the remaining few kilometres, sticking to a gentle, unthreatening speed. Eventually, Station Ares came into view, a long, low block of blackness studded with lights. As the *Reckless Abandon* drew closer, Dev got an impression of its shape: a hexagonal axis with six radial arms, each subdividing into branches and tipped with a field gun.

A standard pop-up offshore naval base, the kind which could be airdropped in kit form and assembled on site in under a week and which was known colloquially as a 'snowflake.' Depending on requirements, it could be configured to provide dockage for a flotilla of medium-sized warships or accommodation for as many as eight companies of Marines.

Station Ares appeared to have plumped for the half-and-half option, its facilities equally divided between dorms and marinas. Dev counted a dozen ships in all, from corvettes to nippy little fast-attack craft. All sported the chiselled, angular design that minimised radar cross-section almost to zero.

A gunboat had been launched to greet the *Reckless Abandon*, stabbing the darkness with a searchlight.

"Ahoy, there," said an amplified voice. "Follow us in."

The gunboat spun about, and Handler trailed obediently after it.

They moored and disembarked, to be met by a welcoming committee of three Marines. The highest-ranking was First Lieutenant Sigursdottir, who snapped them a salute that was crisp, curt and, because they were civilians, just that little bit contemptuous.

"You have permission to come aboard Station Ares, gentlemen," she said. "Apologies for firing on you just now. You were zooming in fast and we're a mite defensive at the moment. It's a good thing you saw sense and halted. If you hadn't, we might have blown you out of the water."

"Itchy trigger fingers, huh?" said Dev.

"Afraid so. The situation on Triton being as it is, we're in a shoot-first-ask-questions-later frame of mind."

Sigursdottir was no more than a metre and a half tall, but somehow made up for it with an erect bearing, as though she felt there was no one she couldn't see eye-to-eye with. She had classic Nordic features – lofty cheekbones, narrow eyes, ash-blonde hair – and her sea-camo battledress barely disguised the bulges of a powerful, athletic physique. Like many a Marine, she looked as though she could bench-press her own bodyweight without breaking a sweat.

Dev was ever so slightly smitten.

"If you'll walk this way…"

He and Handler fell in behind Sigursdottir, who marched them to the snowflake's axis at a fast lick. The other two Marines took the rear, carrying their rifles in their hands rather than slung over their shoulders.

This spoke to Dev about the general nervousness at the base as loudly as the artillery shell had. A pair of unarmed and apparently harmless friendlies were being treated with the same protocols as captive enemy combatants. He imagined that were he and Handler to step out of line, they might expect a bullet in the face. Or, just as likely, in the back.

They entered a building that, like every other one on the base, was single-storey and as featureless as any bunker. They passed communications rooms where staff sat cradled in padded lounge chairs. These people seemed to be staring off into the middle distance, but unless Dev was very much mistaken, they were uplinked via commplant to radar arrays, data-collecting buoys and geostationary observation satellites all over Triton, monitoring the planet for security purposes. There were a few floatscreens for general use, if imagery needed to be shared and communally examined. Otherwise the work was done inside people's heads.

At the epicentre of Station Ares lay the office of Captain Arkady Maddox. It was a bare space with no windows and not much in the way of ornamentation beyond a TerCon Marine flag on the wall and a floatscreen gif gallery of significant moments in the occupant's life, which seemed to consist entirely of parades and medal presentation ceremonies.

The man in charge of every Marine on Triton was in

his mid-fifties, with hair the colour of iron and a grin that revealed teeth like ivory tombstones. Dev recognised in him the hardbitten, highly-decorated top-brass type he had come across countless times during the war, a gruff outward bonhomie masking a harsh, aggressive nature. His handshake was crushingly strong, less a greeting than a test of character.

"Handler," Maddox said. "Good to see you again. And this is Harmer, yes?"

"Dev Harmer, ISS," said Dev.

"So they've made you a fish-man too, eh?"

"In their infinite wisdom."

"Well, I suppose it makes sense. If the natives are restless, deploy an asset who's half-native and can speak the lingo."

"That would seem to be the general idea."

"Lieutenant? Thank you. You're dismissed."

Sigursdottir and the other two Marines saluted, about-turned and left.

"Heck of a good officer, that one," said Maddox. "Takes no shit, gives no shit. The ideal combination. Drink?"

Handler declined, but Dev said, "Don't mind if I do."

"Only have some of the local rotgut, I'm afraid. Distilled from fermented kelp. An acquired taste, but it does the trick."

He uncorked a label-less bottle containing a greasy clear liquid with a greenish tinge, and poured Dev and himself a tumbler each.

"Down the hatch."

"Fuck me!" Dev yelped after his first swallow of the stuff. He exhaled hard and thumped his chest. "Whoof. That clears the pipes."

"And that's why I passed," said Handler, while Captain Maddox guffawed lustily.

"Told you. Takes some getting used to."

"It's like seawater mixed with acid," said Dev. "And fish."

"That'll be the other main ingredient coming through. Bile from the gall bladder of one of the local fish species – runty little sucker that looks a bit like a herring."

"You could have warned me."

"And ruin the surprise? This drink's been known to cause blindness and renal failure, by the way. But it gets a buzz going like nothing else."

"Does it have a name?"

"Don't think anyone's dared give it one. I've heard it referred to as 'double moonshine,' which is reasonably witty, but I reckon leaving it anonymous shows it the respect it's due. Top-up?"

Dev figured he was being judged, so he held out his tumbler. "Go on, then."

The next shot tasted no better than the previous one, but at least this time he was prepared for it. He could feel the alcohol hitting him already, a heat spreading outward from his belly. Quick work. The sensation of peaceful ease it brought was almost worth the disgusting aftertaste lingering in the back of his throat.

"So, Handler, this request you put in…" said Maddox. "You're wanting some of my men."

"As many as you can afford to lend us, if that's all right," Handler replied. "I know it's an imposition, but we'd be eternally grateful."

Dev felt this was the wrong approach to take with a man like Captain Maddox, who respected forthrightness, not politeness. By the same token, Handler should have accepted the offer of a drink, regardless of how much he didn't want it. Still, Handler knew Maddox, this was his negotiation, so Dev said nothing and let him take the lead.

"How many?" Maddox barked.

"We're thinking a contingent of about a dozen Marines," Handler continued. "Unless that's too many. Half a dozen will do."

"A dozen, half a dozen – why should I go along with that? Why should I let you have *any*? We're on code amber right now. Do you know what code amber means?"

Handler floundered. Dev stepped in.

"Strong threat of imminent attack," he said.

Maddox regarded Dev evenly, reappraising him. "There speaks a serviceman. War veteran, yes?"

"As it happens."

"Where did you see action?"

"Easier to name the places where I *didn't*."

"Who were you with?"

"Ninth Extrasolar Engineers."

"Sapper regiment."

"Yes, but they chucked us into just about any firefight going."

"Including Barnesworld?"

"Of course."

"Leather Hill?"

Dev flinched a fraction.

"Ah," Maddox said. "Say no more. Your reaction speaks volumes. Let's have another glass."

They clinked drinks.

"To fallen comrades."

"To fallen comrades," Dev echoed.

"Wasn't there myself," Maddox said.

"Why would you be? It was an inland battle, not littoral or inshore."

"Sometimes wish I had been."

"You shouldn't."

"Why ever not? The decisive clash of the Frontier War. The one where we finally settled the digimentalists' hash. Who wouldn't want to have been there? Glorious moment!"

Dev did not remember Leather Hill as glorious at all. He remembered day after day of grinding, gruelling attrition. Slow advances, desperate retreats, determined re-entrenchments. Troops thrown headlong into the threshing machine of the Polis+ lines. The Plussers pitching everything they had into the fray, every mech, every organic war beast, crab tank, suicide spider, zombie clone battalion, and blade-flailing samurai robot, all the time proclaiming in high, ululating voices the majesty and wonder of their god the Singularity...

It was tempting to put Maddox straight, to point out that Leather Hill had not been a victory but rather the final straw for both sides, a mutual massacre so extensive that it had eventually brought them to the negotiating table to sue for peace and sign a treaty.

But here was a man who relished combat. Lived for it. No amount of slaughter could ever dismay or deter him. Death was just an unavoidable necessity, as far as Maddox was concerned, the fire that he snuggled close to for warmth even though it could burn him. Dev had no hope of persuading him otherwise.

So all he said was, "You had a good war, I'm guessing."

"The best," Captain Maddox replied. "Loved it. Every minute of it. You're not one of those limp-wristed liberal pacifists who'd rather we never got involved, are you?"

"We did what had to be done. I did."

Maddox nodded. "Good an answer as any. It's just that I've met some vets who seem to have turned their backs on the whole concept of fighting. They resent it. It's as though we weren't engaged in a struggle for the human race's existence, as though the decade we spent keeping the Plussers at bay was somehow a complete waste of time and a senseless loss of life." He snorted. "I have no truck with that attitude whatsoever, as I'm sure you've gathered."

"Ahem." Handler looked sheepish. "I fear we're straying from the point, captain."

"Men," said Maddox. "You're after a detail of my men to accompany you south to the Tropics of Lei Gong, where the Tritonians are raising the biggest ruckus."

"I appreciate that it's a big ask."

"It *is* a big ask. As things stand, I'm under-staffed. I could do with another three stations this size, the better to keep an eye on the Plussers."

"There are Plussers on-planet?" Dev said.

"Not that we know of." Maddox waved an arm skyward. "The ones out there. What do you think this base's purpose is, after all? I'll give you a clue: we're not here for the surfing and the seafood."

"Forward reconnaissance," said Dev, "that's what I think."

"Clever fellow."

"There are deep space radio telescopes orbiting above us, peering into Polis Plus territory. All those people we passed on the way in, I thought they were monitoring Triton, but now I see they're not. They're analysing and assessing regional Plusser activity and relaying it to high command on Earth."

"Precisely. This isn't some peacekeeping force I'm in charge of. We're not policemen. Station Ares is a high-value listening post, and it needs to be properly safeguarded. If the locals are busy attacking Terran interests, who's to say we're not next on the list? Meaning I need all hands on deck. That said…"

Maddox rocked on his heels, mulling things over.

"We can't really look the other way and whistle when things are so clearly turning sour," he said. "And TerCon must have a hunch it's the Plussers who are getting the Tritonians all uppity, or why else bring ISS in?"

"Covert Polis Plus plots are kind of our speciality," Dev said.

"And if that's what's happening, then it'd be a dereliction of duty on my part not to help out."

"That's the spirit."

"Tell you what. Yes. You can have your Marines. You can also have a gunboat for them to tag along with you in."

"That's very generous of you," said Handler.

"I'll even throw in Eydís Sigursdottir. Can't spare her, really, but you'll need a decent junior officer to run the show, and she's the best."

"I'm fine with that," Dev said, sounding more eager than he intended.

"Just make sure it's worthwhile. Don't make me look a fool. I'd hate that, and so would you."

Maddox hoisted the bottle of double moonshine and refilled Dev's glass and his own one more time.

Dev would have liked to refuse, because the buzz from the booze was beginning to turn nasty. The room had started to reel and his tongue had gone numb. His host form, after all, had never ingested alcohol before. Its physiology was as pure and untainted as a newborn baby's, its liver a stranger to all intoxicants. And this particular liquor was so strong, even a hardened drinker would have had difficulty metabolising it.

Nonetheless he slugged the shot down in one go, both to seal the deal with Maddox and to prove he had guts.

Next instant, he proved he had guts in another way, by bending double and puking copiously on the floor, much to Maddox's amusement.

When he straightened up, he found he was hopelessly lightheaded. The room was growing grey and distant around him, and Maddox's booming laughter had begun to echo as though they were in a cavern.

Don't pass out, Dev told himself. *Whatever you do, don't –*

10

He came to aboard the *Reckless Abandon*, sprawled indecorously on a bunk in one of the cabins.

He felt awful.

No, that was an understatement. He would have loved to feel awful. Awful was a condition he aspired to.

He felt truly abysmal. Wretched. A half-dead wreck of a man. A bag of pain and ghastliness. His every nerve ending jagged and raw. His muscles so many chunks of suppurating rotten meat. His bones broken twigs.

Just raising his head off the bunk was like wrestling a grizzly bear, an act that was not only a huge, self-lacerating effort, but utterly futile and guaranteed to end in defeat.

For a while all he could do was lie there and moan self-pityingly.

The jetboat was in motion, which did nothing to alleviate his suffering. It leapt and bounced across the water, heaving him up and down as gleefully as a cat persecuting a mouse.

Even dying was preferable to this – and Dev, who had once felt his body being torn to ribbons by coilgun rounds, knew a bit about dying.

The phrase *Never again* tolled in his mind like a bell. He

always seemed to forget that every time he was installed in a host form he was starting over from scratch. His personal history, including a tolerance to alcohol accrued over a lifetime, meant nothing to a virgin, vat-grown body. In that disjuncture between what he remembered about himself and what he currently was, trouble lay.

Finally, through the pulsating haze that fogged his vision, he noticed that someone had done him the courtesy of leaving a packet of Blitz-Go beside the bunk. He no doubt had Handler to thank for that. He fumbled for the packet and popped a couple of the hangover-remedy pills from their blisters. Then he helped himself to a third one. Well in excess of the recommended dose, but screw it.

He dry-swallowed the three pills and waited patiently for them to take effect. Soon enough, specially designed enzymes were coursing round his body, breaking down the acetaldehyde build-up and negating acidosis. He dared to sit upright and, when he could manage that without feeling that he was going to pass out again, to stand.

A bleary, brittle Dev climbed the companionway that led to the *Reckless Abandon*'s main deck. From there he bravely tackled the ladder up to the flybridge, only losing his footing twice.

Handler, at the helm, gave him a commiserative smile.

"You poor bastard. I almost admire you, the way you went for it with Maddox. I've played that game myself. Once. Once was enough. That man has the constitution of an ox."

"Trust me, I'm regretting it. Thanks for the Blitz-Go, by the way."

"No problem. How are you feeling?"

"How do I look?"

"Like crap, frankly."

"That's how I'm feeling."

"I imagine the progressive host form deterioration isn't

doing you any favours either. You're due for another dose of nucleotides."

"Fine. If you say so. Did I screw things up with Maddox? You know, by upchucking all over his floor?"

"As a matter of fact, no. 'Best laugh I've had in ages,' he said, and then ordered some flunkey to come in and clean up the mess."

"Well, that's a relief. So we have our Marine escort?"

"Look to starboard."

Dev turned.

"No," said Handler, "the other starboard."

Dev turned again, and there, some 400 metres away, was a naval catamaran keeping pace with the jetboat. Dawn was coming, and the sleek grey ship stood proud against the silvering sky. Its superstructure bristled with weaponry, from heavy calibre guns to missile launchers. Its twin hulls, with forward-projecting keels, sliced through the water like knives. Dev fancied the catamaran would offer a much smoother ride than the *Reckless Abandon* and kind of wished he was aboard it right now.

"That there is the *Admiral Winterbrook*," Handler said. "Hunter-killer class attack vessel. Named after the hero of the sea campaign on Kapteyn B."

"He went down with his ship, didn't he?"

"But not before destroying the Plussers' submarine-generating facility."

"I'm just saying, is it wise to give your ship the name of someone famous for having his ship sunk under him?"

Handler shrugged. "How should I know? I'm not a navy man. I guess a hero's a hero, whether he died of wounds in battle or of old age in bed. Probably more of a hero, though, if it's the former rather than the latter."

"Still doesn't seem all that auspicious, to my mind," said Dev.

"Tell it to the Marines," said Handler, gesturing at the

catamaran. "Hey, that was a good joke. Don't you think? They're Marines, and I said, 'Tell it to the Marines.'"

"Jokes are even better when you explain them."

"But you didn't laugh. I thought you hadn't got it."

"I *was* laughing. Deep down. Where it counts."

"I read that you like wisecracks. It was in your psych profile. 'Fond of using humour as a means of defusing tension and/or deflecting enquiries into private matters,' or words to that effect."

"I like making wisecracks. Doesn't necessarily mean I like it when other people make them."

"The other thing I read about you is that you give everyone nicknames."

"That's not true. Not everyone. Only if I like you."

"So it's a kind of litmus test. You know you're in with Dev Harmer if he comes up with a nickname for you."

"Something along those lines."

"Do I have one yet?"

"Working on it."

The sun breasted the horizon, dispelling the last of the night clouds that were loitering to the west. Dev noted that the two boats were holding a southerly heading.

"These Tropics of Lei Gong I heard Maddox mention," he said. "What's down there?"

"The name should give you a clue."

"Can't say 'Lei Gong' rings a bell."

"Chinese thunder god."

"Ah. I see. Bad weather. What else?"

"The greatest concentration of settlers on Triton. Three floating townships: Opochtli, Dakuwaqa and Mazu. All within a twenty-kilometre radius of one another. They're known collectively as the Triangle Towns region. The Tritonian insurgents seem to be focusing their attention there. Mazu alone has been hit five times in the past month."

Handler broke off to emit a huge yawn.

"Beg pardon," he said. "I've been up all night. It's starting to catch up with me."

"I can take over," Dev said. "You go down and get some rest."

"You're okay to pilot this thing? Not too sick?"

"Give me my next nucleotide shot and I'll cope. How hard can sailing a boat be? There's the throttle, there's the steering wheel…"

"Ship's wheel," Handler corrected.

"Whatever. The turny thing that makes you go right or left. We're running on autopilot anyway. If I get into difficulties, I'll give you a shout."

"All right. We've a few hours to go before we hit the tropical latitudes. Wake me when we're below the twenty-third parallel."

"Which I'll know we've done because…?"

"Because that big red dot on that map screen there, which is us, has a number beside it, which is our GPS co-ordinates, and when the first bit of that number starts to read twenty-two degrees, then we're –"

"Okay, Captain Condescension. I get it."

"Please tell me that's not my nickname."

"Captain Condescension? Nah. I can come up with something better than that. At the moment I'm edging towards Manhandler, on account of the way you shoved me into the sea yesterday and pushed me under."

"Manhandler," Handler said, as though trying it on for size. "Could be worse."

11

ONE SERUM PATCH later, Dev was left alone on the flybridge, minding the ship while his ISS liaison slept.

After half an hour he was bored. One stretch of seascape looked much like another. So he searched the local commplant directory for 1st Lieutenant Eydís Sigursdottir.

Her personal details were classified, but one of the few perks of working for ISS was high security clearance and the master-key override software that came with that. Soon he had a link for her, and called her. Handler was right: connection times on Triton were ridiculously slow. It was nearly a minute before he got through – he had begun to think Sigursdottir was asleep and had her commplant switched off.

Yeah?

Lieutenant Sigursdottir, how goes it?

Who is this?

Dev Harmer. We met last night.
ISS guy? Charming nature? Dazzling personality? Great sense of humour?

The fish-looking one who came with the other fish-looking one? And who can't hold his drink?

That's me. Hailing you from the *Reckless
Abandon*, currently cruising alongside your fine
and rather intimidating catamaran.

What do you want? It's early.

You're up, though.

I'm CO. Of course I'm up. Wait, how did you
get hold of my commplant address?

I'm sneaky. I only want to say hi. We didn't
really get a chance to chat before, did we?

So?

I thought, as we're working together now, we
ought to get acquainted. Break the ice. Strike
up a rapport.

Why do we have to do that?

Because it'll foster a close professional
relationship.

I have a unit of eight Marines under my
command, all of them well trained, highly
disciplined, and good at taking orders. Right
now, a close professional relationship with
them is the only one I need.

Sigursdottir was going to be a tough nut to crack. But then
Dev preferred it when women didn't make life easy for him.
He was perverse that way.

So what do you do for fun around here?
When you're not busy with your Marine-y
stuff, that is.

Are you hitting on me?

It's called polite conversation. That thing
where you find out things about other people
and they find out things about you and it
becomes a thing. *That* thing.

In my down time I practise my Krav Maga,
hit the weights racks, clock up hours at the
shooting range, and keep on top of my studies
for my diploma in interstellar logistics. And
when I'm not doing any of that, sleep.

Wow. I did say "fun", didn't I? You did hear
that?

We clearly have different definitions of the word.

You don't go for a drink, then? Maybe
download a movie? Grab a pizza and just
chill?

Mr Harmer, I am a member of a Marine force
stationed on one of the remotest Diasporan
planets, more light years from home than I care
to think about, overlooking Polis Plus territory. I
am not here to chill. I am here to do a job.

Everyone needs to let off steam every now and
then.

You're not a Marine, are you?

Come on. I've never met a serving military
person who didn't like to go crazy and let their
hair down once in a while. In fact, you Marines
are famous for it. I remember this one time,
during the war, I was out with some of the
guys from my regiment during a week's R and
R, and we came across a bunch of Marines
who were shit-faced drunk and setting fire to –

Terrific anecdote. I'd love to hear more of it
sometime.

You don't mean that.

No, I don't.

It really is pretty amusing. You see, we were on
Kepler 62F, or was it Kepler 22B? One of the
Keplers, at any rate. Desert planet. And it had

these burrowing meerkat-type creatures, real
pest, got everywhere, loved to chew on cables
and crap under your cot. And the Marines…
Sigursdottir? You still there?

The call had been disconnected. Sigursdottir had hung up. Dev was projecting his thoughts out into a void.

Shame. The story about Marines dousing the meerkat creatures' fluffy tails in ethanol and setting them alight seldom failed to raise a smile. Especially the part where several of the terrified, flaming mammals – someone had dubbed them 'nearkats' – scurried into the mess habitat and it caught on fire and burned to the ground. The Marines ended up facing a disciplinary tribunal and receiving a non-judicial punishment of a forty-eight-hour forced march during which their only food rations were strips of roast nearkat meat.

The point he had been trying to make by regaling Sigursdottir with the story was to show that Marines did know how to have fun. But maybe Sigursdottir wasn't that sort of Marine. Or that sort of person.

Dev suspected, though, that deep down, underneath that stern exterior, she was.

He turned his attention back to the map screen, where the red dot that was the *Reckless Abandon* continued to nudge its way southward. The sea around it was rendered as a patchwork of concentric blobs in various deepening shades of blue, signifying seabed depth. The *Admiral Winterbrook* showed up as a faint secondary dot overlapping the *Reckless Abandon*'s.

All at once a fresh red dot appeared.

Then another.

Dev was gripped by alarm. Other vessels? Popping up out of nowhere?

The explanation was only a little less disturbing.

Blood was dripping from his nose onto the map screen.

He pinched his nostrils shut and went down to the galley for a cloth to staunch the bleeding. Back on the flybridge, he wiped the screen clean with another cloth and waited for the flow of blood to taper off. Eventually it did, but not before the first cloth was almost fully saturated.

So this was how it was going to be, was it? As the host form continued to break down, he could expect more nosebleeds? Perhaps, to add to the merriment, he would start bleeding from other orifices as well. *There* was something to look forward to.

Jetboat and catamaran sped along side by side for another hour, and as Beta Ophiuchi rose further, the air grew humid. Dev's skin began to prickle in the heat. Or was that another manifestation of his deterioration?

He realised he was going to have to be unusually careful on this mission. Not only was he pushed for time, he would not be functioning at peak capacity, and his physical efficiency would inexorably decrease. His body was crumbling under him like an unstable cliff edge. It might give way at any moment.

What he would have to bear in mind, above all else, was the need to data 'port out of the host form before it disintegrated completely. If he failed to get out in time, if his consciousness was still inside this body when its brain turned to mush, that would be that. Game over.

The matrix rig and uplink were back at the ISS outpost at Tangaroa. Whatever else happened, he had to give himself sufficient leeway to return there before his condition got too bad. He only had Handler's estimate of seventy-two hours to go on. It was probably just an educated guess. His host form might have longer, it might not; it might have far less. He would have to play it by ear.

The main thing was not to leave it too late to get back to Tangaroa. There might not be much margin for error.

To be on the safe side, Dev started a countdown timer on his commplant. Approximately sixteen hours had elapsed since he had data 'ported in, so he dialled the clock to $56\!:\!00\!:\!00$ and set it going.

$55\!:\!59\!:\!59$
$55\!:\!59\!:\!58$
$55\!:\!59\!:\!57$

There. Now he had a rough guide to his remaining lifespan. How many people could say they knew, almost to the minute, when they were going to die?

Mr Harmer.

It was Sigursdottir, calling him back. Dev permitted himself a small, secret smile. He might have known she wouldn't be able to resist for long.

Lieutenant Sigursdottir! To what do I owe the
honour?
Don't get all tumescent. This isn't a social call.
Have you looked at your map screen in the
past couple of minutes?
Uh, no, not really.
Do.

Dev glanced at the screen and frowned. There was a new red dot on it, some distance to the south-west. To judge by the map scale, fifty-odd kilometres.

What's that?
It's a licensed scientific research vehicle,
the *Egersund*, Norwegian-owned. I know

that because I've cross-referenced its radar signature with the Triton maritime database, and also because it's sending out a mayday giving its name and position.

It's in trouble?

That's usually what a mayday means.

But what sort of trouble?

Unknown. All we're getting is the automated distress beacon. We've hailed, but no response. We've no option but to go in and help.

Hold on, you mean divert?

That's exactly what I mean. It's a rule of the sea. A mayday cannot be ignored, especially if you're the nearest available ship, which we are. It's our responsibility.

Do I get any say in the matter?

None at all. I'm telling you as a courtesy. We're already changing tack. If you want to stick with us, then you can come along. Otherwise feel free to carry on on your own.

Dev looked to the right. The *Admiral Winterbrook* was veering away from its parallel course, trending westward. The gap between the boats was widening.

He was in a quandary. On the one hand, the sooner they got to the Tropics of Lei Gong, the better. The mission was, after all, time critical; they couldn't afford to be sidetracked. On the other hand, he and Handler had gone to all the trouble of securing an escort of Marines, and now they were going to lose it? That would render the whole trip to Station Ares a waste of time.

There really seemed no choice but to stick with Sigursdottir and her squad.

Handler's down below, snoozing, and we're on
autopilot. How do I alter course?

Log in to the navigation computer. The interface
is pretty straightforward and self-explanatory.
Just draw a vector line to the *Egersund*'s
position. The computer will do the rest.

Roger that.

Don't want to be separated from us, huh?

It's a big ocean. It might be tricky to hook up
again. Plus, we've only just got to know each
other, you and me. It'd be a shame to lose this
connection we've got.

Mr Harmer, sincerely, give it a rest.

Dev followed Sigursdottir's instructions, synching his
commplant with the navigation computer, and the *Reckless
Abandon* was soon coming about to match bearings with
the *Admiral Winterbrook*.

55:55:;3
55:55:;2
55:55:;;

12

THE *EGERSUND* WAS enormous. Dev kept thinking the research ship couldn't loom any bigger, but it kept growing.

It was like an oceangoing skyscraper. Its hull was solid and plain, unrelieved by portholes, a sheer metal cliff face. Its superstructure consisted of a bridge, an accommodation level, and a pair of towering derricks.

Licensed scientific research vessel, Sigursdottir had called it, but Dev couldn't help thinking it was a whole lot more than that. What need did scientists have for something this colossal?

More to the point, how come a ship so huge was sending out a mayday? What could conceivably pose a threat to a titan of such epic proportions?

Closer yet, he noticed that the *Egersund* was listing slightly. It was stationary but leaning at a drunken angle. He could only presume it had been holed below the waterline.

The *Admiral Winterbrook* dropped to dead slow, and Dev did the same, disengaging the autopilot and assuming manual control of the jetboat. The catamaran nosed warily around the bow of the *Egersund*, and Dev followed in its wake.

Still not getting anything on any of the regular
radio frequencies. If someone's aboard, they're
not answering. I'm going to try the loudhailer.

Aye-aye, lieutenant.

You're not a sailor. Don't say that.

"*Ahoy, the* Egersund." Sigursdottir's amplified voice rang
out from the *Admiral Winterbrook*. "*Can anyone hear me?
Signal somehow if you can. What is the problem? Are you
taking on water? Do your crew need rescuing?*"

Nothing from the research vessel. No heads appeared atop
the great promontory of its prow. No arms waved.

As they came round its far side, Dev saw that the sea was
awash with blood. A great frothing patch of crimson spread
out from the hull. It looked as though the *Egersund* was
bleeding into the water from some mortal wound.

No, it wasn't the *Egersund*.

Attached to the ship's flank by cables was the carcass of
a redback whale. The cetacean was floating underside up,
quite dead, its pectoral fins raised towards the sky as though
in supplication or valediction.

The cables were lashed around its tail, and one of the
derricks had begun the process of drawing the beast aft but
had halted for some reason, leaving the redback's flukes
suspended just above the waves.

The *Admiral Winterbrook* and the *Reckless Abandon*
chuntered past the whale. The boats were dwarfed by the
mound of the creature's pink, barnacled belly, and the
redback was in turn dwarfed by the *Egersund*.

The stern of the gigantic ship sported a U-shaped transom,
inset with a ramp almost level with the water. The ramp
was streaked with stains that could have been rust but could
equally have been caked-on blood from the corpses of other
cetaceans. This was where the derrick had been hauling the

redback carcass before something interrupted the procedure. The ramp doubled as a means of getting the bodies aboard the ship and a chute for dumping bones, offal and other valueless parts.

Scientific research my butt.

My thoughts exactly. This is a whaler. A factory ship. I'd heard there were a couple of them operating on-planet, but I reckoned it was just a rumour.

They're collecting whale meat?

There's a market for it back home and in some Diasporan communities. A ship like this can catch, process and flash-freeze several thousand tonnes of redback and load the flesh aboard a goods freighter for distribution.

That'd cost a small fortune. The price per kilo at the restaurant table would be extortionate.

There's people willing to pay it and rich enough to. Japanese tech tycoons, for one.

Nordic interstellar logistics magnates, for another.

Was that a dig, Harmer?

Not intended as such. But it's the Nordic countries and Japan who used to consume whale meat the most and who whined the loudest when TerCon finally abolished it from the menu. Stands to reason they'd be the ones coughing up the cash to buy it from other sources when it's no longer available on Earth. Pricey extraterrestrial whale meat's better than no whale meat at all.

Well, yeah, can't argue with that. Speaking as an ethnic Icelander, I've never had the

urge to eat it myself, but I can remember my
grandfather going on about how much he had
loved *hval rengi* – that's whale blubber soured
with milk.

Seriously?

And *sur rengi* – pickled blubber.

Sounds delicious. I'm amazed you were never
tempted to try it.

Grandpa used to bitch about TerCon
outlawing whaling. But even he had to
admit that if it hadn't been banned outright,
eventually there'd have been no whales left.

Luckily the gene pool wasn't too depleted and
the Comprehensive Repopulation Programme
had a broad enough clone base to bring the
species back from the brink of extinction.

Yeah, but nobody's whaling anymore on Earth.
Seems unfashionable these days. Uncool.

Whereas here, halfway across the galaxy, it's
still okay.

What the eye doesn't see…

The two boats rounded the rear of the *Egersund* and
completed their circuit of the ship. Other than the redback
carcass, there had been no sign of life – or death. The
Egersund appeared to have been abandoned while its crew
were midway through gathering in their latest catch.

So what's the plan, Sigursdottir?

We're going to have to send men aboard.
There may still be crewmembers somewhere,
perhaps injured, unable to communicate. We
can't leave without checking.

Okay. I'll come with.

What? Why?

Curiosity. I'm in intel-collecting mode. What's happened on that ship may be relevant to my mission. It may *not* be, but I won't know unless I take a look for myself.

I'm under orders from Captain Maddox to facilitate you in whatever way I can. I suppose this counts as that.

And you couldn't sound more enthusiastic about it.

Too right. Just get yourself over here pronto.

Aye-aye, lieutenant. Sorry. I mean: yes, ma'am.

13

DEV LEFT HANDLER a message explaining what he was doing. The ISS liaison would find it in his inbox when he woke up.

He then set the jetboat's controls to maintain a steady position a safe distance from the *Egersund* and dived overboard. He surged along underwater, covering the couple of hundred metres to the *Admiral Winterbrook* in just over a minute, a time not even the fastest Pure Olympic swimmer would have been able to equal, although an enhanced Free Olympian might. He ascended the rope ladder that had been lowered over the catamaran's side for him, and was assisted over the gunwale by a powerful hand that clamped over his wrist and pulled.

The hand belonged to a corporal – by far the tallest woman Dev had ever seen, and quite possibly the broadest too. Her grip had been like a bear trap, and he suspected she had been using only a small fraction of her full strength. Laced with augmentations and modifications, the corporal looked capable of pulverising rocks in her fists.

Her name tag said Milgrom, and she was accompanied by Private First Class Blunt and Private First Class Francis. These two women were small compared to her but both sizeable nonetheless, well above average. Bulked out with ceramic-tile body armour and bristling with ammo and ordnance, the three of them were a formidable proposition.

Sigursdottir appeared on deck, and Milgrom, Blunt and Francis all came smartly to attention. The sea-pattern camo on their battledress had been switched to active. Waves of colour, predominantly blue and grey, rippled across the fabric, moving even as the wearers of the battledress stood perfectly still.

"Just pulled this tiddler out of the water, sir," said Milgrom. "Looks kind of shrimpy. Shall we throw him back?"

"Don't tempt me," said Sigursdottir. She gave Dev a once-over from head to toe as his clothing rapidly dripped dry. "You ready for this? You aren't carrying any weaponry."

"I thought this was a rescue expedition. I'll take a gun if there's one going begging."

"Francis, lend him your sidearm. Don't give me that look, private. You've got plenty else to use."

PFC Francis grumblingly unbuckled her hip holster and passed it across to Dev. He fastened it on and drew the gun to inspect it. Could be worse: a Heckler & Koch hypervelocity pistol, which used a burst of piston-generated condensed hydrogen gas to propel sabot rounds at a speed of seven kilometres per second. The holster belt held an ample quantity of spare ammo clips.

"Don't these things have a tendency to jam?" he said. "Fragments of rupture disc get stuck in the high pressure coupling."

"Only on the old models," said Francis. "That there is the HK HVP Mark Two. The rupture discs are programmable plastic now, rather than stainless steel. Under pressure they disperse into a cloud of particles that gets vented out of the muzzle behind the round."

"I believe Mr Harmer knew that already," said Sigursdottir.

"He was just trying to show he's not an amateur. He wants us to know he's got game."

"In a tactful way," Dev said.

"Tact's wasted on me," said Francis.

"And me," said Blunt. "Blunt by name, blunt by nature."

"Well then, in the spirit of bluntness, I don't suppose it'll matter if I mention the words 'all-woman team,'" said Dev.

"Depends what you mean by it," said Milgrom. "If you mean 'I'm not working with a bunch of girls,' then I'd be correcting that opinion sharpish if I were you. Otherwise you could end up like that redback back there, only not as pretty-looking."

"No. All I meant was, Sigursdottir told me she would be sending men aboard."

"I should have specified their gender?" said the lieutenant. "I use the word *men* as shorthand. For your information, everyone on board this boat is female. My entire team – ladies. Girls. With boobs and everything. Is that going to be an issue?"

"Not in the slightest."

"Good. Because if it was going to be an issue, it would be *your* issue, if you get my drift."

"Noted," said Dev. "I've adjusted my attitude accordingly. Please no one cut my balls off."

"Oh, we wouldn't touch your balls," said Milgrom, leaning in so close to Dev that he could smell the chewing gum on her breath and see the stippling of fine dark hairs on her top lip. "It wouldn't be worth our while trying to find them."

Blunt and Francis both chortled. Sigursdottir smirked.

Dev just smiled. "Are we done hazing the newbie? That ship over there may be sinking. Unless you've a few more insults to unload, perhaps we should focus on searching it while we still can. Yes?"

Milgrom grunted, then nodded. "I've not begun insulting you, fish-face. But sure, let's save that for later. Meantime, we've got a ghost ship to explore."

14

THE *ADMIRAL WINTERBROOK* hove to at the *Egersund*'s stern, adjacent to the ramp. Milgrom and Blunt fired grappling guns. The hooks arced to the top of the ramp, trailing lengths of synthetic spider-silk rope behind them and fastened electromagnetically to the metalwork. Milgrom gave the rope on hers an experimental tug to establish that it was secure. Then, with the end of the rope wrapped around her upper arm, she took a running jump and leapt from the catamaran to the whaler.

Blunt alighted beside her a moment later, and the two Marines hauled themselves hand over hand up the ramp. At the top, they launched hoverdrones from wristlets in their forearms. The micro aircraft unfurled rotors and rose to five metres, sporting four-way camera arrays that transmitted images to their commplants.

Eyes in the sky. Eyes in the backs of their heads.

Coilgun rifles unshouldered, Milgrom and Blunt performed a sweep of the aft deck, right and left, mirroring each other. The hoverdrones accompanied them like kites on invisible strings.

Once the all-clear was given, Sigursdottir and Francis sprang onto the ramp and clambered up to join them.

Dev went last. Catching the grappling hook rope as he landed, he clambered up the steep, slimy slope, the smears of old blood making the steel slippery. Unlike the Marines, he didn't have grip-soled boots.

The Marines were already on the move, heading forward in two-by-two formation. Milgrom's and Blunt's hoverdrones whispered obediently along overhead.

The central section of the *Egersund*'s deck was a kind of industrialised outdoor abattoir. There were servo-powered exoskeleton suits fitted with huge circular saws and long serrated blades designed specifically for flensing whale flesh. There were dicing machines you could have driven a van through, with a grid of criss-crossing filaments that reduced whatever was shoved into them to neat, manageable metre-wide cubes. A network of channels carried the spilled blood aft to the ramp.

The stench of rotten meat permeated the air. The channels held a tarry black residue like grisly molasses. The exoskeleton suits stood at attention, hollow executioners awaiting the order to start chopping.

An external staircase led up to the bridge. The hoverdrones remained outside, keeping lookout, while Dev and the Marines entered.

The bridge was unoccupied, but there were indications that whoever had been here had not left willingly. Some of the consoles bore bullet holes, one window had been smashed, and there were still-wet blood spatters on the walls.

Dev noticed something else: a patch of charring on the vinyl upholstery of the captain's chair.

"Flash discharge?" he wondered aloud. "From a plasma beam weapon?"

Sigursdottir shook her head. "Nope. Seen this before. It's a bioelectric burn."

"Huh?"

"Sea monkeys," said Milgrom. "I knew it had to be. Fucking sea monkeys did this."

"Hold on. Sea monkeys?"

"Tritonians," said Sigursdottir. "We're not supposed to call them that," she added, shooting a look at Milgrom.

Her subordinate merely shrugged her massive shoulders. "Tritonians, schmitonians," she muttered. "Sea monkeys is what they are."

"That" – Sigursdottir pointed to the charring – "is what you get when a Tritonian fires a shock lance at point blank range, in air. See the star-shaped scorch?"

Dev recalled the two Tritonians who had saved him from the thalassoraptor. The female had been carrying a weapon which was an amalgamation of coral and a softer organic material. He was guessing that that was a shock lance.

"Tritonians boarded this ship," he said.

"Seems so. A raiding party."

"They're amphibious? My understanding is they can't breathe out of water."

"They can for short periods. As long as their gills stay moist enough, they can extract diffused oxygen from the air. Like mudskippers do, and climbing perch. Crabs too."

"Not the type of crabs you've got, Blunt," said Francis.

"Hey, fuck you."

"From fraternising with Master Chief Reynolds."

"That was you. In your dreams."

"Before settlers came along, the Tritonians never had any reason to leave the sea," said Milgrom. "They probably didn't even realise they could, until they decided they needed to attack humans in their own element. They learned the knack of air breathing pretty fast."

"They can last half an hour, an hour tops," said Sigursdottir. "It's enough."

"So Tritonians were here," said Dev, "but they must have gone by now. The *Egersund*'s been beaming out that mayday for a couple of hours. They did whatever they did, then left."

"Assume nothing."

"The question is, where's the *Egersund*'s crew?"

"That's the biggie, isn't it? I think our next step should be to go below and eyeball what's down there."

15

SIGURSDOTTIR LED DEV and her team into the bowels of the whaler. She and Milgrom took point; Blunt and Francis had the rear. Dev, in the middle, felt like a VIP being protected by a phalanx of bodyguards. The hoverdrones had returned to their roosts on Milgrom's and Blunt's arms like well-trained hunting falcons, folding themselves neatly away into the wristlets.

The Marines held their rifles high, sighting along them, quartering every corner they turned and every room they entered. The four women moved with practised speed and precision, each aware of the others' whereabouts at all times. They were pure military efficiency, a symphony of teamwork.

The *Egersund* groaned softly and insistently, and every now and then a shudder ran through it like a small earth tremor. Dev was conscious of the slight tilt of the floor under him. The ship was skewed to port and aft. He couldn't tell if the incline was steepening or not.

The whaler doubtless had a double hull and watertight partitions between its bulkheads, as any large ship did. Polymer-crystal adhesive injectors as well, to soak up the water and provide a seal. A single, localised rupture in its skin would not be a fatal blow. It would, though, necessitate bringing the ship to a dead stop, if only so that a damage inspection could be carried out.

Dev could only presume that the Tritonians had put a hole in the *Egersund* for precisely that reason – disable the whaler so that the captain had no alternative but to halt. Then they could board with ease.

The search party arrived at the *Egersund*'s mess hall, where Dev half expected to see unfinished meals on the tables. But the room was spick and span. When the Tritonians struck, the crew had been busy outside dealing with the freshly caught redback whale, not having a meal.

Sigursdottir ordered a five-minute rest break. Milgrom kept lookout at the main door while the others set down their rifles and took a load off their feet. A canister of water was passed round, although Dev, pointedly, was not offered any.

He shared with Sigursdottir his theory about how the Tritonians had forced the *Egersund* to stop. She agreed it was the likeliest scenario.

"The thing about these particular indigenes," she said, "is they're not dumb. Don't go thinking they're primitives, savages, whatever. They aren't. They're a sophisticated, technologically adept race. Just because they don't have Riemann Deviation drive spaceships and comms devices wired into their brains doesn't mean they're not every bit as smart as us."

"Crafty buggers as well," Blunt interjected.

"They may have started from a different baseline," Sigursdottir continued. "They may use organic materials rather than predominantly inorganic like we do. But you underestimate them at your peril. Out of the water as well as in, they're to be respected."

"And blasted to bits if they so much as look at you funny," Milgrom commented from the doorway.

"Hoo-rah!" said Francis, and she and Blunt high-fived.

Sigursdottir grimaced. "As you can tell," she said to Dev, "the Tritonians haven't exactly endeared themselves to us in recent months."

"TerCon Marines," said Dev. "Famous for their tolerance towards civilians and non-Terrans."

That almost – *almost* – provoked a smile from the stolid, imperturbable lieutenant. He could see it in her eyes, even if it didn't quite extend to her face.

"ISS operatives," she retorted. "Famous for being sarcastic dickwads."

"I'll have you know I earned us that reputation single-handedly."

They resumed their journey through the *Egersund*'s labyrinthine interior, heading further down, deeper. Signs on the wall pointed the way toward a storage hold, so they followed them until they emerged into a cavernous space, very cold, traversed by conveyor belts, which were currently static. Compressor fans on a dozen huge refrigeration units thrummed reverberantly. Heavy-duty hooks were suspended from the ceiling on pulley chains, swaying ever so slightly as the stationary ship lolled.

Here, at last, were the crew.

There were perhaps forty of them all told. They hung from the hooks, limp and inert, and had, to a man and woman, been eviscerated. Innards lay clumped in heaps below their feet, still attached to their owners, unspooled from gashes in their bellies. Flesh had been stripped away, in some cases clean to the bone. Here and there a limb had been lopped.

Like countless redbacks, the whaler's crew had been methodically and ruthlessly butchered.

"The phrase 'poetic justice' springs to mind," said Dev.

"The lieutenant said the sea monkeys aren't savages," said Milgrom. "This'd seem to contradict that, don't you think?"

They examined the bodies one after another to see if any of them was by some miracle still alive. None was. Dulled, horrified eyes stared down emptily at them. Slack mouths hung open in silent cries of protest.

"Is this everybody?" said Blunt. "The whole crew accounted for?"

"I've patched into the ship's onboard manifest and apparently it has a complement of forty-three, so yes, by a rough head count, I guess this is it," said Sigursdottir. "The Tritonians were thorough. Rounded them all up, marched them down here, strung them up like sides of beef and slaughtered them. Didn't miss anyone out."

"What for?" said Dev. "Why do this?"

"To scare the shit out of us, for one thing."

"Full marks to them, then," said Blunt. "Achievement unlocked."

"But also, more importantly, to send a message. They don't like humans killing redbacks. It offends them."

"Do they regard these whales as sacred or something?" said Dev.

"Not particularly. In fact, they harvest them as well. Use them as a source of food and construction materials. Clothing too. They make their own version of leather from redback hide steeped in the redback's own ambergris. Whalers like this are poaching their game and hence pissing them off."

"There are less drastic ways of showing you're upset," Dev pointed out.

"The Tritonians aren't really big on dialogue and diplomacy," said Sigursdottir. "Ask your friend Handler. He's the one who's supposed to be the ambassador between us and them. Ask him how much success he's had getting them to see things from our point of view or, for that matter, putting their point of view across to us."

"Spoiler," said Milgrom. "Not a lot."

"The history of settler–indigene relations on Triton has never been a happy one," Sigursdottir said. "Mostly it's been a case of the two sides trying to ignore each other as much as possible. Handler and all the envoys before him, they've not been much more than window-dressing. Lip service to the idea of mediation. Something to show we've at least made an effort, we've tried to be reasonable, we've met the Tritonians halfway…"

"So don't blame us if they haven't reciprocated," said Dev.

"Bingo."

"If a single envoy is all we've offered, is it any surprise they're getting militant now?"

"No, but we can all pretend it is." Sigursdottir twisted her mouth in a cynical grimace. "This has been a while coming, but it was always inevitable. People had begun taking the Tritonians for granted, thinking they'd just go on passively accepting our presence."

"No one reckoned that if humans kept pushing them, sooner or later they'd push back."

"Quite. So along comes a whaler like this, and it's just too much of a provocation, far as the Tritonians are concerned. Too intrusive to ignore. Big old ship pulling the planet's largest mammals out of the sea and turning them into steaks – how can they let it be?"

"No excuse for getting quite so radical," said Milgrom, tapping the corpse nearest to her with the barrel of her rifle. "At what point does legitimate grievance become a sanction for mass murder? There's a line, surely."

"Anyone mind if we carry on the conversation somewhere else?" said Francis. "I don't know about you people but this place, these bodies, it's giving me the willies."

Blunt sniggered. "Never heard *you* complain about being given the willies before."

"Skank."

"Whore."

"Bitch."

"Slut."

"Stow it, ladies," barked Sigursdottir. "We all know you love each other like sisters. But Francis is right. There's nothing we can do for these poor bastards, and frankly I'd rather not have them hovering over me like the world's ugliest piñatas. Let's bail and regroup topside. Get some fresh air."

16

THE AIR OUTSIDE might have been fresher, and indeed warmer, but it didn't do much to dispel the chilling memory of the massacre in the storage hold. The *Egersund* was a floating tomb, and Dev felt no great urge to remain aboard any longer than he had to.

Sigursdottir insisted that they perform a search of the ship's forward deck section, the only part they hadn't checked yet. There was the accommodation level underneath the bridge, and a forecastle beyond that. If by any chance a crewmember had managed to escape the Tritonians' depredations, they might be hiding out in one of those places.

The forecastle was home to the *Egersund*'s harpoon cannon.

Or rather, to what was left of it.

The large, swivel-mounted device had been dismantled, vandalised, destroyed beyond repair. The shattered debris lay strewn. This cannon wouldn't launch an explosive-tipped projectile at a redback ever again.

As Dev surveyed the wreckage, he noticed something odd. The distribution of the broken parts was not as random as it first looked. He took a step back to obtain a better view.

Yes, the bits of cannon hadn't just been tossed about any old how.

They had been heaped up. Arranged.

The pattern they lay in was essentially symmetrical. There was a shallow arch over two small circles, and then a pair of lines projecting out at acute angles, each ending in a V-shape.

He studied the pattern from the other side. This way round it resembled a smiley face with strange, angry eyebrows. That didn't seem right. The first view felt more apt, more meaningful. He wasn't sure why, wasn't sure how he knew that, but he was convinced it was the correct way of looking at the pattern. Arch on top, circles, outward-pointing lines at the bottom.

He summoned Sigursdottir over and showed her what he'd found.

"Make any sense to you?"

"None whatsoever."

"I'm not deluded, though, am I? It's something the Tritonians put there. They made it on purpose. Yes?"

"I can't help but think so. A kind of symbol."

"But what's it for? What does it mean?"

"Beats me. Must have some significance for them. Maybe it's a way of marking the ship. Celebrating what they did here."

"Or like a gang sign. A graffiti tag."

"Possibly. Why don't we wake Handler up, get him over and ask him? He might know. He might have seen it before."

"Good idea. He's napped long enough anyway. ISS aren't paying him to –"

A thunderous *boom* resounded the length of the *Egersund*. The ship lurched, throwing Dev and Sigursdottir off-balance.

"What the – ?" Sigursdottir ran to the port-side gunwale and peered aft. The explosion, or impact, or whatever it had been, had come from that direction.

Dev, looking over her shoulder, saw a mist of spray hanging

in the air and, below it, the sea seething white, effervescing. The carcass of the redback bobbed wildly, rocked by the suddenly turbulent water.

"We've been hit," he said.

"No shit," said Sigursdottir.

"The Tritonians. They've come back for more."

"Looks that way. We need to get off this ship before –"

A second *boom* shook the whaler, this time coming from its starboard flank.

"Before that," Sigursdottir finished. "They're not content with leaving the *Egersund* crippled. They want it sunk."

Milgrom and Blunt arrived on the forecastle at a run.

"Sir!" Milgrom said. "I've spotted a Tritonian cuttlefish sub just beneath the surface. Looks like it's going round systematically ramming holes."

"Contact Gunnery Sergeant Jiang on the *Winterbrook*. Tell her to seek and engage."

"Yes, sir!"

"Blunt, where's Francis?"

"Last I saw, she was in the cabins."

"Get her out here, if she isn't on her way already. We are *leaving*."

Milgrom and Blunt activated their commplants and relayed Sigursdottir's orders. Francis appeared a moment later, and the five of them set off at a mad dash back to the stern ramp.

The *Egersund* was struck a third time, then a fourth, a fifth. The whaler was being pierced rapidly and repeatedly and taking on water fast, faster than the sealant injectors could cope with. Dev could feel the ship rolling, wallowing. He and the Marines were going as quickly as they could, given the circumstances. The deck kept heaving this way and that, however, making progress treacherous. You couldn't be certain your foot would land where you wanted it to. It was like trying to run during an earthquake.

Yet another blow from the cuttlefish sub sent all five of them sprawling. The *Egersund* was now letting out a hideous groaning noise. There was a terrifying low rumble as well, coming from deep down inside the vessel – the sound of millions of gallons of seawater flooding in where no seawater belonged.

Sigursdottir dragged Dev back upright by the scruff of his neck, and the five of them continued running.

"What does Jiang think she's playing at?" Francis said. "Why hasn't the *Winterbrook* pinged that sub and blown the fucker in half?"

"Easier said than done," Sigursdottir replied. "Cuttlefish subs can shift. Anyway, that's not our concern right now. Getting our backsides off this thing before it goes down is what matters."

The last hundred metres to the ramp was a rollercoaster of ups and downs and sideways twists. The *Egersund* didn't seem to know what it wanted to do – pitch, yaw, sink – so it did all three at once. Dev felt as though he and the Marines were fleas on the back of an irate mule which wanted rid of them but instead of scratching them off was trying to dislodge them by bucking.

They threw themselves onto the ramp and slid down, spinning helplessly, flailing, until they hurtled off the end, into the sea.

The instant he hit the water, Dev felt his under-lids snap into place and his gills flare. He looked around and saw Milgrom striking for the surface with mighty sweeps of her arms and legs. She was toting at least fifty kilogrammes of equipment, but didn't seem encumbered at all. The other three Marines were swimming upward too.

A large shape flitted at the periphery of his vision. Thalassoraptor? Not again, surely!

No, it was something else. Something that was both sea beast and more than that.

It looked like a huge cephalopod, perhaps thirty metres long, with a smooth conical body covered in mottled markings and a cluster of arms trailing behind its head. It used jet propulsion to move, sucking in and squirting out water through a ventral siphon. A fringe of fine lateral fins helped it steer.

Yet it was not wholly a living thing. The globes of its eyes were hollow and transparent, and inside each sat a Tritonian. The indigenes were clearly pilots, somehow controlling the cephalopod.

This, then, was a cuttlefish sub. And as Dev watched, it darted off, so fast it was almost lost from view in just a couple of seconds. A swift about-face, and it returned just as fast, if not faster, to slam into the stricken *Egersund* with impressive force.

Rivets popped. Seams split. Yet another fissure appeared in the whaler's hull.

Dev, meanwhile, was reeling, semi-concussed by the cuttlefish sub's impact with the ship. His eardrums felt as though someone had punched them with an awl.

The bizarre organic submarine wheeled away from the *Egersund*, preparing to deliver further attacks. Then it seemed to have a change of heart. It came about and coasted towards Dev, manoeuvring with delicate pulses of its fins until it was face to face with him.

Dev trod water blearily. His head had not yet cleared. He felt stunned and groggy.

The cuttlefish sub finned a little closer still so that the Tritonian pilots in their eye socket cockpits could get a better look at him. They exchanged glances across the few metres of cephalopod head between them. Photophores flashed, but Dev could not quite make out what was being expressed. Curiosity? Puzzlement? No, something a bit stronger, a bit more indignant than that.

He tried to 'speak' himself, reaching inside for feelings of surrender and goodwill. He had no wish to be rammed by the cuttlefish sub as the *Egersund* had been. A direct, head-on blow from it would mash him to pulp.

His face tingled but he wasn't sure he was radiating the message he intended. The acquiescent sentiments he was striving to convey seemed muddled somehow. There was apprehension in there. Doubt. A hint of confusion.

It would have been better had he been less dazed. Clarity of mind would have brought purity of emotion.

As it was, the Tritonians' own faces registered jade-green bafflement shot through with ruby-red ripples of contempt. They weren't sure what Dev was saying but they knew they didn't like it.

Or him.

The vast bulk of the *Egersund* continued to sink slowly in the background while the cuttlefish sub thrust past Dev, then swung round so that its arms were facing him.

A pair of tentacles unfurled towards him with a languid, python-like grace. They were lined with suckers and tipped with diamond-shaped pads with a soft, prehensile dexterity. They groped for Dev, and he understood, with a surge of panic, that the Tritonians were planning to take him prisoner. Either that or rend him limb from limb with the tentacles.

The panic was like a bolt of lightning in his brain, a sudden, sharp flash, dispelling confusion.

Dev's hand went to the hypervelocity pistol at his hip. One of the features of the gun – a reason it was a favourite among Marines – was that it worked underwater.

The tips of the tentacles were around him, almost enfolding him, as he brought the HVP up to fire.

Just as his finger tightened on the trigger, however, the tentacles retracted. They re-joined the cuttlefish sub's arm cluster, folding together neatly beneath.

Dev had time to wonder if the pilots were responding to the threat of the HVP. A sabot round could easily sever one of those tentacles.

Then he became aware of a second craft hovering nearby, just behind him. This one had the kite-like outline of a manta or a stingray, with gently undulating wingtips and a tail ridged with dorsal fins.

Another organic submarine, the bulbous eyes mounted at its front housing another pair of pilots.

One of the pilots was busy communicating with the two Tritonians in the other vessel. Dev watched incredibly complex light patterns flicker over their faces, a back-and-forth three-way dialogue. The exchange moved too swiftly and was too convoluted for him to follow properly, but he got the gist of it.

The manta sub pilot appeared to be saying that the human – Dev – was to be left alone. The cuttlefish sub pilots were unhappy about this and felt that no human, not even one who was part-Tritonian, should be immune from harm. Their wrath was great, as proved by the punishment they and their fellows had meted out on the giant surface ship that would soon be afloat no more. No one should escape it.

The manta sub pilot insisted that Dev should be spared. He was...

Dev could not really grasp the next bit.

Different? Unusual? Rare?

He had the impression that the manta sub pilot was talking from experience, as though Dev was a known quantity.

Peering, he realised that they *had* met before. At least, he thought so. It was the female Tritonian who had helped save him from the thalassoraptor. Her co-pilot was the male who had killed the predator deftly with his spear.

Dev wasn't one hundred per cent sure it was the same two Tritonians. He wasn't familiar enough with the indigenes to distinguish them one from another easily. Their features were all somewhat similar, and he hadn't yet worked out which physical characteristics were the crucial ones, the ones to look for in order to tell them apart.

But the female had that scarified nautilus design at her breastbone. How many other Tritonians bore that?

He didn't know the answer, but it was too much of a coincidence to disregard, especially when she was defending him to other members of her race as though he and she weren't strangers.

The question of why the Tritonian couple happened to be here, hundreds of kilometres south of Tangaroa, in the exact same spot at the exact same moment as Dev, was something he would have to address later. For now, he was simply glad that the female was interceding on his behalf, making the case for him being allowed to live.

It looked as though she was winning the argument, too. The Tritonians in the cuttlefish sub were exhibiting less hostility, more consent. The lights on their faces suggested that they considered themselves satisfied with the havoc they had wrought on the *Egersund* and its crew. One more human death, one fewer – what did they care?

If sighing had been possible underwater, Dev would have breathed a sigh of relief.

Three things happened next, in quick succession.

First, the *Egersund* seemed to have had enough. It had taken on too much water. It could no longer stay upright. It gave in.

The whaler slowly capsized, with a roar of tortured metal and roiling water. It was like watching a mountainside collapsing, a steady, unremitting black avalanche. The sea erupted into a nightmare of turbulence as the ship's quarter-million tonnage bore down into it, and down, and further down.

Dev felt himself being pushed bodily backwards by the wake of the ship's collapse. Both the cuttlefish sub and the manta sub were shaken about, too.

The second thing that happened was that hands seized Dev under the armpits and he was hauled away from the capsizing *Egersund* and the Tritonian submarines. He glimpsed diving gear – wetsuits, full-foot swim fins, compact oxygenated-crystal rebreathers – and could only assume he had been grabbed by Marines from the *Admiral Winterbrook*. The divers had turbine-driven jetpacks on their backs and were forging through the water at close to twenty knots.

The third thing was a subaquatic explosion, a fireball blossoming somewhere by the Tritonian vessels, a sphere of brilliance encased in a glassy shell of bubbles. The detonation was sharp-sounding, a brief noise-spike amid the ongoing cacophony of the *Egersund*'s demise.

The afterimage of the explosion lingered in Dev's retinas like a gibbous moon as the Marines spirited him further and further away from the scene of chaos. They were travelling so fast that he found it hard to breathe. All he could do was keep his head tucked in, open his mouth as wide as it would go, and suck in as much as he could of the water surging past.

He hoped he could last. He hoped he wouldn't black out. He hoped the Marines would slow down before he did lose consciousness and couldn't force water through his gills anymore. He hoped he wasn't going to become the first amphibious human being ever to drown.

17

BY THE TIME Dev was safely aboard the *Admiral Winterbrook*, the excitement was over.

The *Egersund* was gone, plummeting through thousands of fathoms into the icy gulfs of Triton's ocean, dragging the redback carcass with it. An oil slick, a smattering of flotsam and a patch of troubled sea were all that was left to show for it.

The manta sub and the cuttlefish sub were gone too. Gunnery Sergeant Jiang had deployed three torpedoes against the Tritonian vessels. After the first of them detonated, the submarines had dived; the next two torpedoes had been fired more to deter a return visit than in hopes of scoring a hit.

Dev's subaquatic saviours were Private Reyes and Private Cully, the team's diving experts. Their brief had been to drag him clear of the danger zone, then rendezvous with the catamaran once Jiang had determined that the Tritonians had skedaddled. The fact that they had almost killed him during the rescue was not something Dev would hold against them. Alive was alive, however you got there.

Sigursdottir tore into him, demanding to know what he'd thought he was doing. "Why didn't you head for the surface like the rest of us? Why'd you hang back? What was going through your tiny little mind?"

"It's complicated. There was that cuttlefish sub…"

"So you thought you'd stop and sightsee, is that it? Just float there like an idiot, making a target of yourself."

"I was communicating. The Tritonians were curious about me, and I had an idea I might be able to negotiate with them."

"And then another bunch of them came along, and you were basically pincered. They could have taken you out any time they liked. Lucky for you, Reyes and Cully were suited up and ready to go. I had them on standby just in case. If they hadn't swooped in and grabbed you when they did…"

"Don't get me wrong, I'm not ungrateful. But even if the Tritonians in the cuttlefish sub weren't going to listen to reason, the ones in the manta sub would have. They weren't like the other lot. They were a different kettle of fish – wait, is that racist?"

"Different? In what way?"

Dev shrugged noncommittally. "Less radical, I suppose. Moderate. I don't know for sure, but I'm wondering if not all Tritonians are the same. There are factions. Different degrees of resentment. They're not all fanatical human-haters."

"You're saying there are good Tritonians as well as bad ones?"

"Seems so."

"Well, duh," said Sigursdottir, rolling her eyes. "Of course. We'd be nuts if we thought every last one of them was a ruthless revolutionary. *That* would be racist. Trouble is, in the midst of a conflict situation you can't necessarily tell the sheep from the goats and you don't have time to make distinctions. You have to assume every indigene is an enemy combatant and act accordingly. Otherwise you might make a mistake – the sort of mistake you don't get the chance to learn from."

"I don't disagree with that," Dev said. "But if you want to create more of those ruthless revolutionaries, lobbing torpedoes indiscriminately at friendlies and hostiles alike is a good way of doing it. Friendlies can turn into unfriendlies fairly quickly."

"Yes, well, thanks for the advice, Harmer, and fuck you. I could have left you down there. I could have told Reyes and Cully to stay put on the *Winterbrook* and not risk their necks to save yours. If I didn't have my orders, I probably would have. For you to stand here and lecture me on how to deal with insurgents – that's the icing on the turd. I've been stationed on Triton for three long years. I know how shit goes down on this planet. You don't come waltzing in out of nowhere and tell me how to do my job. You don't have that right."

There were witnesses to this exchange, which took place on the *Admiral Winterbrook*'s bridge. Corporal Milgrom was there, and so was Gunnery Sergeant Jiang, a woman so petite that next to the hulking Milgrom she looked like a schoolgirl. Even the diminutive Sigursdottir stood a head taller than her. Jiang's size spoke of an upbringing on one of the ergonomically compact Sino-Nipponese asteroid collectives. No one was that short except by design.

Milgrom, for her part, stood menacingly at Sigursdottir's shoulder to let Dev know that everything her commanding officer said, she backed to the hilt – the hilt of the shimmerknife she was lovingly fondling. Jiang outranked Milgrom and was the second most senior Marine on board, but it was clear which of them regarded herself as Sigursdottir's XO and adjutant.

Dev was annoyed that the *Admiral Winterbrook* had attacked the manta sub, but he knew that antagonising Sigursdottir any further would be counterproductive. The Marines were tolerating him at best. It would be pointless to give them a reason to actively hate him.

"Look, all right," he said. "What's done is done. I don't want to get into politics or counterinsurgency tactics or any of that. Handling the Tritonians, that's your concern. Mine is trying to establish how far Polis Plus is involved in their activities, if at all. So you do your thing, I'll do my thing, and let's somehow meet in the middle. Okay?"

Sigursdottir was somewhat mollified, but evidently couldn't let him off in front of her subordinates. She said, "Yeah, well, stop behaving like a prize chump and that should be possible. By the way, your nose is bleeding."

"Shit." Dev put a hand to his face and came away with a glistening palmful of blood. Sigursdottir sent Milgrom to fetch a first aid kit, and shortly Dev had a coagulant-impregnated absorption pad pressed to his nose.

"Got a sanitary napkin if you'd prefer," Milgrom said with a grin.

"This'll do fine, thanks."

"Must've been the torpedo," said Sigursdottir. "Shockwave burst your sinuses."

"Must have been. Hold on a second. Call coming in."

Harmer? Handler. What's up? I got your message, and when I came out on deck, there was a massive ship sinking and the *Admiral Winterbrook* firing torpedoes left, right and centre. I leave you alone for a few hours...

Yeah, you missed some big fun, Manhandler. I'll fill you in when I come back over. I'm probably going to need more of your magic medicine, too. I've started getting nosebleeds. That's a bad sign.

No, really?

"I should be getting back to the jetboat," Dev said to Sigursdottir. "Handler's giving me grief."

"Off you go, then," said Sigursdottir. "Missing you already."

"Yeah," said Milgrom, wiping away an imaginary tear. "Don't be a stranger, you hear?"

18

THE TWO BOATS resumed their journey south. Next on their itinerary was a refuelling stop at the township of Llyr, some 300 kilometres away on the fringes of the Tropics of Lei Gong.

After Dev had brought Handler up to speed on recent events, he asked him about the symbol the Tritonians had made out of the wreckage of the harpoon cannon.

Rather than describe it verbally, he drew a simple picture using his commplant's sketch function and beamed it to Handler:

"Ring any bells?"

Handler sucked his teeth. "Yes. I've seen this once or twice before."

"What does it mean?"

"It's religious. Iconography."

"Representing...?"

"Ah, that's just it. There isn't much data to go on, I'm afraid. I've done a correspondence course in Tritonian anthropology. It's one of the requirements for the job. But if I tell you that the course lasted just a couple of hours, it should give you an idea how much we know about these people's behavioural patterns and belief systems."

"Not a lot."

"Next to nothing. They're a hard race to study, for the obvious reasons. They live underwater and communicate using a visual language which is difficult to converse in for anyone who isn't modified the way you and I are. There aren't many xeno-anthropologists who are prepared to have their DNA rearranged so drastically. The quest for knowledge and academic advancement has its limits, it seems. In fact, only one guy has ever made it all the way out here to learn about Tritonian society, and he didn't bother with altering himself."

"What did he do instead?"

"Tried artificial solutions," said Handler. "Professor Robert Adams, his name was. Arrived here in '65, couple of years after the first wave of settlers. He used scuba gear, deep-dive suits, and a specially-made helmet fitted with an LED mesh to mimic photophores, run by a heuristic translation program."

"You say 'tried.'"

Handler gave a wry smile. "It was a noble effort. He lasted less than a month. Software, no matter how sophisticated, can't hope to pick up a language that's emotion-based."

"Way I see it, it's as close to telepathy as anything."

"That's it. Prof Adams's program was applying algorithms to patterns that defy mathematical analysis. The software could copy the Tritonians' light patterns but not comprehend them. It couldn't correlate their meanings and build a dictionary. Essentially, Adams was a parrot, echoing what was said to him without knowing what he was saying. To the Tritonians it must have come across as a joke. Or worse."

"An insult."

"Which," said Handler, nodding, "may be why one of them took umbrage and ran him through with a spear. Adams said the wrong thing by accident, or else the Tritonian just couldn't bear the sight of this blank mechanical face shovelling out phrases at random. It offended his sensibilities."

"Like the Uncanny Valley."

"Right. Just as human forms inhabited by Plussers seem 'off' to us, Adams seemed 'off' to the Tritonians."

"And he got stabbed for it."

"Near fatally. He recovered, but since then no one else has been very keen to conduct research into this field, surprise, surprise. Whatever we know about Tritonians has come from envoys like me engaging with them on a day-to-day basis, gleaning whatever we can as we go along – snippets here and there that build into a picture, like a mosaic."

"And speaking of pictures…"

"Yes." Handler reviewed the image Dev had sketched. "What you have there is something called either the Ice King or the God Beneath the Sea. Take your pick. The names are the closest approximations we can manage."

"And who or what is the Ice King?"

"That's the big question, isn't it? Far as we can gather, it's both a creation myth and some kind of apocalypse myth. The Ice King is an ancient, all-powerful god. Many millions of years ago he ruled the planet, his frozen domain. But it was just him and a few animals for company, and he was bored and lonely. So, he melted the ice, turning it to water and thus creating the world as we know it today. In that way he made a home for people – Tritonians – to live and flourish in."

"But if it used to be ice and he's an *Ice* King…"

"Exactly. It was an act of supreme self-sacrifice. He couldn't live here himself anymore. So he disappeared into the oceans, and since that time he's been asleep somewhere, lying dormant."

"Right, and don't tell me, but when the time comes, when it's the end of days, he'll awaken from his slumber and rise again to destroy everything."

"Something along those lines," said Handler. "There will come a time when the world is overrun with sinners and unbelievers, and that's when the Ice King will return, to wreak chaos and devastation and eliminate all who do not follow his ways. The seas will run red with blood. Only the faithful, his loyal acolytes, will survive."

"Nice. So we have a religious sect on Triton who believe the Ice King, the God Beneath the Sea, is due a second coming any day now, and the righteous will be spared while the infidels will all die horribly."

"It seems some religious tropes are universal."

"And these fanatics are the ones spearheading the attacks on settlers. They count humans among the heathen."

"The symbol appears to confirm it. There was a rumour going round that it had been found at the scene of at least one other attack, daubed on a wall in the victim's blood. But that was only hearsay, so I didn't pay it much attention. No hard evidence, pictorial or otherwise."

"Well, we've got it now," said Dev. "Sigursdottir and I both saw it, plain as day. What I can't figure out is what the symbol's meant to represent."

"Beats me too. Is that curve the sky? The firmament?"

"Maybe the circles are Triton's moons."

"What does that make the forked lines, though? Lightning?"

"Or it might be some sort of pictogram. A hieroglyph?"

"It might be, if the Tritonians had a written language, which they don't. Communication is always done face-to-face with them. Everything is visual and personal. They couldn't write anything down because it would become meaningless when detached from its emotional content. It would become verbal garbage, like Professor Adams's LEDs."

"Yeah, I can see that. Also, how would you write in moving lights? What medium could you use?"

"I'm sure the Tritonians could figure that out if they wanted to. A very simple symbol is probably the closest they get to representing an abstract concept in concrete form. Aside from that, they just light-speak to one another. In the same way, the story of the Ice King has never been formally enshrined. It's a saga, a tale told by poets and parents, passed on from one generation to the next. Oral tradition."

"I've seen another symbol," Dev said. "A cutaway of a nautilus shell."

"Where?"

"On a Tritonian. Remember yesterday? When you nearly got me eaten by the thalassoraptor?"

"That wasn't my fault!" Handler protested hotly.

"I know, I'm kidding. But one of the Tritonians there had the nautilus design on her chest. Ritually scarred into her skin."

Dev refrained from mentioning that he had seen the same design – the same Tritonian – again today, just now. If, as seemed to be the case, the two indigenes at Tangaroa had followed the *Reckless Abandon* all this way, why? What were they after? He could think of no answer that wasn't worrisome, and he felt Handler needn't know about it just yet. The straight-laced, high-strung ISS liaison had enough on his plate already.

Besides, it might be nothing. Coincidence. A false alarm.

"Ah, the nautilus," Handler said. "It's a reasonably commonplace motif. I've seen it a few times when I've been interfacing with the locals. I've seen other designs as well – fish skeletons, a redback, something that looks a bit like an octopus. They could just be decoration, but if you ask me, they may well signify familial or tribal affiliation."

"Like wearing clan tartan."

"Yes, or else denote social rank and status, like the Maoris' *moko* tattoos."

"Or membership of a gang. They could even be prison tats, I suppose. What if an octopus represents an eight-year jail stretch for a Tritonian criminal?"

"An intriguing proposition."

"I'm joking, Manhandler. Well, sort of. Half joking."

"It makes as much sense as any other theory. Perhaps Tritonian scarification is there to show that you're a bad guy, a hard case, not to be messed with. Someone could put together an amazing doctoral thesis on this topic, couldn't they?"

"If only there was a xeno-anthropologist out there with the balls to become a fish-man and find out."

"I wouldn't recommend it," said Handler. "I can't remember much about the procedure except that it felt weird and really, really hurt. Especially when my gills broke through."

Dev gave a sharp intake of breath, not in sympathy but in actual pain.

"Are you all right?" Handler asked.

"No."

Tiny electric shocks had started shooting down into Dev's jawbone from his lower teeth at the back. He touched the side of his face, probing. He was gentle as anything, hardly exerting any pressure with his hand, but all at once, a molar came free from its gum bed.

He plucked it from his mouth with thumb and forefinger. The tooth had fallen out whole, roots and all. It sat in his palm, smeared in blood and looking larger than it had any right to be.

Handler winced. "Ouch."

Dev inspected the gap in his gum with the tip of his tongue. It felt huge, a bottomless pit. Suddenly, spontaneously, the adjacent molar also fell out. He spat it onto the deck, along with more blood.

"Oh, this fucking sucks," he said. "First nosebleeds. Now I'm losing teeth. What next, my gonads?"

"Ten minutes after I gave you a shot, too."

Dev consulted his countdown timer.

52:14:39

"Is there anything else we can do to slow down the whole falling-to-bits thing?" he said.

"Not that I'm aware of. It's not as if we can order you up another host form and transfer you across into that. Not in time, at any rate. We don't have a growth vat of our own on Triton."

"Not considered important enough, huh?"

"We're a lesser ISS outpost," Handler admitted. "Not fully equipped. The body you're in was supplied by the central hub and delivered weeks ago. It's been sitting in a stasis solution ever since. We'd have to wait several more weeks before we could get hold of a replacement."

"Then I'll just have to muddle along with what I've got, won't I?"

"Afraid so."

19

LLYR WAS MUCH larger than Tangaroa, a manmade archipelago covering some five square kilometres. This far south the air was noticeably warmer and moister, and large grey clouds boiled on the horizon. They had crossed the 23rd parallel and were officially in the tropics.

The skin-prickling which Dev had felt earlier in the day returned with a vengeance. As Handler guided the *Reckless Abandon* into a berth beside the *Admiral Winterbrook* at Llyr's main marina, Dev rubbed his bare forearms, and eventually started scratching. He stopped when he realised that his fingernails were raising red welts.

"Looks like you're developing a reaction to heat," Handler said. "Hives. Another sign that your host form's malfunctioning – your immune system's going into overdrive."

"Any suggestions for remedies, Panhandler?"

"I thought I was Manhandler."

"I'm trying names out for size."

"Well, for what it's worth, I prefer Manhandler. And my suggestion is, try a dip in the water."

Needing no further invitation, Dev leapt off the jetboat. The water was lukewarm but cooler than the air, blissfully so.

He luxuriated in its tepid embrace, performing slow somersaults and barrel rolls.

A tiny fish popped up in front of his nose. It was as long and thin as a pencil, with a pair of pea-sized eyes perched at the front, quite out of proportion with the rest of it. The eyes made the fish look goofy and comical, and Dev couldn't help but smile.

The fish goggled at him inquisitively. Dev held up a finger, and the creature scooted backwards with wafts of fan-shaped gossamer fins. Then timidly, inch by inch, it crept forward again.

Dev waggled his finger, and the fish mirrored the action, flexing its body. He wondered if it thought his finger was a prospective mate that could be seduced with a few neat dance moves.

You're barking up the wrong tree there, my friend, he wanted to tell it.

Abruptly, a dozen identical fish appeared alongside the first as if answering some invisible summons. They all seemed fascinated by his finger, like professors investigating some new scientific phenomenon. They converged on its tip, eyeing it beadily.

Then there was a whole shoal of them, more than Dev could count. They filled his field of vision, a thousand sinuous silver ingots.

The frontmost of them – it may have been the original one, but with so many lookalikes to choose from Dev had lost track – nudged right up to his finger. Its soft lips opened and closed a few times. It looked like a reluctant Romeo, trying to pluck up the nerve to go in for the kiss.

Then a spike darted out from its mouth, pricking the fingertip. Dev snatched his hand back. Almost instantly, his finger went numb as far as the first knuckle joint.

As if taking their cue, other fish from the shoal flashed

forwards and jabbed their pointed tongues into him. He felt pinpricks everywhere – arms, chest, legs – and the pain in each instance was followed immediately by a brief tingling sensation, then numbness.

He swept his arms wildly at the fish, who flickered out of his reach then swarmed back in around him. Now he was being stung from behind too, on his back, his calves, the nape of his neck.

He thrashed and flailed, churning the water. The tiny fish had him completely surrounded, walled in, cocooned. Their tongues, half as long as their bodies, snaked out and nipped. He batted the creatures away more violently than ever, smashing them, snapping them in two, but always there were new ones to take the place of the ones he killed, an endless supply of the little nightmares.

He stopped trying to fight them – it was futile – and focused his mind on escape instead. He struck out for the surface, clawing through the wriggling, writhing mass of fish, and as soon as he hit air he made for the nearest refuge, which was the dock. He could feel his limbs getting sluggish, his muscles weakening. The shoal stuck with him, still stinging him wherever they could even as he hauled himself out of the water onto dry land.

He collapsed prone on the dock, panting hard. He was shuddering all over and his vision was blurred. He was aware of people assembling around him – legs, combat boots, sea pattern camo fabric. He heard dim, distant laughter, and then felt the burn of a hypodermic injection in his thigh.

Slowly the shudders subsided and sensation returned to his skin. His breathing stabilised and his eyesight cleared.

Handler was hunkered down on his haunches, looking concerned. The entire team of Marines were ranged in a semicircle, looking less concerned.

"Harmer," Handler said. "Dev. Look at me. How are you feeling? Are you back with us?"

"Yes. Fuck. Yes, I think so."

"You were going into anaphylaxis. I gave you an epinephrine shot."

"I offered to urinate on you," said Milgrom. "I would have if the lieutenant hadn't stopped me. Just remember that. I was prepared to piss all over you. That's the kind of girl I am."

"It wouldn't have worked," said Sigursdottir. "Urinating on stings to relieve the inflammation – that's an old wives' tale."

"Who said anything about inflammation? I just thought it'd be amusing."

"Your generosity is appreciated," Dev said, struggling to sit up. "Urghh. Those little fuckers. They seemed to cute as well."

"Stickerfish?" said Handler. "They are cute – until they start stabbing you with their tongues."

"Once they've put enough neurotoxin into you that you're paralysed and helpless," said Milgrom, "they start snacking on you, nibbling off your skin, burrowing into your flesh. They've got sharp little teeth." She grinned with relish. "It's not pleasant."

"Really? Because it sounds like an absolute hoot."

"Well, the good news is the feeding frenzy only last about five minutes. Once they've filled their bellies, the stickerfish just go. The bad news is, by then there's enough blood in the water to attract a big predator. Either way, you're a goner."

"Is there anything in this stupid sea that doesn't try to kill you?"

"Nope. That's one of the joys of Triton. It's a wonder they don't make this place a holiday resort."

Handler reached out and helped Dev to his feet. "Actually Triton isn't as bad as all that. The corporal is exaggerating."

"No, I'm not."

"You've just been desperately unlucky, that's all."

"Unluckiness seems to be the defining characteristic of this mission so far," Dev remarked. "But maybe that's about to change. Maybe I've had my quota."

He wouldn't have laid money on it, though.

20

GUNNERY SERGEANT JIANG remained with the boats, tasked with replenishing their fuel tanks. Triton was plentifully supplied with deep-sea deposits of methane which, in liquid form, drove almost every vessel on the ocean. A few kilometres north of Llyr lay a couple of the drilling rigs that tapped the gas from the seabed and condensed it. They were crowned with feathers of blue flame, burning off the over-pressure to protect the plant equipment.

The refuelling would take a couple of hours, so in the meantime everyone else – Dev, Handler, the other Marines – headed for the centre of town to find a place to eat.

On Sigursdottir's orders, all weapons and body armour were removed and left behind on the boats. This was temporary shore leave, and standard etiquette applied.

On an esplanade that skirted one of Llyr's larger domes was an open-air food court. Cafés and restaurants served local staples, either fish-based or derived from homegrown algae crops. There were also stalls selling imported treats at eye-watering prices. A can of soda would set you back an average week's wages; a bar of chocolate twice that.

At a large communal table Sigursdottir ordered tapas

for everybody. Dishes arrived in dribs and drabs, brought by a slender young waiter who seemed intimidated by the Marines, and with good reason.

"Ohhh, yeah," said Milgrom, watching him walk away to fetch more food. "Look at that tight butt. I'd grab myself two handfuls of that and just tear."

"Kind of skinny," said Blunt. "I prefer a man with a bit of meat on him."

"Like Master Chief Reynolds, you mean?"

"Will you shut the fuck up about Master Chief Reynolds?"

"I would, but he's just so *dreamy*," Francis cooed, fluttering her eyelashes.

Blunt clouted her round the head. Francis just giggled.

"I like 'em skinny," said Milgrom. "Less resistance with the skinny ones. You can really show 'em who's in charge." She wolf-whistled at the waiter. "Isn't that right, gorgeous? I know what you want. You want me to slap you down on the ground and straddle you. Ride you 'til you're worn to a nub. Am I right?"

The waiter smiled wanly, no doubt thinking of his tip. So to speak.

Dev sampled everything on offer. Battered lumps of fish. Fish in sauce. Fish roe. Greasy fish-tasting globs. Assorted types of shellfish and mollusc. Chunks of algae cut into shapes and cooked to resemble vegetables. Yet more fish.

Fortunately there was beer, to rinse the fishiness out of your mouth. Fermented-seaweed beer, to be precise, but it was close enough to the real thing – and a great deal less hazardous than double moonshine.

The drunker Milgrom got, the worse she behaved. She pawed the hapless waiter whenever he went by. She flirted crudely with a group of men at the adjacent table, who began by encouraging her but after a while got bored and started studiously ignoring her. She bellowed out dirty, but admittedly very funny, jokes. Stern looks from Sigursdottir would quieten her for a while, but then she would begin again.

Blunt, Francis and the other privates weren't much better. They took the corporal's rowdiness as a licence to vamp it up themselves.

Dev could see that Sigursdottir was cutting her troops some slack. They were on shore leave. They should be allowed to make the most of the down-time and fool around a little.

He feared, however, that things were going to get out of hand, and that it might happen faster than Sigursdottir realised.

He wasn't sure what it was, but there was a mood hanging over Llyr. Something in the air. He sensed it without being able to put his finger on it. During the walk from the marina to the esplanade he had noticed furtive looks from the residents, a shiftiness in the presence of the Marines. People going about their daily business had stiffened as the team went by, relaxing when they were gone.

It had occurred to him that this could be how the settlers normally reacted around the military. There was an inherent tension, a simmering mistrust. Servicemen often had that effect on civilians.

What he was reminded of, however, was the way crooks acted whenever the police showed up. Even the most hardened criminals shied away from cops, doing their best to look innocent, which of course only served to make them look guilty. Dev had seen it a lot during his misspent youth. Law enforcers were like searchlights. You didn't dare look at them directly. You lowered your gaze and turned away, waiting until their attention was no longer on you.

As far as he knew, Llyr was an ordinary town. Law-abiding. Everything above board here. So why were the residents behaving as though it wasn't?

He could feel the tension deepening as the Marines got louder and more raucous. Sigursdottir finally detected it too, and began hissing orders to her subordinates, trying to keep them in line. Around their table, a hubbub of discontent was rising. Not just in the restaurant but across the esplanade, locals were turning their way, scowling. Wariness was mutating into resentment.

"I think we should leave," Dev said to her.

"I think so too," Sigursdottir said. "There's a weird vibe here, and my men aren't helping."

This statement was truer than ever of Milgrom, who now made a lunge for the beleaguered waiter, shunting her chair back and enfolding him in a bear hug.

"Feel those tits, little boy?" she growled. His head came level with her chest. "How'd you like to get your paws around those bad mamas?" She buried his face in the deep valley of her cleavage. "What d'you say? You and me, having a dance together. And by dance I mean sex."

"Milgrom." Sigursdottir got to her feet. "That's enough. Let him go. You've had your jollies. Poor kid's scared out of his wits. It's time we got back to the boat."

"But sir, do you know how long it's been since I had a man? A girl gets tired of her own hand, y'know."

"Corporal Milgrom." Sigursdottir moved a step closer. "I have given you a direct order. You have to the count of three to obey. One. Two."

"All right, all right!" Milgrom shoved the waiter away, so hard he banged into a table, toppling glasses. "I was only playing. Can't a girl have a little fun? He was into it, too."

"We'll take our bill, please," Sigursdottir said to the pale-faced waiter.

Behind him, the diners whose drinks had been spilled grumbled in complaint. Sigursdottir offered to buy a round of refills. The gesture did not seem to placate them.

"Keep your money, bitch," one of them said.

"Better still," said another, "shove it up your snatch."

That was all the excuse Milgrom needed. With a cry of "*Bastards!*" she threw herself at the diners. There were five of them, fishermen with shaggy beards and outdoor-work physiques. As one, they rose to the challenge.

Sigursdottir yelled at her to stand down, but it was too late. Milgrom had a fire of belligerence in her stomach and a commanding officer's honour to defend. She was a ball of righteous, beer-fuelled fury.

The fight did not last long. Five men, no matter how burly, were no match for a hulking, body-modded Marine.

But then other settlers joined in. And so, accordingly, did the other Marines. Both sides piled in against one another, while Sigursdottir shouted to be heard above the fray, vainly attempting to restore calm.

That was until someone swung a fist at her. Then she got embroiled in the whole fracas too.

Dev, though not averse to a punch-up himself, decided he couldn't afford to get involved in this one. His ailing host form was in sorry enough shape already. He had no wish to add bruises and possibly broken bones to its litany of woes.

Handler was in a state of abject terror, cowering and cringing as furniture and crockery flew and the air resounded with yelps of pain and the thuds of blows. Dev seized him by the collar and dragged him through the milling throng, shunting people aside to clear a path.

They made it out of the restaurant onto the edge of the esplanade.

Then their way was blocked by a couple of locals.

"You're with those Marines, aren't you?" snarled one of them.

"No," said Dev.

"Yes, you are," said the other. "We saw you sitting at their table."

"Okay, we are. But not *with them* with them, if you get my drift. We're just sort of heading in the same direction as them. Fellow travellers."

One of the men drew a knife. The kind of knife you gutted fish with. Big fish. The blade was wickedly curved, its lower half serrated for sawing through bone.

The other local brandished a short-handled gaff hook.

"You two look sort of like fish," he said. "Let's see if you slit open just the same way."

21

HANDLER WHIMPERED. DEV shoved him backwards, putting himself between the ISS liaison and the pair of locals.

"I've got this," he said. "Leave it to me."

But he wasn't as confident as he sounded. This body was resilient, yes, with good reflexes and above-average strength, but he couldn't rely on it. It might crap out on him at any moment.

Best just to get the fight over and done with as quickly as possible, then.

The man with the gutting knife shifted to the left. His friend with the gaff hook prowled to the right. Swiftly Dev sized them up, assessing which was the greater threat. Gutting Knife, he decided. He was the wirier of the two, and a wicked, jagged gash on his cheek suggested he was no stranger to violence. No stranger to pain and injury, at least.

The gash looked relatively fresh, too, no more than a week old. Still inflamed at the edges, and Dev could make out the faint ladder mark of subdermal smart-stitches, there to tighten and draw the wound shut before dissolving when their job was done. A work accident, Dev assumed, although he couldn't rule out it being the result of a fight.

Dev feinted at Gaff Hook, causing him to take a step back, then rushed Gutting Knife. With a forearm block he batted aside the blade, accompanying the attack with a stiff-fingered strike to the throat.

Gutting Knife jerked his head back just enough to dull the impact. It paused him in his tracks but wasn't the crippling one-and-done hit Dev had been after.

Gaff Hook came in from the side, weapon raised for a downward slash. Dev spun and rammed the heel of his palm into the man's elbow as the hook descended. He heard and felt a *crack*, and Gaff Hook yelped. The elbow had been dislocated, that arm rendered useless.

A warning cry from Handler, and Dev swivelled just in time to see Gutting Knife lunging at him from behind. He twisted out of the path of the blade and gave its wielder a rabbit punch to the kidneys as he stumbled past.

Gutting Knife went down with a whooping, strangulated gasp, while Gaff Hook, having transferred the hook to his other hand, swiped at Dev sideways. Dev reared away from the weapon's swing, butting up against the steel balustrade that bordered the esplanade's waterside edge.

Over Gaff Hook's shoulder he saw at a glance that the brawl at the restaurant was losing steam. Most of the locals involved now lay unconscious or incapacitated on the floor, and Sigursdottir was marshalling her troops, coaxing them into a withdrawal before word spread and more opponents arrived. Corporal Milgrom alone was still fighting, overcome by a sort of berserker rage. She had just smashed a plastic chair over someone's head and was brandishing one of its snapped-off legs like a cudgel, inviting anyone within earshot to come and have a go if they thought they were hard enough.

That was all Dev had time to register before Gaff Hook renewed his assault. With one arm hanging limp and his weapon in his off hand, however, he was unbalanced and clumsy. Dev had only to pivot on the ball of one foot, and Gaff Hook lumbered headlong, helplessly, into the balustrade.

It was too tempting and too easy just to pitch him over the top rail of the balustrade, but that was no reason not to do it. Dev grabbed him by the seat of the trousers and flipped him heels over head, sending him somersaulting into the sea. Gaff Hook surfaced immediately, spluttering, and hauled himself one-handed through the water to grasp the balustrade for support. His hook was gone.

Dev debated whether to stamp on Gaff Hook's fingers so that he was forced to let go and keep swimming, or pretend to help him out onto dry land only to dunk him back under. Some further humiliation was in order, he felt. He wasn't going to let the bastard off that lightly.

"Dev?"

Handler's tone was querulous and frightened. Gutting Knife had recovered from the kidney punch sooner than Dev expected and, while Dev was busy dealing with Gaff Hook, had got back to his feet and seized Handler by the scruff of the neck. His blade hovered at the ISS liaison's throat, and he looked more than ready to use it.

"I'm sick of you people," he growled. "I know you two aren't sea monkeys, not exactly. Frankly I don't know what the fuck you are. But you look enough like sea monkeys that it makes no difference in my mind. Those buggers are determined to screw things up for the rest of us, and I've had it up to here with that. Them. You."

"Put the knife down." Dev darted another glance at Sigursdottir and the other Marines. They were all engaged in defusing Milgrom's drunken battle frenzy, restraining her and trying to drag her away. They weren't going to be any help to him in this situation right here. They had their hands full. Milgrom was bellowing and resisting, and not about to come quietly.

"I don't think so," said Gutting Knife. He nodded at the blade and at Handler. "This is how sea monkeys should be treated. We've tried being all sympathetic and understanding and reasonable with them, and where has that bleeding-heart bullshit got us? Nowhere. They've just taken it for weakness and stepped up their campaign against us. Know how I came by this cut on my face?"

"I didn't think it was a shaving accident," Dev said. He was playing for time. "Why not tell me about it?"

"I got it fending off one of the fuckers from my boat. He boarded while I was laying out my nets. Just popped up out of the briny onto the main deck, bold as you please, like this was his property and I was trespassing, and not the other way round. Had one of those ivory spears they like to carry. Well, I wasn't going to stand for any of that crap, was I? Neither were my shipmates."

"Of course you weren't. Now please, let my guy there go."

Gutting Knife pressed the cutting edge of the blade harder against Handler's skin. Handler hissed in panic and shot Dev a frantic, pleading stare.

"So we laid into him," Gutting Knife continued, "the three of us: me, my bosun, my first mate. He was an agile bastard, I'll give him that. Hopped about the place like a flea. But he was young, inexperienced. Looked like he was a teenager, maybe, no older than that. Reckon he was trying to prove his manliness or something, the way kids do."

"So it was three grown men versus a child. You must be proud of yourselves."

Handler glowered, his eyes saying, *Antagonise him, why don't you?*

But Dev knew he was going to be able to end the standoff only through patience and needling. He wanted to lull Gutting Knife into a false sense of security and at the same time keep him rattled. That way, with Dev veering between guile and aggression, Gutting Knife wouldn't be thinking straight; couldn't be sure whether or not he was being played. His confusion would eventually give Dev an opening, an opportunity to leap in and neutralise him.

Or so Dev hoped. Nothing was guaranteed here except Gutting Knife's unpredictability. There could be a successful outcome, or there could be Xavier Handler on the ground, windpipe slashed wide, aspirating his own blood.

"We did what we had to," Gutting Knife said. "How were we to know he wasn't an ambush? How were we to know there weren't a dozen more of them about to jump out and surprise us? We took the sea monkey out; anyone would."

"But not before he got you a good one to the face."

"Yeah, and he paid for it. He's still..." Gutting Knife blinked and twitched his head. "He paid for it all right. That's all I have to say."

All at once the man was looking guilty as sin and Dev was getting the same aura of defensiveness and furtiveness off him that he'd noticed earlier among the other townspeople. If anything, it was stronger with Gutting Knife, more overt.

There wasn't time to cross-examine him, however. Out of the corner of his eye, Dev spied Gaff Hook clambering up the balustrade, shedding water. If Gaff Hook chose to go on the offensive again, Dev's attention would be divided and he'd be in no position to save Handler. The ISS liaison's fate would be entirely up to Gutting Knife.

Dev needed to wrap things up right now. No more pussyfooting around.

"Listen, this can go either of two ways," he said. "You kill him, and I beat the shit out of you. Or I get to you before you kill him, and I still beat the shit out of you, only not so badly. You walk away."

"You're saying whatever happens, I lose. Are you trying to negotiate with me here? Because it doesn't seem like you've got the hang of bargaining."

Handler appeared to agree. His gills were flapping and flaring anxiously.

Dev signalled reassurance to him using his photophores. Their glow was less perceptible out of the water, in broad daylight, but Handler got the message nonetheless.

Dev then, using the same medium, warned him to brace himself.

"What are you doing?" Gutting Knife demanded. "That fucking light-show stuff. Stop it! It isn't natural."

"Last chance," Dev said. Gaff Hook was on this side of the balustrade now, lowering himself awkwardly, hampered by his bum arm. "Give up, and I'll go easy on you."

Gutting Knife sneered.

Dev flashed an alert to Handler, urging him to shunt himself backwards.

Handler, to his credit, did as requested, with scarcely any hesitation. He pushed his shoulder hard into Gutting Knife's chest, with almost his whole weight behind it.

Briefly, Gutting Knife was taken aback.

Dev sprang. He grasped Gutting Knife's blade hand in both of his before the man could recover his equilibrium. He twisted it round sharply and savagely enough to separate the carpal bones from the radius and ulna.

Gutting Knife could only scream at the sudden, searing pain. The blade fell. Dev pressed home the advantage, bringing his adversary to his knees with a stamp to his instep, then stoving in a few ribs with a vicious toecap kick.

After that there was little Gutting Knife could do except writhe on the ground in agony, clutching his side.

There was little Gaff Hook could do either except make a run for it. His friend had been disarmed and reduced to a pitiful, howling wreck. He had no desire to end up the same way, and he could tell he wouldn't stand a chance, injured as he already was, against the weird half-human, half-Tritonian hybrid. Cradling his limp arm, he scuttled away as fast as his legs would carry him.

"Well done," Dev said, patting Handler on the biceps. "You did good."

The ISS liaison looked relieved but still shaken. "He could have… He nearly…"

"But he didn't, did he? That's the main thing. And you were a part of it. You acted. Give yourself a pat on the back."

The Marines had finally got Milgrom under control and were hustling her towards the food court exit. Sigursdottir beckoned commandingly to Dev and Handler.

"We are out of here," she said. "Now. Most ricky-tick."

As they made their way towards the boats, Dev remarked to her, "That could have gone better."

"Don't gloat, Harmer. Don't you dare. I'm pissed off enough as it is. This is on me. I let it get out of hand. I should have nipped it in the bud while I could. Maddox will tear me a new one when he finds out."

"I won't tell if you won't."

"Of course I'm going to tell. I'll have to give him a full report. You can't just cover an incident like this up. Even if I personally don't let him know, he'll hear about it some other way. Someone from Llyr will blab, or even lodge a formal complaint. It's inevitable. And then I'll be even deeper in the brown."

"Okay," Dev said. "Well, let's deal with that when it happens. But when you do file your report, don't overlook the fact that the locals were behaving in a squirrelly fashion before things kicked off. There's something not right here, and they don't want us knowing what, and that might be why they were as ready to have a scrap as you people were to start one."

"You know this?"

"Normally I'd call it a gut feeling and that'd be as far as it goes, but the guy I just put in intensive care back there blurted out something that makes me almost certain this town has something to hide. A guilty secret."

"And you think we should find out what it is."

"I think it would be a gross dereliction of duty, lieutenant, if we didn't."

22

THE TWO BOATS sailed away from Llyr into the gathering dusk at speed, putting as much distance as possible between them and the township. So long and good riddance.

Once Llyr had disappeared over the horizon, however, the *Reckless Abandon* and the *Admiral Winterbrook* both came to a dead stop.

Half an hour later, as night fell, the Marine catamaran launched a URIB, an ultralight rigid-hulled inflatable boat, seven metres long and powered by a near-silent electric inboard motor. Manning the central helm console was Private Reyes, with Private Cully at the bow, crouching by the forward-mounted 12.7mm machine gun. The only other occupant was Dev.

Sigursdottir had needed some persuading – but not a lot – to grant Dev permission to return to Llyr. Once he had explained to her just what he thought the townspeople were hiding and how it could be advantageous to the mission, she had given him the go-ahead.

"At least we might be able to salvage *something* from this fiasco," she had said.

Handler had taken a little more convincing, and Dev had

had to remind him that he was answerable to Dev, not the other way round, so canvassing his opinion was more a courtesy than anything. Handler acknowledged this and said that as long as he himself didn't have to go back to Llyr, he supposed he was okay with the idea.

"Spoken like the truly sensible person you are," Dev had said, adding, "I'm toying with Can Handle Himself In A Fight as a nickname. How about that?"

"Bit of a mouthful," Handler had replied, "but it's the best you've come up with so far."

Triton's twin moons were rising as the URIB bounded across the waves, retracing the course the two bigger boats had just travelled. The collision-damaged one, designated Luna A, was the larger of the satellites but also the more distant. Its intact counterpart, Luna B, was smaller but nearer. By some quirk of astrophysics, their orbits positioned them so that they appeared to be of identical size when viewed from the planet's surface. Set close together, they gazed down from the sky like a pair of pearly, cataracted eyes.

The moons' light lent the sea an opalescent dazzle, while the URIB's wake shimmered a sparkling green as the boat's progress disturbed the bioluminescent phytoplankton. Soon, manmade illumination was added to the mix: the lights of Llyr, harsh yellow and white against the night sky.

Reyes slowed the URIB to a crawl.

"Close enough?" she asked.

"It'll do," Dev replied. "Don't want anyone spotting us."

"We'll hang back here. You get in a jam, send out a call and we'll come running. Otherwise we'll wait, and you can RV with us when you're done."

"Cool. Thanks."

"Don't leave it too long," said Cully. "Reyes's conversation gets very boring very quickly."

"Hey!"

"And she has a tendency to nod off during recces and stakeouts."

"No, that's you."

"Only because you're so dull you send me to sleep."

Dev tuned out their banter, focusing on Llyr. About four klicks, he estimated. Shouldn't be a problem, as long as his body played ball. Since the outbreak of hives earlier, there hadn't been any fresh symptoms of decay – no more bleeding, no further rashes. Dev felt slightly dizzy, but that was all, and it might be nothing more than mild seasickness. Handler had offered him a nucleotide top-up before he left, but there hadn't been time to fit it in. He would have it when he returned.

With a farewell nod to the two Marines, Dev dived overboard.

The sea rumbled around him as he swam. The further he got from the URIB, the more he became aware of a plethora of marine sounds. The water was not silent. It was alive with noises – a cacophony of clickings, moans, shrill keening ululations. They came from unseen creatures communicating across distances or finding their way through the darkness by echolocation. Dev felt like he was crossing a crowded bar.

Then there were the visible signs of life, no less plentiful. Lights flashed far below him, flickers of brilliance in every colour of the rainbow. These belonged to the inhabitants of the benthic zone, that realm of perpetual night, and it was like soaring high above a fireworks display, a welter of pulsing fluorescence.

In the shallows, meanwhile, myriad fauna surrounded him – finned things, soft things, cartilaginous things, shelled things, top-lit by moonglow and starshine. Some were hideous, with snaggle teeth or vampiric fangs or lifeless jet-black eyes set beneath beetling brows. Others were fascinating and beautiful, crowned with flowing fairytale fronds or elaborate horny growths, like something a child might dream up. Others still were drab and nondescript, shoals of matt-grey small fry as alike as peas.

Not knowing which species were dangerous and which weren't, but not wanting to take any chances, Dev gave them all a wide berth. Any creatures that didn't dart out of his way as he approached, he diverted around or swam under.

He was glad of the HVP at his hip, especially when something large and streamlined loomed up beside him and kept pace with him for a while. It was at least three metres long from its pointed nose to its sickle-shaped tail and it moved with the purposeful ease of a shark. It seemed curious about him but never strayed closer than about thirty metres, so that he couldn't get a clear view of it, only glimpses of a murky silhouette.

Eventually the big fish lost interest and swam off, but Dev remained on his guard for several minutes after. The beast might still be shadowing him, just from a greater range. He wasn't taking anything for granted, not in this relentlessly deadly ocean.

From time to time he popped his head above the surface in order to re-establish his bearings. Llyr's domes, with their jewelling of lights, drew ever nearer.

He reached his destination twenty minutes after leaving the URIB. Having studied a local insite map of the township beforehand, Dev had identified a number of possible targets, but the simplest and most straightforward was an artificial beach, a narrow shelf of sand that sloped down to the waterline. A huge, fine-meshed cage extended around it into the sea, creating a lido that was safe for recreational bathing.

Dev slithered over the pontoons marking the outer rim of the cage and glided through wavelets to the beach, which was deserted except for a couple sharing a smoke. They were young, in their mid-teens.

As he padded across the sand towards them, he caught a bitterly aromatic scent wafting to him on the breeze. He immediately recognised it as cannablast – ordinary marijuana cross-spliced with vroomshroom, a psychotropic fungus found on the forested planet Tau Ceti E.

Even though vroomshroom had not been shown to have any long-lasting side effects and the high it produced, while acute, was only short-lived, it was still classified as a class-A drug, meaning cannablast was borderline illegal.

Dev suppressed a smile.

Good for these kids.

Good for him, too.

They didn't notice him until he was almost on top of them. The boy made a half-hearted, ham-fisted attempt to hide the joint, masking it inside his cupped palm, while the girl stared up at Dev, frowning in puzzlement. They were both pretty stoned. Their eyes shone glassily in the moonlight.

"Are you...?" the girl said. "What *are* you? You're a bit like... but you're not."

"You must be that dude," said the boy croakily. "The one who represents us to the Tritonians. Our whatchemacall – ambassador. Right?"

He had mistaken Dev for Handler, which was understandable. As far as most settlers knew, there was only one amphibious human on the planet.

"Shit, you're not here to bust us, are you?" The girl's expression turned fraught. "Oh, man, Ty, I said we shouldn't smoke outside. I told you. I knew someone would catch us."

The boy called Ty said, "He's not anybody with any, like, legal power. He can't arrest us. Can you, mister?"

"No," said Dev.

"See, Aletha? Relax."

"You grow that yourself?" Dev asked, gesturing to the poorly concealed joint.

Shy pride lit up Ty's face. "Yup. Got a mini hydroponics lab set up in my cupboard at home. Seeds cost a fortune, but worth it. I mean, what else are you going to do to pass the time out here? I don't even want to *be* on this shit hole. It's a pimple on the butt-end of the galaxy."

"Yeah," said Aletha, "but Dad thought it'd be an adventure for us. Get away from it all in the back of beyond. Live off the land, so to speak. A new start after our mother waltzed off with her zero-gee yoga instructor."

Brother and sister, Dev realised. Not boyfriend and girlfriend.

"So he's off farming kelp all day, happy as a pig in shit," said Ty. "Only good thing for me and Aletha is he's too busy to keep tabs on us."

"He's got a girlfriend, too, so he's kind of distracted," Aletha added. "As long as he doesn't get an alert from TerCon Curriculum that we've fallen behind with our schoolwork, we're pretty much left to our own devices."

"Okay," Dev said. "Well, here's the deal. I should report you to the authorities for cultivation and possession of a controlled substance. Difficult for me not to, really, since as an ambassador I'm sort of the authorities myself."

Their faces fell.

"But you could do me a favour instead, and in return I won't breathe a word to anyone."

"Name it," Ty and Aletha said, practically in unison.

"I have reason to believe that people in Llyr are keeping a Tritonian imprisoned."

The two kids exchanged looks.

"I haven't heard about any –" Ty began, but Dev cut him off.

"Don't try bullshitting me. Everyone in town knows about it, including you. A Tritonian, a male, probably around your age, got taken captive by some fishermen a few days ago. He's somewhere here, and I'd like to know where."

It was partly bluff. Dev wasn't 100% certain.

But he remembered how Gutting Knife had broken off mid-sentence when describing how he had dealt with the Tritonian who boarded his boat: *Yeah, and he paid for it. He's still...* And he had lamely corrected himself: *He paid for it all right. That's all I have to say.*

He's still paying for it. That was what he was going to say.

And if the Tritonian was "still paying for it," that implied he was in Llyr, being held against his will and most likely abused. Which would explain the townspeople's collective antsiness when a squad of Marines had turned up. They'd thought someone had squealed and the military had come to investigate.

"I haven't got all night," Dev insisted. "You might as well come clean."

Ty and Aletha looked truly intimidated, and he hated playing the bullying, mean-spirited establishment figure with them. He understood exactly how they felt: trapped on Triton, thousands of light years from anywhere worth being, bored, resentful, craving some kind – any kind – of escape. He'd known a young man just like them, fond of narcotics and resentful of parents and officialdom. He had *been* that young man, and there were words for the way he was acting now and the kindest of them was hypocrisy.

"Well..." said Ty defeatedly. "All I've heard is rumours. Word is they're keeping him somewhere in town, but I genuinely, sincerely don't know where. I'd say if I did."

"Your best bet is to try the Moot," said Aletha.

"The Moot? What's that?"

"It's like a bar and town hall, both at once. Place where the adults go to get drunk and have these long rambling debates about town politics and such. Air grievances. Blow off steam. Mostly so they can enjoy the sound of their own voices."

"Closest thing Llyr's got to a law court and a town council," said Ty. "Someone there will have more information than we do. Bound to."

"I can't just go up to random strangers and ask questions," said Dev. "I'm not exactly inconspicuous."

"Sorry. It's all I can suggest."

Dev sighed. "So where do I find this Moot? Save me looking it up on a map."

"Main dome," said Aletha. "Right in the middle. This time of evening, they'll be getting started. All you need to do is follow the sound of people arguing. You can't miss it."

"Okay. One last thing. That hooded top you've got on, Ty. Mind if I take it?"

"Is that a rhetorical question?"

"Not really."

"Am I going to see it again?"

"Frankly, not likely. But you're a good kid, and you know what's being done to that Tritonian is wrong. Helping me, even in a small way, is helping him."

Nodding, but still reluctant, Ty parted with the top. "Control buttons on the left cuff, if you need them. The fabric can waterproof itself, and thicken and release heat if things turn chilly. Hood's got three settings: full, half, and snood."

Dev slipped the top on. "Look, I'll be honest with you," he said. "I don't give a shit about that joint. Go for it. Get cannablasted. Have some fun. And if you can figure out a way of leaving Triton any time soon, do. Hop a gulf cruiser, get the fuck out, and go and live someplace decent, somewhere with a bit of excitement. Somewhere *you* want to be and where you're wanted."

Ty and Aletha gaped at him.

"I mean it. Take it from someone who's been there. Been you. Screw your dad and his midlife crisis and his back-to-nature crap. You're smart, both of you, and you deserve better than this."

Dev strode off, hitting the button that raised the hood to full, so that his face would be shrouded from sight.

As the hood telescoped up around his head, he heard Aletha say to her brother, "Who *was* that guy?"

Ty replied, "The voice of truth, sis," and took a long, hissing toke on the joint. "The voice of truth."

23

LLYR'S MAIN DOME offered a few Terratypical home comforts, after a fashion. There was an area of parkland, with threadbare grass and a handful of sad, stunted trees. There was an attempt at a shopping mall, a two-tiered gallery of stores selling clothes, knickknacks, kitchenware and dried goods. There was a nightclub made out of three standard habitat cubes shoved together, and next to that, a strip club called Venus In A Shell.

It was all bit scraggy and gimcrack, but then what could you expect from a small community perched on – to use Ty's colourful phrase – a pimple on the butt-end of the galaxy?

The Moot wasn't hard to locate. As Aletha had advised, Dev followed the sound of voices, a babble which echoed all the way up to the dome's apex. It led him through the parkland to a plaza, where benches and tables were laid out in the open, encircled by a ring of lampposts. Drinks were being served at a roofed bar in the middle of the space. Dev counted perhaps twenty locals, variously sitting or standing, necking beer and liquor. He loitered just outside the plaza's perimeter, in a clump of shrubbery beyond the reach of the lamplight, and observed surreptitiously for a while.

More people arrived in dribs and drabs. Not much debating was taking place as far as Dev could see, until, when the numbers swelled to about fifty, it seemed as though a quorum had been reached. Someone climbed onto a table and began complaining about an offence his neighbour had committed. Siphoned off fuel from his boat, was the gist of it.

The neighbour then got up and refuted the accusation. He was no thief, he said. The two of them had had a verbal agreement. If one happened to run short of fuel, he could borrow some off the other with having to ask permission.

The first speaker responded that he hadn't thought the agreement still stood. They'd made it several months ago. Wasn't there some sort of expiry date on these things?

The problem was thrashed out in public. Friends and acquaintances weighed in on either side. Eventually a solution was reached, by consensus. The fuel would have to be repaid in kind, and to avoid future misunderstandings the agreement was officially annulled. Both parties consented to the decision and sealed the deal with a handshake.

Dev watched a couple more interpersonal disputes get resolved in a similar manner. It was mob rule in action. Raucous, confrontational, ramshackle, but it seemed to work.

Then the conversation at the Moot turned to the bust-up with the Marines that afternoon at the food court. There were grumbles about the troops' general rowdiness and misbehaviour, and it was proposed that a message be sent to Station Ares outlining what had happened and requesting disciplinary action.

The suggestion was shot down, however. Several of the townsfolk were strongly of the opinion that the incident should be left to lie. Raising a fuss would be counterproductive. The phrase 'unwanted attention' kept cropping up.

By that stage, Gaff Hook had come sidling into the Moot. His arm was in a sling, his bare elbow encased in a stabilising brace with a healing-pad inlay. He was far from the only townsperson present nursing an injury from the brawl, but he seemed to reckon he had come off worse than most, aside from his friend Dietrich.

"Poor bastard's still in the infirmary," he said. "Doc says he'll be there for a week at least and not fit to get back to work for a month. That's a month he and his crew aren't fishing. A month with no money coming in for them and their families."

Someone proposed a whip-round for Dietrich, who Dev had to assume was the gash-faced Gutting Knife. Someone else muttered darkly that Dietrich didn't deserve charity for having potentially brought trouble to their door. The Marines, they said, hadn't stopped by for any reason other than refuelling and some onshore R and R. Now, though, they may have cause to think something funny was up. They might have gone for reinforcements, and when next they came to Llyr, it mightn't be a social call.

"What are you saying, Snodgrass?" demanded a powerfully built, grizzled man who had been the loudest and most frequent contributor to the debates and whose opinion everyone else seemed to defer to. If Llyr had been the kind of place to have an elected mayor, Dev reckoned this fellow would have fulfilled that role. He bore a kind of settled self-confidence and had the demagogue's habit of emphasising a point by thumping something with his fist – a table, his own chest, the palm of his other hand.

"I'm just saying maybe now's the time to cut our losses, McCabe. Forget that Dietrich ever brought anyone here. Make the whole thing go away."

McCabe scowled, and Snodgrass bobbed his head, an unconscious gesture of submission.

"A thought, that's all," Snodgrass added hastily. "Just floating an idea."

"Nothing is changing," McCabe declared. "Nothing whatsoever. If you haven't got the balls for this, Snodgrass, that's your lookout. No one's asking you to be involved. But you've no right to ruin other people's fun. Clear?"

"Yes, McCabe."

"Good. Glad we've got that straight. I'd hate to think you were poking your nose into other folk's business. Anybody else take Snodgrass's side? Anybody back him up?"

The Moot was, for once, quiet.

"Thought as much," said a satisfied McCabe. "Those Marines screwed up, and they know it. Picking a fight like that... If they've any sense, they'll sweep the whole thing under the carpet, act like it never happened. We don't have anything to worry about from them, you mark my words."

The meeting, and the drinking that went with it, continued for another hour, but nothing further was said about the Marines or about the subject which McCabe had clamped down on so firmly. In that respect, his word, it seemed, was final. No alternative viewpoints would be brooked.

Dev had a ringleader. McCabe was the man in charge of the captive Tritonian. McCabe, therefore, was the man he had to watch and follow.

Eventually, with several bottles of beer inside him, McCabe got up to leave the premises. A group of his cronies took their cue and went with him, among them Gaff Hook, whose name Dev had learned was Chlumsky. They ambled away from the Moot, and Dev, still fully hooded, followed after them at a distance.

24

HE ALMOST LOST them in the maze of bridges and lesser domes at Llyr's fringes. He couldn't tail them too closely since this area of town was more or less deserted and there was a risk he'd be spotted. He hung well back and used their voices and footfalls as guidance whenever he no longer had visual contact. McCabe and his cronies were, thankfully, in a rambunctious mood, and the noise they were making carried far, even above the constant lap of waves and the squeal of bridge hinges.

They ended up at a boatyard with a repair shop attached, a low utilitarian building advertising itself as McCabe's Mechanics and Chandlery.

"Now I see why you're such a big shot, Mr McCabe," Dev muttered to himself. McCabe fixed boats. People had to be nice to him, otherwise that motor stayed bust or that hole didn't get patched. No transportation, no livelihood.

McCabe and followers disappeared inside the repair shop.

There was a window near the main door, its panes encrusted with salt, cloudy but still just transparent enough to see through. Dev crept up to it, knelt and peered in.

In a room full of tools, workbenches and cutting and welding gear, McCabe approached what appeared to be a large box covered by a tarpaulin. He whipped the tarpaulin away to reveal a steel-framed, glass-sided tank which looked like something he himself had constructed specially. It held a few hundred cubic litres of water – filthy water, brackishly green, with assorted lumps of waste matter floating in it and gnawed fish bones littering the bottom.

Just visible inside the tank was a figure. A young male Tritonian lay slumped in one corner, shackled with chains.

As Dev looked on, McCabe hit a switch, and a hoist in the ceiling started turning with a mechanical whine, drawing a length of chain from the water and reeling the Tritonian out.

The indigene hung inert, insensible, as McCabe used the hoist to guide his dripping form clear of the tank and lower him until his toes just touched the floor. He stirred a little as he realised he was no longer immersed in his natural medium. His gills began to pulsate, working to breathe.

McCabe slapped his face, and the Tritonian's eyes flew open.

"Wakey-wakey, sushi breath," McCabe said, his words just audible to Dev. "We're back. It's time to party again."

The Tritonian's face rippled through shades of mauve and magenta, a weary plea for mercy.

One of McCabe's cronies cupped an ear. "What's that? Sorry, I can't make out what you're saying. No speakee sea monkey."

There was guffawing and general amusement.

"He's probably offering to give us all a blowjob if we'll let him go," someone commented.

"Eurgh! I wouldn't even if he was female," said someone else. "And have my dick all stinking of fish?"

"Doesn't it anyway, after fucking your wife?" said another.

"You leave my missus out of it."

"He certainly smells a bit like pussy," said Gaff Hook, a.k.a. Chlumsky, leaning close to the Tritonian and sniffing.

"No, more like rotten eggs. Sewage."

"That could just be because most of us have taken a dump in that tank."

"They all smell bad, sea monkeys," said McCabe. "Doesn't bother 'em. Stench doesn't travel underwater."

Dev noticed that the Tritonian's body was covered in cuts and contusions. His scales were dull, his skin sloughing away in places. Anyone could tell he was in pretty bad shape, barely this side of death.

Dev felt his temper rising, his fists clenching. McCabe and the others must have been systematically torturing the Tritonian ever since Dietrich brought him in. He was just a kid, and his only crime had been jumping aboard Dietrich's boat with a spear in his hands, no doubt in a fit of youthful bravado. He was being made to pay for the sabotage and damage his race were inflicting, a scapegoat for the insurgency, a whipping boy these settlers could take their frustrations out on.

"Who in the name of fuck are you?"

Dev whirled round, to see three men had stolen up behind him.

"Never mind," said the middle man.

Dev caught a glimpse of a short truncheon with a double-pronged tip.

Something crackled.

Pain coursed through his midriff. His legs, suddenly numb, gave way as though chopped by an axe. He crashed down, twitching helplessly, his body no longer under his control. Faintly he could smell burning flesh. *His* flesh.

Another crackle. Another paroxysm of agony.

Then nothingness.

25

A SLAP TO the cheek. Hard.

Dev awoke.

He was trussed up in chains, like the Tritonian. Fastened to a tubular steel chair. The hood had been pulled back, exposing his head.

Blearily he looked around. McCabe was bent over him, hand drawn back to deliver a second slap if required. The Tritonian was nearby, still suspended from the hoist and now in evident respiratory distress, his gills opening and closing frantically as they dried out. Slowly suffocating.

"Yeah, that's him all right," Dev heard Chlumsky say. "The guy who gave me and Dietrich so much grief. Near broke my fucking arm. Sneaky son of a bitch, he is. Doesn't fight fair."

"Two of you, armed, against one of me?" Dev croaked, dry-mouthed. "You have a strange definition of fighting fair."

"But you know kung fu or something."

"No, I don't. I know dumb fu, the ancient art of dealing with morons."

One of McCabe's cronies sniggered.

Chlumsky bristled. "Who are you calling a moron?" he snarled.

"You, moron. Truth is, weapons or not, you and your friend Dietrich were hopeless. Easy meat. Pre-schoolers would have been more of a challenge."

"Enough!" McCabe smacked Dev round the face again, open-handed but still with force. "You were outside eavesdropping on us. Spying. Lucky thing Kelso came by when he did with his fish stunner."

"I brought it to use on *him*," said Kelso, pointing the device at the Tritonian. "Saw you sneaking around and... Well, a couple of five-million-volt jolts later, here we are."

"Yeah," said Dev. "Thanks for that. All that electricity – I haven't felt this lively in years."

He didn't feel good at all, truth be told. There was a sore patch on his belly, the skin singed where the fish stunner's electrodes had been applied. The muscles in his abdomen and upper torso, meanwhile, ached from the fierce contractions they had undergone as the current surged through them.

His commplant was down, too, which was a more pressing concern. The electric shock had overloaded it and knocked it out of commission. It was rebooting, but he had no idea how long that might take. Until the commplant was functioning again, he couldn't send a distress call to Reyes and Cully aboard the URIB. He was on his own.

He didn't even have the hypervelocity pistol anymore; not that he could have used it, hogtied as he was. It hung in its holster belt from a tool rack on the far side of the repair shop.

"Question is," said McCabe, "why have you come back? And where are those Marines?"

"That's two questions."

McCabe hit him once more, this time with a closed fist.

It hurt.

"Tell you what," Dev said, spitting out blood. "Let the Tritonian go, and Marines don't descend on this location all guns blazing. They're already here, waiting for the go from me, and they can bring a shitstorm down on your heads. All it'll take is a single message. I can call them in or call them off. Your choice."

McCabe studied him carefully, and Dev took the opportunity to check McCabe out in return. He was looking for Uncanny Valley, the weird vacancy in the eyes which was the mark of a Polis+ agent wearing an organic human form. Plusser infiltrators often set themselves up as agitators and firebrands. People like McCabe, in other words. People well placed to stir up discord and discontent. If Polis+ was behind the Tritonian insurgency, then they might have agents rabble-rousing among the settlers as well. After all, tensions heightened more quickly if both sides were being goaded from within simultaneously.

"What are you looking at?" McCabe said, squinting.

"Nothing," Dev replied.

And there *was* nothing. Nothing untoward, that is. McCabe's eyes were normal. No absence of emotion in them. None of that telltale, vaguely indefinable unrealness. No Uncanny Valley.

There were other tests Dev could apply – he could ask a series of questions about faith and divinity designed to provoke an extreme response from the religiously pious Plussers – but he didn't feel he needed to. He was satisfied that McCabe was wholly human.

"I've given you my terms," he said. "The Tritonian goes free, and you and your friends get to live."

At present, it was still an empty threat. His commplant remained out of action. There was at least a progress bar now, however, informing him that the commplant was getting its shoes back on. The bar currently stood at 30%.

McCabe considered Dev's statement, then said, "Bullshit. I can tell when people are lying. Your Marine pals aren't anywhere near. Where's their boat, that catamaran? Someone would've said if it had been seen. Any of you guys heard anything?"

Headshakes all round.

"See? What I think, fish-face, is that you're alone. The Marines left, and you stayed behind to save this guy." McCabe jerked a thumb at the Tritonian. "I don't know how you found out we had him. I'd guess maybe there's some kind of sea monkey grapevine that you're plugged into. It doesn't matter. Here you are, on this little solo rescue mission of yours. Not going so well, is it?"

Dev shrugged as much as the chains would allow him to. "Now that you mention it, no. At least put the kid back in the water. Can you do that much for me? He's going to die if you leave him exposed to the air much longer."

The Tritonian's head had sagged and his gills were twitching fitfully, barely moving.

McCabe assessed the indigene's condition, then gestured to one of his cronies. "Okay. Stick him back in the tank. He's no use to us dead."

As the hoist whirred into life, he said to Dev, "We can get a few more days' entertainment out of him if we're careful."

"Keep him just alive, you mean?"

"Exactly. That's the trick. Mess with him as much as he can bear but no further. Let him rest in between. Feed him. Pump air through the water in the tank to re-oxygenate it. We can make him last."

"You're a sadistic motherfucker, you know that?"

McCabe just laughed. "I'm not the one who started all this. Us settlers, we were prepared to get along. Live and let live. There aren't even that many of us, relatively speaking, and the planet's big enough, right? Got more than enough resources for everybody. Plenty of fish in the sea."

He jabbed a finger in the direction of the tank. The

Tritonian was submerged again and his breathing appeared to be normalising, the beat of his gills becoming regular.

"It's them. His kind. Their fault. They wouldn't play ball, would they? Wouldn't share. They had to get uppity. Turn terrorist. And even then, after the troubles started, we gave them the benefit of the doubt. We tried to be decent about it."

He leaned close to Dev.

"Well, no more Mr Nice Guy. That stops here. It's time to teach the natives a lesson. Show them we're not to be fucked with. If the powers-that-be aren't going to fight back – if the Marines who should be protecting us won't do their *job* – then people are going to take matters into their own hands."

"Is torturing one Tritonian to death really going to make that much difference?" The progress bar on Dev's commplant had reached 63%. *Come on*, he urged it. *Hurry up. What's taking you so long?*

"Who said anything about 'to death'?" said McCabe. "We'll stick him back in the sea eventually, when we feel we've made our point. He can return to his people and explain what happened to him. He'll be an object lesson. A message."

"Oh, that'll work. The Tritonians will back right off then. I can just see it. They won't – y'know – regard it as a provocation and come and attack Llyr in force, or anything."

"Sneer all you want, but I've thought this through."

"No, you haven't. You're pretending it's a cunningly laid plan. You may even believe it. But all it really is, McCabe, is cheap, spiteful playground tactics. Dietrich managed to snag a Tritonian, and you saw a chance to demonstrate how big and bad you are. Toughest dude in town. 'Not scared of Tritonians, me. Watch me beat this one up. That's how much I hate them.'"

"Hand me that fish stunner, Kelso," McCabe said.

"You going to zap me?"

"Crossed my mind."

79% on the progress bar. Nearly there. Dev had to keep stalling.

"To shut me up, I suppose," he said. "Because I'm saying stuff you don't want your friends to hear. Because you know it's true."

"Or it could just be I find you intensely annoying."

84%. If McCabe jolted him with the fish stunner, the commplant would fritz again.

Dev had to delay him just a little bit longer.

"Listen, McCabe. Here's the deal. I'm with Interstellar Security Solutions."

"ISS. One of those mercenary spooks. Is that so?"

"Yes. I'm on Triton to defuse the situation, the unrest, before it spirals out of control."

"Good luck with that."

"I'm appealing to you, human to human – don't do something really regrettable, something you can't come back from. Release me, release the Tritonian, before it's too late."

90%. Getting there.

"Too late for what?"

"You can still walk away from this, with no repercussions."

"Hate to say it, but he has a point, McCabe," Kelso piped up. "If he's ISS, that's something else. A whole level of hot water we don't want to end up in."

"*If*," McCabe said. "He's lying, ya idiot! Anything to save his skin."

"This body is a host form," Dev said, "a vehicle for my downloaded consciousness, purpose-built so that I can interact with Tritonians as well as with you lot."

McCabe shook his head slowly. "No, I reckon what you are is what you look like, an interspecies ambassador. Another one. Chlumsky says he and Dietrich faced off against two of you. You're the other guy's replacement, that's my guess.

He's training you up before he steps down from the job. Or vice versa."

"Sounds plausible," Dev said, "but I assure you it's not the case. I *am* ISS."

96%. Almost. Almost. Just a few seconds more.

McCabe brandished the fish stunner, hefting it in his hand. "I doubt a real ISS operative would admit it so openly. Aren't they supposed to be secret agents or some such?"

"Field operatives. Not necessarily covert. We advise, participate, recruit and develop assets, collaborate with locals, forge alliances. We don't like to advertise ourselves, but we don't hide in the shadows either."

98%.

McCabe pondered.

"Nah," he said. "You're someone who's got too inquisitive for his own good, that's all. Ambassador or not, you've made a major mistake."

"And you're going to kill me for it? To cover up what you've been doing here?"

"Kill you? Probably not. Maybe just show you the real state of interspecies relations on Triton right now."

He thumbed the switch on the fish stunner, activating the power cell.

99%.

Come on, come on.

"So you won't forget," he continued. "And you'll never be able to pin anything on us, by the way. Go whining to your TerCon paymasters, it won't help you. You won't be believed. No one in this room will have seen anything. Your word against ours. There's a dozen of us, and we'll deny it 'til we're blue in the face."

McCabe didn't look round to check that he had his cronies' consent. They were browbeaten, in his thrall. Whatever he told them, whatever rules he laid down, they would go along with.

His grin was broad and cruel.
100%.

Commplant online.

Reyes! Cully!

McCabe brought the fish stunner forward and poised the electrodes beside Dev's neck.

"Brace yourself," he said.

I'm at McCabe's Mechanics and Chand—

Lightning exploded in Dev's head.

26

McCABE HAD DIALLED down the voltage on the stunner. Now, instead of producing a knockout-level charge, it merely caused pain.

Excruciating pain.

Dev writhed, the muscles in his neck and chest contorting. The chains dug into him as he twisted and strained spasmodically against them. The chair legs rattled on the floor.

It may only have lasted a handful of seconds, but for Dev it was a white-hot, timeless forever. When McCabe eventually withdrew the stunner, he continued to twitch and shudder for a full minute afterward.

The involuntary movements gradually ebbed and faded. Dev tasted metal at the back of his throat. His ears were singing.

He was just starting to catch his breath when McCabe shocked him again.

This time he felt his eyeballs bulging as though they were going to erupt from their sockets. His teeth clenched so tightly together that three of his molars cracked.

As the pain and convulsions subsided, Dev heaved air in and out his lungs, coughing and wheezing. A string of drool leaked down from one corner of his lips.

"How's that?" McCabe asked. "Sparky enough for you?"

"Not as bad as… your body odour," Dev panted out raspily. "Personal hygiene… not a big thing… on Triton?"

McCabe chuckled as though this was one of the wittiest remarks he had heard in a while. Then his smile dropped and he jabbed the stunner into Dev's groin.

Dev nearly blacked out. It felt as though a hand was reaching up from between his legs into his abdominal cavity and giving his innards a good, hard twist.

"You know," he said when the pain had abated and his thoughts were no longer a senseless jumble, "there are certain people… who'd pay to have that done to them… and you're *giving* it away."

"What does it take to shut you up?" McCabe said wonderingly.

"I don't know… big guy. Nothing you're capable of."

McCabe looked set to use the stunner on Dev a fourth time, but then had a better idea.

"Haul the sea monkey out of the tank again," he said, and his cronies scurried to obey. "You care about the natives," he told Dev. "Maybe more than you care about yourself. Why else would you have risked your neck to save this one?"

"Don't," Dev said.

"Don't give him a going-over with the stunner? Why not? I was planning to anyway, but I just realised it'll be a lot more enjoyable if you're still awake and watching. You'll feel it almost as strongly as he does. Two for the price of one."

Dev lunged at McCabe, teeth bared. A futile gesture. There was a tiny amount of slack in the chains but not nearly enough. He didn't even get close. All he succeeded in doing was thrusting the chair forward a few centimetres.

"Ah-ah!" said McCabe. "Easy, boy. Bad dog. What were you hoping to do? Chew me to death?"

"If it came to that. Leave him alone, you bastard. Carry on electrocuting me, by all means, but the Tritonian – he's suffered enough. He's just a kid, for fuck's sake."

"A kid who's a terrorist. Once you decide to be a terrorist, age ain't nothing but a number."

Dev seethed impotently as the Tritonian was set dangling before McCabe. His commplant was offline once more and stubbornly refusing to reboot. He suspected it had gone into enforced hibernation, executing a shutdown protocol in order to preserve itself against the electric shocks. External reactivation would be required, probably a full software reinstallation too.

He could only hope he had got his message out to Reyes and Cully in time. There'd been barely a second between the reboot completing and McCabe zapping him. It was possible the distress call had not been transmitted at all. Help was not coming. The cavalry was not on its way.

McCabe strolled in a circle around the Tritonian, who eyed him dully, halfway between hatred and despair.

Dev made one last attempt to plead with him. "I know you don't really want to do this, McCabe. You have a hard-man reputation to keep up; I get it. You're eager to impress your friends. But can't you see how wrong this is? That boy over there is guilty of nothing except hot-headedness."

"He attacked Dietrich on his boat."

"Alone. With nothing but a spear. Against three full-grown men. Only today, I've seen what Tritonians can do when they're properly being terrorists. It's not pretty. A lone kid waving a handweapon around isn't nearly on the same scale. We've all been that age. Who of us hasn't done something just as stupid when we were young, thinking we're being ballsy and grown-up?"

He seemed to be getting through to McCabe's cronies at least. Some of them were shuffling their feet and making discontented noises. Others had the good grace to look ashamed. They had consciences, buried deep somewhere within.

Too deep, however, to overcome their fear of their ringleader, who remained defiant and unrepentant.

"How are they ever going to learn," McCabe said, "if someone won't teach them a lesson?"

He levelled the fish stunner in front of the Tritonian's face.

"This is going to leave a mark," he said.

The Tritonian cringed. He had seen what the device could do. He had been watching McCabe use it on Dev.

Dev tried to send him a message of reassurance and solidarity, his face aglow, but the Tritonian wasn't looking. His gaze was fixed on the stunner's electrodes, which were inching closer and closer to him. McCabe was prolonging the awful anticipation, relishing the indigene's naked dread.

There was the sound of glass breaking, followed an instant later by the thud of something landing on the floor and rolling.

A metallic ovoid, tossed in through the shattered windowpane.

No one apart from Dev recognised what it was. The townspeople stared in incomprehension as the object trundled to a halt close to McCabe's feet. They were even more dumbfounded when tiny pores popped open all across its surface.

Clearly none of them had encountered a subsonic incapacitator before.

Dev groaned inwardly.

This was not going to be pleasant.

27

THE SUBSONIC INCAPACITATOR didn't detonate as such. It simply emitted a ten-second pulse of infrasound too low to be heard but powerful enough to be felt.

The effect was instantaneous. Everyone within a five-metre radius who wasn't bound in chains, which meant everyone in the repair shop except for Dev and the Tritonian, staggered where they stood. Some collapsed. Others grabbed whatever they could for support. It was as though a miniature, localised earthquake had just hit.

For that reason a subsonic incapacitator was popularly known as a 'knee trembler.'

A subsidiary effect, which also applied to nearly all of those present, was spontaneous and uncontrollable projectile vomiting.

For that reason a subsonic incapacitator was even more popularly known as a 'vom bomb.'

The townspeople succumbed, bending double and puking out the contents of their stomachs. The Tritonian was sick too, coughing a pale yellowish fluid down his front.

Dev alone managed to resist, although only just. The initial infrasound burst sent a wave of queasiness surging through him, and the acrid reek of vomit that swiftly permeated the air afterwards triggered a sympathetic gag reflex. He swallowed down the gorge rising in his throat, refusing to give in.

McCabe, he was delighted to see, was on all fours, arching his back like a dog, copious amounts of partly digested food and beer gushing out of his mouth.

A booted foot smashed the door open, and in came Reyes and Cully, mouths and noses masked, coilgun rifles sweeping.

The two Marines took in the room at a glance and saw it was fully pacified. Anyone not still disorientated by the subsonic incapacitator and emptying their guts out had their hands in the air, cowering meekly at the sight of the rifles.

"Harmer!" Reyes barked. "Are you okay?"

"I'll be better once someone undoes these chains. And that Tritonian's too."

Cully released him, while Reyes saw to the Tritonian. The indigene crumpled as the chains came loose, and Reyes took his weight on her shoulder.

"Are we good to go?" Cully asked, stepping carefully around a quivering, quailing local and the puddle of vomit he had created.

"Almost," said Dev.

He retrieved the HVP holster belt from the tool rack and fastened it on. Then he went over to McCabe, who was still retching and spitting out ribbons of bile. He picked up the fish stunner and waved the tip in front of McCabe's nose.

"I should shove this where the sun doesn't shine and hold the button down 'til the power cell runs dry," he said. "But I'm not that petty."

McCabe looked up at him, whey-faced, pathetic, bedraggled.

"Well, not quite," Dev amended, and clobbered McCabe over the head with the stunner. He pounded until McCabe was left lying face down in his own vomit, bleeding from one ear, unconscious.

"How are you ever going to learn," he said, "if someone won't teach you a lesson?"

Dev and the Marines exited the repair shop, Reyes and Cully supporting the Tritonian between them. The URIB lay moored in the boatyard, tethered to a pier. The Marines clambered into the boat, laying the indigene flat on the footboards at the stern. Dev stepped aboard just as Cully was casting off.

Reyes started the motor and threw the URIB into a tight, banking one-hundred-and-eighty-degree turn. Within moments Llyr was falling away behind them.

"Touch-and-go," Cully said to Dev, "but it seems we got there in the nick of time."

"Yeah. You cut it fine, but it beats not at all. Thanks."

"Sorry about using the Thunder that Brings the Chunder, but we couldn't have done anything else. Lethal force against unarmed civilians is prohibited."

"It was perfect, Cully. Really."

"Was it worth it?" She nodded at the Tritonian. "He doesn't look too healthy."

"Nor would you if you'd just spent several days being beaten and half suffocated. Speaking of which..."

Dev removed Ty's hooded top and thrust it into the sea until the fabric was sodden. Then he swaddled it around the Tritonian's throat to help keep his gills moist.

"Think he's going to make it?" Cully asked.

"He'd better, after all this. You won't believe what I just had to go through."

"If that scorch mark on your neck is anything to go by, I can hazard a guess." Cully nodded in sympathy. "You know, the lieutenant has her doubts about you. Thinks you're headstrong and undisciplined. A loose cannon. But I think you're okay, Harmer."

"High praise indeed."

"Milgrom's not your biggest fan, though."

"Not yet. Now *there's* a loose cannon."

"But also a good woman to have at your back in a firefight."

The URIB scudded onward, and Dev continued tending to the Tritonian, repeatedly re-soaking and reapplying the hooded top. The kid's face radiated random colours, running through the entire visible spectrum. Dev found it indecipherable. It was, he presumed, equivalent to a human mumbling feverishly, talking gibberish.

At one point the kid's eyes snapped open and he was briefly lucid. His face flashed a mellow green glow of gratitude before he lapsed back into semiconscious incoherence.

"You're welcome," Dev said. "Now just hang in there. Won't be long."

Within half an hour they rendezvoused with the *Admiral Winterbrook* and the *Reckless Abandon*.

As the URIB sidled up alongside the catamaran like a duckling re-joining its mother, Dev wrapped his arms around the Tritonian and rolled overboard with him.

He stayed submerged, supporting the youngster, waiting for him to revive. Minutes passed, and the Tritonian started to stir. Cautiously Dev released him, leaving him to float unaided but remaining within arm's reach. He wasn't going to let him make a break for it, not without pumping him for intel first. The kid might be only an amateur insurgent, but that didn't mean he knew nothing about the real insurgents.

A loud splash heralded the arrival of Handler in the water. He shone curiosity and exasperation at Dev. Dev figured that he had been sent down by Sigursdottir to check on the rescued Tritonian and find out Dev's intentions.

Dev signalled that the Tritonian was coming round and they would soon be able to ask him questions. He still hadn't quite got the hang of the visual mode of speech, judging by the frown and the amber-and-magenta puzzlement on Handler's face, so he repeated what he had 'said' using supplemental hand gestures to get his meaning across.

Handler registered comprehension, and joined Dev in treading water, while the Tritonian continued to show signs of emerging from his stupor. Dev was glad Handler was with him, since the ISS liaison spoke the indigenes' lingo fluently while he himself had yet to master it. He stood to get more out of the kid with Handler there to translate.

All at once the Tritonian was awake and alert, but no sooner did this happen than Dev became aware of a commotion in the water. Something sizeable was coming towards them, creating a powerful disturbance, a vibration he could feel viscerally.

No, not just something.

Several somethings.

Silhouettes loomed in the darkness. Any fish in the vicinity scattered. Dev counted three – no, four – large shapes. They homed in on him, Handler and the Tritonian. They were sea creatures of some sort, but they moved with a weird purposefulness and precision, in a converging formation. Almost as if...

Tritonian vessels. Among them was a manta sub, very like the one Dev had encountered at the *Egersund*, and which had intervened when he was being menaced by the cuttlefish sub. The one that appeared to be piloted by the couple he had first run into at Tangaroa.

Seated in the hollow globes of its eyes were the female and the male from before. He recognised them mainly by the nautilus-pattern cicatrix tattoos on their chests.

The other subs surrounded the two humans and the young Tritonian: a second, slightly smaller manta sub, a sub with the skeletal fins and lantern-jaw underbite of an anglerfish, and a tall, stately one which somewhat resembled a seahorse.

Dev could see how the situation might look to the Tritonians. He and Handler were in close proximity to one of their kind who bore injuries consistent with torture. He wouldn't blame them for jumping to the wrong conclusion: that the two hybrid humans had been responsible for the abuse.

Worse, the Tritonians would be well aware of the Marine boat floating overhead, just as the Marines were doubtless aware of the arrival of the Tritonian submarines. Sigursdottir might perceive the subs as a clear and present danger and respond with a pre-emptive strike.

Things were liable to turn nasty at any moment.

28

THE FEMALE TRITONIAN ducked out of her piloting station in the manta sub's left eye. A few seconds later she emerged from the lipless rectangular slit of a mouth and swam forward, shock lance in hand.

Dev's own hand drifted towards the HVP, hovering over the grip like a gunslinger's, ready to draw. Just a precaution. Just in case.

As the Tritonian neared, Handler's face emanated a greeting, albeit one that was shot through with pale yellow streaks of anxiety. Dev settled for polite amiability and what he hoped was innocence.

Ignoring them, the Tritonian went straight to the youngster and examined him all over, inventorying the lacerations, the bruises and the peeling scales. Then came a rapid exchange of dialogue, colours on both their faces shifting too fast for Dev to follow the conversation easily.

As near as he could tell, the female was quizzing the kid, her interrogation shot through with anger and concern. He was answering hesitantly but truthfully about his capture on Dietrich's boat and subsequent ordeal at the hands of McCabe and friends in Llyr.

A couple of times the female aimed what appeared to be suspicious glances at Dev and Handler before resuming her grilling of the boy. The kid eventually got round to explaining that one of these hybrid humans had helped him get away from his captors. Dev saw embarrassment and conflict on his face, as though he was having trouble reconciling his appreciation for what Dev had done with his resentment of humans as a whole. It seemed he couldn't fathom why one of the enemy had treated him with compassion and not the cruelty the others had shown. It was confusingly unexpected.

Dev wondered why the kid hadn't simply lied and accused him and Handler of being his torturers. It would have been easy enough to do so, and the other Tritonians would have no reason to disbelieve him. The idea of landing the two humans in trouble must at least have crossed his mind. If he hated the species that much, he could have overcome his scruples and framed Dev and Handler. Vengeance from the other Tritonians would have followed swiftly and been total. The anglerfish sub alone, with its palisade of jutting, spiny teeth, could have made mincemeat of them.

Then it dawned on Dev that the kid *had* to tell the truth. All Tritonians did. An emotion-based language made lying impossible. Each of them could tell at a glance if another was being evasive or insincere. It would be literally written all over their faces.

Tritonians, by that logic, were the most honest race in the known universe. They had no choice in the matter. Whatever they communicated, they had to feel, and whatever they felt, they had to communicate.

Now the female was looking at Dev and Handler, Dev particularly, with newfound admiration. Or so Dev thought. Those round black eyes of hers were hard to read, and her facial expression varied only minutely. A stone might have been less inscrutable.

That was until her photophores flared green, with veiny pulses of pink trending outward from the corners of her mouth. Thanks and congratulations, it said, unmistakably, clear as day.

Dev beamed back a smile in incandescent form. He had the impression that he had earned more than the female's esteem. He had in some way justified a judgement she had made about him; passed a test he hadn't even known he was taking.

Handler propelled himself forward. With tensions de-escalating, he became more confident. His ambassadorial side asserted itself.

He insinuated to the female that he and the other humans were on an important mission which would benefit everyone on the planet, settlers and indigenes alike.

No one here bears any ill will towards your people, he said. The rescue of the boy is surely proof of that.

He begged her, in the name of peace, not to instigate an assault on Llyr. The perpetrators of the boy's kidnap and abuse had been punished. Retaliation against them was not necessary and would only add to the breakdown in relations between her race and humans.

Dev chipped in with a plea of his own. Would the female mind assisting him? He needed to show her something, up on the boat. Something she might be able to clarify for him.

Wariness flickered yellowly on her face. I suspect a trap, she said.

He assured her it was no trap.

She wavered. Pondered.

Then she replied that she had no alternative but to agree to his request. She touched the young Tritonian on the shoulder, indicating that she owed Dev a debt. I'm putting my trust in you to continue to act with the forthrightness and integrity you've demonstrated so far. These are qualities that are uncommon in your kind but prized by mine.

Is that why you've been following me? Dev asked. Why you took my side against the people in the cuttlefish submarine? Because I behave like a Tritonian?

More so than an ungilled, yes.

Ungilled carried derogatory connotations. But it was no worse than sea monkey, Dev thought, and was biologically accurate if nothing else.

You intrigue me, she continued. The way you dealt with the reptile.

The thalassoraptor.

You had no weapon, she said. You ought to have died. You are either insane or foolish.

I've been called both, Dev said.

But you might also be exceptionally courageous. I feel that you are someone we can work with. Someone who may serve as a bridge between us and your kind. Am I wrong?

I hope not.

I have persuaded others to join me in trailing you, so that we may all of us assess your worth.

That explains this lot, said Dev, indicating the other subs. Friends of yours?

Likeminded individuals.

And your... husband? He was referring to her manta sub co-pilot.

Cousin. I am unpartnered. Now, shall we float here all day talking or shall we go to your boat so that I can see whatever it is you wish to show me?.

Of course.

She instructed the boy to board the manta sub and wait there. As he swam off, she projected a message to the other Tritonians present. I'm accompanying the humans, heading above the surface. I won't be gone long.

Within the cockpits of the manta subs, the anglerfish sub and the eel sub, faces glowed, offering reluctant acquiescence.

If I fail to return, she added, you know what to do.

It was a threat, and not a very thinly veiled one. If these ungilled imprisoned or harmed her, they should be destroyed.

29

BARELY HAD THEY broken the surface – Dev, Handler, and the Tritonian – and climbed onto the dive deck of the *Reckless Abandon* than they heard Lieutenant Sigursdottir calling across from the *Admiral Winterbrook*.

"Harmer, what the actual fuck is going on? There are Tritonian craft below, and you're inviting one of the occupants onto your boat? I'm sure there's a rational explanation."

"There is," Dev yelled back. He could just make out Sigursdottir at the starboard rail of the catamaran, flanked by Milgrom and Blunt.

"Message me and tell me about it."

"Can't. Commplant's down."

"I can see she's got a shock lance. If you're acting under duress…"

"We're not."

"But if you are, I can have men over there in seconds."

"No need. Really. Handler can fill you in on the details." Lowering his voice, Dev said to the ISS liaison, "Fire her a quick message, will you? Say everything's okay, nothing to get her panties in a bunch about."

"I'll phrase it a little more tactfully, if you don't mind."

"Yeah, I would. Main thing is she backs off and stays backed off. I'm not going to get much useful out of our fishy friend here if a herd of Marines comes stampeding in."

Handler's gaze defocused as he composed the message to Sigursdottir. Dev meanwhile ushered the Tritonian up to the *Reckless Abandon*'s main cabin. She walked with little of the grace that she swam with. The steep staircase from the lower deck to the upper gave her particular trouble. She stumbled flat-footedly at the top, and Dev sprang reflexively to catch her before she could fall. She shrugged off his hand with a pale flare of irritability, insisting she could manage on her own.

Dev apologised. I meant no insult.

She tripped as she stepped over the raised threshold of the cabin door, and this time Dev left her to fend for herself. She managed to recover her footing with as much dignity as she could muster. Dev could imagine how clumsy she must feel, going from the supportive buoyancy of water to the unforgiving emptiness of air. She was out of her element, in a realm where you were obliged to hold yourself vertical when moving and where gravity was all at once a treacherous foe, always ready to undermine you.

He showed her to a chair, inviting her to sit, and she sank into it with some relief. He begged her patience. I need to prepare something.

His commplant was status-signalling that it had insite connection and could be restarted. He ordered a complete restore, with all cached data to be downloaded from remote backup.

While he waited for the mental *beep* that would tell him the commplant was back online, Dev watched the Tritonian surveying her surroundings. The cabin furniture, with its sleek, rounded lines and artificial fabrics, seemed to fascinate her, as did the small galley nook and the recessed ceiling lighting. She remained on her guard, however, warily fingering the coral handle of her lance, as if drawing security from it.

"Dev," said Dev. He accompanied the word with the facial colouration that meant he was introducing himself formally.

The sound of his voice startled her, and her grip on the lance tightened.

"Dev," he repeated, injecting friendliness into his voice and smiling.

"Doesn't mean a thing to a Tritonian, tone of voice," Handler said, entering. "They can't differentiate kindness from anger, sadness from amusement, anything from anything. Spoken speech in general is just noise to them. You might as well be oinking like a pig. Same with facial expressions. They don't use them so they have no idea what yours are for."

Dev persevered anyway, offering his name a third time, projecting the friendliness now in lights.

The Tritonian responded with a complex configuration of swirling geometric patterns.

Dev frowned at Handler. "Am I right in thinking that's her name?"

"Yes."

"But it feels more like... an attitude. Determination. Resolve. With a sense of justice thrown in."

"That's who she is and what she is," said Handler. "The patterns she just used are unique to her, like a fingerprint. She'll have refined and developed them over the years as she matured. They're her perception of her own personality, the image she portrays to others. It's not a name in sense that you or I understand. It's deeper than that, an emotional autograph, a declaration of her inner self."

"I was hoping for something a bit more practical, something I can use when referring to her out loud. She can't just be 'that Tritonian over there.' How about Ethel?"

"Ethel?"

"There was a singer, Ethel Merman, a century or so Pre-Enlightenment."

"Merman. I get it. Did you happen to have that fact at your fingertips?"

"No. I ran a search earlier, after I first met her. Mermaid, merman, that sort of thing. Just in case. 'Ethel Merman' cropped up, and I made a mental note."

"Well, you can call her what you like, verbally. It'll be just a meaningless burble to her. But if you want to address her by name in a way she'll understand, reproduce the light patterns she showed you a moment ago. That's how it works."

"I don't know if I can."

"Yes, it's tricky."

"I'll give it a shot anyway."

Dev concentrated, summoning up what he hoped was the same cocktail of emotions that the Tritonian had displayed, each ingredient in the correct proportions.

If her show of scornful amusement was anything to go by, he failed dismally. She repeated the patterns, and he tried again to replicate them. He still didn't get it right, but her amusement was no longer quite as haughty this time around, so he assumed he had made a better job of it.

He then lobbed a question at her. The scar tattoo on your chest – what does it represent?

At first he thought he hadn't expressed himself clearly enough, since the Tritonian he had chosen to name Ethel looked blank.

What came next, however, was a slew of concepts that lit up every corner of her face. The regularity of the nautilus shape, the mathematical progression in the size of the chambers within the shell, the spiralling steady growth of it, the sturdiness, the rigidity, the support it provided, the pride it instilled in her...

Dev looked at Handler. "I'm not sure I got all of that. Did you?"

"Think so. The nautilus is a badge of some sort, an emblem of a social movement. It's all about evenness and solidarity – strength in numbers. The more of you there are, the greater you are. You augment one another."

"And you all stem from a common point of origin. You all share the same core ideal."

"That's it. Fairness. Reasonableness. Interdependence."

Dev turned back to Ethel and asked if she was the leader of this Nautilus Movement.

Her answer was curtly negative. It doesn't have leaders, only members. We work together towards a mutual goal. No hierarchy is necessary when everyone is in agreement about their aims.

Dev would have pressed her for details, but Ethel began to display impatience. My time in the air is limited. What is the reason you have brought me up here, other than to ask your fumbling questions?

Ethel, Dev realised, was not a woman to be trifled with. She and Sigursdottir should meet, he thought. They would get on like a house on fire. Or end up at each other's throats. Either way, sparks would fly.

His commplant announced that it was working once more, with a proviso:

> Operational efficiency compromised.
> Processing speeds may be reduced.

The countdown timer resumed its deathwatch-beetle ticking:

43:04:41

Dev searched through the backed-up data and found his sketch of the design the terrorists had left on the *Egersund*, the symbol Handler had identified as representing the mythical Ice King. He switched on the cabin's floatscreen unit and transferred the sketch to that. It hovered in midair, projected by helium-neon lasers.

Ethel's reaction was immediate and fierce. She leapt to her feet, her face flushing with furious contempt. Jabbing her shock lance for emphasis, she seethed about the danger the Ice King posed, the threat to peace and stability, the rampant bloodshed that was being carried out in the name of the God Beneath the Sea.

So many statements tumbled out of her, and the lights on her face conveyed such an intensity of passion, that she veered close to becoming unintelligible. She ranted about the followers of the Ice King, who justified murder if it was committed in his name. She asserted that they were everything the Nautilus Movement stood against, beating the cicatrix on her chest to underscore her point.

"Religious extremist terrorists," Dev said to Handler. "They're the ones heading up the insurgency."

"And the Nautilus Tritonians are their sworn enemies, or at least an opposing political faction."

"Rationalists versus zealots. Remind you of any recent intergalactic conflict, by any chance?"

Ethel was still venting her spleen against the followers of the Ice King as Dev and Handler simultaneously received a call from Sigursdottir.

> Sonar's registering activity due east of us, near the surface. Five klicks and closing. Looks like a shoal of large fish, but the pings they're sending back are all shapes and sizes and they're moving more like something manmade.
>
> More Tritonian vessels?
>
> That'd be my guess, Harmer. Handler told me

that the female you've got there is a friendly,
and presumably so are the rest of them
directly below us. Question is, are these other
ones friendlies too? Speed they're coming
suggests not. Looks more like an attack.

Let me check.

Dev asked Ethel if she was expecting company. Other Nautilus types maybe? Have you arranged a rally?

Ethel said no and, picking up on the concern on Dev's face, hurried out of the cabin. Dev raced after her, in time to see her perform a supple, parabolic dive over the rail. She hit the water with scarcely a splash.

Not looking promising, lieutenant, but I'd
advise you to hold fire 'til we know more.

No can do. I'm not endangering my men's
lives on an unknown. We're going to action
stations.

The *Admiral Winterbrook* began turning, coming about to face east. At the same time, Dev saw a Marine – someone tall and bulky, had to be Milgrom – rush towards the point-defence gun that was rising through a hatch from below decks at the bows. She slotted herself into the bucket-seat and put the gun through its paces experimentally. First she rotated it through its full firing arc, to ensure that the platform bearings were in working order and ran smoothly. Then she elevated and lowered the four barrels. It was as though the gun were nodding, swaggering, confident in its power.

Somewhere on board the catamaran, an alarm klaxon was hooting.

How far away now, Sigursdottir?

Two klicks, and they're not slowing. All the
signs are it's hostiles

Dev scanned the seascape, looking for evidence of the
approaching Tritonian craft. He saw distant streaks of
luminescence in the black water, running in parallel, like a
meteor shower scoring the night sky. They were the wakes
of large objects underwater, zooming in fast. He estimated
there were a dozen of them at least.

Handler appeared at his side. "If those are insurgent
vessels, are they coming for us or the other Tritonians?"

"Beats me. Either way, they have the numerical advantage."

"The *Admiral Winterbrook* should even up the odds. It's
armed to the teeth."

"Even so, there's a limit to what a surface boat can do
against submarines."

"You're not contemplating going down there to help out.
You *are*, aren't you? You're crazy. What difference can one
man make?"

"I'm a disruptive influence," Dev said. "You read my
psych profile. I have a knack for causing chaos. So I'll bring
a bit of that to the party."

"Well, I'm sure I can't stop you. At least let me give you
your next dose of nucleotides first. Hold you together a little
longer."

Handler deftly applied a fresh serum patch to Dev's arm.

"Good luck," he said. "Try not to get yourself killed."

"The motto I live by."

Dev dived.

30

THE NAUTILUS TRITONIANS had circled the wagons. The four submarines were huddled together, braced for attack and ready to repel. If a fight was in the offing, they were meeting it head-on, not fleeing.

Dev was duly impressed.

He swam to Ethel's manta sub, positioning himself in front so that she could see him through the cornea of its cockpit.

I'm on your side, he said. An extra pair of hands.

Leave, she replied. We don't need you.

You might find you do.

Very well. If you insist on staying, don't get in the way.

I'll do my best.

The other group of Tritonians were almost there. They were travelling in an assortment of vessels, led by a cuttlefish sub. Dev was certain it was the same cuttlefish sub that had sunk the *Egersund*. Its mottled markings looked familiar.

With it were a pufferfish sub, a swordfish sub, a sub not unlike a moray eel, and others that defied categorisation, comparable to no Terran marine creatures Dev knew of. One resembled a bone disc, with sharp points protruding from its circumference. Another was what might result if a salamander and an umbrella somehow mated and spawned.

Ethel and her co-pilot cousin eased the manta sub forward to meet the cuttlefish sub face to face. The cuttlefish sub and its entourage halted, and Ethel attempted to parley. She advised the new arrivals to turn around.

One of the cuttlefish sub pilots, serving as spokesman for the group, responded with disdain.

You have no authority over us, he said. We answer to a higher power. We do the Ice King's bidding.

There is no Ice King, Ethel said. He's a figment. A fantasy.

That's where you're wrong. He is real, and he is awakening. He is stirring in the deeps, soon to lead us in liberating our world.

So you say.

So we know. His hour has come. We're on a pilgrimage to find him, and when we do, we will follow him wherever he leads and do whatever he asks of us.

You worship nothing but an empty dream.

We worship might and freedom and a future no longer blemished by the stain of the ungilled. That's what the Ice King promises us.

You're using faith to legitimise slaughter, said Ethel. I don't like these gill-less interlopers any more than you do, but there are ways we can live alongside them.

Peaceful coexistence? Now that is an empty dream!

They're not all bad. They can be reasoned with, if we only try.

Easier just to kill them.

Your acts of sabotage and murder don't do anything except make them angry and incite retaliation. I'll show you.

Ethel beckoned behind her, and she was joined in the eye socket by the kid who had been held captive on Llyr.

This boy is one of yours, she said. Like you he fights against the ungilled, but unlike you he's suffered the consequences.

I know him, said the cuttlefish sub pilot. He put himself forward to join us, but we turned him down. Too young. He has not grown into a name yet. When someone's old enough to know his own name, then we'll embrace him, but only then.

You have standards. You're noble.

Sarcasm, it seemed, was burnt-orange in colour.

We can't be responsible for the lives of children, said the cuttlefish sub pilot.

I tried to prove my worth, the kid said. I hate the ungilled. I hate them even more after the things they did to me.

He was taken prisoner, said Ethel. Abused horribly. You see the marks on his body. This is what happens when you resort to violence. You get violence in return.

It's to be expected, the cuttlefish sub pilot said without regret. All who are hurt or who perish in our cause are sacred martyrs. They will be avenged. The Ice King will bring a reckoning against the ungilled who steal the creatures that are our property and pollute the water with the filth of their machines, who've invaded our world and violated its sanctity, who've claimed our seas as their own and squat above us in their shadow-casting settlements as though they are our lords.

I believe that too! the boy declared.

You're a brave one. If you were just a little older, you'd deserve a place in our ranks.

Why not now? I belong with you. I'm prepared to do anything in the name of the Ice King.

So saying, the kid hauled back and struck Ethel a vicious blow across the side of the head. She hadn't seen it coming. She reeled away, stunned.

Seeing this, her cousin darted from his station, plunging into a sort of access duct that ran from one side of the manta sub's head to the other, a link between the eye socket cockpits.

The boy, meanwhile, snatched up Ethel's shock lance, which was resting in a purpose-built niche beside her seat. He moved towards her with the weapon held out menacingly. Ethel, still dazed, floated helplessly, vulnerable.

Dev didn't think Ethel's cousin was going to reach her in time. He himself, outside the sub, wasn't much better placed to help.

Unless…

He drew the HVP and fired straight into the manta's gaping maw.

The sabot round punched a hole in the mouth's interior, hitting one of the spongy filter plates the manta used to sieve its food source – microscopic organisms – from the water. The wound was relatively small, to a beast that big, but deep and piercing nonetheless.

Dev's gamble paid off; the living submarine flinched and recoiled in pain.

The sudden lurch threw the kid off-balance. He blundered against the outer membrane of the eye, and the next instant Ethel's cousin reappeared at the other end of the access duct. The eye now had three Tritonians crowded in it.

The cousin lunged at the kid, who twisted round to face him, thrusting the shock lance forward. The two of them grappled with weapon between them, their faces ablaze with antagonism.

The boy's hand closed on a lever on the lance's handle.

There was a brilliant blue flash.

Ethel's cousin juddered, then went limp.

The boy looked aghast, startled, horrified... but also triumphant.

The cousin drifted away from him, slowly spinning. No question, he was dead. His arms began to rise in a kind of crucifixion pose. His head lolled.

Ethel emerged from her stupor, took in the situation at a glance, and launched herself at the kid with lightning streaks of pure naked fury forking across her face. She seized the lance off him and aimed.

Whether or not she actually intended to use the lance against him, she never got the opportunity.

The Tritonians in the cuttlefish sub saw that the boy was in danger. He was their ideological kin. They could not simply leave him at Ethel's mercy.

The cuttlefish sub jetted forward with a powerful squirt of its siphon. The other subs alongside it followed suit.

The vessels of one Tritonian faction joined battle with the vessels of another, and what ensued was one of the bizarrest battles Dev had ever known.

31

SUPERSIZED SEA CREATURES clashed in a tumult of lashing tentacles, threshing tails and snapping jaws. Dev almost forgot that these were submarines, steered by pilots. The giant beasts seemed simply to be doing what came naturally, instinctively: competing with rival species, employing the arsenal of weapons and defensive measures which evolution, that great quartermaster, had equipped them with.

The moray eel sub lunged at the seahorse sub, mouth open wide to reveal rows of backward-hooking teeth. The seahorse danced agilely aside, avoiding the eel's rippling serpentine rush. With its prehensile tail it caught hold of its assailant just behind the gills. The eel arced its head round but couldn't reach its target. It began turning in circles, but as long as the seahorse kept its grip and hung on, the eel could not sink its teeth in.

The swordfish sub went for the anglerfish sub, slashing at it with its long, sharp-edged bill. The anglerfish tried to bite back, but the bony blade was moving too fast. Its fierce sweeps drove the anglerfish back and opened up cuts in its flanks and belly. The anglerfish couldn't get close enough to bring its fangs to bear.

The other manta sub, the one not piloted by Ethel, engaged with the pufferfish sub. Although the manta dwarfed the pufferfish, it had trouble utilising that advantage. Whenever it swooped in, the pufferfish inflated like a balloon, projecting an array of stiff spines that could pierce the thickest hide. The manta veered away each time, aborting the attack to avoid injury.

As for Ethel's manta sub, it was enmeshed in the cuttlefish sub's arms and struggling to break free. Dev could see Ethel and the body of her cousin in its left eye socket cockpit. There was no sign of the kid. Presumably he had fled once the battle started. Ethel herself was preoccupied with manipulating the controls, which consisted of a waist-high column festooned with knobbly protrusions.

Under her ministrations the manta thrashed its wings and flexed its body, but the cuttlefish had it tightly clasped. No amount of writhing was going to detach those arms with their lining of finely serrated suckers.

And now another vessel was jockeying above the manta, looking for an opportunity. This sub had elements of turtle in its makeup, and elements of jellyfish. A thick keratin shell protected all of its body except for the underside, from which hung a curtain of transparent, coiling tendrils.

It was attempting to drape these tendrils onto the manta sub's back. The manoeuvre was delicate and required precision. The turtle-jellyfish's pilot was trying to keep the tendrils from accidentally making contact with the cuttlefish sub's arms. Dev could only assume there were venom cysts embedded in those dangling gelatinous tubules.

Sure enough, when the turtle-jellyfish sub finally managed to touch the manta sub's cartilaginous skin, the manta immediately arched and convulsed. It was clearly in terrific pain, and as Dev watched, its efforts to break free of the cuttlefish sub's clutches grew feebler and more uncoordinated. Ethel wrenched and hammered urgently at the controls, but her vessel had become unresponsive.

The turtle-jellyfish sub was poised to attack again. The venom in its tendrils must be some kind of paralytic neurotoxin. Another dose would bring the manta sub to a complete standstill, possibly even kill it. Already the cuttlefish sub was exploiting its weakened state, probing the cornea of its left eye with its tentacles. They could undoubtedly pop the eye open and drag Ethel out, Dev thought. Once the manta sub was rendered entirely helpless, there'd be nothing to prevent it.

Dev made a beeline for the turtle-jellyfish sub. It had only one point of vulnerability that he could see. Its pilot sat suspended beneath its shell in a blister-like pod, just ahead of the tendrils.

Dev swam close enough to bring the pod within the range of the HVP. With the battle raging around him in a surge of bubbles and swirls of bioluminescence, he took aim.

Then it hit him – a clench in his gut, a wallop of pure agony. He doubled up, almost losing his grip on the pistol. It was like the worst stomach cramp imaginable, the kind you got with severe food poisoning or some awful gastric infection.

He glimpsed the turtle-jellyfish descending towards the manta again, that mat of dangling tendrils ready to stroke a bare patch of the other sub's wing.

Even as his innards twisted inside him, seeming to tie themselves in knots, Dev raised the HVP. His host form might be rebelling, it might be doing its utmost to undermine him, but he would not let it get the better of him. Fuck the pain. Fuck it. Fuck it and fuck ISS and fuck exponential cellular breakdown and fuck absolutely *everything*.

He lined up the shot again, eyeing down the barrel of the HVP and centring the pilot blister in the fluorescent triangle formed by the front sight's inverted V and the rear sight's matching topless trapezoid.

The sabot round burst the blister, and also the head of the Tritonian inside.

The turtle-jellyfish sub drifted away, caught by some current, and Ethel's manta sub was spared a second stinging.

Ethel was far from out of trouble, though. The cuttlefish sub's tentacles were squeezing the cockpit eye, making its membranous cornea bulge alarmingly.

Stomach still cramping, Dev pawed his way down through the water to the two entangled subs.

Elsewhere, the worshippers of the Ice King appeared to have the upper hand. The seahorse had been torn free from the eel by a third sub, and now the two enemy subs had joined together and were ripping it asunder between them.

The anglerfish sub was reeling from the swordfish sub's onslaught, blood billowing from a score of gashes in its body.

The second manta sub was faring somewhat better. It had abandoned the pufferfish sub and moved on to a sinuous, cylindrical craft gifted with a round mouth full of concentric rings of teeth. The manta was clobbering the parasitical, lamprey-like nightmare with its wings, pounding relentlessly so that the pilot of the other sub was unable to do anything except retreat.

Dev swam under Ethel's manta sub and navigated through the thicket of the cuttlefish sub's clinging arms. Buffeted by the forces of the contest between the two vessels and stricken by waves of pain from within, he nevertheless made it to the manta's mouth.

He ducked into the opening and straightaway spied a sphincter set in the roof of the mouth, directly above him. It was tight shut, but would, if open, admit a person, or so he reckoned.

There was no other visible entry point. The filter plates were too narrow, and anyway would lead only to the manta's oesophagus and stomach. He prodded the sphincter experimentally, and sure enough, at the touch of his fingers, it dilated, revealing a vertical shaft. He swam in, and the aperture sealed itself behind him.

A couple of metres up the shaft, he came to a three-way junction. Two narrow tunnels branched left and right – the access ducts to the eye socket cockpits – while a third headed along the manta's dorsal line, towards the creature's tail. He took the turn to the left cockpit.

As he clawed along the duct he tried not to think about the fact that he was inside the body of a living entity. The rigid, uneven walls around him were manta flesh. He was travelling through the meat of the beast via a passageway that had been burrowed out specially for that purpose. Claustrophobia and a vague repulsion warred within him, but they at least took his mind off the pain in his intestines.

He reached the cockpit just as the cornea succumbed to the pressure put on it by the tentacles. The membrane burst with a sickening rending sound, and within seconds the diamond-shaped pad on the end of one of the tentacles had slithered through the jagged tear and was probing for Ethel.

She scooped up her shock lance and gave the tentacle a jolt that deterred it, but not for long. It was back, groping for her, within moments. She pressed the lever on the shock lance again, but this time there was no flash, no bioelectric discharge. Either the weapon had run dry or it needed a while to build up its energies for the next shot.

Dev shouldered in beside her and fired the HVP at the tentacle. From point-blank range, the sabot round practically sheared the pad off. The tentacle withdrew smartly in a cloud of dark blood, the pad still clinging on by just a shred of gristle.

Ethel showed appreciation.

Dev said, I'm sorry about your cousin, with a nod at the corpse now curled foetally on the floor.

A shiver of blue crossed Ethel's face, so dark it was almost indigo. I'll grieve when I have time to grieve. Come on! It's not safe in this eye anymore.

She slid into the access duct, Dev close behind. They crossed over to the other, still intact cockpit, where there was a control column identical to that in the cockpit they had just vacated.

The cuttlefish sub hadn't loosened its grip on the manta sub, but the injury to its tentacle had given it pause for thought. The pilots were trying to regain command of their vessel, frantically pressing the buds and pulling the stalks on their control columns in various permutations. The cuttlefish remained recalcitrant, unwilling to do as told. It had been hurt – the tip of a limb all but amputated – and its survival instincts were at odds with the wishes of its masters.

The control columns, Dev realised, were patched directly in the creatures' nervous systems. The animals retained the lower orders of brain function, the ones that regulated breathing, heartbeat, digestion and so on. The pilots ran everything else.

The subs were, in effect, zombies, with their Tritonian crews providing purpose, motivation and guidance. Yet even mindless, obedient slaves balked when they were confronted with something which caused pain or presented a clear threat.

Ethel grabbed the largest stalks, a matching pair, and flipped them to and fro. The manta sub seesawed from side to side. Had Dev been standing rather than floating, he would have been tossed violently about. The same for Ethel. As it was, Dev felt the water within the cockpit churn around him while he remained more or less stationary. The wonders of hydrodynamics.

The manta sub tore itself away from the cuttlefish sub's arms.

As the limbs flailed loose, Ethel threw the manta into reverse. The sub glided backwards with a few beats of its vast wings, before Ethel propelled it forwards again, at ramming speed.

The cuttlefish sub was still drawing its arms together, gathering itself, as the manta sub struck. The manta's momentum and greater bulk sent the cephalopod spinning away.

The cuttlefish's pilots barely had time to regroup and right their vessel before the manta struck again. The leading edge of one wing hammered it straight between the eyes.

Ethel didn't stop. She kept butting, battering and bashing the cuttlefish sub remorselessly, giving no quarter, not letting up until the creature was pounded into submission.

Eventually the cuttlefish just hung in the water, its limbs splayed, showing no voluntary movement. There wasn't any external damage that Dev could see, but some of its internal organs must surely have been ruptured. Nothing, least of all a pulpy-bodied invertebrate, could endure the kind of punishment the manta had been dishing out and remain unscathed.

In its eye socket cockpits, its pilots floated dazed and bewildered, only just conscious. Dev almost felt sorry for them. They could hardly have anticipated how brutal and ferocious Ethel's retaliation would be. Though part-paralysed by the turtle-jellyfish sub's sting, the manta sub was still formidable, and once it had shaken itself free, it had proved that the cuttlefish sub was no match for it – especially with a vengeful, unforgiving Ethel at the helm.

Ethel scooped up her shock lance. I'm going out there to finish this, she said.

You mean kill those two?

Tempting, but no. They are the ones who can halt the battle. They can call off their allies and lead them in a retreat. I will make them do so. They are bullies, and will quickly comply once I threaten them.

Dev did not doubt that, but he wasn't sure there was much of a battle left to end. From what he could see, Ethel's side were in poor shape. The anglerfish had been sliced to ribbons by the swordfish. The seahorse sub was now in several pieces, gently dispersing.

Only the other manta sub remained intact, and it was beleaguered on all side by enemy vessels, harrying it. The manta fought back, giving as good as it got, swatting at any opponent who came within reach, but the constant siege was wearing it down. Either it or its pilots were tiring. Sooner or later it would reach the limits of its endurance and, exhausted, fall victim to its assailants.

Ethel inserted herself into the access duct, only to come reeling back a split second later. Blood erupted from her shoulder, mushrooming outward.

The Tritonian kid emerged from the duct, carrying a short knife fashioned from some animal's tooth. Dev noticed ornate decorative patterns carved in the ivory, intricate scrimshaw. He took in this detail even as he moved to intercept the boy.

In the name of the Ice King! the kid said, slashing at Dev with the knife. Die, ungilled scum!

Dev seized his wrist and pivoted his hand back against itself. Instantly the knife slipped from his grasp. Dev batted the weapon behind him, out of reach, then wrenched the kid's arm round and yanked it up behind his back until his fist was lodged between his shoulderblades.

He hated using this level of force against a minor, but the kid needed to be pacified. His fanaticism made him more dangerous than someone of his tender years would otherwise be, or indeed ought to be.

The kid kicked at Dev with his heels, trying to worm his way free. Dev increased the compliance hold by driving the kid's hand even further up his back.

Then the kid did something unexpected. He performed a back-flip, paddling hard with his legs until he was above Dev, then behind him.

Dev kept his hold on the boy's wrist, but now the kid was where the knife had fetched up. He seized it and stabbed at Dev, who had to relinquish his grasp on the boy in order to evade the knife thrust.

There's gratitude, he said. I rescue you from a mess that was largely of your own making, and this is how you repay me.

Shut up! The kid chased up the comment with an insult likening a part of Dev's anatomy to a string of excrement hanging from a fish's anus.

Dev was about to close in on the kid with a view to disarming him once more, when Ethel sprang up behind the boy. Her shoulder was bleeding copiously, casting a pall in the water, but nonetheless she snaked an arm round the kid's neck and clamped her other hand over his knife hand.

Holding the knife at bay, she proceeded to squeeze both sets of his gills flat. It was a perfect chokehold. The kid strained and twisted, but Ethel maintained pressure. He kicked at her in vain.

Soon he was juddering, dancing on the spot. Then his head rolled back.

Unconscious.

Dev waited for Ethel to let go.

She didn't.

He's out cold, he said. You can stop now.

Ethel answered with a look of steely-blue calm.

He's not a threat anymore, Dev said. He's neutralised. If you keep that up, you're going to kill him.

He deserves it.

Maybe, but he's still only a boy. Still without a name. Can you do that? Can you murder someone that young in cold blood? Whatever he's done, whatever his beliefs, you can't have his death on your conscience. You know you can't.

He then projected her name at her, her real name, with its connotations of resolve and justice, the former tempered by the latter. Her 'emotional autograph,' Handler had called it.

Her true self. He used it imploringly, to remind her who she was, to bring her to her senses.

It worked. Ethel swept her arm away from the kid's neck, her face suffused with dun-coloured disgust. The kid's gills reopened, pulsing in autonomic reflex.

He was lying in wait, she said. He'd have found that knife in my cousin's sleeping chamber. It was my cousin's prize possession, a gift from his father. I'm angry that he caught me unawares. I'm even more angry that he dared to use something so cherished on me, dishonouring the man whose life he ended.

I understand. But you've done the right thing.

Have I? said Ethel sullenly.

A spike of pain registered redly on her face. She pressed a hand to the wound in her shoulder.

At the same time, Dev experienced another of those stomach cramps, this one unusually savage.

Ethel, seeing this, said, You are hurt too?

It'll pass. I think. You look like you should do something to stem the bleeding.

It'll pass, too. I think. Besides, there is still a fight going on out there. She retrieved her shock lance. It's my job to end it.

Barely had that last statement faded from her face than an almighty explosion rocked the manta sub.

32

IT WAS A deep *whoomph* that reverberated through the water, accompanying a suddenly expanding sphere of brilliance that sprang into life not far above the other manta sub and the horde of Ice King worshipper vessels around it.

All the subs recoiled from the blast, shunted downward and apart by the pressure wave.

That's not one of our weapons, said Ethel to Dev. Unless I'm mistaken, it's one of your people's.

She wasn't mistaken. Even as the subs recovered from the shock, Dev saw a pair of barrel-shaped objects descend towards them, twirling lazily.

Depth charges.

The *Admiral Winterbrook* was joining the fray.

Brace yourself, he warned Ethel.

Nearly simultaneously – *ba-bam!* – the depth charges detonated. The swordfish sub and the lamprey-like sub were both caught in the blast radius. Their bodies burst wide open, spilling out shredded internal organs and fragments of shattered bone.

The other Ice King subs were sent reeling, as was the second manta sub.

In Ethel's manta sub, she and Dev were hurled against the back wall of the eye socket cockpit. Their limbs tangled with the kid's and each other's, and it took a few moments to extricate themselves.

During that time the scene outside changed drastically. The Ice King subs scattered, careering vertically down into the depths or horizontally off into the black water, out of sight. One of the cuttlefish sub's pilots had recovered enough to take control of the vessel again and join the frantic exodus. The second manta, meanwhile, limped round towards Ethel's craft.

Will they attack again? Ethel asked Dev. A third wave of those metal weapons?

I don't know. If the aim was to drive the Ice King guys off, then no.

You aren't certain.

The ungilled up there like to be thorough, and in this situation it's not that easy telling friend from foe among your people.

The two manta subs waited side by side, their occupants peering anxiously upwards. Ethel was poised to execute a steep dive at the first sign of another depth charge. She had instructed her colleagues in the other manta to be ready to do the same.

Seems we're okay, said Dev at last. They've worked out who's who and they know the bad guys are gone. They've stood down from action stations.

You weren't confident that would happen.

I've learned to take nothing for granted where combat is concerned. In the heat of battle, anything can go wrong and probably will.

You're a fighter. It was more a statement than a question. One whose business is defeating others in conflict.

She was trying to say soldier, but there was no direct analogue for the word in her vocabulary.

I used to be, Dev said.

No, you are. It's your life. Your nature. I saw it when you took on the thalassoraptor, and also when you were first confronted by the cuttlefish sub. You aren't just any ordinary ambassador. You're half us, half ungilled, as with all the ambassadors, but you have talents they don't. You're more than they are. More dangerous. More determined. More of a doer than a talker.

That's because I'm not actually an ambassador.

Briefly Dev outlined his status as an ISS field operative and his reasons for being on Triton. He didn't go into the niceties of host forms and data 'porting, partly because he didn't want to overload Ethel with extraneous detail but mostly because he wasn't sure that Tritonese could be stretched to express such concepts.

The cramping in his stomach had eased a little. Either that or he was adjusting to it. Still, it wasn't going away. He was keen to get back to the *Reckless Abandon* and dose up on painkillers at the first opportunity.

Before that, though, he would pick Ethel's brains further.

I realise this probably isn't the best moment, he said. You're injured. You've just lost your cousin.

Say what you have to.

Like I told you, I'm here to stop the insurgency before it gets out of control. Anything you can tell me about the Ice King and the people who worship him, anything at all, would be handy.

Ethel cast a bitter glance at the still unconscious kid. Her hand was clasped to her shoulder, pinching shut the edges of the wound he had given her.

He would be able to enlighten you better than I can, she said. What I do know is they're mad. The worst kind of mad, because they think they're sane. There's a legend that the Ice King made the world the way it is.

Yes, I've heard as much.

They say, too, that he sleeps in the ice at the heart of the world and will awaken when the time is right, in our direst hour of need. Some people claim he's watching over us all the time, checking on us. The moons that shine down through the roof of the world are, it's said, his eyes. They judge us constantly, and if we're found lacking, sometimes the Ice King will conjure up a vast storm overhead, to remind us to behave. Like a parent warning a naughty child.

The syzygy storm.

But it's only a story, Ethel went on, with the Tritonese equivalent of a shrug. The moons are just moons, and the storm is just a storm, if an unusually severe one.

So there's no way any of this stuff could be true? There is no Ice King?

You have to ask?

I do.

If he does exist, I have seen no credible evidence.

His followers seem pretty convinced about him.

They're deluded. They've taken a fiction and constructed a faith around it. It enables them to justify their actions against your kind.

Amid the indignation on her face he saw traces of sympathy, but it was not for humans.

You don't completely disapprove of what they're doing, he said.

I don't approve of their methods, the brutality they resort to. Nor do I approve of how their movement can lure in the young and corrupt them, as with this one. All the same I have no great love for you ungilled. I would prefer it if you'd never come to our world. I feel as much of a grievance against you as anyone else does. You don't belong. You aren't welcome.

That's a shame.

Isn't it just.

No, I meant because I was hoping you'd stick with us — me and my group. We could do with having you along. You know how things work around here and you're good in a fight. Frankly, we need someone like you onside.

After what I just said?

About not loving the ungilled? Yes. Whatever your personal feelings, whatever your animosity towards us, you want a peaceful resolution to the situation, like I do.

Any kind of resolution would be good, but a peaceful one would be best.

Well, that puts you, for better or worse, on the same side as me.

Those blank, black eyes of hers scrutinised him.

I have followed you quite some distance already, I suppose, she said. And you've borne out my initial judgement of you, so far.

Is that a yes?

It is. Besides, she added, someone should keep an eye on you. You and the ones with you up there. To keep you from getting into too much trouble.

Or causing it.

33

DEV RETURNED TO the *Reckless Abandon* long enough to swallow a gulp of analgesic gel and brief Handler on the latest developments. Then he swam across to the *Admiral Winterbrook* and brought Sigursdottir up to speed too.

"Congrats, by the way," he said. "You did absolutely the right thing, dropping depth charges. Targeted the aggressors and avoided any collateral damage."

"A commendation from you brightens my day," Sigursdottir replied drolly. "I can sleep easy, knowing Dev Harmer has complimented me on a job well done. Beats any medal."

"Glad you appreciate it."

"Wasn't exactly rocket science, though. Not for trained Marines. We sonar-tagged every single vessel, both the incoming lot and the ones already here. When we saw the hostiles overwhelming the friendlies, I gave the order to step in. The person you really ought to be thanking is Gunnery Sergeant Jiang. She programmed the charges to go off with pinpoint precision."

"I'll give her one of my coveted commendations too," Dev said, "but later. First things first. I've got a funeral to attend."

He plunged into the sea again, where the debris from the battle was in the throes of being eaten. All sorts of marine life, from tiny fish to hulking great predators, were busily consuming the carrion from the destroyed subs. There were feeding frenzies here and there among the shoals of small fry that collected around free-floating chunks of flesh, while the larger creatures gnawed sedately and masterfully at the carcasses themselves, abandoning their meals only if a still larger creature came along and muscled in.

It wasn't just the subs that were being devoured either. The bodies of the Ice King worshippers were getting nibbled and slowly pulled apart. One of them even became the rope in a gruesome three-way tug of war between a trio of shark-like monstrosities. They yanked it this way and that until an arm tore loose, and then the remainder of the corpse was sundered it two at the waistline.

At some distance from this grisly banquet, Ethel and her allies were gathered in the shadow of the two manta subs, which hovered dumbly above them, providing shelter with their giant, gently wafting wings. Ethel had dressed the wound on her shoulder using a sponge and strips of something that looked like seagrass.

The pilots of the seahorse sub had perished along with their craft. One of the anglerfish sub's pilots had been killed too. The other had survived, sustaining a broken arm during the hammering assault by the swordfish sub.

With the addition of Ethel's cousin, that meant four bodies now waited to be given Tritonian last rites.

It wasn't a funeral service as such, but it had a ceremonial aspect to it and was conducted with all due solemnity. The bodies were lined up in a row and each was assigned some personal belonging of their own, a single item which was attached to them by a tether of braided kelp. In the case of Ethel's cousin it was his knife. For another of the bodies it was a bivalve shell with a drawing of a relative etched into its nacreous interior. Treasured possessions for the dead to take with them to their watery graves.

The mourners, led by Ethel, announced each body one after another by name, celebrating their respective characters. Her cousin, it transpired, had been brave and steadfast with a wicked humorous streak.

Then, their faces shining a solemn greyish blue, the Tritonians drew knives and slid the blades through the corpses' ribcages deep into their chests, with practised precision. Blood came out but also a stream of bubbles, and Dev realised that the bodies' swim bladders, which occupied pretty much the same space inside them as a human's lungs, had been pierced. The bubbles were the gas inside the sacs escaping.

The bodies began to sink. The mourners watched them descend with dashes of turquoise farewell cutting through the grieving blue on their cheeks and foreheads.

Afterwards, Ethel swam over to Dev.

We're coming with you, all of us, she said. The others have agreed to be a part of your mission.

Thank them for me.

Where are you intending to go?

Further south, most likely. That's where the focus of the insurgent activity is.

We'll follow.

Where's the kid?

In my manta sub. Still unconscious, securely tied up. He's going nowhere.

What do you plan on doing with him?

I ought to return him to his drift cluster, wherever that may be. Send him home. Let his people deal with him as they see fit. It would be the fair and conscientious thing to do. But I'm not feeling very fair or conscientious towards him right now. Besides, the detour will cost us time, and you'd probably prefer not to have any more delays.

For what it's worth, I think we should hang on to him anyway, Dev said. If he knows anything more about the Ice King and the Ice King's worshippers, anything at all, it'll be useful. We can pump him for information when he comes round.

Ethel signalled agreement. I hope we don't have to use force to get him to talk. Then again, in some ways I hope we do.

34

BACK ABOARD THE *Reckless Abandon* once more, Dev found Handler up on the flybridge, seemingly staring into the distance. It was the trance-like gaze of someone in the middle of a commplant conversation.

"Who are you talking to?" he asked.

Handler blinked and held up a finger. After several seconds, he said, "Captain Maddox. I've just been letting him know where we are."

"Geographically or figuratively?"

"Both."

"I'd have thought that was Sigursdottir's job, not yours."

Handler looked furtive. "Maddox asked me to send him updates," he confessed finally.

"About me," said Dev.

"Yes. Not that he doesn't trust you, I hasten to add, but he's given you a squad of Marines..."

"And he wants to know, from a third-party source, that I'm taking good care of them. I haven't broken the toys he lent me to play with. Understandable, I suppose."

"I should have said something. I would have, if Maddox hadn't told me to keep it strictly between him and me. I feel like I've betrayed you."

Dev shrugged. "It's all right. Maddox seems like a hard man to say no to."

"That's putting it mildly."

"Why don't you bring me in on the conversation? I might as well have a word with the grumpy old bastard myself."

"You won't tell him you know? He'll go mad if he finds out I've given the game away."

"Promise."

"Okay then."

Dev felt a tiny cerebral *pop*, like an airlock opening, as his commplant was patched in to Handler's.

> Captain Maddox. Hope you don't mind me horning in. I assume you called Handler because you've been having trouble getting hold of me.

Yes. He says you've been underwater a lot. Incommunicado.

> I have.

And I hear there've been some shenanigans.

> If by shenanigans you mean progress, then yes.

A pitched battle of some sort? Tritonian versus Tritonian?

> The upshot of which is that I've recruited allies from among the indigenes. They can provide insider intel and they're well motivated to support us both tactically and logistically.

Fair enough. Always good to have some locals in your pocket. Hearts and minds. Even so, I'd watch my back if I were you. Can't trust sea monkeys, any of them. Slippery buggers in every sense.

Noted, but what we have here is a "my
enemy's enemy" scenario. These are Tritonians
who want the insurgency reined in every bit as
much as we do.

If you say so. Handler also tells me you're
having a spot of bother with your host form.
Sustainability issues. Specifics?

You don't really want to know the specifics.
They're pretty grim, trust me. Bleeding. Pain.
Lost teeth. I'm half expecting a leg to fall off at
any moment.

He's keeping you going, though?

Handler butted in eagerly.

Regular shots of stabilising nucleotides,
Captain Maddox. I think they're helping.

Not making it worse, at least. They're the
maintenance this old banger needs to keep it
on the road. Actually, captain, you've been on-
planet a while, haven't you?

Maddox transmitted a heartfelt sigh.

Too long, it feels like sometimes.

I'd like to run something past you, if that's okay.
You too, Handler. This Ice King business…

Ah yes. That. Superstitious bullshit, of course.
The terrorists' little fantasy. Their god. Like
Polis Plus and their Singularity. Ugh. Carte
blanche for evil.

It's fair to say there's a level of conviction
among these fanatics that's easily the equal of
the Plussers'. It might even be greater.

So?

Well, I've just heard a reference to "the ice at the heart of the world". It's where the Ice King is supposed to be sleeping.

Again, so?

So, just spitballing here, but what if there's a place? An actual location that's, I don't know, sacred to the Ice King's worshippers. Somewhere they go to pay their respects and say prayers and do whatever else they do to earn his favour. Some sort of church or temple that's perhaps also a refuge.

Somewhere that matches the description "the ice at the heart of the world"?

That's what I'm thinking. How about one of the ice caps? Somewhere in the polar regions, at least?

Handler chipped in.

Triton does have ice masses at the poles, but they're not huge and they're subject to seasonal variations. In summer they shrink from around 20,000 square kilometres to a quarter that size.

It's summer now.

Midsummer, almost, and on top of that the planet's in an interglacial period, a geological epoch between ice ages. The ice caps are pretty much as small and thin as they could ever be, just a fragile crust on the sea's surface, a scattering of broken-up floes. It's highly unlikely anyone has sited a temple there.

Granted, but you never know. It's occurred to
me, you see, that the insurgents might have a
home base they operate out of.

Captain Maddox responded to that idea with enthusiasm.

I like the sound of this. Somewhere we can
hit them, you're saying. Where their leaders
and main players congregate. The head of the
monster. Cut it off and the insurgency's dead.

Handler came back in.

Not really the *heart* of the world, is it, though?
An ice cap. That's more the top of the world.
Or the bottom.
Maybe I misinterpreted the remark. Maybe
something got lost in translation.
Or maybe it's literally the heart of the world.
The core.
Go on, Handle With Care. Sounds like you've
had a eureka moment.
Triton used to be an ice giant, remember?
And there's ice at the very centre of it still.
I'm talking a solid ball of permafrost several
thousand kilometres in diameter, the nub of ice
that was left after the planet greenhoused. A
significant amount of that is methane clathrate,
a form of frozen water with methane trapped
in its crystalline structure.
The same methane the settlers extract and
use for boat fuel.
And the same methane whose release
contributed significantly to Triton's atmospheric

warming all those millions of years ago.

Which gave us this charming world of water
we're all enjoying being on so much. Any
chance that ice ball might be where the
insurgents go to hole up?

A couple of dozen kilometres down? Where
the pressures are so immense they'd crush
you flat in an instant? I very much doubt it.

Fair point.

No, what I'm getting at is, is this the truth
behind the God Beneath the Sea myth?

The whole thing's a metaphor?

Yes. The Ice King *is* the creator, but only in
the sense that he's the methane gas that
made Triton what it is now. The Tritonians
have anthropomorphised a global geological
event into a divinity. He's the embodiment
of the warming process that resulted in the
environment they now inhabit. He's a racial-
memory narrative of how the world as they
know it came to be.

And he's still 'sleeping', as it were, in the ice
core. He's the latent methane. I get it.

If we look at the Ice King symbol in that light, it
takes on a new meaning.

Those bits at the bottom aren't lightning forks.
They're arrows. They show the direction the
methane took, permeating upward into the
atmosphere.

Seems reasonable to assume.

Well, so much for the myth. After all that, it's
nothing but hot air.

Maddox laughed, with a touch of ruefulness.

Oh, well. No convenient terrorist base for us to take out.

Shame. I really thought I was on to something.

Your best bet, Harmer, if you want my advice, is simply to stay on course. Keep going south and do whatever you can in the Triangle Towns region. Word of warning, though.

Bad news? I can never have enough of that.

Weather satellites are indicating a severe low-pressure system building in the Tropics of Lei Gong, with a high-pressure system coalescing around it. That's a recipe for a typhoon. You'll want to keep an eye on that.

You're right, I will.

Also, do you know about the syzygy conjunction?

When Triton and its moons line up in a row?

Please don't tell me that's happening as well.

Due tomorrow.

Shit. Really?

Sorry to be the bearer of bad tidings.

Will there be a storm?

Uncertain. Syzygy storms can't be predicted. You can't be sure if one's going to crop up, let alone where. Too many variables. But there's always a chance, especially down there in Lei Gong.

The way things have gone so far, I wouldn't bet against it. Fuck my fucking luck.

Triton's not been a bed of roses for you, has it, Harmer?

Bed of nails, more like.

The call ended there, and shortly afterwards the *Reckless Abandon* and the *Admiral Winterbrook* got under way again. As the boats picked up speed, Dev checked the sonar. The red dots representing the manta subs were keeping pace with them.

A strong breeze arose, whipping up choppy waves crowned with creamy phosphorescing foam. In the sky, suspended amid the constellations, Triton's moons glared down. They appeared to have edged closer together since Den had last looked at them.

The eyes of the Ice King, Ethel had called them.

Dev, like any sensible person, did not believe in gods and had no time or sympathy for those who did. Rationalism was the Terran orthodoxy, after all. Nonetheless he couldn't shake the eerie feeling that the moons were somehow watching him, and their gaze seemed more focused now than before, more intense.

More forbidding.

Angrier.

35

OVERNIGHT, DEV AND Handler manned the helm in shifts, two hours on, two hours off. The navigation computer was perfectly capable of steering the jetboat without supervision, but both men felt safer knowing one of them was up top keeping an eye out, in case something sudden and catastrophic occurred. It helped make the two hours of sleep that bit sounder and more restful.

Past midnight, the wind sharpened and the sea swell deepened. The *Reckless Abandon* rollicked along, automatically making tiny course corrections so that it cut into the waves with its bow rather than let them hit it abeam, thus reducing their impact. The *Admiral Winterbrook* was doing likewise, so that the two boats etched parallel zigzagging paths, responding to every minor alteration in the wind's direction while still maintaining their southerly heading.

Dev watched the two red dots of the manta subs on the sonar with envy. A hundred metres below the surface, Ethel and the other Tritonians weren't getting buffeted about by the elements and jigging right and left erratically. Their journey was straight and smooth. Plain sailing.

During the handovers between shifts, Dev would exchange a few words with Handler. On one occasion, the ISS liaison asked if Dev really didn't mind that he had gone behind his back, reporting to Captain Maddox.

"You seem to be taking it in your stride," Handler said. "I'm surprised you haven't made more of a fuss."

"I doubt you had a choice in the matter. I can't hold it against you," Dev said. "Can't even be annoyed with Maddox. That's what top brass do if they've got any sense: cover all the bases."

"I've not been spying on you, if that's what you're thinking. This isn't some conspiracy."

"I'm sure it isn't."

"Arkady Maddox might be an unreconstructed old warhorse..."

"Couldn't have put it better myself."

"...and he doesn't suffer fools gladly..."

"Again, no argument."

"...but he's not a bad person. He's just focused, purposeful. Likes things his own way."

"That's how you get the scrambled egg on your dress cap, and how you keep it."

"At any rate, you caught me at it and the secret's out. In a way I'm relieved. Thanks for not letting on, when you were talking to him."

"No harm done. In future, just keep me in the loop when you're keeping him in the loop. Okay?"

"I can do that."

The next time they swapped roles – Handler heading up to take the helm, Dev going down to his cabin for some shuteye – Dev said, "I've been meaning to ask. This boat of yours. Who came up with the name *Reckless Abandon*?"

"I did. It's not my boat, though, technically. TerCon supplied it for the use of us ambassadors."

"Ah, I see. And because it doesn't belong to you, you don't really care what happens to it. *Reckless Abandon*. Might as well call it *I Can Bash Around In This Thing All I Like And It Doesn't Matter Because The Government Will Pick Up The Tab For Any Damage*."

"No. That's not it. Actually, it's what came over me the first time I drove the boat, the first time I gunned the engine on the open sea and really *drove*. Seriously, Dev, this thing's so fast! Up until then it had always been known as *Diplomat One*, and that just seemed too boring and prosaic, completely unsuitable, so..."

Dev chuckled. "You're a dark horse, Handler. Hidden depths."

"Thanks. I think."

At the subsequent handover, Handler made sure to give Dev a fresh dose of nucleotides.

"I can't tell if these shots are making any difference," Dev said.

"How do you feel right now?"

"Headachey. Nauseous. That could simply be seasickness, I suppose. My sea legs still haven't quite come in. But look at this."

He held up his hands. The skin was speckled with tiny purple blotches, particularly around the wrists and knuckles.

"I noticed one shortly after my last shot. I didn't think anything of it, but then about an hour ago I realised all these others had appeared."

"Subcutaneous bleeding. Capillaries spontaneously bursting around the joints."

Dev grimaced. "At least it's internal. Not as nasty as having the stuff pour out of your nose."

"Painful?"

"A little, but analgesics are keeping it at bay."

"I really regret that this has happened to you," Handler said.

"Not as much as I do. I'm just glad a treatment was available. I'd be screwed otherwise."

"ISS are prepared for every contingency," Handler said. "This probably isn't the first time there've been problems with the host form assembly process."

"You're probably not wrong."

Dawn broke while Dev was minding the controls, and the early sky was as red as any he'd seen, a riot of carmine and crimson. Even after the sun rose and the redness faded, the prospect was no less gloomy and worrisome. Huge clouds were amassing on the horizon, taking on menacing shapes – like anvils and battleships, towering and iron-grey.

He consulted his countdown timer. It registered a little shy of 32 hours remaining. He was over halfway through his allotted three days, and he couldn't help but ask himself how much he had actually achieved on Triton in that time. He had obtained a military escort, had fathomed the insurgents' mindset to some degree, and had enlisted the co-operation of indigenes opposed to the insurgency. Apart from that, though, what had he accomplished? Was he any closer to ending the conflict?

Sometimes the missions that ISS sent him on seemed overwhelming, almost impossibly difficult. It was as though the company didn't want him to earn his 1,000 points and redeem his own body. Once or twice he even wondered whether they were sending him from pillar to post just for the sheer fun of it, deriving some sort of sick pleasure from the trouble they put him through, the teetering odds he faced. The way kings, or for that matter gods, liked to toy with ordinary mortals, just because they could.

But that assumed that the higher-ups at ISS cared about him at any other level than as an asset. His struggles didn't *amuse* them. Didn't concern them, either. All they wanted from him was results, preferably supplied in the most cost-effective manner possible, with the least fallout, the fewest legal ramifications.

Handler brought up coffee, and the two of them drank it side by side on the flybridge, mesmerised by the slow, stately swirl of the cloud formations. The sea had grown wilder than ever, and they stood with their knees bent to counteract its wayward buck and sway. Keeping the coffee in the cups, preventing it from slopping over the sides, was some feat.

"What's that?" Handler said, pointing.

Dev squinted. It looked like another cloud, but wasn't. It was too upright. Too dark.

"Column of smoke," he said.

"You sure?"

"I don't think it can be anything else. What's in that direction?"

Handler referred to the navigation map screen.

His expression turned grim.

"Dakuwaqa," he said. "It's the northernmost of the –"

"Of the Triangle Towns," said Dev. "I know. Shit."

> Sigursdottir? Are you seeing this? At your eleven o'clock.

Just spotted it. It's Dakuwaqa, we reckon.

> Yeah, looks that way. Lot of smoke. Can't be good.

No shit. Are all you ISS types this sharp or are you a special case?

> I'm not just clever, I have dazzling charisma too.

If you think that, then you're doubly deluded.

> We should investigate.

If you're referring to your ludicrously inflated self-image, then no, we shouldn't. We should leave that well alone. But if you mean

Dakuwaqa, then duh. Of course. It's what
we're here for.

Ten to one we're looking at the result of
insurgent activity.

That's not a bet I'll be taking.

Handler set course for Dakuwaqa. The *Admiral Winterbrook* changed bearing too, and the manta subs duly tailed along.

The smoke column was huge, its summit level with the tops of the tallest clouds. As the boats drew nearer to it, Dev recalled how he had once seen an entire city on fire during the war, a libertarian commune colony on a world called Roark which had succumbed to a bombardment from Polis+ dreadnoughts in near-planetary orbit. That black, roiling perpendicular plume had looked much like this one. He feared he knew all too well what they were going to find when they arrived.

36

Dakuwaqa was burning.

All of Dakuwaqa was burning.

Every dome habitat, every algae farm, every fishery, the tidal power barrages, the desalination plant, the marinas. Every inch of every structure in the township was swathed in flame and contributing to the vast pillar of smoke that loomed over it like a black ghost.

The heat was so intense, you could feel it on your skin even at a distance of 300 metres, which was as close as the *Reckless Abandon* and the *Admiral Winterbrook* dared get.

The roar was deafening, a great crackling bellow of combustion that rolled across the water.

There was nothing they could do. Dev, Handler and the Marines were able only to look on in horror. Horror and awe, because in the face of such wholesale devastation, a sense of smallness and humility was unavoidable.

Then there were the bodies.

Bobbing in the water. Many of them charred. Some face down, others face up.

Sea creatures were jostling over them, gorging from below, lending the bodies a ghastly kind of animation. They twitched and thrashed as countless sets of unseen teeth tugged on their flesh. Sometimes the dead even seemed to be trying to swim, limbs splashing ineffectually, the feeble crawl of the doomed.

Ash fell from the sky in a thin black snow. Embers hissed into extinction as they hit the sea.

Milgrom and Blunt sent up their hoverdrones to overfly the scene. The likelihood of finding anyone alive in the midst of that holocaust was slim verging on nil. A search had to be carried out all the same, just in case. There might be some pocket of the township still intact, as yet untouched by the blaze, where survivors were hunkered down, praying for rescue.

The hoverdrones flew high around the edge of the vast thermal, surveying. Their rotor fans carved weirdly beautiful vortexes in the smoke.

Their cameras, however, relayed nothing to their controllers' commplants – nothing but footage of fire and ruin. Milgrom and Blunt summoned them back, and they swooped obediently to their perches on the Marines' wristlets and folded themselves flat.

"This is awful," said Handler. He looked sickened, as well he might. Even a Frontier War veteran like Dev was finding the sight of a shattered township and a sea of corpses hard to stomach. "I've never seen anything like it before."

"Be thankful for that."

"I had no idea the insurgents would be capable of... *this*. It's just insane. They've gone too far."

Dev pulled up data on Dakuwaqa's population from an insite. The township was – had been – home to approximately six thousand. Like its companion towns Opochtli and Mazu, it was a thriving community. The warm, fertile waters of the Tropics of Lei Gong yielded the densest and most easily harvested fish stocks, compensating for the not always congenial climate. The methane mining was good here, too.

Six thousand men, women and children – slaughtered.

The worshippers of the Ice King had proved, once and for all, that they meant business.

Question, lieutenant. How did they manage it? Up until now the incidents have been relatively small-scale. This is a major step up. They've either adopted a new tactic or they've got some weapon we don't know about.

That's what I'm thinking. They could have overrun the place with sheer numbers, I guess, then torched it as they left.

But there'd have been resistance, surely. And the settlers would have had time to get a distress signal out. This happened suddenly, without warning, too quickly for anyone to react. Nobody was able to retaliate or escape. It's like the insurgents used a bomb...

But they don't have bombs.

Something similar to a bomb, then. I mean, look at the way some of the domes are caved in. It's hard to tell through all the smoke and flame, but can you see? It's as though they were struck from above. Crushed, almost. As though they had things land on them.

I see that. And then those same things set them alight. But the Tritonian weaponry I've encountered so far has all been hand-to-hand. Have you heard of them deploying anything with this level of yield?

Not before now. But the evidence of my own eyes is telling me the status quo has changed. And with Dakuwaqa gone, where's going to be next?

Opochtli or Mazu, I'd imagine.
We've got to send a warning. Get both
townships to evacuate.

Good idea. We should also head for one of
them ourselves, whichever's nearer. Try and
overtake the insurgents before they can launch
another attack of the same magnitude. We're
going to have to be extra careful, though.
Remember the *Egersund*?

What about the *Egersund*?

The people who carried out the massacre left
a vessel behind, didn't they? To finish the job.
The rest of them moved on after they'd done
killing the crew, but the cuttlefish sub hung
around in order to sink the ship and us with it.

Your point being…?

It was a trap. Straight out of the terrorist
playbook. You commit an atrocity, knowing
that someone is bound to come running.
Then, to cause maximum carnage and
outrage, you spring a sneaky follow-up attack
and take out the people who've just arrived.

Like in the days of suicide bombers. One of
them would blow up the marketplace, then
when the cops and ambulances turned up,
a second suicide bomber would take care of
them too.

Or there'd be a second improvised explosive
device with a delay fuse to catch the people
who went to the aid of the people hurt by
the first improvised explosive device. Who's
to say the insurgents haven't done the same
thing here, just like at the *Egersund*? We need
to keep our wits about us and proceed with

caution. I wouldn't put it past these cunning
bastards to have left another trap for us.

The two boats moved off slowly, giving Dakuwaqa a wide
berth and making sure to stay upwind to avoid catching any
stray embers from the blaze.

I've managed to hail Mazu, Harmer. The head
councillor there was already concerned after
contact with Dakuwaqa was lost. He knew the
place had gone dark but had no idea why.

· And now that he does…?

He's implementing a full, township-wide
emergency evacuation. Every functioning boat
is going to embark as many passengers as
will fit and get the fuck out of there as fast as
it can.

Great. What about Opochtli?

Not so great. We're not getting through.
Private Fakhouri is multiple-messaging
everyone on the town's contacts list insite. Not
a single reply yet.

Fakhouri. Dev remembered her from the tapas restaurant on
Llyr. A quiet and unassuming individual with dark, intelligent
eyes, she had seemed happy for Milgrom, Blunt and Francis to
hog the limelight. From what he could tell, she was a stickler
for protocol and accuracy, as befitted a comms specialist.

Fuck.

Might just be some kind of signals
interference. Typhoon brewing. Maybe that's
playing havoc with the satellite relay.

You don't think that anymore than I do.

No, I do not.

Then Opochtli's our next port of call.

"Uhh, Harmer?"

"Yes?"

Handler gestured at the sonar screen.

Dev scowled. "What in the name of sanity is that?"

Less than a kilometre ahead sat an amorphous shape, like some pale red amoeba. It was perhaps half a kilometre across, and it lay more or less directly in their path.

"Whatever it is, it's not a single entity," Handler said. "It's diffuse. A mass of... something. Some*things*."

"Fish? A shoal?"

"Hard to say. The sonar profile is similar, but not the same."

"Where did it come from?"

"It just appeared a moment or so ago. Like it welled up from below."

"We should divert around, just to be on the safe side."

"Already on it."

"Good work."

Sigursdottir...

Seen it. Any ideas?

Not a clue, but it's big and anomalous and I don't like it for both those reasons.

Me either.

It's also... Shit. Yes. I think it's moving. As in, trying to cut us off.

It didn't seem possible, but the amoeboid mass on the screen was indeed moving. It was shifting as if to intercept the boats, its central mass thinning as it extended towards them. Dev thought of a pseudopod unfurling. An arm reaching out to curb them.

Looking ahead, all he could see was a dark patch in the churning whitecaps, where the sea's surface was that little bit less wrinkled, a little smoother. It didn't give much indication as to what lay beneath.

He noted, however, that the manta subs had pulled back. They were no longer keeping pace with the jetboat and the catamaran.

That was most definitely not a good sign.

"Handler, bring us about," he said. "I still have no idea what that thing is, but we can't go round it and we certainly don't want to go over it."

Handler disabled the navigation computer and took manual control. He threw the *Reckless Abandon* into a tight U-turn.

At that moment, Dev realised to his dismay that a second amoeboid shape was manifesting on the sonar screen.

Right behind them.

It occupied the space between the surface boats and the manta subs, cutting the two sets of vessels off from one another.

Encirclement.

They had been well and truly suckered.

Was this what had wrecked Dakuwaqa, Dev wondered? Was this the insurgents' weapon of mass destruction?

If so, he, Handler and the Marines were deep in the shit.

And if it wasn't, if it was something else...

Then they were, he suspected, just as deep in the shit.

37

THE AMOEBOID SHAPES on the sonar screen were closing in, extending and bending together to form a rough oval, with the two boats corralled within.

Still there was nothing visible to the naked eye except a greasy smoothness on the sea's surface, somewhat like an oil slick. Now and then Dev caught a glimpse of a brown, whip-like *something* bulging out of the water, there and gone in a split second. Limb? Body? Tentacle? He couldn't tell.

Handler spun the *Reckless Abandon*, looking for a way out, but in vain. The two masses finished merging and became one, shutting off all channels of escape.

And now it began contracting around the boats, like a noose tightening. The area of clear water inside it shrank fast. Handler had to nudge the *Reckless Abandon* up beside the *Admiral Winterbrook*. There was nowhere else to go, no more wiggle room.

On the catamaran, the Marines were preparing to fight. Milgrom manned the forward point-defence gun, the targeting system of which was now slaved to her commplant. Jiang had torpedoes primed and ready to fire.

They got a heads-up from Sigursdottir.

Hang on, gentlemen. We're going to fight our
way out. It's going to get loud.

It got loud. The point-defence gun's quartet of barrels
boomed, sending volleys of 12.7mm fragmentation rounds
into the water in broad, sweeping arcs. A torpedo shot out
of its tube in the catamaran's left hull like a seal slipping off
an iceberg. It furrowed straight ahead, detonating some fifty
metres from the *Admiral Winterbrook*, raising a funnel of
white water mingled with fragments of dark, pulpy tissue.

The net result of these heavy-ordnance attacks was...

Nothing.

The oval mass just kept on narrowing in remorselessly,
undeterred. The *Admiral Winterbrook* might as well have
been chucking paper darts at a wall, for all the effect its
firepower had. Sigursdottir seemed to realise as much,
because no more torpedoes were forthcoming and the point-
defence gun soon stopped its strafing.

All at once the hollow, tightening oval on the screen became
a solid and the two boats were fully engulfed. The mass had
swamped them. There was no distinguishing their sonar
signatures amid the pinkish cloud that had subsumed them.

Dev peered over the side of the jetboat and saw dense,
tangled rods of living matter seething in the water. They
were lobed and fluted, with here and there a blister of some
sort, a pouch the size of his fist. His nose was hit by a strong
brackish smell that took him back to a school trip to the
seaside in his youth.

Could it be...?

Then the *Reckless Abandon*'s engine died.

Handler hit the ignition. Yanked the throttle handle back
and forth.

No good.

"We have power," he said, flustered. "Just no propulsion."

The boat's computer flashed up an explanation. The pump intakes were blocked, so the engine had automatically shut down to protect itself from overheating.

"That stuff's clogged them up," Dev said. "Any way of clearing them?"

"Apart from going down into the water and doing it by hand? No."

"I wouldn't get into the sea right now if you paid me. I'm not sure what this shit around us is, but climbing into it doesn't strike me as the way to find out."

Next moment the *Admiral Winterbrook* stalled too.

Our propellers are snarled. What are we up against here, Harmer?

Beats me, Sigursdottir. Best guess, some kind of seaweed.

Seaweed?

What it looks like. Smells like, too.

Seaweed doesn't move of its own accord. It doesn't surround you and deliberately paralyse your boat.

This seaweed does. It reminds me of bladderwrack. That brownish crap you find washed up on the beach or clinging to rocks below the tideline. Only... I think it might be sentient.

You're shitting me.

I don't make the biological rules here, Sigursdottir. It's Triton. This is Tritonian fauna. Or flora. Whichever. Both together, maybe.

And it has a brain?

Some kind of collective intelligence. That or it's being manipulated.

By insurgents?

Why not? Tritonians use zombified sea
creatures as submarines and have guns made
of coral and soft tissue that fire bioelectric
discharges. I don't think weaponising a vast
clump of kelp is beyond them.

Well, we're immobilised. That's the fact of the
matter. We'll just have to figure out a way of
cutting ourselves loose.

If being immobilised is the worst that happens
to us, we should be thankful.

Ever the voice of optimism, eh, Harmer?

A day and a half on the wretched piss-ball of a
planet has taught me not to expect anything to
work out well.

Dev hoped this would be the worst of it.

But it wasn't.

The plant began to surge out of the water. Strands of it coiled together into thick ropey vines which spiralled up the flanks of both boats like ivy growing at time-lapse speed. The vines made slobbering wet sounds as they slapped their way up the hulls, the awful moist kiss of slimy vegetation on fibreglass and steel.

"It's climbing the boat," Handler said. "It's trying to board us."

Dozens of the plaited vines of bladderwrack crawled over the gunwales, probing their way onto the lower deck. The *Admiral Winterbrook* was in the same predicament, entwined all around in a questing, squirming mesh of seaweedy growth.

Milgrom leapt from the seat of the point-defence gun and began slashing away with a shimmerknife. A couple of other Marines came out on deck to help her, but it was hopeless. For every vine they severed, another slithered up to take its place.

Dev pulled out his HVP as a tendril of the bladderwrack began climbing the ladder to the flybridge.

"Wait!" Handler cried. "You'll damage the boat."

"I think the boat has more to be worried about than a hole from a sabot round. So do we."

"Sorry. You're right. Fire away."

Dev blasted the encroaching twist of seaweed in two, also managing to blow out a chunk of deck.

It made very little difference, however. The severed vine fell away but the stump carried on regardless, worming its blunt tip up the rungs and wrapping offshoots of itself around the handrails for added support.

"Shit," said Dev. "This is not going to work."

The *Reckless Abandon* lurched under them. The bladderwrack had a firm stranglehold on the boat and was lashing further vines around it and flexing them ever tighter.

"I think it wants to pull us under," Handler gasped.

"I think you're right."

"What are we going to do? Tell me you have an idea, Harmer. Please! Tell me there's a way out of this."

Dev's mind had gone blank. He couldn't think of anything. The *Reckless Abandon* was listing rearwards. The bladderwrack was everywhere, glistening strands of it all over the boat, driving through doorways into the cabins.

He and Handler couldn't simply jump overboard. He doubted they would last long once they landed in that oozy morass of stems and air sacs. They would be mired, sucked down, suffocated.

What about crossing over to the *Admiral Winterbrook* somehow? The Marine catamaran was still level in the water.

He doubted it would last much longer, however. Only a matter of time before the bladderwrack covered it too. And they couldn't reach it anyway. The gap between it and the *Reckless Abandon* was a good five metres, too wide to leap.

They were screwed.
Both boats were as good as lost.
Unless...

38

"HANDLER," DEV SAID, "where's the fuel tank on this thing?"

"Just aft of amidships."

"Port or starboard?"

"Both. One on either side."

"Below or above the waterline?"

"Just above."

Dev leaned out from the flybridge and fired several rounds into the side of the boat in a diagonal line.

All the shots punched ragged gouges but it was the last three that actually drew blood, as it were. Liquid methane spurted out in a trio of clear, jetting streams. The fuel spread quickly, dispersing to form a viscous, iridescent layer across the water and the bladderwrack.

The sentient seaweed recoiled, evidently finding the methane noxious. Not noxious enough, however, to release the *Reckless Abandon*. If anything, the plant seemed peeved that someone was trying to poison it. The vines redoubled their efforts to drag the jetboat down.

"So much for that plan," Handler said, on the verge of despair. "All you've done is piss it off."

"I'm not finished yet."

JAMES LOVEGROVE

Dev had in fact been hoping that the fuel spill would drive the bladderwrack away. Since it had failed in that aim, he had no choice but to resort to Plan B, something a little more drastic.

"Handler, listen to me. We're going to have to jump ship."

"Abandon the *Reckless Abandon*?"

"Afraid so."

"But you said it would be suicide to –"

"I know what I said, but circumstances have changed. We have a shot at getting through this, but the price is you're going to have to kiss your boat goodbye."

Handler groaned.

"It's fucked anyway," Dev said brusquely. "But it can at least buy us a chance to get clear, and maybe save the *Admiral Winterbrook* into the bargain."

"You're going to scuttle it?"

"In a manner of speaking. Wait just a second."

> Sigursdottir, does that point-defence gun of yours have incendiary ammo?

We can load some. Why?

> See the fuel pouring out of the *Reckless Abandon*?

Gotcha. Say no more. What's the timescale?
How long do you need?

> How long's it going to take to load that ammo?

No more than thirty seconds.

> Then that's our timescale.

He disconnected the commplant call, only to find that Handler had quit the flybridge. The ISS liaison was scooting down the ladder, taking care not to touch the wreathing, writhing bladderwrack.

"Where the fuck are you going?" Dev shouted.

"Your nucleotide shots," Handler called back. "I have to get them."

"Oh, you…"

Dev bit back a curse and flew down the ladder after him. Handler ducked into the main cabin, stepping over the vines that now infested the floor. Dev followed.

In the confined space the bladderwrack's stench was repulsive, rotten as well as briny. The vines had fastened themselves to anything that was fixed in place, wrapping around the bulkheads, the bolted-down seats, the table legs, every projection and fitting. If Dev and Handler stood still even for just a few seconds, the bladderwrack would latch on to them too.

"Handler, this is the worst possible moment for heroics."

"I just need to…"

Handler was grappling with a cupboard door, unpicking the vine holding it shut.

Dev, after a brief inner debate, went over to assist. Together they managed to tear the vine loose from the door handle.

Inside the cupboard lay the shockproof metallic case that stored the serum patches. Handler grabbed it, and he and Dev raced back out on deck.

Dev didn't know how much time they had lost. More than they could reasonably afford, he reckoned.

The *Admiral Winterbrook*'s point-defence gun was swivelling, coming to bear. Fuel was still gushing from the *Reckless Abandon*'s perforated tank. The slick it had created across the top of the bladderwrack was now some sixty or so metres in diameter, and still growing. The air above the slick was shimmering as the methane, released from the pressurised containment that kept it cooled and liquefied, began to evaporate.

"Come on!"

Dev grasped Handler by the scruff of the neck and hauled him up the sloping deck to the bows.

"If this works, we should get an opening to dive in."

"'If'? 'Should'?"

"Give me a break. I make these things up on the fly. Desperate measures are never an exact science."

The gun began blazing. Nitroamine explosive rounds raked the methane slick, and in a flash, the sea was on fire.

The bladderwrack collectively convulsed, the entire expanse of seaweed responding as one. It churned and roiled.

"You've hurt it!" Handler crowed, exuberant.

"I don't think so. I don't think it can feel pain the way you or I do. But it's smart enough to know it doesn't want to burn."

The vines interlaced around the *Reckless Abandon* were no longer clinging to it quite so tenaciously. In the water, the bladderwrack was breaking up. It less of a dense knotted mass and more of a loose agglomeration.

This was the best – the only – opportunity Dev and Handler were going to get.

Dev threw Handler off the front of the *Reckless Abandon*. The ISS liaison plunged into the midst of the bladderwrack, clutching the case of serum patches to his chest. Dev was right beside him.

Not a moment too soon, either, as the flames on the sea found the source of the liquid methane. One of the *Reckless Abandon*'s fuel tanks, then the other, went up. The entire jetboat rose clear of the water as it exploded, and when it came back down it was in two pieces, broken in the middle like a snapped branch.

Dev heard, saw and felt the explosion, a burst of brilliance behind and above him, even as he clawed down through the coils of bladderwrack, pulling Handler along. He ignored the slap and clench of the vegetation, focusing solely on pressing onwards, getting to the bottom of it and out.

How deep was this matted mess of seaweed anyway? How far down did you have to go to be free of it?

It looked as though he might never find out, because the bladderwrack began to coalesce around him and Handler. The seaweed had detected the presence of the two humans, intruders. Even disorientated by the fire raging on the surface, it still remembered its job was to seek and destroy.

Dev felt strands of it reaching for him, groping for purchase. He could barely see. Everything was a field of ravelling, snaky brown plant matter.

Then he and Handler were snarled in it, snared. They could no longer move. Up, down, in every direction, the bladderwrack crowded in on them, stifling, crushing.

The more Dev struggled against it, the firmer its python-like embrace became.

It was going for his neck.

It was determined to clamp his gills shut.

And there was nothing he could do to stop it.

39

HE FELT A push from below, a surging rush.

Then he and Handler were rising, as though a giant cupped hand was lifting them.

Dev glimpsed the outline of a huge rounded rectangle below, like a hole coming up to swallow them.

Which was exactly what it was.

Ethel, you fishy beauty.

The rectangle was the mouth of a manta sub – Ethel's, it had to be – and it engulfed them, scooping them up inside as the vessel ascended vertically at speed. The sub was ploughing a path to the surface through the bladderwrack, taking Dev and Handler with it.

Dev deftly hooked an elbow over the rim of the manta's mouth, keeping a tight grip on Handler with his other hand. The sub's incursion had torn them free from the bladderwrack's grasp, but fronds of the seaweed were still battering them and twisting around them as they rose. He clung on grimly against the onslaught.

Then, all at once, they were soaring into the air. The manta sub shot up like a rocket, five, ten, fifteen metres clear of the sea, shedding bits of bladderwrack as it went.

Reaching apogee, the manta turned with its wings outstretched and began a surprisingly graceful descent. It didn't fall so much as glide, several tons of sea beast coming down at a low angle and hitting the water with a hefty but controlled wallop, a bellyflop mitigated by the mattress of bladderwrack the sub landed on.

All the same, the two humans in its mouth were nearly jolted free. Only by hanging on for dear life was Dev able to keep himself and Handler from being ejected like morsels of bad food.

The manta sub had come to rest not far from the *Admiral Winterbrook* and the shattered, sinking wreck of the *Reckless Abandon*. Fire burned across a swathe of the sea, and for a moment Dev thought he and Handler had been saved from the bladderwrack only to face a worse fate. The manta sub was surely stranded, helpless. How could it burrow back down through the seaweed without a run-up to achieve the same impetus it had used in its ascent? And the flames were spreading...

But he had underestimated both Ethel and her vessel.

The manta sub started to rock and shudder. It seemed to be floundering, thrashing about in panic.

No.

It was moving.

It was using its wings to propel itself across the bladderwrack, lurching forward like an elephant seal on dry land. There was nothing elegant about the procedure. It was a cumbersome lollop, demanding a huge amount of effort and achieving very little. The sub wasn't getting anywhere fast.

But it was getting *somewhere*. A few metres at a time, it was crawling over the swampy morass of bladderwrack.

Dev and Handler were tossed violently around inside the manta's mouth. There was nothing to grab onto for support except the creature's gill arches, but even after Dev had established a handhold and foothold here, and made Handler do the same, they still found themselves being bounced bruisingly up and down. Dev felt it worst in his cracked molars, which sent bolts of pain into his skull with every bump his body suffered.

How long the torturous journey lasted, Dev had no idea. It was probably no more than four minutes, but it felt like forty. The manta sub's exertions grew increasingly urgent. With no water flowing into its mouth and through its gills, it was running out of oxygen.

Then it was past the edge of the bladderwrack and plunging headlong into open water. It shook off the last few strands of seaweed still adhering to its body, and soon it was planing smoothly through the water once more, at home in its natural element.

Dev thrust himself out of its mouth. He offered a quick flash of gratitude to Ethel, who sat at her piloting station in the manta's intact eye, before shooting up to the surface.

The *Admiral Winterbrook*.

The Marine catamaran was, for all he knew, still marooned in the centre of the bladderwrack, surrounded by burning liquid methane. If Sigursdottir and her team had taken the option of abandoning ship the way he and Handler had, then they needed retrieving from the seaweed too, and quickly. Once he had assessed the situation, he would go back down and get Ethel to attempt another rescue operation if one was needed.

At first all he could see was a coruscating wall of fire. No sign of the *Admiral Winterbrook*. Tongues of flame licked upward from the sea, rising from a coal-black bed of burnt, shrivelled bladderwrack.

Had Sigursdottir found a way out? Or had her boat gone down with all hands, either consumed by the fire or dragged under by the sentient seaweed?

No reply.

Shit. That could mean only one thing.

Dev tried to console himself with the fact that the Marines had been professional soldiers. They had signed on the dotted line knowing the job brought with it a risk of getting killed. They hadn't been forced to join up, as he had. They hadn't been part of TerCon's juvenile offender conscription programme and offered the not-really-a-choice of military service or a spell in prison. They had been well aware of what they were getting into and how they might come out of it: feet first.

All the same, he couldn't help feeling at least partly responsible for their deaths. If not for him, the eight of them would even now be sitting safe and sound at Station Ares, rather than plummeting into the icy depths of Triton's ocean. Their final resting place lay so far from Earth that the light reaching it from the Sun, one of the fainter stars in the night sky, was twenty thousand years old.

He would have to break the bad news to Captain Maddox. That was a conversation he wasn't looking forward to. He imagined the grizzled old bastard would not take kindly to losing eight of his complement, a favoured lieutenant among them. He foresaw bellowing. Not to mention the threat – and perhaps the application – of physical violence.

A low, steady rumble caught Dev's attention, and he looked up. There, to his left, was the *Admiral Winterbrook*, hoving into view around the edge of the field of bladderwrack. It had emerged from somewhere behind the curtain of flames, which had been screening it from his sight.

What's that? Harmer, your signal's breaking up. Repeat.

I said, you made it.

Ah. Yes. Well, we owe it to you, I suppose. When the seaweed started burning, it lost its grip on us. Like it got frightened and forgot what it was meant to be doing. Jiang goosed the motor and we reversed out. Been looking for you since. We thought *you* might not have made it.

Well, I'm here.

Sorry, say again. You keep cutting out.

My commplant must be misbehaving.

That'll be why we can't get a GPS fix on you.

I'm about five hundred metres off your port bow. Look. I'm the one in the water, waving.

Got you. Where's Handler?

Down below. He's safe.

Hooray.

Sigursdottir?

Yeah?

I'm glad you're okay. And your men too. Even Milgrom.

Didn't catch that.

I said I'm glad you're —

Still not hearing anything. Just static.

You bitch, you're screwing with me, aren't you?

That I heard, loud and clear.

Dev laughed. No room for sentiment, not in Sigursdottir's world.

As the catamaran wheeled round towards him, he set his commplant to run a diagnostic on itself.

The results were dismaying, if unsurprising. Not only had the shocks given him by McCabe damaged its operational efficiency, the commplant was now suffering from intermittent power supply. It drew bioelectricity from the user's own physiology, specifically the action potentials in the nerve fibres, and wasn't presently getting a consistent, reliable flow of juice from Dev's host form. The cellular breakdown must be interfering with electrochemical reactions in his body.

It often affected commplants in the elderly and those with neurological disorders. The low-resistance electrodes and power harvesting circuitry found input harder to come by, and so the device performed less well. The usual remedy was the surgical installation of a pinhead-sized lithium polymer ion battery to boost its charge and normalise function.

Dev had neither the time nor the wherewithal to adopt that solution. He would just have to make do and hope for the best.

In the meantime, Opochtli beckoned.

He had a township to save.

40

THERE WAS A hastily convened conference.

Dev and Sigursdottir stood on the rear deck of the *Admiral Winterbrook* with Ethel and Handler. The catamaran was en route to Opochtli, and finding the increasingly high waves heavy going. The sky had darkened, the weather turning from blustery to squally. A warm, frenetic rain had started to fall, while sea spray burst over the *Admiral Winterbrook*'s twin prows with every wave the boat ploughed into, much of it vaulting over the superstructure and reaching all the way aft to soak the three humans and the indigene.

"And she has no idea what we're up against?" Sigursdottir said, eyeing Ethel.

It was the first time the two women had been in close proximity to each other, and the Sigursdottir was as wary of Ethel as the Tritonian was of the Marine lieutenant. For all Dev's assurances that Ethel was an ally, Sigursdottir had yet to be convinced. Ethel, likewise, seemed mistrustful – perhaps forgivably – of the woman who only yesterday had ordered her manta sub to be torpedoed. Her hand never strayed far from her shock lance.

"She has no clue what these Ice King guys used on Dakuwaqa?" Sigursdottir continued.

"None," Handler replied, relaying Ethel's answer. He, like Sigursdottir, had to raise his voice above the seethe of the sea and the whip of the wind. "Whatever it is, she doesn't believe it's Tritonian in origin. She says her race would never manufacture something quite so destructive."

"Not even religious fanatics? The same people who just sicced a dirty great clump of living seaweed on us?"

"I suppose it's possible," Ethel conceded, via Handler. "But I don't know where or how they built it, if they did. What if, instead, they've somehow got hold of ungilled weaponry? What if they're using some of your own explosive devices against you?"

"She has a point," Dev said. "Maybe they've raided an armoury and stolen a bunch of missile launchers. What we saw at Dakuwaqa could, I suppose, have been caused by rockets packed with high-ex cluster-bomb submunitions. Thistledowns, for instance."

"The dispersal pattern wasn't right for Thistledowns," said Sigursdottir. "The bomblets' targeting would have been much more uniform and precise. Besides, the only military-grade armouries on this planet are ours, and there've been no thefts from them that I'm aware of. Captain Maddox would go apeshit if something like that happened. Man runs a tight ship, and a security breach on that level – he'd roast the poor sucker responsible alive, and every one of us would hear about it."

"Somebody else has given them weapons, then."

"Plussers?" Sigursdottir blinked rain out of her eyes. She was the only one present who had to. Dev and Handler's nictitating membranes clicked protectively into place when exposed to water, while Ethel had no eyelids at all, her eyes quite comfortable with being wet.

"Stands to reason," Dev said. "It's the perfect set-up for them. A world on their doorstep which we've very cheekily come along and claimed for ourselves. A faction of the indigenous race that wants rid of us. Slip the insurgents a bit of high-end ordnance, light the blue touchpaper and retire. A little proxy war and they don't have to get their hands dirty or risk a single casualty."

"The Ice King worshippers are in league with your enemy?" Ethel said after Handler had finished explaining who Polis+ were and the state of chilly hostility that existed between them and the Terran Diaspora. He had had to coin a special Tritonese term to convey the concept of AI sentiences: 'Number Folk.' "I don't know. They're independent and righteous. Too proud to accept assistance from outside."

"You sure about that?" said Sigursdottir. "Even if it's assistance that gives them a winning edge?"

Ethel's face went a muddy, equivocal ochre. "Having seen what they're prepared to do – slaughter thousands in their god's name – I'm not certain anymore. About anything. I don't understand these people. Perhaps I never will."

"It could be that they're receiving help from Polis Plus without realising," Dev said. "Plussers are tricky fuckers, we all know that. They could have infiltrated the Ice King worshippers. There could be agent provocateurs within their ranks who've convinced them that non-Tritonian weapons are the way forward."

"Aren't you trained to spot Plussers lurking in organic host forms?" said Handler.

"It's a skill I've acquired. Trouble is, I've not been able to apply it yet. I haven't had a chance to sit down with any insurgents and see if I can weed out ringers."

Dev also had his doubts that the standard test questions would work on Tritonians. Their expressions and mannerisms were so different from humans', not to mention their mode of speech, that the usual deviations from the norm – the quirks and atypical responses you had to watch out for – weren't applicable.

An alien masquerading as a human was one thing. An alien disguised as another species of alien – then all bets were off. How could you tell which behavioural patterns were anomalous? It would be as though the Plusser was wearing two masks. Doubly impenetrable.

Besides, the true marker of a Plusser occupying a human host form was that unnerving deadness in the eyes, Uncanny Valley. And Tritonians' eyes were naturally blank and inexpressive.

You could also make a Plusser agitated by mocking the race's religion. Since the Tritonian insurgents were themselves religious zealots, however, exploiting that topic to provoke a reaction from them meant nothing. They would be just as touchy about it as any Plusser.

"I've a good mind to call Maddox and ask for reinforcements," Sigursdottir said. "This is bigger than we thought, bigger than we're equipped to deal with. We need backup."

"You mean leave Opochtli to the mercy of the insurgents?" said Dev. "No way."

"You're in no position to give me orders, civilian. If I think waiting for reinforcements is a good idea, then waiting for reinforcements is what we're going to do. Maddox can mobilise all of Station Ares and have three hundred heavily armed Marines here in no time."

"In no time? How long do you reckon it'll take them to arrive?"

"Best-case? Twelve hours."

"Opochtli will be toast by then. Maybe Mazu too. By all means have Maddox deploy. The plain truth, though, is that right here, right now, it's all on us. Me, you and your

Marines, and Ethel and her pals. We're less than twenty klicks out from Opochtli and, like it or not, we're the best and only chance that town has."

"It may already be too late. The attack may already be over."

"We don't know that," Dev said, "and now's not the time to start second-guessing ourselves. Whatever weapons the insurgents have, it's up to us to stop them. Nobody else can. I wouldn't be surprised if we're hopelessly outnumbered. Outgunned as well. But holding back and waiting for support simply isn't an option. I'm sorry, but that's just how it is."

Sigursdottir squared her shoulders. It occurred to him that he might have pushed her too far.

"I bet you think that was a stirring speech, don't you?" she said.

"I was going for impassioned, with a hint of rousing."

"I'd still be within my rights to halt this boat and not go any further. I have a duty of care to my team. It would be crazy to send them into a firefight they probably can't win. That's just not sound tactics."

"Agreed. But wouldn't you say you had eight *exceptional* soldiers on board, yourself included?"

"Oh, you sly bastard."

"Capable of meeting any challenge, however great?"

"Shut up."

"And isn't it your sworn responsibility to protect colonists on Triton from harm? Isn't that the sole reason you Marines are garrisoned here?"

"I hate you, Harmer."

"Only because you know I'm right. Believe me, I don't much relish the prospect of what we're heading into. I'm shitting bricks about it, in fact. Insurgents with enough firepower to level a town and no qualms about using it – what's to love about that scenario? But if the alternative is sitting on our backsides and doing nothing while Opochtli burns, then that's no alternative at all."

Sigursdottir gave him a look that was equal parts resentment and resignation.

"I'll tell you this," she said finally. "If Corporal Milgrom was out here right now, she'd go down on one knee and ask you to marry her. That is a woman who loves having the odds stacked against her. She's been itching for a proper, no-holds-barred scrap ever since she came to Triton."

Dev mimed a profound shudder. "Marry Milgrom? I'd rather take my chances with a thalassoraptor."

41

I DON'T TRUST him.

This was from Ethel as the manta sub coasted along in the *Admiral Winterbrook*'s wake. She had summoned one of the Tritonians from the other sub to pilot hers while she went topside for the conference. Now she was back at the controls, the other manta alongside, all three vessels bound for Opochtli.

Say that again? said Dev.

I said I don't trust him.

Dev wondered if he had misinterpreted the sentence both times, perhaps got the gender wrong.

The ungilled soldier? he said, meaning Sigursdottir.

No. Not her. She seems straightforward enough, as far as I can tell. Even honest.

From a Tritonian, that was a compliment indeed.

No, it's him, Ethel went on. The other hybrid like you. The ambassador.

Handler, she was talking about.

Yeah? Dev injected a note of offhandedness into the remark.

He's careful about what he says. Too careful.

Maybe he just has trouble with your language.

You don't seem to, not anymore, and he's been here longer than you.

I'm a quick learner, Dev said glibly.

What he was reluctant to admit, even to himself, was that he had his own misgivings about Handler. It wasn't just the business about the call to Captain Maddox, although that bothered him more than he had let on. Handler's loyalties should lie with ISS first and foremost, and he shouldn't have allowed Maddox to bully him into spying on Dev. At the very least he should have confided in Dev, telling him up front that Maddox had asked him to keep an eye on his progress and report back. More troubling than the deed itself was the duplicity involved.

Troubling, too, was the way Handler had gone to fetch the case containing the nucleotide shots when he and Dev were supposed to be leaping overboard. He had put himself in danger doing that, and while it seemed like a brave, selfless act, Dev wondered if it truly was. Mightn't it have been something else, something more?

A thought kept nagging at him, a correlation between events. If he was wrong, if it was just coincidence, than he had nothing to worry about. If he was right, however, then a conspiracy was afoot and he needed to watch his back. The insurgency wasn't the only threat to stability on Triton.

You don't like him either, Ethel said.

You just couldn't hide anything from a Tritonian. You couldn't prevent your feelings leaking through any more than you could keep your cheeks from flushing when you were embarrassed.

Put it this way, Dev said. *I'm revising my opinion about him. He's polite, but sometimes politeness is deviousness in disguise.*

I think I understand what you're saying.

Some concepts are difficult to express in Tritonese.

I'm amazed how you ungilled, with those gurgling noises you make, communicate anything at all.

We manage. Now, if you'll excuse me a moment.

Where are you going?

To see if that kid has come round yet.

Do you think he'll know something about the Ice King worshippers' weapons?

Frankly no. But it can't hurt to ask.

The kid was awake and attempting to free himself. As Dev entered the sleeping chamber which had belonged to Ethel's late cousin, he found the youngster struggling against his bonds. The kid froze as soon as he saw Dev, his face turning a surly yellow.

Saying nothing, Dev checked the cords binding the youngster's wrists and ankles together in front of him. Made of plaited plant fibre, they were strong and tight. The knots looked secure. No amount of straining would work them loose.

Doesn't look too comfortable, Dev said. I imagine your muscles are starting to seize up, being stuck in the same position for so long. They'll be cramping soon, if they aren't already. Your hands and feet will be going numb, too. You'd give anything to be untied and able to swim around again.

The kid's reply wasn't quite Go fuck yourself but it was unmistakably in that vein.

Dev hunkered opposite him. The sleeping chamber wasn't large, a cartilaginous burrow just long enough to stretch out in, if not quite tall enough to stand up in. Bioluminescent polyps on the ceiling radiated a faint amber glow.

I'd be willing to release you, he said. You're not important to me. Just tell me how your Ice King cronies were able to raze an entire ungilled settlement.

So I am important to you, the kid sneered.

No. You're nothing. But if you know something useful, anything, that makes you slightly better than nothing.

I know that the ungilled's days on this world are numbered. I know that the Ice King lives and you are all going to die.

Okay. Dev moved towards the door, another of those sphincter apertures that dilated when pressed to permit you to swim through. I gave you a chance.

Hateful scum! Fish-belly slime! You're no better than the ones who put me in that tank and tortured me.

And you're just an ignorant little punk who needs to grow up and learn the different between hating and being right.

Dev could have been talking to his own younger self. He mused on this irony as he left the kid in the sleeping chamber, face an inferno of insults.

He was satisfied that the kid hadn't anything to offer in the way of relevant information. Beneath all the bluster and the aggression he was just a scared adolescent who had fallen in with the wrong crowd and knew it, but didn't have the nerve to extricate himself. One day he would figure it out – if he didn't get himself killed first playing the tough guy.

Back in the cockpit with Ethel, Dev watched her guide the manta sub into a dense swarm of phytoplankton.

Feeding is necessary, she said.

The other manta sub joined them, and the two vessels turned cartwheels and figures of eight through the phytoplankton, scooping great swathes of the microscopic organisms into the mouths with the aid of their cephalic lobes. With their eyes modified into cockpits, the mantas were effectively blind, but electroreceptors at the fronts of their heads detected the bioelectric fields of other living organisms.

Replenished, fuel stop over, the mantas chased after the *Admiral Winterbrook*, soon catching up with the catamaran again.

Dev estimated they were now no more than five kilometres out from Opochtli. He scanned the deep, fathomless waters ahead for signs of activity, insurgents' vessels, *something*.

Perhaps Sigursdottir had been correct. Perhaps they were already too late. The attack was over and the Ice King worshippers had moved on.

Then he saw it.

At first he wasn't clear what he was seeing.

It was immense. It was a vast black silhouette, ponderously moving.

It seemed to be an island underwater.

Was it Opochtli, sinking? Had the township been demolished and was now slowly subsiding into the sea?

But it was moving horizontally, under its own steam.

It was gigantic and it was *alive*.

Dev felt a prickle of fear. Nothing that big could be an organism. Nature had its limitations. The largest creatures that had ever existed on Earth were all sea dwellers, from the blue whale to the megalodon. But they were still a couple of dozen metres in length at most.

This thing could be measured in hundreds of metres.

Ethel decelerated, bringing the manta sub to a near halt. He didn't blame her. She looked as alarmed as him.

What is that? he said. Have you see anything like it before?

I haven't. But look at the shape of it. The colours on her face were several shades paler than they ought to have been. If she had been using human speech, her voice would have trembled. We know that shape.

The behemoth was flat and round, like a discus. Dev could just make out segmented limbs, principally two great arms tipped with pincers. Oar-shaped legs at the rear rowed it to and fro, while an array of thinner, more delicate legs kept it balanced in the water.

If it resembled anything, it was a crab. But he didn't think that was what Ethel was getting at. She meant something else, something she evidently felt he would find familiar.

A moment later, he had it.

It could only be the symbol the insurgents had left on the *Egersund*'s forecastle, the one he had made a sketch of and later shown to Ethel, prompting a tirade of disgust and anger from her.

What he had taken for sky, moons and lightning forks – or directional arrows – were actually the carapace, eyes and forelimbs of a crab.

This very crab.

He was looking at a myth made real. A story in the flesh. A god incarnate.

He was looking at the Ice King.

42

THE ICE KING was foraging, plucking at objects that floated on the surface and stuffing them into its maw with its pincers.

As the manta sub inched closer, Dev tried to make out what it was feasting on. He had a pretty good idea, and the thought turned his stomach. But he needed to be sure.

Gathered around the gargantuan crab were smaller beasts, an entourage of Tritonian subs, dwarfed by the monstrosity they attended. Ice King worshippers, congregating around their deity.

Beyond them lay Opochtli. Even from below, Dev could tell that the township had been attacked already and now lay in ruins. Flames glittered above the sea's surface, distorted and refracted by the tempestuous waves. Beneath, debris was tumbling, twirling languidly, a slow-motion snowfall of rubble spiralling down into the dark depths.

The Ice King continued reaping the spoils of the havoc it had caused. It was taking its pick from the bodies floating round Opochtli, scavenging just like any ordinary crab, eating greedily.

Some of its prey weren't even dead yet, settlers who had hurled themselves into the sea to escape the destruction of their home, only to find that swimming away could not save them. The Ice King fastened pincers around them and drew them down, writhing helplessly, into its mouth, where its mandibles sawed the bodies into swallowable morsels.

What do we do? Ethel asked, appalled. How do we fight… that?

Not with a couple of manta subs, that's for sure, Dev replied. I'm going to head up to the Marines, see if they've got anything on board to tackle it with.

Even as he swam from the manta sub's mouth to the surface, however, Dev doubted the *Admiral Winterbrook* had the capability to do any significant damage to the Ice King. The crustacean's shell looked to be several metres thick all over. That much chitin would be as effective a protection as the ablative plating safeguarding gulf cruisers against meteor strikes and collision damage. A torpedo or depth charge might chip away at the top layer, but would never penetrate deep enough to cause fatal harm.

He hailed the catamaran via commplant as he broke surface, and shortly after was aboard and on the bridge. There he joined Sigursdottir, Handler, Milgrom and Jiang.

"Perhaps if we aimed for a weak spot, we could at least give it something to think about," Jiang said, after Dev had described the Ice King to them. What she lacked in stature, she made up for in steely focus. "Maybe even cripple it."

"I don't think it has a weak spot," said Dev.

"Limb joint? Mouth? Eye?"

"Possibly, but you haven't see this thing. Not with your own eyes. It's a fucking *beast*. Like something out of an old Toho Studios movie."

"I have to admit we thought we had a sonar malfunction when it first popped up on the scope," said Sigursdottir. "And before you ask, I know there are survivors out there. We've spotted one or two, at any rate. We've seen them get dragged under. We'd go in and try to pick up as many as we can, but…"

"But," said Jiang, "the sheer amount of water that thing's displacing, coupled with the treacherous conditions, makes it impossible. We'd be swamped if we tried. It wouldn't be a rescue mission so much as a suicide run."

"It sucks balls," said Milgrom, tight-lipped, "but you have to weigh up the risk-to-reward ratio. All we can do is figure out some way to make that motherfucking monster pay for what it's done."

"It's the actual Ice King?" said Handler to Dev. "You're quite convinced about that?"

"Ethel reckons as much, and if she does, then so do I. I'm not saying it's genuinely a god, of course not. But it seems like someone's managed to build a creature that's big enough and powerful enough to pass for a god. And by 'someone' I obviously mean Polis Plus."

"How? Engineered it?"

"Why not? You should have seen some of the Frankenstein abortions the Plussers dreamed up and threw at us during the war. Nothing as humungous as this, but still hideous enough to give you nightmares."

The pack of marauding caniforms on Epsilon Indi A sprang to mind, as did the troll-like commando things on 55 Cancri D. Dev would never forget them. He had led a dozen-strong team of sappers into the cave system where the creatures hid between their night-time harrying raids on Diasporan farmsteads, with a view to planting munitions and bringing the roof down on their bulbous, misshapen heads. The op was a success, but not casualty-free. The trolls – pallid, agile, spidery-limbed, needle-fanged – kept slipping silently out of crevices to tear out throats or twist necks.

The organic host forms the Plussers created were somehow worse than the inorganic. Their carbon-and-tungsten mechs were at least logical in design, sleek, cunningly modular, sometimes even possessing a lethal beauty. Polis+ had less affinity with flesh, and what their minds conceived often betrayed that. They had no sense of how evolution shaped and refined an organism, the symmetry of it, what went with what. They just threw attributes together, gene-splicing indiscriminately, hitching the properties of one species to the properties of another any old how. Whatever worked. Whatever fulfilled the intended function.

The results were seldom short of ghastly.

The Ice King, if nothing else, was pure arthropod, a recognisable entity – just magnified to colossal proportions, to besiege townships and singlehandedly reduce them to rubble. It was ugly even by crab standards, but the true horror of it was its phenomenal, mind-boggling size.

"Never mind who made it or how," said Milgrom. "How do we end it? That's the question here."

"The *Winterbrook* doesn't have the firepower, I know that," said Jiang, more than a little ruefully. It pained her to admit that her boat's armaments weren't up to the task. "A vessel like this is meant for littoral work, mostly – landings, inshore river assaults, engagements in shallow water. It can take on a gunboat, say, but not a battlecruiser. And it'd be safe to describe that thing down there as sitting at the battlecruiser end of spectrum."

"A nuke would sort it out," said Sigursdottir.

"Do you have any?" said Dev. "Like maybe a satellite-launched ICBM we could call down?"

Sigursdottir shook her head. "None. The only satellites orbiting Triton are communications-relay ones."

"And spy-in-the-sky ones, trained on Polis Plus territory."

"You know about those?"

"Captain Maddox told me, although I'd already guessed. Station Ares is forward reconnaissance."

"Yes, and it's safe to say that Polis Plus know it too. It'd be stupid of us to sit here, perched right on the Border

Wall, and *not* be taking a peek over at their comings and goings. But as long as we're only looking, and they know we're only looking, and we know they know, and that's as far as it goes..." She smiled thinly. "Détente, right? Everyone's happy."

"So I suppose kinetic-rod bombardment is out, for the same reason."

"Yup. Anything floating up there in orbit that even smelled like a weapon would have the Mainframe Council screaming peace treaty infringement. It'd be too overt, too much in their faces. The Plussers just couldn't turn a blind eye to that."

"But you have nuclear bombs at Station Ares. Please tell me you do."

"No."

"Shit."

"We've got something better. A couple of Sunbakers."

Sunbakers were fusion warheads which, in the microsecond before impact, fired a burst of high-energy x-rays at a hydrogen fuel pellet suspended inside a gold-plated hohlraum shell. The result was an explosion which, for the brief duration of its existence, rivalled a main sequence star for temperature and intensity.

"Kept under lock and key," said Sigursdottir, "in case of need."

"Independently propelled?"

"No. Ship-mounted artillery shells."

"But Maddox could get them here..."

"And will," Sigursdottir said resolutely, with finality. "Once I give him a full sitrep, he'll order them to be broken out and deployed."

"You'll have to impress on him that they're the only thing that's even got a chance of killing the Ice King."

"Don't worry, I will."

"But it's going to take half a day to get the Sunbakers here," said Jiang. "What happens in the interim?"

"What do you mean?" said Dev.

"Well, we can't just let the Ice King roam free, can we? There are other townships in the vicinity. Mazu's the obvious next target."

"It's being evacuated," said Sigursdottir. "Should be cleared by now."

"Even so, the Ice King can still clobber it and leave several thousand people without homes and livelihoods, racking up several millions' worth of property damage into the bargain. And I can name at least two other settlements – not as big as any of the Triangle Towns, but still juicy targets – within a hundred-click radius."

"We have to keep the über-crab occupied, is that what you're saying?" said Milgrom.

"No, but keep tabs on it and be ready to wade in if it looks like it's getting set to stomp somewhere else."

"Gunnery Sergeant Jiang," said Dev, "you've taken the words right out of my mouth. Until the Sunbakers arrive, the Ice King is our responsibility. Let's just keep our fingers crossed and hope Crabzilla's had its fill of killing for now."

43

"YOU'RE AVOIDING ME."

Dev was steadying himself on the rail of the *Admiral Winterbrook*, preparing to dive overboard and re-join Ethel. Handler had followed him out from the bridge onto deck, hurrying to catch up.

"No, I'm not," Dev said. "What gives you that idea?"

"The way you rushed out just now. I was trying to attract your attention."

"Didn't see. Sorry."

Handler looked at him sceptically, as well he might, since Dev had indeed ignored the ISS liaison's obvious hand-flapping attempts to catch his eye, and hadn't made much of a pretence about it either.

"Well, you're due your latest nucleotide shot. If you'll wait a minute, I can fetch one."

"Yeah, about that. I'm going to do without from now on."

"What? That's crazy."

"Might be." On reflex, Dev checked the countdown timer:
30:12:11

"I'm just wondering if the cure isn't worse than the disease."

246

"Don't be ridiculous," Handler snapped. "Of course it isn't. The serum patches are all that's standing between your host form and catastrophic collapse. Without them, I tell you, you'll start dissolving into pure foaming protoplasm. Do you want that?"

"Fun as it sounds, no, I don't."

"It'd be an accelerating cascade. Within two hours, three at most, your body will begin falling apart. And once the process is under way, once the ball gets rolling, there's nothing you or I or anyone can do to stop it. My guess is it'll take an hour all told. An hour of screaming, haemorrhaging agony. Everything that's inside you, pouring out in a great gush."

"You paint such a vivid picture. Still, I'm going to pass."

Handler clutched the air despairingly. "Why? We're a good half-day's journey away from Tangaroa and the transcription matrix. If you want to data 'port out safely, you'd have to start heading back now, and even then there's no guarantee you'd make it in time. Come on," he cajoled, "have the next shot. It'll only take a moment."

"You want the honest truth, Handler?" Dev said. "I've come to the conclusion that your precious nucleotides aren't making any difference. No, scratch that. They *are* making a difference. Just not a positive one."

"How can you say that?"

"Easily. You may not have noticed, but every time you stick one of those patches on me, not long afterwards I get sick. Something nasty happens like a rash, or spasms of pain, or bleeding."

"Coincidence," Handler said with a dismissive flick of the wrist. "Or it could simply be that your immune system is abreacting. It doesn't recognise the nucleotides as helpful. It's mistaking them for a virus or bacteria – an enemy."

"I'm no medic, but that sounds unlikely."

"I'm no medic either. All I know is I'm trying to keep you alive and well for as long as I possibly can, so that you can complete your mission, and you for some inexplicable reason are rejecting my help. Besides, you're wrong."

"I am?"

"Yes. You got sick *before* I even put a patch on you. Remember? Almost as soon as you came round after being installed, you complained of a severe headache. Like your skull was, and I quote, 'full of lava.'"

Dev couldn't deny it. "Installation's never pleasant."

"You said you felt much worse than usual."

"Maybe the half of me that's human is allergic to the half of me that's fish."

"Facetiousness is often what people resort to when they know they're losing the argument."

"And condescension is often what people resort to when they know they haven't got a hope of winning the argument. Look, Handler, I really don't have time for butting heads like this. The biggest fucking crab in the universe ever is going on a rampage, accompanied by a horde of religious nutcases who are under the impression it's their god and it's come to save them. Our job is to turn it into seafood chowder. That's my priority right now."

"But you'll never succeed if your host form gives out on you."

"I'm gambling on surviving long enough to pull it off."

"Without nucleotides? Not a chance. I insist you take the next dose."

Dev climbed onto the deck rail, swaying as a particularly heavy wave hoisted the *Admiral Winterbrook* onto its back and then, as if changing its mind, set the boat down again the other side.

Handler laid a firm hand on his shoulder.

"I'd let go if I were you," Dev said in a low voice.

"As your ISS liaison," Handler said, "I demand that you do as I ask."

"Take your hand off me or I'll break it."

"You wouldn't dare. Think how our employers would view that. Think of your one-thousand-point quota. How many points would ISS deduct for maliciously injuring a co-worker? I don't know the answer myself, but I suspect it's quite a few."

"Might be worth it, just to wipe that patronising smirk off your face."

"Harmer, please." Handler's tone became wheedling, conciliatory. "This antagonism – it's unnecessary and counterproductive. I'm on your side. I'm trying to do what's best for everyone."

Dev gave an exaggerated, emphatic shrug. Handler got the message and, to appease him, lifted his hand away.

"Just come inside with me," he continued. "Lieutenant Sigursdottir let me stash the case of patches in her cabin. I went to all that trouble, retrieving it before the *Reckless Abandon* went down. You wouldn't want me to have done that for nothing, would you?"

"All right then," Dev relented with a sigh. "You lead the way. I'll be right behind."

Handler, satisfied, turned away from him.

Next instant, Dev scrambled over the rail and propelled himself into the heaving sea. Handler's yell of thwarted exasperation was cut off as Dev hit the water.

He half expected Handler to dive in after him and carry on the discussion in Tritonese. Evidently, though, the ISS liaison felt the point – and Dev – didn't merit pursuing.

There was only the tiniest niggle of doubt in Dev's mind that he was right about the nucleotide shots. They *were* making things worse for him. It was simple cause-and-effect. Symptoms of cellular breakdown cropped up almost immediately after each dose.

So, was the treatment unsuitable? Had Handler been given bad advice by ISS?

Or was the batch of nucleotide serum contaminated somehow?

Both were possibilities, and both were unpalatable.

But there was a third, even worse possibility.

Sabotage.

44

THE ICE KING was moving on.

With its retinue of Tritonian subs, the God Beneath the Sea – now, more accurately, the God *In* the Sea – left Opochtli behind. Its physical appetite had been sated. Perhaps its appetite for destruction too. For the time being, anyway.

Mighty, water-warping kicks of its paddle-like hind legs drove it away from the township, setting up a turbulence that turned the sinking debris into a raging blizzard.

The manta subs took refuge in deeper strata of the ocean as the chunks of flotsam hurtled past like meteors. They stayed there until things calmed.

The Ice King had been unaware of the subs' presence, or of that of the *Admiral Winterbrook*. It had been preoccupied. Its assembled worshippers hadn't spotted them either, too busy gawking at their god's awe-inspiring display of power to look in any other direction.

This, Dev mused, was just about the only advantage he and his allies had going for them. They had observed the Ice King from a safe range and managed to remain unobserved themselves.

The trick now was to stay on its trail and not get caught.

The moment the behemoth or its entourage of Tritonians caught sight of them, it was game over. A creature that could singlehandedly obliterate a township would have little trouble with a Marine catamaran and a pair of manta subs.

Once it got up to speed, the Ice King travelled fast. Dev estimated it was achieving perhaps fifteen knots, which was remarkable considering just how much of it there was to shift. The kicking of its hind legs resonated through the water, a low, quaking *boom-boom-boom*. The wake it generated buffeted the manta subs about even at a steady one-kilometre distance.

Ethel was still coming to terms with the notion that a piece of her people's folklore had been brought to actual, physical life.

You're telling me someone made that? she said.

The *Number* Folk are master engineers, Dev said, and crazy with it. They can manipulate the smallest particles of existence, much like we can, but they do it with far less restraint. They're not afraid of pushing the boundaries. For them it's a technical exercise. For us, it's tampering with our own essence. We're inhibited about it, whereas they don't care. They go for broke.

But who would envisage a god as a giant crab?

I don't know much about gods. It's not something my race really concerns itself with anymore. But as I understand it, deities have taken all sorts of shapes and guises over the centuries. Plenty of them have been animals, or part animal.

All the same — a crab?

In the stories about the Ice King, is he described at all?

No. I always assumed he looked like one of us.

I think — no offence — but the aim here was to produce something a bit more impressive than just another Tritonian. Something alien and unknowable. Something that would intimidate as much as enthral.

Something that'd be hard to kill, too.

Exactly. But also there's the symbol to consider. The Ice King symbol has been around for ages, hasn't it? Since as long as anyone can remember. It represents the creation myth. And the moment you laid eyes on the actual Ice King out there, you connected the two of them, it and the symbol, didn't you? The association was instant.

Realisation dawned on Ethel's face, exquisitely rosy. Because the symbol happens to look like a crab.

Meaning a crab would be the logical choice for the Ice King's incarnation, Dev said. The Number Folk drew on the pre-existing image to determine what physical aspect the god would take, in order to make it instantly recognisable, familiar. Life imitated art. Or rather, life was obliged to follow art.

How did it get here, then? Ethel asked. It didn't just appear. It didn't drop from the sky. Where did it come from?

Fairly good question. I've seen something similar before. Not the same proportions, but the same principle.

On Alighieri, the last planet he visited before this one, Dev had met a Professor Sunil Banerjee, a zoologist who had aided and abetted a Plusser agent in developing an oversize version of a specimen of the local fauna, the moleworm. The Plusser, going by the intentionally nondescript alias of Ted Jones, had then used the giant moleworm as part of a plot to take over the Diasporan helium-3 mining operation on that world.

Somebody on Triton had pulled off much the same feat, only on a far grander scale.

Who and how, Dev had yet to ascertain. More and more, though, he was convinced that there was an active Polis+ infiltrator presence on Triton and that it was better entrenched and embedded than any he had encountered before. Foes in high places.

Put simply, he told Ethel, it was grown. Either from scratch or using an existing creature. It was cultivated in secret and then, when it was ready, let loose.

Hard to keep anything so large hidden.

But not impossible on a world that's virtually one hundred per cent water and relatively sparsely inhabited. Anyway, the Ice King didn't have to remain a secret for very long. Once it reached maturity, the sooner people found out about it, the better.

In order that its worshippers would rally around it.

Yes. In order that word about it would spread and it would draw the faithful to it.

So saying, Dev exited the cockpit and went to the sleeping chamber where the insurgent-wannabe kid was being kept.

He hooked a hand around the bonds binding the kid's wrists and ankles together, and dragged him out, roughly but not too roughly.

Back in the cockpit, he showed him the Ice King.

There it is, he said. That's your god.

The kid's face was flushed with a beatific golden glow. He's real. I knew it. I knew it!

Dev explained that the crab was an artificial being, nothing more. A hoax perpetrated by means of ungilled science. A monstrous fraud.

But the kid saw only what he wanted to see.

He came, he said. Rumours started going round. Stories about a commotion in these parts. Upheaval. An arrival. Something huge. It was taken as a sign. An omen. And it was all true. He has arisen. He has come.

No, that thing came, said Dev. That thing came, and a whole bunch of insurgent types got wind of it, went for a look, and said to themselves, "A-ha! The Ice King. The God Beneath the Sea. Must be." Because what they found is vast and menacing and ugly and powerful. It fits the bill. It's everything they've been wishing for and longing for. It's a figurehead they can get behind.

Blasphemy! the kid declared, affronted. Don't speak that way about our god.

Whoops. Too late. Guess I'm doomed now.

You are. All of your kind are. With the Ice King leading us, nothing can stop us. His might will sweep our enemies aside. He will purge the ungilled and purify the world.

You're being played, Dev countered. That massive great crab has been put here simply to give the uprising a focus and an added impetus. It's here to make the waverers commit. Anyone who was undecided about signing up with the insurgency, won't be anymore. Who wouldn't want to be part of the holy army, now that you've got yourselves a living, breathing weapon of mass destruction?

Face it, said Ethel to the kid, you've always known the ungilled colonists could beat you in a straight fight, with their superior weaponry and technology. That's why you and your fellow insurgents were restricting yourselves to hit-and-run tactics. Sneak attacks and vandalism. But not anymore.

No, not anymore, said the kid with pride. Now, everything has changed. Today is the day we were promised so long ago. Today is the day we take back our world.

Not necessarily, said Dev. *You may find that, come this afternoon, your beloved Ice King won't be looking nearly so impressive.*

What are you talking about?

I know people who know people who've got a weapon that's capable of taking out your so-called god, and they're not afraid to use it.

Liar. That's not true.

You'll see for yourself, soon enough.

You're making it up, the kid protested. *Trying to confuse me. Get me doubting. I don't believe you. It's a bluff. Nothing can harm the Ice King! The Ice King is immortal. The Ice King is forever.*

Yeah, yeah, said Dev breezily. *Just you wait.*

Ethel was finding the kid's ideological fervour harder to dismiss than Dev was. Dev could see she was itching to hurt him. Her hands were squeezing the manta's fleshy steering stalks hard, as though she wished to throttle them, and raw contempt glowered on her face in shades of pewter and puce. Her cousin's killer and a staunch upholder of a dogma she was ardently opposed to – she had every reason to despise the kid.

Before she could lash out, perhaps even kill him, Dev hustled the kid out of the cockpit.

Do what you like with me, the kid said defiantly. *I'm not scared. If I die at your hands, I die knowing that my god is going to avenge me.*

I'm not going to kill you, Dev said. *Can't you get that through your thick skull? That woman back there – she's the one you have to worry about on that score, not me. In fact, I may have just saved your skin. Again. So pay attention.*

The kid looked away in obstinate refusal.

Dev grabbed his head and forced it back round so that they were face to face again.

I think you're a good person, he said. *I think that deep inside you there's a lonely, frightened boy who's got himself further into a situation than he intended and is looking for an exit. It's scary where you are and it seems even scarier trying to wriggle free, so you're staying put. That's no way to live.*

The kid's jet-black, saucer-like eyes stared at Dev. Was he

getting through to him? Was what he was saying making any sense to him whatsoever?

Being an insurgent might have seemed like the answer to all your problems, he went on. *It might have made you feel grown-up and manly. It might have given you an outlet for all that adolescent angst and aggression. But look what it's also done. It got you imprisoned and tortured. It's turned you into a murderer. It's ruined your life.*

Still nothing from the kid. Except – was that a brief, faint flicker of remorse? A stippling of rueful blue, gone in a moment?

It's not too late, though. You can still turn things around.

How? said the kid. Surly and morose but also, just discernibly, inquisitive, imploring.

Search me. That's something you'll have to work out for yourself.

They had arrived back at the sleeping chamber. Dev prodded the door to open and shunted the kid in through the irised aperture.

The kid floated to the floor of the room and lay there on his side, passive in his bonds.

He was thinking.

As far as Dev was concerned, that was an encouraging start.

45

MAZU SEEMED TO be the next stop on the Ice King's itinerary. The gargantuan crab was certainly heading in the right direction, maintaining a roughly south-easterly course.

To Dev this was proof – not conclusive proof but near enough – that his theory about the Ice King was correct. It wasn't marauding at random. It had purpose.

That surely indicated that the consciousness of a Polis+ agent had been installed in the creature, just as had occurred with the giant moleworm on Alighieri. The Plusser's sentience was now infused into the network of ganglia that served as the crab's brain, and was firmly in command, like the driver at the wheel of a juggernaut.

Opochtli had been just the latest on the hit list. Mazu would follow, and the Ice King would keep on going, systematically and methodically decimating townships and accumulating worshippers with every fresh conquest until it had an entire regiment of devotees in its thrall. Insurgents everywhere would draw inspiration from it, take heart from its example. Their ranks would keep swelling, new recruits would keep flooding in, until eventually the uprising achieved critical mass and all-out war erupted between indigenes and humans.

Dev could imagine Polis+'s Mainframe Council rubbing their hands with jubilation over that.

All this, of course, was assuming the Ice King was allowed to continue its rampage unchecked. Those Sunbakers couldn't arrive soon enough, as far as Dev was concerned.

Onward the Ice King swam, Mazu-bound

Then a drift cluster came into view.

The Tritonian town floated at a depth of some two hundred metres, borne along by the prevailing current at a sedate, stately speed.

It resembled, more than anything else, a papier-mâché model of some complex molecule. Spheres of varying sizes were linked together by a lattice of spokes, fashioned from the spinal columns of redback whales.

The spheres themselves were lumpy agglomerations of coral, cultivated to give them windows, doorways and occasional long towers which served as tethering posts for living submarines. Bioluminescent lighting twinkled both indoors and out, giving the spheres the look of ghostly mobile constellations.

Each sphere, Dev reckoned, could comfortably house a hundred residents. They were gnarled, globular apartment blocks.

He could see that the Diasporan settlements on the surface had been built deliberately to mimic the design of a drift cluster. It was clearly the most practical way to organise habitation, both on and under the sea.

Of the two kinds of architecture on this world, human and Tritonian, Dev knew which he preferred. The drift cluster was just as functional as Tangaroa, Llyr, even Station Ares, but it had an eerie, otherworldly beauty too. It was an undersea fantasy of organic materials, constructed from things that had once had life or still had a life, not a single squared-off corner or smooth contour to be seen, hand-crafted and rough-hewn, fairytale, enchanting.

Cunning, also. Though large and sturdy and weighing many tons, the drift cluster had neutral buoyancy. Between the porous coral and bone, and their broad distribution, the drift cluster was far lighter than it appeared, yet still heavy enough to remain submerged at a consistent depth. It was poised perpetually, elegantly, between rising like a bubble and sinking like a stone.

It glided towards the Ice King, moving north-westerly; their paths set to converge.

The Ice King detected its approach and, as Dev would have expected, made moves to divert around it. The subs following the Ice King did likewise, tiddlers emulating the parent fish.

The drift cluster, after all, was home to Tritonians. It was not a lair of the hated humans. The Plusser agent within the Ice King had no reason to attack members of the insurgents' own race. A wise god doesn't alienate his worshippers.

Consternation reigned at the drift cluster nonetheless. Like panicked ants from an anthill, the inhabitants emerged in their droves. Some came out to gawp, some to flee, and some to wave weapons at the passing titan. These valiant defenders must have realised that knives, shock lances and tusk spears would be useless against so vast a beast, but better to brandish something than nothing at all.

The Ice King swam on, serenely aloof and unconcerned. The drift cluster trembled in its wake, but was not affected by its close encounter with a god.

But then...

On a whim, or so it seemed, the Ice King turned.

It's coming back, said Ethel. Why is it coming back?

The behemoth sidled up to the Tritonian town, both practically the same size as each other. Its eyes, huge but beady, flicked back and forth beneath the beetling brow of its upper carapace. It was appraising the drift cluster, curious, almost quizzical, as though it was trying to make up its mind about something.

Then, without further ado, it struck.

An immense pincer came crashing down, cracking open one of the drift cluster's spheres as though it were an egg. Dev could imagine how the Ice King had done exactly the same to the domes of Dakuwaqa and Opochtli, rearing out of the water to pound the townships mercilessly with its claws.

A score of Tritonians were hurled from the shattered sphere, spilling out like the candy in some horrendous piñata. Most swam away in terror, but a few simply floated, stunned insensible, or worse.

The Ice King slammed its other pincer onto the next sphere along, with the same results. The drift cluster shuddered and lurched. The bone spoke joining the two spheres fractured into its individual vertebrae.

Just about every Tritonian in the town scattered. The mass exodus spread in all directions except towards the Ice King. Dev saw adults herding small children before them and carrying infants in their arms; others dragged along the elderly, infirm and injured.

A handful of stalwart defenders remained, and some of these swam down to unfasten a large, tightly-meshed net that was attached to one of the lower spheres.

The net floated free and, from captivity, a large clump of vegetation unfurled. It was bladderwrack, the same stuff that had snarled up the *Reckless Abandon* and the *Admiral Winterbrook* just off Dakuwaqa.

The Tritonians prodded it with shock lances, goading it away from the drift cluster and towards the Ice King. The bladderwrack obediently went on the attack, extending several tangles of fronds out to the monster, trying to ensnare its limbs.

The Ice King made short work of it. The bladderwrack did its best, but the gargantuan crab tore the mass of sentient plant matter apart as though it were candyfloss. The drift cluster's main deterrent became, under the Ice King's snipping, slashing pincers, just so much shredded detritus.

The Ice King turned back to the drift cluster and began hammering it again with gusto. Dev was reminded of an infant, brutally and cheerfully dismantling a toy. Outer walls of coral, painstakingly trained in the desired shapes, collapsed into jagged fragments and clouds of powder. The honeycombed architecture inside was laid bare – chambers, tunnels, concourses – itself reduced to smithereens by further tremendous, scything swipes of the Ice King's claws.

It wasn't until the drift cluster was half wrecked that the true artistry of its design became clear. The entire structure began to wallow from side to side, like something in great pain. Then, all at once, the remaining unbroken sections split from one another. The spokes disintegrated. Some of the intact spheres started to rise, while others plummeted. A perfect balance had been catastrophically disrupted.

The whole extraordinary artefact fell to pieces, leaving the Ice King chasing the unbroken spheres, batting at them before they could get away from it.

The monster tired of the game pretty quickly and decided instead to eat a few of the drift cluster's submarines. The zombie creatures were still attached by ropes to an intact tethering pylon, which was reeling through the water in pirouetting freefall. The Ice King wrenched subs off it and shoved them into its mouth one after another, gobbling down a whole smorgasbord of species, following fish with cetacean and cetacean with cephalopod and cephalopod with giant mutant tadpole thing.

Hope you get a bellyache, Dev thought.

He was seething with anger, an anger stoked by helplessness and inadequacy. At that moment, all he could do – all anyone could do – was look on from the sidelines while the Ice King pursued its campaign of wanton demolition and slaughter. Until Marines from Station Ares brought those Sunbakers, there was no other choice. The only weapon available to him was the hypervelocity pistol, whose sabot rounds would have been as much use against the God Beneath the Sea as spitballs.

He did have the presence of mind to wonder why the Ice King had turned on the very people it was supposed to be liberating. Had its Plusser puppetmaster made a mistake? Had attacking the drift cluster been a tactical aberration? A technical glitch? Or was there some motive behind the action that he couldn't as yet discern? Did it serve some wider purpose?

Even as Dev was pondering these questions, Ethel abruptly bent the steering stalks as far forward as they would go. The manta sub beat its wings hard, accelerating from stationary to top speed.

The other manta was galvanised into action, its pilots loyally copying Ethel and falling in step beside her sub.

We're going to help some of these people, right? Dev said. The ones with children, maybe? Let them hitch a ride with us?

Ethel barely glanced at him out of the corner of her eye. No. There's no point saving only a handful of them, not when they're all at risk.

What are you proposing?

What do you think?

You're not seriously —

But she was.

The manta subs were making directly for the Ice King.

46

DEV GAPED IN disbelief.

Whoa there! he said. Stop! Now!

The glare of his demand was reflected on Ethel's skin, a super-bright yell. She couldn't have failed to see it. She ignored him nonetheless.

He thrust himself into her eyeline.

What are you hoping to achieve? A pair of manta subs against that thing? It eats vessels like these for breakfast. Literally. I've just seen it.

Move, Ethel snapped, pushing him aside.

You're going to get us all killed.

You don't strike me as someone who's frightened of dying.

I'm not — not if it's worthwhile. But I'm against pointlessly throwing my life away. It's a policy of mine.

I have no intention of pointlessly throwing my life away, or yours, or anyone's.

Well, you're doing a fairly good impression of someone who's about to.

You need to trust me.

I don't know you well enough to trust you.

Then you might as well make yourself useful instead.

How?

By shutting up, for starters, Ethel said. Also, by going to the other cockpit.

You want me out of the way, huh?

No, you ungilled ignoramus. Most submarines work better if there are two people in charge, especially when there's danger involved. I want you to co-pilot this thing with me.

Co-pilot...?

A sub is more responsive if two people are operating the control columns in unison. When it receives commands from both, it accepts them better and processes them faster. And for what I have in mind, this manta's going to need a lot of persuading and every bit of agility we can coax from it.

I've never driven anything like this before, Dev said. You know that, right?

Who else is there? That boy? A sulphur-yellow pulse of disgust. All *you have to do is pay attention and follow my lead. It's easier than you think.*

You're sure about this?

Co-piloting is at its most efficient when both pilots are related in some way, ideally by blood, Ethel said. *Failing that, if they've developed a bond over time. My cousin is no longer with us, and I can't say we've really bonded, you and me. All the same, you're far from stupid, and you seem to pick things up quickly. And you're all I've got.*

Number one in a field of one.

Indeed. Now go!

Dev swam through the duct connecting the chambers and planted himself behind the other control column. Currents surged and swirled within the spherical confines of the cockpit; the manta sub's speed was forcing water through the rip the cuttlefish sub had made in the cornea. Dev had to scissor his legs around the base of the control column in order to stay anchored and in place.

He grasped the steering stalks with both hands and looked across the manta's mouth to the other cockpit. Ethel flashed him a word or two of encouragement and he answered with a mixture of trepidation and bravado.

Both mantas plunged into the field of debris which had until a couple of minutes earlier been a drift cluster. Ethel deftly navigated around the boulders of coral and the dislocated sections redback vertebra. The subs soared and swooped and side-twisted, threading the three-dimensional, rapidly changing maze. It was the directest route to the Ice King, and the only one that afforded any sort of cover. Neither the 'god' nor its worshippers would see them coming.

Dev felt the fleshy stalks twitch and tense in his hands. He sensed them mirroring the activity of the other control column.

He had assumed there was a second cockpit on this and every Tritonian sub simply for the same reason that many aircraft had dual yokes: redundancy. A spare was needed in case one set of controls malfunctioned or one of the pilots became unable to fly.

But now he understood that the adaptations which the Tritonians had made to these animals reflected their bilateral symmetry. The control columns tapped into both sides of the creature's nervous system. Each alone gave a pilot mastery over it, but both in conjunction made that mastery absolute.

He began operating the stalks, matching his movements to Ethel's. The stalks, he realised, worked much like the differential control sticks on a tank or other tracked vehicle. Each ran one of the manta's wings. The further forward you pushed it, the harder the wing on that side would beat. Pulling back on the stalk flared the relevant wing, applying braking power.

He let the stalks themselves guide him, taking his cue from them as much as from Ethel. The sensory link between the two control columns made this comparatively straightforward. His principal job as co-pilot, it seemed, was to reinforce whatever the other pilot did.

Nevertheless, there were one or two hair-raising moments. Either he misinterpreted what the stalks were telling him or he anticipated Ethel's next manoeuvre incorrectly. Then the manta sub would veer crazily, or dip like a kite during a sudden lull in the breeze, or threaten to go into a pancake spin.

That led to several near-misses in the debris field, and only Ethel's experience and rapid reflexes saved them from a nasty collision.

Just relax, she flashed to Dev from her cockpit. Go with it. Don't overthink it.

Which was easy for her to say, but this was Dev's first time at the helm of a manta sub. And, moreover, he was having to learn in the worst possible circumstances. It was like having skis strapped to your feet on your starter lesson and being shoved down a black run rather than the nursery slopes, with an avalanche chasing you for good measure.

Then the mantas were out of the debris field, emerging into clear water between it and the Ice King. They had come through unscathed, for which Dev could take little of the credit but about which he was more than a little relieved.

Alarming as that escapade had been, it was nothing compared with what came next. Dev had a feeling Ethel wasn't zooming towards the gargantuan crab simply to get a better view of it. Her plan was more drastic and foolhardy than that.

Unfortunately, he was right.

We're going to attract its attention, she announced to him and the Tritonians in the other manta sub. We're going to make ourselves bait and lure it away from here.

That sounds like a totally sensible and sound idea, Dev said, picturing the sarcasm on his face as the deepest shade of orange imaginable, something like burnt tangerine.

If we keep our wits about us and collaborate...

We'll still probably get mashed to pulp or wind up as a tasty crab treat.

It's us or the people from the drift cluster, one or the other. The Ice King is going to go after them eventually, if it hangs around much longer. They can't outswim it.

And a manta sub can?

A manta sub should be able to. And outmanoeuvre it too.

Only should?

As long as we stay alert and focused. Now, enough whining. We're doing this.

Dev didn't think he had been whining, just sounding a note of caution. Ethel was harsh in her judgements. All the same, he could see the sense in what she was proposing.

The manta subs dived towards the monster.

Here goes nothing, Dev thought grimly.

47

HE HAD A moment of sudden clarity as the Ice King's vast, hideous face loomed in front of him, a kind of epiphany.

I feel fine, he thought.

It was the first time since arriving on Triton that he could say in all honesty that there was nothing physically wrong with him. There were no aches, no pains, no nausea. No dragging undertow of illness. No nagging feeling that something was amiss, something was *missing*.

He was *healthy*. That was the word. He felt sharp and alert and on top of things. Firing on all cylinders. The full ticket.

It might, of course, have been due to the adrenaline coursing through him, the fight-or-flight response triggered by the obvious hazardousness of the undertaking. That could be what was honing his thought processes and banishing bodily discomfort. Adrenaline was a great sweeper away of cobwebs, wasn't it? A great, if temporary, anaesthetic as well.

But there had been plenty of previous instances during this mission when he had been in danger: the thalassoraptor, coming under fire from Station Ares, hand-to-hand combat on Llyr, the bladderwrack... None of those had sparked the same heightened, zingy clear-headedness he was currently experiencing.

It was almost as though up until now he had been too under par to appreciate just how under par he was. Right from the outset, he hadn't been himself, or rather it had been a struggle to be himself. He had been on the back foot, error-prone, forever missing a beat.

He hadn't noticed because he had started out from a pretty low baseline – the skull-lava headache – and after that things had never improved more than marginally and seldom for long. Constantly at the back of his mind there had been the knowledge that his host form was compromised and would last seventy-two hours at most. Awareness of his body deteriorating had overshadowed everything else, like a curse.

From this he could only infer that he had done the right thing rejecting Handler's regime of nucleotide shots. They weren't therapeutic, they were toxic. And either the ISS liaison knew that, which meant he was a liar and a traitor, or he didn't, which meant he was a dupe, someone's patsy. Dev resolved to find out, at the earliest available opportunity, which of the two it was.

In the meantime...

The manta sub swooped so close to the Ice King that Dev could make out every section of its mouth parts, all the articulated segments that meshed neatly together and could manipulate and dissect prey as nimbly as fingers. They were slimed with gore and speckled with shreds of torn flesh.

He and Ethel danced the sub right in front of those big-as-a-baseball-diamond eyes. The invitation couldn't have been plainer. *Come and get it, big boy. Nice juicy manta. All yours. Free grub. Just reach out a grab a bite.*

The Ice King gazed, perhaps mesmerised, perhaps uninterested – it was hard to tell. Dev kept a watchful eye on the pincers. They were at rest, but at any time they might come roaring up, eager and grasping.

The sub continued dancing, appetisingly – or so Dev hoped. The manta itself was not a willing participant in the plan. He could feel that through the stalks. It didn't like exposing itself so blatantly to any predator, and its electroreceptors were telling it that here, perilously nearby, was a predator deluxe. Dev and Ethel were having to fight to keep it in position. Had there been only one pilot in charge rather than two, the manta might have won; but beneath their combined wills, it submitted. Just.

The Ice King, however, still wasn't taking the bait. Was its stomach full, no room for anything more?

Or did the Polis+ agent inhabiting it know that something was awry? Perhaps the Plusser thought the manta sub was too obviously making a target of itself. Perhaps Dev and Ethel had overplayed their hand.

Then, fast, astonishingly fast – almost too fast – the Ice King made a grab for the sub.

One pincer rocketed through the water, yawning wide, its serrated inner edges like the fangs of some vast dragon.

Without hesitation, in unison, Dev and Ethel sent the manta into a steep climb. The creature beat its wings as rapidly as it could, surging upwards at full tilt.

At the limit of the Ice King's reach, the pincer snapped shut, crashing together.

It missed the tip of the manta's tail by centimetres.

The manta sub cleared the sea's surface and flew over the long, raging waves for a span of several seconds before slamming back into the water with an impact that nearly dislodged Dev from the control column.

Down it went again, to come face to face once more with the Ice King.

The crab was indisputably interested now. Its mouth parts rippled as though it were gnashing its teeth or voicing threats. With a kick of its hind legs, it lunged for the manta, both claws outstretched.

Dev and Ethel threw the sub into full reverse, even as the two sets of pincers converged on it. The thought crossed Dev's mind that Ethel had sorely overestimated the manta's capabilities and underestimated the Ice King's. The crab was swifter and quicker-witted than she'd realised.

Then the other manta sub darted in. It wove a spiral around one of the pincer arms enticingly, divertingly. The Ice King, suddenly presented with two potential snacks instead of one, lost focus. It couldn't decide which to go for. It made a half-hearted snatch at the new arrival, before turning back to the first sub.

By that time, Dev and Ethel had retreated out of reach. The Ice King set off after their sub, seemingly forgetting about the second sub, for all that it was closer.

Together Dev and Ethel flipped the manta around and poured on speed. The Ice King gave chase.

They had succeeded in making a target of themselves. They had the Ice King's undivided attention.

Which was all well and good, but what, Dev wondered, were they going to do for an encore?

48

JUST KEEP GOING. That appeared to be Ethel's plan. Keep the manta swimming flat out, and let the Ice King follow. As long as they stayed ahead, they would be fine. But not too far ahead. They didn't want the Ice King to lose heart and give up pursuing them. They had to be sure it remained interested.

Every so often, they spun the manta round to look back and check that the Ice King was still on their tail.

The first time they did this, Dev was startled to see just how much distance lay between them and the gargantuan crab.

Hardly any at all.

The Ice King was hot on their heels, its pincers aloft and flared, waving like titanic battle-clubs. Its eyes glinted with an avaricious inner light. Dev had been hoping the manta might have a lead of at least fifty metres on the behemoth, but in fact it was more like a dozen.

That wasn't anyone's idea of a safety margin.

He and Ethel somersaulted the manta sub to face forward again and urged it to flap harder and faster than ever. The manta, to be fair, needed little encouragement. In its dim, stunted brain it might have been asking itself why its pilots had voluntarily placed it in harm's way, but its overriding imperative was sheer survival.

When Dev and Ethel next turned the sub for a look back, the Ice King was that little bit further away. Still not far enough for comfort, but at least it wasn't hulking directly behind them.

Then it was.

The Ice King had been between kicks. As its hind legs gathered for each thrust, its forward momentum briefly slowed and the manta sub gained ground. The next kick made up the difference.

The manta whirled round once again, while the great chitinous cliff that was the Ice King continued to hurtle after it. The crab was as remorseless as any bloodhound, as implacable as any shark. Dev felt that in some way the hunt had become personal. The Ice King did not wish to be cheated of its prize. It was honour-bound now to catch the manta sub, come what may. Nobody, nothing, should escape it.

The third backward look they took was the briefest yet, a mere glance, that was all. The Ice King was no further away, but no nearer either, which was a relief.

Dev also observed that none of its worshippers were with it anymore. He couldn't see them tagging along in its wake. The only Tritonian sub anywhere in sight was the other manta with Ethel's Nautilus allies in it, keeping just to the Ice King's rear.

Reflecting on this as the manta resumed its desperate flight, he could only conclude that the worshippers' subs were unable to keep up.

That or, more likely, the Ice King's unexpected and unprovoked assault on the drift cluster had taken the worshippers by surprise and they were still trying to process the turn of events. What did it signify? Why had their god mauled a Tritonian community when it was supposed to be attacking only ungilled settlements? Where was the divine justice in that? What was the Ice King thinking?

God moves in mysterious ways.

Dev vaguely recalled hearing that line some time back. It came, or so he thought, from that book which no one read or owned anymore, the Bible. Whoever had quoted it would have been using it ironically or for shock effect. Even just mentioning God – as in capital-g God – could provoke outrage in the Post-Enlightenment era, a blasphemy against rationalism, a heresy in an age of atheism.

God moves in mysterious ways. You weren't supposed to question your deity's actions or motives, you were just supposed to accept them. Unthinkingly. Unblinkingly. Like a sheep.

But this particular 'god' had behaved so out of character, so wrongly, that its worshippers were bewildered and taken aback. Maybe, even now, a chill of doubt was creeping into their hearts. They were beginning to ask themselves if they had made a mistake, if their faith was misplaced. Unfounded, even.

As the manta sub swept onward, Dev looked across at Ethel and said, How much longer can we keep this up?

As long as necessary, was the reply.

But we're well clear of the drift cluster by now.

We'll carry on until we're absolutely certain the Ice King won't return there.

And when our manta subs get tired...? They will sooner or later.

Ethel's response manifested as a dim, ambiguous mix of cobalt and charcoal-grey. The Ice King may tire first.

Rendering the phrase "And pigs might fly" into Tritonese was tricky. The nearest Dev could get to it was And flying fish mightn't fly, which made very little sense even to him and was met with stony incomprehension from Ethel.

As the chase continued, Dev wished he had some way of communicating with the *Admiral Winterbrook*. He was confident the catamaran was still overhead, doggedly tracking the Ice King. Sigursdottir may well have deduced from the sonar imagery what the manta sub was up to. At the very least she would realise the monster and the sub were locked in a deadly pursuit.

What she ought to know was that there was a Polis+ conspiracy afoot on Triton and that a passenger on her boat, Xavier Handler, was involved somehow. Handler might well be a mere pawn. He might, though, be instrumental in the plot.

He might even be a Plusser himself.

The notion, as soon as it popped into Dev's mind, made his stomach go sour. A Polis+ agent masquerading as an ISS liaison. The Plussers somehow managing to infiltrate Interstellar Security Solutions. Putting one of their own right into the heart of the corporation that made a profit from combating them.

Shit.

That would be a kicker, wouldn't it? The ultimate inside job.

And yet, if true, there was a certain bravura audacity about it. You almost couldn't help admiring the Plussers' nerve.

The manta seemed to sense something. Dev felt it faltering, as though it was in a quandary.

He looked across quizzically at Ethel, who was also puzzled.

They turned the sub, only to find that the Ice King had dropped back. A gap of over two hundred metres had opened up between them and it.

The Ice King simply floated. It looked inconceivably cunning to Dev just then. Inscrutable and calculating.

What's it waiting for? he said.

I don't know, said Ethel. But I have a very bad feeling about this.

Think it's had enough? It's going to head back to the drift cluster?

It better not.

They nudged the manta towards the crab with a few tentative wingbeats.

The Ice King remained put, observing them with those dark, leeringly knowing eyes.

Is it... messing with us? Dev said. Trying to sucker us in?

You mean beat us at our own game? Not sure, but I wouldn't put something like that past it.

Let's hold back. I'm not letting myself get played by a string-of-shit-hanging-out-of-a-fish's-anus crab.

Ethel showed amused surprise. You've picked up some bad language.

It's the company I've been keeping.

The strange standoff stretched on. The Ice King exhibited nothing but a steady, enigmatic patience, as imperturbable as a granite monument. If Dev hadn't known better, he would have thought that its mouth parts were fixed in a sort of smile.

The Polis+ agent inside it had an ace up his sleeve. That was the only conclusion Dev could draw. The Plusser knew something Dev and Ethel didn't.

Hold on, Dev said. Where's the other manta? Where are your friends?

Ethel scanned the sea immediately surrounding the Ice King.

They were riding its wake, last time we looked, she said. Right behind it.

Where are they now?

Ethel's face went a sickly shade of green, the colour of dread.

They wouldn't have abandoned us, she said. Never. "The more of us there are, the greater we are." What's happened to them?

It was as though the Ice King had been waiting for her to ask. This was its cue.

Its mouth parts unfurled, revealing that they were clasping an object, something they had been masking from sight.

The other manta sub.

The Ice King loosened its grip on the sub tauntingly, just a fraction, to give Dev and Ethel a better view. In the manta's eye socket cockpits, the two Tritonian pilots exuded panic and terror, jaggedly jarring hues of red and green. The manta itself squirmed in the clutches of the crab's mouth parts, stuck fast, trying in vain to break free.

No!

Ethel rammed the steering stalks forward. Dev wrenched his pair of stalks back.

Don't, he warned her. *That's what it wants.*

Their manta dithered, paralysed by the conflicting commands it was receiving.

We can't leave them to the Ice King's mercy, Ethel insisted. *We have to go and help them.*

The Ice King doesn't have any mercy. This is a trap. It must have known all along your friends were there, at its rear. It spun round, grabbed them, and now this. It wants us to move in. It wants us within pincer range.

Let go of those stalks, Ethel demanded. *Now.*

We'll all die if I do.

We can save them.

I doubt it.

They're not your friends. They're mine. Do as I say, you heartless ungilled bastard.

It was one of the toughest calls Dev had ever had to make.

I can't, he said. *The Ice King is going to kill them whatever happens. Don't you see that? They're as good as dead.*

The crab's mouth parts tightened somewhat, forming a cage around the manta and its pilots, an inescapable imprisonment. The two Tritonians peered out through the bars of their jail like condemned convicts, and Dev watched their agony of fear turn to resignation. They, too, had realised that their situation was hopeless.

No, Ethel said, desolate.

The Tritonians signalled fatalistic defiance across the space between the Ice King and Ethel's manta.

Don't forget us, one said.

Make sure the monster pays, said the other.

I promise, said Ethel.

Wearily, reluctantly, she eased back on the steering stalks. The manta edged away from the Ice King.

The gargantuan crab saw that its bluff had been called. The manta in front wasn't coming to the aid of the one in its maw.

The mouth parts moved sideways and apart so as to grasp the manta by the wings. Then, with a slow, cruel deliberateness, as though making a point, the Ice King proceeded to tear the sub apart.

First it tore the manta in two, like a wishbone. Then it dissected the still twitching halves piecemeal, ripping through cartilage, rending inner organs, splintering bone.

It managed to save the cockpits, and the Tritonians inside them, for last.

There was an expression of almost palpable malice on the Ice King's face as it clamped its mandibles around the manta's eyes and crushed them.

The corneas burst.

Then, as the Ice King continued to apply pressure, the Tritonians burst too.

Ethel displayed nothing but fiery red loathing.

Dev felt much the same.

In a final act of spite, the Ice King did not actually consume any of the manta or its pilots. Instead, as if in sheer contempt, it spat out the whole mess in a churning billow of sundered flesh and ruptured innards.

Not good enough even for me to eat, was the message.

And Ethel received it loud and clear, and her hatred curdled to blind rage, and she slammed the steering stalks forward again, and before Dev could counteract the command, the manta was flying straight at the Ice King.

49

DEV TRIED TO pull the manta out of the kamikaze divebomb run it was making. He wagged the steering stalks this way and that, but the manta only wobbled, didn't deviate. Ethel had pure, furious determination on her side. Of the two of them, she was imposing the fiercer will on the manta. Her face screamed revenge.

The Ice King filled Dev's field of vision from end to end, every crevice and craggy contour of its front end visible in sharp relief. It looked eager to greet them. Its mouth parts yawned wide, exposing the cavernous, toothless grotto that was its gullet. Moments from now, it would be feasting on the manta that had led it such a merry dance.

There was method in Ethel's apparent madness, however.

At the last possible instant, just as it seemed the manta was going to pitch headlong into the Ice King's mouth, she thrust the stalks out to either side and squeezed a nodule on the control column with one knee. The manta veered downward.

The crab's mouth parts gesticulated wildly as the sub shot past them, plummeting on a perfect perpendicular trajectory. Down into the depths it went, travelling at such speed that Dev lost his grip on the control column. He sprawled against the rear of the cockpit, pinned by the force of the water jetting in through the rift in the eye's outer membrane.

The sea darkened. The silvery light filtering down from the storm-tossed surface faded to grey, then to the colour of ashes, then to a thin, feeble gleam like dawn on a cloudy day.

Soon the light had leaked away altogether, and there was nothing but blackness.

Still the manta descended, its pace not slackening. The rush of water within the eye socket was just about the only evidence Dev had that the creature was moving. Visually, there were no clues. Everything outside was like ink, pure unfathomable void.

Then he glimpsed lights.

It was the same firework-display illumination he had seen during his nocturnal swim from the URIB to Llyr. It seemed more distant than he remembered, deeper down. He assumed the marine fauna responsible for it took refuge in lower strata of the ocean during daytime, rising after sunset when the ambient light from above dwindled almost to nil. To them, a surrounding darkness was comfort. It was what they were used to. Home.

As the lights brightened and enlarged, Dev felt a twinge in his ears which developed rapidly into pain. How far down was the manta sub? And how much further did Ethel intend to take it?

The water began to feel sluggish as it passed through his gills, not to mention cold, as numbingly cold as an arctic wind. It was like breathing iced soup. Every inhalation and exhalation became laborious, an effort.

And the pain in his ears only increased, until it was a bone-drilling, temple-tormenting agony.

The water pressure was now intense, a hundred atmospheres or more, and the temperature many degrees below zero. Dev could endure it for the time being, but not for much longer, not if they kept on going.

Yet they kept on going. The manta did not slow. Ethel drove the sub relentlessly down towards the scintillating patterns of living light, deeper and deeper. Now Dev could hear cracking sounds coming from his skull, the bones of his cranium grinding together along their suture lines. His head felt as though it was going to implode. He knew he was beyond the point where a human diver could safely venture even in a pressurised aluminium-alloy exosuit. No one should be this far down, unprotected.

They came to the place where the benthic creatures dwelled, the abyssal realm.

Here, at last, Ethel reduced speed and levelled the manta out. The sub hovered, not quite at rest, and Dev recovered his bearings and peered outside, squinting through his haze of head pain.

It was like something out of a dream.

The worst dream imaginable.

A phantasmagorical cavalcade of sea creatures swept past the cockpit's corneal membrane, things that didn't belong in any bestiary, things that had no place in a sane and ordered universe. They seemed like evolutionary castoffs, abortions of nature that had been consigned to this oceanic dungeon because there was nowhere else to put them and they were better left where no one could see them. Lit from within by their own garish bioluminescence, they teemed back and forth, prowling and clashing.

One was like a bundle of balloons, pallid gas-filled sacs that swelled and shrivelled at different times, inflating and deflating in accordance with some indefinable pattern.

Another was a ribbed hexagon of skin several metres wide that moved through the water by folding itself into complex geometric shapes.

There was a largish armoured fish that at first glance seemed to be giving a smaller fish a piggyback ride, until

Dev realised that the hanger-on was attached by tentacles which pierced the larger fish just behind the head through a chink in its plated hide. The hitchhiking fish was a parasite, feeding off and controlling the other, using it as a combined larder and transportation. A horrid symbiosis.

A colony of hydrozoa split into its hundreds of component parts to overwhelm its chosen prey, a doughy, lumpen thing with a face like a clown in a police mugshot. The tiny anemone-like creatures swarmed over their quarry, stung it to death, sawed off a chunk each with minuscule corkscrew teeth, then coalesced back together in a clump to dine, while the chewed, riddled corpse they left behind sank from sight.

Something a bit like a coelacanth sauntered by, ancient and unhurried, with what appeared to be a dozen tumours dangling from its belly. These were in fact semi-transparent egg sacs, and a developing foetus nestled in each, suckling on pre-digested food piped to it from its mother's intestinal tract.

Something revoltingly phallic throbbed along with peristaltic convulsions of its body. When a potential aggressor wandered near, the rubbery tube of meat started everting, prolapsing its intestines through its anal orifice and sucking them back in. It rolled itself inside out like this, over and over, confusing its foe and probably, if Dev's own reaction was anything to go by, nauseating it too. Eventually the predator, deterred, decided to turn elsewhere for a meal, alighting on a tiny shrimp, which looked as though it would be a delicious mouthful – except that it wasn't a shrimp at all but a decoy, a shrimp-shaped growth perched on the proboscis of a megamouthed carnivore who promptly swallowed the hapless, bamboozled mark in a single gulp. The trickster didn't last long enough to enjoy its ill-gotten gains, however, as it was harpooned from below by a spiny projection shot from the snout of a broad, flat crustacean, which reeled the victim in. The crustacean gnawed on the flexing, still living body in a leisurely manner, until...

But Dev had had enough. Disgust overcame fascination. There was only so much of this grotesque, hallucinatory spectacle he could take. He had done psychedelics in his youth, not often but often enough to know the slippery, lurid delusions a mind could come up with. This was worse; it didn't have the consolation of being imaginary.

The manta sub was profoundly uneasy in the midst of the milling crowd of deep-sea horrors. It shied away whenever any of them swam close, and Dev could feel distinct tremors of anxiety running through it. It yearned to be back up in the warm, friendly waters of the photic zone – if perhaps not as much as Dev did.

Especially when a blobby, spongy animal resembling a brain with fins began nudging through the rip in the cockpit cornea. Dev lashed out with a foot, and the brain blob oozed away, disgruntled.

He decided he would prefer the security of an intact cockpit, and so he wriggled along the duct to the other eye socket. Movement, physical effort, made his head hurt worse. The pain almost blinded him. Nonetheless he persevered and struggled on through to the other side, slithering down beside Ethel, who looked to be in as much discomfort as he was.

How long –? he began, but she interrupted.

Shhh, she said. She pointed upward.

Something was moving about above them.

Something enormous.

The Ice King.

It had followed them all the way down and it was hunting for them in the dark, looking for them amid the throngs of benthic wildlife. The kicks of its hind legs, the force of its immense bulk pushing through the water, generated powerful currents that rocked the manta. What Dev had taken for fits of trembling was the turbulence set up by the Ice King as it cruised to and fro, roving, searching.

The glowing, ghastly fauna outside reacted to the Ice King's presence with a weird apathy. They were too busy preying on one another, caught up in their endless cycle of kill-or-be-killed, to care much about this new arrival, however abundantly vast it was. In a carnage-filled arena, what was one more gladiator?

Are we supposed to not talk at all? Dev asked, trying to keep his 'voice' as muted as he could. In case the Ice King spots us?

Ethel answered in equally subdued tones, It's not the Ice King I'm worried about. It's everything else. Down here, light is all. Light attracts, repels, communicates, misleads...

So keep it low, that's what you're telling me. If we don't want to draw unwelcome attention from the freak show out there.

Speak only when necessary. If they can't see us, they won't notice us. As long as we're silent and the manta stays stationary, we're invisible.

Really? One of those things was trying to get into the other cockpit a moment ago.

It must have bumped up against the manta by accident, that's all.

If you say so. Can I ask why we're hiding out here?

It was the only place I could think of to go. Somewhere where we could pause. Regroup. Where, if we're lucky, the Ice King won't be able to find us.

Too many other creatures. Too many lights. Interference. I get it. Losing ourselves in a crowd. But the pressure is...

Unpleasant, yes.

Mistress of understatement, Dev thought.

You'll just have to put up with it, Ethel went on.

How long do you reckon the Ice King will go on looking before it gives up?

Your guess is as good as mine. Once he moves off, we'll resume following him as before, stealthily.

Okay, but –

Ethel covered his face with her hands.

Outside the cockpit, a subaquatic spider was staring in.

It might not have been a spider in the strict taxonomic sense, but it was sufficiently arachnid to merit the comparison. Big as a limousine, it had a smattering of eyes, a profusion of thin spines that looked like hairs, and a pair of pedipalps set below its mouth. With these long, spindly forelimbs it began gently touching the cornea of the eye, exploring its outline, getting a sense of its shape and texture.

The manta sub recoiled, which only increased the sea spider's inquisitiveness. Ethel laid a steadying hand on the steering stalks, and the manta obediently went stock still.

The sea spider spent a couple more minutes investigating the source of the lights it had caught sight of: Dev's and Ethel's conversation. It appeared not to understand why there was a barrier separating it from them. The pedipalps quested over the cornea like the hands of a sculptor over a block of raw marble, assessing it for strengths and weaknesses.

Dev had never been as repulsed by any living being as he was at this one. The feeling intensified when the sea spider's mouth parts opened and a pair of fangs extruded from within. A seam of fluorescent yellow venom was visible through the translucent material of each fang, running down the middle. It didn't help that the fangs themselves were the size of his forearm.

The manta sub remained immobile, and Dev could only admire its self-restraint. If the sea spider had been touching *him* like that, he could never have endured it the way the manta was.

All the same, the manta was starting to quiver, and this time it wasn't a result of the commotion caused by the Ice King passing overhead. The creature was becoming fractious, unstable.

Delicately, ever so delicately, Ethel tugged on the steering stalks. The manta shrank back from the sea spider, centimetre by centimetre, with the tiniest wafts of its wings.

The sea spider was all set to head after it, still curious. Then a ribbed hexagon-of-skin animal, possibly the one Dev had spied earlier, flopped onto it from above like a dropped carpet.

A battle ensued, sea spider and skin hexagon wrapping themselves around each other, all legs and triangles, fangs and umbrella folds. Dev didn't much care which of them won the fight. If they both killed each other, so much the better.

The manta sub found a volume of clear water, a hollow among the shimmering multitudes, and halted.

Above, the Ice King continued to search.

50

TIME PASSED. DEV'S head pulsed. Now and then the manta sub shook as the Ice King swam by.

Sometimes the gargantuan crab got close, alarmingly so. The water became a mass of sweeps and swirls, rumbling like a rock slide.

The Ice King was being thorough, no question. The chase, as far as it was concerned, was anything but over. Manta was still dish of the day. It just needed to find it.

An hour ticked by in the abyssal fathoms, two hours, three, with distant flashes and crackles of light erupting all around and every now and then an animal appearing directly outside the cockpit, supple, lugubrious, ghostly, grim. Each seemed more repugnant than the last, as though there was an Ugliest Organism Alive contest under way and the winners were being announced in reverse order.

After a while, though, Dev became used to the deep-sea creatures' universal unloveliness. Grace and beauty weren't advantages down here. To survive in this ruthlessly Darwinian environment it was best to be tough and mean, to be the sum of your offensive and defensive capabilities and no more.

The kid.

Suddenly, with a start, Dev remembered that the Tritonian kid was still aboard, trussed up in the sleeping chamber. The poor bastard would be experiencing the same pressure pains as he and Ethel were. It wasn't fair just to leave him there, alone and suffering, without at least checking up on him.

Dev scooted back along the manta's dorsal duct.

The kid lay listless, groans trickling across his face in thin pink rivulets.

Dev felt his first real pang of compassion for the young Tritonian since discovering him in the tank at Llyr. Almost on a whim, he decided to untie him.

He remained on his guard as he undid the knots. There was a chance the kid was faking. He was playing possum, hoping someone would take pity and free him, and then he would make his move. This could be some elaborate escape bid.

If he felt anywhere near as bad as Dev did, however, that was unlikely.

Sure enough, the kid did nothing once the bonds around his wrists and ankles were removed. He continued to lie there, even as Dev massaged his hands and feet to get the blood flow going again.

Eventually he looked up and said wanly, Where are we?

Dev explained as succinctly as he could.

The Ice King... smashed up a drift cluster? the kid said.

Afraid so. Like I told you, your god doesn't seem to differentiate between friend and foe, Tritonian and ungilled. It's just a big, mean, hungry bastard. Whatever takes its fancy, it kills and eats. Like it's trying to do to us now. You've felt the manta sub shaking, right?

Yes.

That's your holy crab, stomping around upstairs. It can't seem to get its head round the idea that we've managed to elude it.

It's... It's not a god after all, is it? the kid said falteringly. He was both ashamed by the realisation and, it seemed, relieved. I've been an idiot.

No. Well, yes. But also, you've been young.

I – I killed that man, that woman's cousin, for nothing. The kid writhed in a paroxysm of self-recrimination. *How can I ever apologise for that? How can I make up for it? I can't, can I?*

I don't think so. Not easily. I think all you can do is live with it, learn from your mistakes, and make sure you never fall for anyone's line of fishcrap again.

I heard one of them speak, one of the Ice King's worshippers. He stopped off at our drift cluster, not long ago. He talked about fighting back against the ungilled. He talked about a glorious revolution. He swore that our god was coming back and would lead us. He was so convincing.

Zealots often are. Fanaticism spawns fanaticism. It spreads from person to person. It's like a disease that way.

People tried to shout him down. They wanted to drive him out from the cluster. But there were enough of us who were curious to hear what he had to say, so we voted and he stayed, and he spoke some more, and by the end of it I felt he was right. The ungilled don't belong here. They should be gone. They take and they taint. Why should we have to put up with that any longer?

I'm not saying the ungilled are blameless, Dev said. *Probably we shouldn't be here. For all sorts of reasons. But it's not as if we were oppressing you Tritonians, at least not until all this insurgency business blew up. We're an inconvenience, you never asked us to come to your world, we never asked your permission to be here, but it could have been a lot worse.*

Perhaps there are some people who just want an enemy. They're spoiling for a fight. Like I was.

Yes, and they can dress it up as politics, they can dress it up as religion, but what it comes down to is they like having someone to hate. They use it to define themselves.

You say that like it's something you have personal experience of, the kid said.

Once, maybe, I did. When I was your age. Authorities were my enemies. Whatever they stood for, I was against. Nowadays, my enemies are whoever the authorities point me at and tell me to fight.

Which, Dev thought, *is pretty ironic. Not to mention sad.*

But this is kind of heavy stuff to be discussing at the bottom of the ocean, he said. *My head's already killing me, and so are my gills with all the effort of breathing. Thinking is an added pain I can do without.*

The kid's face erupted into bubbles of blotchy saffron laughter.

Do you have a name? Dev asked. I mean, I know it takes your kind a while to figure a name out for yourselves, you don't get given one by your parents, but...

It's not ready yet, the kid said. It's changed even just lately. As it stands right now, it's....

The colours he displayed spoke of frustration, regret, guilt, and a faint glimmer of optimism.

Looks raw, Dev said.

Needs work, yes. Could be tidier. The mix isn't right.

But I like it. It's something to build on.

51

WHEN HE LED the kid to the cockpit, Dev did not expect Ethel to be happy either that the kid was there or that he was no longer tied up.

And she wasn't.

She confined herself, however, to a few acerbic comments about murderers who should be in captivity and would-be insurgents who thought they knew all about life but knew nothing. She also muttered that the cockpit was too small for all three of them to be in it.

She had seen the kid's face. That was why she wasn't angrier. It was shot through with contrition, sincere remorse. Dev doubted she would ever be willing to forgive him for his crime, and no one could blame her for that. But at that moment the kid seemed to hate himself more than she could possibly hate him, which satisfied her desire to see him suffer.

Besides, something else had happened.

The Ice King, she said. I think it's moved on.

How can you tell? Dev asked.

Haven't you noticed? No more disturbances in the water. There haven't been for a while.

Doesn't mean it's gone. We've established it's a cunning son of a bitch. It could be doing what we're doing, lying still, waiting. The moment we show ourselves, bam!

We can't stay down here indefinitely. Much longer and we'll be doing our bodies irreparable damage.

Then let's go up, Dev said, but carefully. Really carefully. First sign of anything remotely crab-shaped, we zip straight back down.

Ethel tilted the manta so that it was facing upwards at a shallow angle. With a nudge on the stalks, the sub began to ascend.

We have to do this slowly, she said. Rise too fast from this kind of depth, and you get what we call the crawling misery.

Decompression sickness, Dev thought. Dissolved gases in the body expanding and forming bubbles, causing joint pain, skin itching, numbness, seizures, embolisms, paralysis, even death. Commonly known as the bends.

Divers could get it. Astronauts on extravehicular activity jaunts could get it. Anyone involved in an extreme depressurisation event could get it.

Tritonians too, apparently.

Dev kept watch for movement, for the slightest hint of anything untoward, as the manta climbed out of Triton's netherworld. He knew it was a waste of effort. In this pitch blackness they would never see the Ice King coming until it was right on top of them, and probably not even then. But he couldn't simply turn his back and *not* look. That would be tempting fate too far.

The herds of benthic animals thinned, and their firework lights fell away. There was just the dark, and gradually, the dark lessened.

Or so Dev thought. Again and again he detected a tinge of grey in the water outside, only for it to disappear, phantom-like, as though it had never been.

His eyes, he realised. An optical illusion. His vision trying to give him what he wished for.

The ascent seemed interminable, the blackness unending, and there was the ever-present sense that the Ice King was lurking nearby. Even now the gargantuan crab might be spying on them, stealthily mirroring their progress, keeping them in its sights, ready to pounce when they least expected. By breaking cover they had played right into its hands. Its pincers. Whatever.

The first indication that they were truly putting the abyssal realm behind them was Dev's headache easing. The iron band that had been clamped around his skull unclenched. The pain retreated to his ears and sinuses, and then receded altogether.

Then he noticed that the sea was quite definitely less dark. He glimpsed faint, paler patches, moving like feathery swirls of fog.

At around the same time, he became aware that he was breathing with almost no effort, his gills no longer heaving the water through them. The joy of not having to fight to get oxygen into your system!

Ethel sent the manta sub into a helical climb. Since they could now see, however dimly, it made sense to scan around them as they continued to rise. Before, when the Ice King could have been anywhere in the dark, it hardly mattered which direction the manta was facing in. This way, tracing a lazy spiral, they might at least have some warning of its approach.

The world revolved outside, getting lighter and lighter by the minute. There were fine, glinting specks, blooms of plankton, and now a shoal of metallic-shiny fish no bigger than a fingernail each, like flakes of platinum. There was life – the more normal life of the bathyal realm. This level of the ocean was still fraught with potential hazard, as all of Triton was, but it lacked the ceaseless grisly slaughter of the zone below. Lacked the loathesome rogues' gallery as well.

No Ice King, though. If the God Beneath The Sea was stalking the manta sub, it was staying well out of sight.

In fact, Dev suspected the crab was nowhere hereabouts anymore. Once it had resigned itself to its inability to catch the manta, it had chosen to forget all about that failure, cut its losses and move on. Probably it was now in search of a new target, something it could take out its frustrations on. Mazu was the likeliest candidate.

The arrival of the photic zone, with its brightness and comparative warmth, was as welcome as sunshine after a tornado. Dev could hardly bring himself to believe that they had made it back up here unscathed. He relaxed his shoulders, which he had been subconsciously hunching throughout the ascent. His nerves, taut as wires, loosened.

The manta halted some ten metres below the surface and hung there, inert and languid. The creature was exhausted from its exertions. It needed rest, according to Ethel, and food.

So do we all, I reckon, Dev said. *But I, personally, don't have that luxury. I have to reconnect with my ungilled allies up top.*

In particular, he had to have words with Handler. The ISS liaison was due an interrogation. Dev was determined to get to the bottom of the nucleotide serum business. Aside from obliterating the Ice King before it could wreak anymore mayhem, securing a confession out of Handler was paramount.

He knew just how to go about getting one, too.

52

WHILE DEV HAD been below, the storm had grown to epic proportions. The sea swell was ferocious. Waves swept him up high, showing him an expanse of raging water as far as the eye could see, kilometre upon kilometre of grey turmoil, before cresting over his head, smothering him in foamy whiteness, and collapsing away under him, dropping him at stomach-knotting speed. The wind moaned, and rain clattered on his skull from a sky that was like wire wool from horizon to horizon.

If this wasn't the notorious syzygy storm, he'd hate to see what was.

In the troughs between the waves – the all-too-brief lulls before the next surging incline of water shovelled him up dizzyingly fast – he attempted to make contact with Sigursdottir. His commplant registered the feeblest of signal strengths. The storm lay like a thick, deadening blanket between him and the nearest available satellite.

To make matters worse, Dev was physically drained, meaning the commplant had less juice to draw on. The effort of keeping his head above water was placing further demand on his metabolic batteries. He had only a few minutes, he guessed, until the commplant went into automatic shutdown. His window of opportunity was closing rapidly.

Then: connection.

Harmer? Harm—

And the signal went.

Call interrupted. Retry?

Dev responded to the commplant's prompt with an okay. With the squall hissing in his ears, rain pounding his scalp, he listened for the click of connection in his head.

Sigursdottir, don't speak, just try to get a GPS fix on me so that you—

Again, the signal went.

Call interrupted. Retry?

"No shit I want to fucking retry," Dev said aloud, and instantly regretted it as seawater slapped into his mouth and he swallowed half of Triton.

Third time was the charm, sort of.

Harmer, there's no way we're going to be able to locate you and zero in, not in all this mess. Needle in a haystack – and someone's shaking the haystack. We're on course for Mazu. Do you read me? Mazu.

Mazu. I read you. Why? I thought there'd been a full evac.

There has, but your dirty great crab has just

popped up on sonar again and it's heading that way. We don't want to lose track of it a second time, and as long as it doesn't sink again, beyond sonar depth, we won't. Can you gargle after zone cream?

That was how the end of the sentence sounded, at any rate. The sense of her words was lost in a churn of interference.

Sorry. Say again.

I said, can you get there under your own steam?

Yes, I think I can.

That was gibberish. Repeat.

Yes, I think I can get there under my own steam.

Nothing further from Sigursdottir. The signal had gone yet again, and this time Dev's commplant couldn't get it back. Every attempt met with resounding silence.

So, Mazu it was. The Polis+ agent who was driving the Ice King had a checklist of Diasporan townships and was crossing them off one by one. The Plusser didn't know Mazu was empty, and it might not make a difference anyway. Another ungilled settlement sunk, another milestone on the journey to full-blown, worldwide revolution.

Dev ducked back under, dived down to the manta sub, and brought Ethel up to speed on the situation.

I'll get you there, she said, and coaxed the reluctant manta back into motion. I can't promise we'll go fast but we'll make it.

Thanks. I don't expect anything more from you than a lift to the township. You've done so much already. Lost so much.

This is still my fight. I'm more determined than ever to see it through to the end. How are you bearing up?

I just gave you the answer to that, Ethel said flatly.

First your cousin, now your friends...

She glanced at the kid, who was skulking at the back of the cockpit, glum-faced.

His "god" has a lot to answer for, she said.

It's not my god, the kid muttered. Not any longer.

The Ice King's worshippers also have a lot to answer for. I should like to see them pay a penalty for what they've done, but right now, even more than that, I'd like to see the Ice King itself pay. If you ungilled genuinely have a way of killing it...

Oh, we do, said Dev.

Then you can count me in. I want to be there when it dies. Witness it with my own eyes, up close.

Trust me, you don't want to be too close. The weapon we'll be using — let's just say the results are best seen from a distance. A considerable distance.

Fair enough.

What I still can't work out is why the Ice King went for that drift cluster.

That puzzles me too. It seems so arbitrary. If it were just an animal, I might understand. But you claim it's being controlled from the inside.

The drift cluster wasn't by any chance a Nautilus Movement stronghold? Dev hazarded.

Not to my knowledge, no. But even if it was, the Ice King didn't seem to care if innocent bystanders got hurt. Children, for example.

Well, if what it did has cured a few insurgents of their religious fever, that's something, Dev said. Now all we have to do is eradicate the source of the disease. The Ice King's second coming is about to be cut short.

And good riddance, the kid said, with feeling.

Ethel looked at him with surprise – and something that bore a more than passing resemblance to approval.

53

Mazu.

Last surviving Triangle Town.

Its domes and outlying marinas and algae farms rode the enormous sea swell. Each roller sent a ripple through it, making its various sections rise and fall in succession, from one end to the other. The bridges that linked them all canted up and down, hinges strained to the limit. The entire township resembled a caterpillar, flexing fluidly.

The storm was doing its level best to break Mazu apart, but so far the place was holding together.

Once the Ice King got here, that would all change.

It seemed that the manta sub, although it had travelled at less than maximum speed, had made good time. The *Admiral Winterbrook* was already on the scene, but of the Ice King there was no sign. Both vessels had beaten it to its destination.

Dev transferred from the sub to the catamaran, where the first thing he did was head for the bridge and brief Sigursdottir about the attack on the drift cluster and the ensuing game of cat and mouse which had led to him and Ethel hiding out in the deepest possible reaches of the ocean.

Jiang, at the helm, listened in, and Milgrom entered shortly before he finished and caught the tail end of his summary.

"You've had yourself a morning," Sigursdottir remarked.

"You can say that again."

"Don't mistake this frown on my face for sympathy, though. I'm not happy. Thanks to you, we lost track of the Ice King."

"Temporarily."

"Yeah, we lucked out. Picked it up again. But I thought the whole big idea was to keep tabs on it. That's what we agreed on."

"Ethel kind of scuppered that. Like I said, it killed a couple of her friends and she knew we'd be next if she didn't do something drastic. She was also trying to help the people from the drift cluster. They might well have been next on the Ice King's hit list."

"Very noble."

"Nice piece of buck-passing there," said Milgrom, unwrapping a protein bar and taking a big bite. "Blame the sea monkey."

"No," said Dev. "I take full responsibility. For everything. But corporal, for what it's worth, I'd be obliged if you didn't call her a sea monkey."

"Ahh, you're sweet on the fish lady. That's nice. You two going to spawn together, huh? Make thousands of nice little caviar babies?"

Dev was tired, irritable and hungry, and the sight of Milgrom munching on food, when his own energy levels were low and his stomach was growling, was pretty much the final straw. Insults and banter he could handle, but it felt as though she was eating in front of him solely in order to mock him.

"Go fuck yourself," he said.

"Only way I can guarantee myself a decent lay," Milgrom shot back with a smirk and carried on gnawing on the bar.

"So, you must really like the taste of fish."

"Seriously, shut up or I will shut you up."

"You're not man enough."

"With all due respect, screw you."

Milgrom took a step towards him. "'Screw you' I can take. But anyone who *with-all-due-respect*s me deserves a pasting."

Dev's hands balled into fists. It was neither the time nor the place to get into a scrap, but Milgrom was really rubbing him up the wrong way. A joke was a joke, but Ethel didn't deserve the disrespect she was getting.

And that protein bar looked so delicious, too.

Sigursdottir moved between them as they eyeballed each other. "You two need to either have a punch-up or get a room. I can't make up my mind which. But at this precise instant, you are both going to stand down and back off. The Ice King is still inbound and we have to decide on the best course of action. Gunnery Sergeant Jiang, how far away is it?"

Jiang checked the sonar screen. "Four klicks and closing. Not going too quickly. Looks kind of arrogant to me. Taking its time, like it knows Mazu's a sitting duck."

"I don't need your interpretation of the thing's psychology," Sigursdottir snapped. She was under immense strain and trying, not wholly successfully, to keep it from showing. "Just the facts. How soon 'til contact?"

"Ten minutes tops."

"Okay. I say we pull back to a safe distance. Let this play out as it will. There's nothing we can do to stop Mazu getting clobbered. It's strictly observe-and-report for us. Then, once the Ice King moves on, we resume pursuit duties until such time as the Sunbakers show up."

"Which'll be when?" Dev asked, shooting a surly glance at Milgrom, who shuttered her eyes at him sneeringly.

"They're on their way aboard the *Astounding*. That's a combat hydrofoil, fastest boat Station Ares has. Maddox is captaining it himself."

"We're honoured."

"High priority. Also, nobody but himself has clearance to launch a Sunbaker. Current ETA is…" Sigursdottir looked to Jiang.

"Oh-four-hundred hours," said Jiang. "A little under five hours from now. Could be longer, though. They're going at flank speed, but they'll lose headway if the storm gets any worse."

"It could get *worse*?" said Dev, only half facetiously. The *Admiral Winterbrook* was seesawing from stem to stern and shuddering violently with every wave that crashed over its bows. The world outside was one mass of angry water, from the sea itself to the pelting rain.

"Syzygy storm," said Milgrom. "Not for wimps."

"Yes, it could get worse," Sigursdottir said. "Winds haven't yet topped hurricane force, and the meteorological satellites are predicting they might. Seventy per cent probability."

"Wishing I hadn't asked now," Dev said. "All right, so we're sacrificing Mazu to Crab Features. Shame, but as a wise man once said, 'Sometimes you have to lose a town to gain a planet.'"

"Who said that?" Milgrom challenged. "I've never heard that before."

"Actually I made it up. But it still applies. Now, just out of curiosity, where's Handler?"

"Last I saw of him," said Sigursdottir, "he went off to bunk down in one of the communal cabins."

"He's been keeping a low profile," said Milgrom. "Think all the excitement's been getting too much for him, poor lamb."

"Just head down and aft," said Sigursdottir. "You'll find him. Don't be long, though, or you'll miss the show."

"I only want a word or two," Dev said.

"Sounds ominous."

"Hopefully it won't have to be."

54

"DOWN AND AFT" meant negotiating a narrow companionway down from the bridge to an even narrower corridor on the lower deck. The staircase underfoot pitched and yawed as the boat rocked.

The first cabin door Dev tried, he disturbed Reyes and Cully, the diving team, catching some shuteye in bunks fitted with form-hugging intellifoam mattresses. Reyes had some very uncomplimentary things to say about him intruding on their slumber after they'd been up half the night on watch duty, and Dev backed out with an apology.

The second door he tried, the bunks were empty, but Blunt and Francis were on the floor, lying on their sides in sixty-nine position. They were going at it hammer and tongs, clothing askew, eyes shut, heads pecking, tongues flicking, so into each other that they didn't even register Dev's presence. All that talk about the handsome Master Chief Reynolds earlier, he mused as he glided the door shut. Private Blunt and Private Francis were wherever-you-can-take-it women, it seemed. Any port in a storm.

Third door, paydirt. Handler occupied a berth above Private Fakhouri, the comms specialist. She was lying on her back, arms folded behind her head, with the coma stare of someone watching or listening to entertainment.

Handler, by contrast, was in a semi-doze, and was startled – to say the least – when Dev grabbed him by the collar and dragged him out of the bunk and into the corridor.

"What the – ? Who the – ? What – ?" he spluttered. "Harmer! What are you doing? What is this?"

Dev slammed him against the wall, forearm to throat, pinning him in place.

"No time for niceties," he said. "Straightforward question. Give me a straightforward answer, and maybe this'll go okay. The nucleotide shots. What are they really?"

"I don't know what you're –"

"Wrong! You had your chance, blew it. Now we do this the hard way."

"Harmer, have you gone mad? Help! Someone help!"

Fakhouri emerged from the cabin just as Dev was about to frogmarch Handler off down the corridor.

"Hold on," she said. "What's all the fuss? Where are you taking him?"

"ISS business, Private Fakhouri," Dev said. "This is between me and Handler. Nothing to concern you."

"Harmer's assaulting me," Handler remonstrated. "For no reason whatsoever."

"No reason?" said Dev. "All right then. How about this? Do you believe in a supreme being?"

"What?"

"Do you believe in an afterlife? Do you live comforted by the falsehood that, when you pass on, your soul becomes subsumed into the Singularity?"

"Where is all this coming from?"

"How does it make you feel when I tell you that on Earth, during the Enlightenment, we began to treat religious fundamentalism as a mental illness?"

Handler blinked in disbelief. "You have got to be joking. You're using the Provocation Sequence test questions on me? You're trying to out me as a Plusser? *Me?*"

"How does it make you feel," Dev persisted, "when I deny your fantasy god? Does it make you angry? Does it offend you down to your so-called soul?"

"Look into my eyes," Handler said. "Look deep. Are these the eyes of a Plusser? Do you see Uncanny Valley in them?"

"Hard to tell, with those extra lids."

"The extra lids don't make any difference." The ISS liaison let out a high-pitched laugh with a touch of hysteria in it. "I can't believe you honestly suspect me of being a digimentalist in disguise. How ridiculous."

"Well, if you *aren't* Polis Plus, maybe you're working for them without knowing it."

"Hypnagogic exposure, you mean? They've brainwashed me into doing their bidding? You're really reaching now, Harmer. Can this get any more absurd? Next you'll be claiming I'm collaborating with the insurgency."

"Had crossed my mind."

"What's brought on all these accusations? The serum, yes? Because you think it's made you unwell? We've been over that. You were unwell when you started."

"What if that's because you gave me one of those shots *before* I came round on the mediplinth?" Dev said.

Handler tried to dismiss the suggestion with a sigh, as though he had never in his life heard something so implausible.

But there was a fraction of a second's delay before the sigh came out. The tiniest of hesitations.

Bingo.

Dev knew, then and there, that he had hit the nail on the head.

"How would I ever know?" he went on. "Why would I suspect? There'd be no evidence. The microneedle patches don't leave a mark on the skin. Not a trace to show that you'd already pumped me with a few millilitres of whatever it is that's been fucking my host form up."

"Wild speculation."

Dev shoved Handler against the wall again. "Then how come I haven't felt better since coming to Triton than I do now, hours since my last dose?"

"If you ask me," Handler said in slightly strangulated tones, because Dev's forearm was once more pressing on his windpipe, "the irrational behaviour you're exhibiting is precisely because you *haven't* been keeping up with the nucleotide shots. Your brain is starting to go. Could be there's some intracranial bleeding you're unaware of. It's affecting your cognitive processes, making you think that insane things are true."

Briefly, for a fleeting instant, Dev felt that what Handler was saying was possible. It made a kind of sense. All of this – his suspicions about Handler, the aggression he was feeling towards him, the way he'd let Milgrom get under his skin a short while earlier – was just the newest manifestation of his host form's gradual decline. His mind was growing unstable, a kind of dementia setting in. What if the final, irreversible breakdown of his body had started? His brain could be turning to Swiss cheese inside his skull, driving him to madness, and he simply didn't realise.

No.

"No," he said. "Nice try, though. You almost had me. Now come on." He yanked Handler away from the wall. "I know just how to get you to talk, and you won't be able to lie."

"I'm not lying."

"Maybe you are, maybe you aren't. We can prove it either way by getting you outside and underwater. We speak in Tritonese, and there's no way you can pull any shit on me. Tritonians always tell the truth, remember? They can't help themselves."

Handler let out a bleat of protest, and at the same time Fakhouri drew her sidearm – standard Marine-issue polymer-frame 9mm automatic, with a magazine full of self-steering fragmentation rounds and a DNA-coded grip to prevent it being wielded by anyone except the rightful user. She aimed it at Dev.

"Stop," she said. "I'm not completely clear what's going on here, but you, Harmer, are threatening that man, and I can't let you do that. Not on a Marine boat, under Marine command."

"Fakhouri, please," said Dev, "put the gun away. I appreciate you think you're doing the right thing. You're not."

Reyes and Cully were now out in the corridor too, drawn by the ruckus. Cully's hand stole towards her own sidearm, while Reyes positioned herself beside Fakhouri's shoulder, a gesture of solidarity and support. She had her colleague's back.

"He fully intends to hurt me," Handler said. "You've seen him. The man's a loose cannon. You need to pacify him."

"And you," said Dev, "are a treacherous sack of shit who's been undermining my mission from the very beginning, and I'm going to find out why."

"Treacherous sack of – !"

"And conniving. Tell them, Handler, how you've been spying on us on Captain Maddox's behalf."

"Spying on 'us,' Harmer? Spying on *you*, maybe. Why would Maddox ask me to keep an eye on his own troops? Especially when he's in regular contact with Lieutenant Sigursdottir."

"An ISS liaison in cahoots with a senior military officer – that's not standard operating procedure."

"We're not in cahoots," said Handler. "I've just been acting as an extra pair of eyes for him. In fact, you might say, thanks to my association with Maddox, that I could be considered an honorary Marine."

It was a blatant attempt to appeal to Fakhouri, Reyes and Cully and, to Dev's dismay, it worked.

"You should let him go," Reyes said to Dev. "I'm sure we can sort it all out like mature adults, without anybody hitting anybody."

"Yeah," said Cully. "You seem like a good guy, Harmer. I think we're all a bit overwrought. If you'd just calm down…"

"Handler said Harmer might have something wrong with his brain," said Fakhouri. "Something about medicine he has or hasn't been taking, if I've been following the conversation correctly."

"Medicine?" said Cully.

"That's just a bluff," Dev said. "Handler's trying to do a number on me. And on you."

"Your word against his," said Reyes.

"Why don't I put this hypervelocity pistol against his head?" Dev said, nodding down at his own hip. "Then we'll see whose word we can rely on."

"Don't even think about it," said Fakhouri, sighting down the gun barrel at Dev and tightening her index finger to achieve first pressure on the trigger. Her legs were braced apart, knees softened to absorb the rocking motion of the catamaran and keep her upper body steady. The expert stance of someone trained to use a firearm on a boat in high seas. "You're going to let go of him, and then we're going to walk up to the bridge, nice and slow, and we're going to talk things through in front of Lieutenant Sigursdottir in a civilised manner, and that way nobody gets a dirty great hole in them."

Dev weighed up the options: trying to disarm Fakhouri, going for his own gun, swinging Handler round to use as a human shield, or simply surrendering. None of them seemed particularly beneficial or appealing.

He very much didn't want to get into a shooting match with the Marines. He would in all likelihood come off worst, since he didn't have a drawn weapon and Fakhouri did. Plus, there were three of them and only one of him. More to the point, they were all supposed to be on the same side.

He didn't want to surrender either, because then he would have lost control of the situation, for the time being at least. Who knew when he would get another crack at Handler? The ISS liaison was aware that Dev was wise to him now and wouldn't let himself be collared so easily again. He might even beg protection from Sigursdottir, so that Dev would find it difficult getting another chance to interrogate him.

"Harmer," said Fakhouri. "I'm waiting. Haven't got all day."

Then Jiang's voice sounded over the *Admiral Winterbrook*'s PA system.

"All hands to the bridge. I repeat, all hands to the bridge. Contact imminent. Report fully prepped, armed and armoured. This is not a drill."

Fakhouri, Reyes and Cully exchanged glances.

"You two go get kitted out," Fakhouri said. "I'll keep the ISS contingent covered. Then you can escort them upstairs while I get ready myself."

"Affirmative," sad Reyes. "Cully, you heard the woman. Double time. Let's hustle."

Fakhouri held Dev at gunpoint and Dev in turn kept Handler pinned to the wall, and this uneasy tableau remained in effect until Reyes and Cully returned from the boat's armoury in full battle gear.

Blunt and Francis appeared too – clothing straightened, hair a little mussed – and that was when Dev finally had to admit defeat. He took his arm away from Handler's neck with a grunt of frustration. Handler managed to look affronted and peeved, but there was also a twinkle of vindication in his eyes that could have been taken, if you were looking for it, as a sign of guilt.

Reyes and Cully took charge of both Dev and Handler and bundled them up to the bridge...

...where, amid the rollercoaster ups and downs of the waves, they had ringside seats for the Ice King's attack on Mazu.

55

EXCEPT THE ICE King *didn't* attack Mazu.

The gargantuan crab circled the township, seeming cautious, unconvinced. Again and again it poked its face speculatively above the surging waves, as though something about Mazu struck it as not quite right, as though it was looking for something that wasn't there.

"What's it up to?" said Jiang.

"Suspicious and unimpressed," said Milgrom. "Like a dog sniffing at its bowl. 'Kibble *again?*'"

Sigursdottir was torn between watching the Ice King and wanting to know why Reyes and Cully were treating Dev and Handler like captive prisoners.

"Explain," she said, drawing an index finger back and forth in the air to indicate the two non-Marines. "What's up with the ISS guys? They under arrest?"

That was when Fakhouri made her entrance.

"They were having a row," she said. "It got heated. I cooled it down."

"A row about...?"

Dev glanced sidelong at Handler. It took every ounce of self-control he had in him to say, "A misunderstanding.

Handler and I have conflicting views on a certain set of facts. You know how it is."

"No, I don't know how it is, and what's more, I don't care. Have you settled your differences?"

"Yes," said Handler firmly.

"No," said Dev. Then: "Yes."

"That's what I want to hear. I will not tolerate squabbling on my boat, not from my men and not from civilians. You, Harmer, seem to be going out of your way to antagonise people today. You'd better stow that shit, or else. We don't have a brig on the *Winterbrook* but we've got a galley you wouldn't like to be shut up inside. Place is a health hazard."

"Message received and understood."

"Now, if you don't mind, I'd rather pay attention to what matters, which is that freakazoid crab monster out there."

Sigursdottir turned back to the windows, which were under siege from sheeting torrents of seawater and rain, so much so that the ultrasonic inducer field that was supposed to be keeping the glass clear and dry couldn't cope.

The Ice King was still giving Mazu a wary once-over.

"Maybe it always does this," Blunt said. "Checks out the opposition before going in for the kill."

"That's not what it did when it attacked the drift cluster earlier," Dev said. "It barely thought twice."

"So what's different about Mazu?" Jiang wondered.

Dev thought he knew. "If you ask me, it's people."

"There aren't any on Mazu."

"Exactly. This thing likes people. It likes to kill them and eat them. It's a forager carnivore and it needs a lot of food to keep it going, and it's unsure about Mazu because it's not detecting any prey there."

"Is that true?" said Sigursdottir.

Dev shrugged. "I can't swear to it."

The Ice King sank under the surface once more, but this time didn't re-emerge.

"So it might wander off now," said Sigursdottir. "Go in search of a meal."

"Unless it decides to trash Mazu just for shits and giggles," said Francis.

They waited. The syzygy storm continued putting Mazu through contortions, like a cruel gymnastics coach, but the Ice King appeared to have decided to leave the township alone.

"Uh-oh," said Jiang.

"Gunnery sergeant, you had better clarify that remark," said Sigursdottir, "quick smart."

"On the sonar. The Ice King. It's coming this way."

"Full reverse thrust! Now!"

The *Admiral Winterbrook*'s engines had been holding the boat in position, making constant micro adjustments in order to resist the sweep of the storm. Jiang threw the throttle back as far as it could go, and the catamaran began to move. Progress was sluggish at first, but then the propellers gained traction in the water.

The Ice King neared. It was swimming just below the surface, pushing a localised tsunami in front of it, a crescent-shaped wall of water five metres high that was gathering size and impetus with every second.

"Do you think it's after us?" said Francis.

"Doesn't matter if it is or it isn't," said Milgrom. "Fucker's going to swamp us either way."

"Unless it changes course," said Blunt.

"Everybody, hang on to something," Sigursdottir ordered. "Even if the Ice King passes right below, we can ride it out. This boat's built to handle the worst nature can throw at it."

She sounded confident. She looked confident. But the confidence didn't extend to her eyes, which were tight with apprehension.

Hands reached out to grab consoles, bulkheads, seat backs, wall-mounted cupboards, whatever was fixed in place and bolted down. Milgrom lodged her hands flat against the ceiling, using her augmented strength to chock herself in place.

Handler, Dev noted with satisfaction, was trembling like a kitten.

"Don't worry," he said. "I'll look after you. Just like you've been looking after me."

"Funny."

"You could come clean now, if you want. Seeing as we might not live through this. Admit you've been poisoning me."

"The only thing I'll admit to is realising that you were having doubts about me when you stopped making up stupid nicknames for me and started calling me by my surname again."

"That wasn't a conscious decision."

"Get this through your thick skull, Harmer. I'm no villain, no traitor. I'm a follower of orders, just like you."

"Yes, but whose – ?"

"Here it comes!" said Jiang.

"Brace! Brace! Brace!" Sigursdottir yelled.

The wall of water struck. The *Admiral Winterbrook*'s bow rose, and rose, and kept on rising. The angle of pitch steepened until it was approaching vertical. People leaned, clinging on hard to whatever support they had found, all except Milgrom, who stayed wedged between ceiling and floor like a pillar. Voices were raised in shouts that were not quite screams.

"It'll right itself!" Sigursdottir called out. "It'll right itself! The boat is *not* going to go over!"

For a moment her prediction almost seemed to come true. The *Admiral Winterbrook* teetered, twin keels exposed to the air. The catamaran felt as though it was about to lunge forward and slap back down into the water. Its stabilisers moaned as they fought to compensate, redistributing ballast.

But then, with slow, heavy inevitability, the boat inclined further up.

Up to perpendicular.

And then a fraction beyond.

Past tipping point.

"Oh, shit!" someone cried.

Jiang lost her grip on the main console and went tumbling with a thud against the rear wall.

The windows showed nothing but furious sky.

A rushing sensation.

A feeling of falling.

Down the *Admiral Winterbrook* went. Straight down at first, like a post being driven into soil, and then backwards down, toppling.

Over onto its superstructure.

Slamming belly up into the sea.

56

THERE WERE BODIES in freefall. A colliding, helpless chaos of limbs and heads and torsos. The shouts were now pure, plain screams as the ceiling became a repository for a tangled mass of men and women. Bodies sprawled among the light fixtures, dazed and groaning. The windows were a gallery of seething bubbles and subaquatic gloom, and from somewhere above and to the rear of the boat came the shrill whine of propellers churning empty air.

Sigursdottir, pushing up to hands and knees, addressed her troops. "Is everyone okay? Anyone hurt? Sound off!"

Milgrom, Francis, Blunt, Fakhouri, Reyes and Cully all called out their names, some hoarsely, others with more vigour.

"Jiang," said Francis. "Jiang's non-responsive. Think she hit her head when she slipped backwards."

"Tend to her. Harmer? What's your status?"

"Ouch."

"Handler?"

"I'll live."

"All right. First things first. Here's your no-shit-Sherlock update for the day: we've capsized. We need to get off ASAP.

No way the *Winterbrook*'s going to stay afloat for long like this."

"Lieutenant, we're shipping water already," said Blunt.

One of the windows had cracked, and cold sea was oozing in through the fissure. A couple of the other windows had been loosened in their frames by the boat's somersaulting impact. Water was welling up and leaking in around the panes.

"That settles it," said Sigursdottir. "No time for taking stock or gathering supplies or any of that. Reyes, Cully, you're our best swimmers. Grab Jiang. You're responsible for her."

"Aye-aye, sir."

"Brace yourselves, folks." Sigursdottir pulled her gun and took aim. "We're about to get wet."

"And not in a good way," said Milgrom.

"This is going to happen fast. Deep breaths. Oxygenate those lungs. Get ready for a big influx of water in three... Two... One!"

She fired off several rounds in swift succession, blowing out five of the windows in a left-to-right arc.

Glass shattered. The sea gushed in. Five geysers flooded the bridge at fire-hose pressure, filling up the space from ceiling to floor in a matter of seconds. Electronics sparked and died. Lights extinguished themselves like snuffed candles.

The Marines swam for the hollowed-out windows, towards the shafts of dim, grey daylight that were now the only source of illumination. Dev saw Handler thrash forwards, barging ahead of Francis even though she had to hold her breath where he could breathe normally. Reyes and Cully grappled with the unconscious form of Jiang, one exiting ahead to reel her out, the other staying behind to push.

Sigursdottir made sure everyone else was out of the boat before squeezing through a window herself.

What she failed to notice, as she kicked for the surface, was that Milgrom hadn't got away. The huge Marine was jammed in one of the windows. She had managed to wriggle her head and shoulders through but had got caught around the chest thanks to her bulk and her body armour. The ceramic tiles on her flak vest had snagged on the frame.

She didn't panic. She began patiently, painstakingly trying to extricate herself. When tugging at the flak vest didn't work, she undid the straps.

Still no joy. She couldn't reach the lower straps, on the other side of the window. She was stuck fast.

Dev doubled back. He signalled to Milgrom that he was going back inside the bridge to assist her. He shimmied through one of the adjacent windows and jackknifed towards Milgrom's legs.

The Marine corporal had the sense to keep still. Flailing legs would not have helped the situation. She was aware that Dev was the only solution to her predicament and she just had to stay calm and trust him.

Dev unfastened the lower two straps of her flak vest, but there was still one strap in the middle, right beneath the edge of the window frame, that neither he nor she could get any access to.

He spotted a shimmerknife attached to Milgrom's calf. Did shimmerknives work underwater? Time to find out.

He unsheathed the knife and switched it on; the blade began to vibrate. He slid the blade flat under the last remaining strap, doing his utmost to keep the cutting edge away from Milgrom's stomach. Then he twisted the knife through 90° and dug up against the strap, which parted as though made of liquorice. The blade even cut a nick in the steel of the window frame.

There was an explosion deep in the heart of the *Admiral Winterbrook*. Water had reached the engine room, and the motor had blown. The entire boat shrieked and shook, and the inverted bridge began to tilt around Dev.

Milgrom still wasn't free. She was trying to wriggle out of her flak vest, extricate her arms from the arm holes, but there wasn't enough slack.

Dev ducked back outside. The *Admiral Winterbrook* was taking on water fast, its stern getting heavy. Milgrom had only moments before the catamaran lost what little buoyancy it had left and began to sink with a vengeance.

Her cheeks were bulging. Her eyes said it all. She needed to breathe, and soon. It wasn't a case of willpower, mind over body, not anymore. The inhalation reflex was becoming impossible to resist. By remaining calm she had extended the amount of time it took her body to use up the oxygen in her bloodstream, but now the carbon dioxide buildup was reaching a peak. She was close to breakpoint, when she would have no choice about trying to get some air into her lungs.

She indicated to Dev that it was no good. She was going down with the ship.

He curtly gave her the finger and applied the shimmerknife to the yoke of her flak vest.

Accuracy and precision didn't come into it. No time. He sliced from arm hole to collar, on the left side then the right, in the process managing to gouge out a sliver of Milgrom's shoulder by mistake. Blood blossomed, but he had released her.

Milgrom breast-stroked urgently upwards, with Dev hauling her, adding his speed to hers.

She broke surface with an almighty sucking gasp.

Meanwhile the *Admiral Winterbrook*'s tail end, thoroughly waterlogged, dipped down amid a maelstrom of bubbles and minor explosions. The catamaran, racked with shudders, riddled with jagged holes, seemed not to want to go gently into the waiting darkness below, seemed to be resisting every inch of the way.

But the darkness was inevitable.

Like its namesake, the *Admiral Winterbrook* had fought
its last battle and had lost.

57

Up on the surface, the Marines were fighting a losing battle of their own, against the relentless sway and crash of the syzygy storm.

Reyes and Cully struggled to keep Jiang's face above water while trying not to get overwhelmed themselves by the waves.

Milgrom found it hard to catch her breath after her near-drowning. The sea kept sloshing into her mouth and choking her.

"Together!" Sigursdottir called out. "Everyone! Bunch up and stick together. Don't get swept away. Grab hold of the man next to you if you have to."

Dev front-crawled over to her. "Mazu," he said. "We have to get there. It's our only chance."

"The storm's driving us away from it."

"Then we swim harder."

"Easy for you to say, fish-man. You're built for this. And you're not carrying a couple of dozen kilos of equipment."

"You're not a quitter, lieutenant. Woman up. It's Mazu or die."

Just as Sigursdottir was marshalling the Marines and pointing them in the direction of the township, Blunt yelped a warning.

"Ice King. Ten o'clock."

The God Beneath the Sea, not content with sinking the *Admiral Winterbrook*, was coming back for the humans who'd been aboard the boat. It must have thought itself very clever to have shaken these tasty morsels loose.

"Francis!" Sigursdottir shouted. "You're right in its path. Swim, woman. Swim!"

The Ice King was just below the surface, cutting against the angle of the waves. Francis had drifted some twenty metres from the rest of the group. There was no doubt the gargantuan crab had her in its sights. She was the nearest to it, and although she started swimming with all her might, the Ice King was easily going to outstrip her.

"Come on!" Blunt urged. "Francis, move your stupid fat butt! The bastard's gaining on you!"

Francis cast a glance backwards. The leading edge of turbulence that marked the Ice King's progress was approaching fast, faster than she could possibly go herself.

She halted.

"Francis! No!" Blunt cried.

Treading water, Francis reached down with one arm to detach something fastened to her belt.

"No, you fucking bitch! Don't you dare!"

But Francis ignored Blunt's pleading. She produced a Ninety-Nine Point Nine, a grenade that sent out a wave that disrupted the quantic interaction inside atoms, collapsing electron shells against their nuclei. The name derived from the fact that well over 99.9% of an atom was empty space, and this was the factor by which the grenade shrank everything within a programmable distance of its epicentre.

Quickly she thumbed the radius dial on the Ninety-Nine Point Nine, then grasped the detonation lever and thumbed out the safety pin.

Blunt howled words, becoming incomprehensible in her horror and despair.

Francis nodded to her, as if to say everything was okay, this was just what she had to do. She seemed aware that she was making a futile gesture, that she wasn't going to *kill* the Ice King by any means. She was going to make it pay for her, though. It wouldn't get her for free.

Then a vast pincer shot up from the water, clamping round her waist. Francis screamed shrilly as she became wedged between two of the serrations and the pincer applied bone-cracking, gut-bursting pressure.

She let go of the detonation lever, and a split second later there was a loud rending noise, not unlike a burp, as a three-metre-diameter sphere of matter condensed instantaneously down to the size of a poppy seed.

Encompassed within that sphere was all of Private First Class Francis and a sizeable chunk of the Ice King's pincer.

The Ice King emitted a sound that Dev would quite happily have gone to his grave without ever hearing again, a cross between a screech and an earth tremor. It thrashed its injured pincer around, spraying gobs of grey-blue blood in all directions. The Ninety-Nine Point Nine had gouged out a perfect, clean-edged cavity in the claw. The wound was far from life-threatening – the equivalent of a person losing a pea-sized section of the ball of their thumb – but it clearly hurt.

"Yeah, motherfucker!" Blunt crowed, weeping. "Take that, bitch! That's what you get! And there'll be more of the same if you come for me."

"Let's go, Marines," said Sigursdottir. "Francis has bought us some breathing space. Don't waste it. Make it count."

And they swam, into the teeth of the storm, powering through the waves that endlessly, endlessly tried to beat them back.

Even as they inched closer to Mazu, Dev kept looking over his shoulder. The Ice King had sunk out of sight. He hoped it had slouched off somewhere to tend to its wound, but he doubted it. The bastard thing wasn't going to give up that easily. He knew from experience just how remorseless and tenacious it could be.

It reappeared – or rather, the tsunami that heralded its presence did.

The Ice King was coming for them yet again.

There was no point yelling a warning, urging everyone to swim harder. It would have been redundant. They were already going as fast as they could.

The tsunami curled, crested, swelled. Reyes and Cully, with Jiang between them, were lagging at the rear of the group. They would be first when the Ice King caught up – first to be pincer-grabbed and eaten.

But then they rose from the water. It was as though they were being lifted, all three of them, and were suddenly surfing rather than swimming.

Dev beheld this weird sight, asking himself if it was some tidal miracle, some bizarre trick of the waves or currents that was buoying the three Marines up and along.

Blunt was scooped up by the phenomenon next, then Handler and Fakhouri.

Finally it came for Dev, Milgrom and Sigursdottir.

All at once the nine of them, Marines and ISS employees alike, were skating along the surface faster than they could possibly have swum.

And Dev was grinning. Grinning like an idiot.

Because underneath them was something solid, a black, rubbery, undulating mass, and it was Ethel's manta sub, and it was ferrying them on its back, keeping them ahead of the Ice King, whisking them like a magic carpet towards Mazu.

58

THE MANTA SUB swerved to a halt beside Mazu's western marina, where every berth stood empty after the mass exodus.

The humans on the manta's back scrambled off onto the pontoons.

There wasn't time to pause or retrench. The Ice King was still coming. With Sigursdottir leading the way and Reyes and Cully stretchering Jiang by the arms and legs, the group ran for cover.

The manta sub dived, seeking cover too.

The fleeing humans reached the gateway that linked the marina with the rest of the township, just as the Ice King hit the outer edge of the marina.

Literally hit, barrelling straight into the pontoons, which bucked and buckled under the impact.

Fakhouri lost her footing and stumbled, but Dev grabbed her, and everyone kept on running. They ran across a footbridge that leapt up and down under them like something in a funhouse at a fair. They ran round the perimeter walkway of a residential dome, then across another footbridge to a dome housing the power-distributing substation for the tidal barrages.

Sigursdottir waved them to a halt, and they hunkered down, sheltering in the lee of the substation dome.

"Milgrom, surveillance. The rest of you, take a breather, but get ready to run again if Milgrom says run."

Milgrom sent up her hoverdrone over the marina. Its stabilisers worked hard but still it careened and yawed crazily in the high winds.

Reyes and Cully, panting hardest of anyone, gladly set down the still unconscious Jiang.

"We owe your Tritonian lady friend," Sigursdottir said to Dev.

"Yeah," he replied. "Not bad for a sea monkey, eh?"

Milgrom didn't so much as twitch.

"And Francis," said Blunt. "Owe her too. She died delaying the Ice King. Only wish she could have taken that fucking great cunt of a thing with her."

"She set the Ninety-Nine to maximum radius," said Fakhouri, "and it was like a paper cut to that monster."

"Maybe a couple more Ninety-Nines, well placed...?" Reyes suggested optimistically.

Sigursdottir shook her head. "Nothing we've got on us is going to do anything but piss the Ice King off even more than it's already pissed off. When the Sunbakers get here, that's another story. Milgrom, what's the creature's status?"

"Hear those noises?" said Milgrom.

Above the wail of the syzygy storm came the sound of crashing and crunching – manmade structures being violently dismantled.

"That's the marina getting the urban renewal treatment. The Ice King's having a field day turning pontoons into kindling."

"It won't stop either," said Handler. "Not until Mazu has gone the way of Dakuwaqa and Opochtli."

"Actually, you may be wrong there," said Milgrom. "It's just started backing off, seems like."

Now only the storm was audible – the wind keening, the sea roaring.

"Yeah, it's withdrawing. Starting to do that circling thing again."

"Prolonging the agony," said Cully. "It knows we're here. It's toying with us."

"It realises we're trapped," Reyes chimed in. "It can take all day if it wants. I've seen a killer whale do this with a sperm whale calf it's already wounded. The orca just trails the calf, occasionally going in for a bite or just to thump it with its nose. Enjoying the victim's helplessness."

"Or," said Dev, "if there's a Plusser inside the Ice King, like I think there is, he's calculating the best way to get to us."

"What if he – it – whichever – loses interest?" Sigursdottir said.

"I don't think there's much danger of that, judging by past performance. If only there was."

"No, this isn't wishful thinking on my part. I'm concerned. The Ice King could maybe decide there aren't enough of us to make hunting us worthwhile anymore. Why trash a whole township, go to all that trouble, just for nine humans? We're not even a snack. There's richer, easier pickings elsewhere."

"I don't see how that's a bad thing," said Handler. "We get to live."

"Yes, but another township, fully populated, suffers," said Sigursdottir. "Also, we'll have lost track of the Ice King. Right now, we know where it is because it knows where we are. If it trundles off, it could go anywhere."

"I get what you're driving at," said Dev. "I don't like it, but I get it. For better or worse, we have the Ice King where just we want it."

"This is where the *Astounding* is heading for. This is our last reported position, and without the *Admiral Winterbrook*'s comms array we'd have no way of getting a message through to say that the target has moved on, if it does. Commplants are useless until the storm blows over."

"And there's not a boat to be had anywhere," said Milgrom, "so we can't follow the Ice King to keep track of it."

"Ethel could in her sub," Dev said, "but we'd still have the same communications issues."

"What it boils down to," said Sigursdottir, with grim resignation, "is our mission parameters have just changed, yet again. We're no longer monitoring the Ice King. Our job now is to keep it here, by any means necessary, until the *Astounding* arrives."

"Fuck me," said Reyes.

"Not while there are dogs on the street," said Cully, which raised a bleak laugh and a smile or two.

"How long do we have to do that for?" said Blunt. "Not fuck Reyes, obviously. Keep the Ice King here."

"It's four and a bit hours until the earliest likely rendezvous with the *Astounding*," said Sigursdottir.

"Four hours, twenty-one minutes, to be specific," said Fakhouri.

"During which time we try to make the Ice King not forget about us but also try not to get ourselves killed?" said Cully. "That's kind of a tall order."

"Did you join the Marines for fun, Private Cully," said Sigursdottir, "or did you join the Marines because you wanted challenges in your life?"

"Challenges, sir. To become all that I can be, sir."

"Good answer. So here's our new objective, people. For the next four hours, twenty minutes at least, we're going to be playing hit-and-run with Crabcakes out there, until such time as Captain Maddox turns up and cooks it with a Sunbaker. We bug it and annoy it, and do all we can not to get massacred in the process. Got that?"

A round of *aye-aye*s and *roger that*s from the Marines.

"Awesome. Harmer, Handler, you're welcome to sit this one out. This is military business."

"Not a fucking chance," said Dev. "But you, Handler, should maybe find somewhere to hole up."

"Given the extent of my combat experience, that might be wise," Handler said. "I can watch over Gunnery Sergeant Jiang until she recovers."

"Appreciated," said Sigursdottir.

Dev opened his mouth to suggest that she oughtn't to trust Handler with Jiang.

"Something to add, Harmer?"

"Just that…"

No. Handler would never be that stupid, that foolish. If something bad happened to Jiang while she was in his care, who would be the most obvious suspect? Him. Handler knew that Dev was waiting for him to incriminate himself further somehow. His continued wellbeing hinged on Jiang's continued wellbeing.

"Nothing, lieutenant."

"Good. So let's check weapons, count ammo, work out a strategy…"

As the Marines got in a huddle and conferred, Dev pulled up the countdown timer on his commplant once again. He hadn't halted it even after deciding that the deterioration of his host form was a fraud. It read:

26:33:47

He reset it for the new deadline.

04:20:00

Until the *Astounding* was due.

That was the minimum length of time he and the Marines had to engage with the Ice King and keep it occupied in order to allow Maddox to come and deliver the coup de grâce. What was once an indicator of Dev's theoretical allotted

lifespan was now the Ice King's.
And, he hoped, no one else's.

59

MILGROM SIDLED UP to him.

"This isn't going to be easy for me to say..." she began.

"Then I'm going to relish it all the more," Dev said.

"Yeah, well, screw it. You needn't have done what you did back there at the *Winterbrook*, when it was going down."

"No, I did. Nobody else could have. Except maybe Handler. So, nobody else."

"Yeah. Useless limp-dick fuck, that guy. I saw the way he pushed past Francis, trying to get out."

"Sorry about the shoulder, though."

Milgrom flexed the joint, which had been sprayed over with healant-impregnated synthetic skin. "Nano-surgeons are knitting up the damaged tissue, and artificial endorphins are doing the rest. It's cool. I'm just trying to say I'm in your debt – and I fucking hate that."

"Being in someone's debt? Or mine in particular?"

"Both."

"Tell you what," Dev said. "We're quits if you give me a couple of the protein bars you Marines have all got stashed in your emergency ration pouches. I'm famished."

"Deal."

* * *

THE COUNTDOWN TIMER stood at:
$$03{:}51{:}08$$

So far, the Ice King had confined itself to prowling around Mazu, nothing more. Every so often Blunt or Milgrom would risk their hoverdrones to the storm and confirm that it was still inspecting the township's outskirts. Fakhouri had established a closed-loop link between everyone's commplants, converting Mazu's principal satellite uplink into a local-network relay hub. They could communicate remotely with one another, just not with the wider world.

Dev felt better almost straight away after wolfing down the protein bars. Hunger and tiredness were what had been making him cranky and unreasonable – not, as Handler had glibly tried to convince him, intracranial bleeding. Once again, the ISS liaison had been trying to pull a fast one.

Dev still couldn't figure out what Handler's agenda was. What did he stand to gain by making Dev less efficient at his job? Who did it benefit? Not Handler himself. Polis+? The insurgency? Who?

It was maddening. Behind the scenes, Dev knew, someone was pulling strings. The trouble with fighting an alien enemy who could hide within people, who could pass for human, was that they could be anyone, anywhere. You could never be sure who to mistrust.

"Okay," said Milgrom. "Looks like the Ice King might be thinking about ditching us."

"Who's nearest it right now?" said Sigursdottir.

"Blunt."

Via commplant, Sigursdottir instructed Blunt to open fire. From Mazu's northern end came the sound of gunshots.

Did you score a hit?

Blunt confirmed that she had. The Ice King was suddenly interested in that corner of the township.

Then move, Marine! Get out of there!

There was a cacophony of destruction. Blunt had been positioned at Mazu's tidal barrages. They now succumbed to the Ice King's pounding claws.

Blunt? Private Blunt? Are you all right? Do you copy?

Blunt's voice came over the shared link eventually.

I made it out. Skin of my teeth. Ice King's made quite a mess of things.

03:27:52
The Ice King became curious about a series of small fires that Reyes and Cully had set on the artificial beach on Mazu's south side. It seemed entranced at first, then it exploded with rage and smashed up both the beach and the adjacent promenade.
03:05:03
The Ice King revisited the ruined marina and began probing there. Something had lured it: the sound of a human voice, shouting and yelling. Fakhouri had rigged up the loudspeakers from a nightclub with a microwave receiver and was transmitting to them from her commplant. The noise fascinated the Ice King until it realised it had been hoodwinked. Then, in what looked like a fit of pique, it demolished not only the speakers and what was left of the marina but a nearby warehouse dome as well.

02:41:14

Some high-ex grenades lobbed into the water by Milgrom from Mazu's main algae farm brought the Ice King bursting clear of the sea. Milgrom, executing a series of huge augmented leaps from growth bed to growth bed, just managed to get away with her life. The algae farm was a write-off.

02:33:20

Blunt struck again, loosing off a salvo of ultra-velocity coilgun rifle rounds from a vantage point on top of one of Mazu's taller domes. She aimed for the Ice King's face with sniper accuracy, and got its attention. She slid down the dome and jumped for safety an instant before a giant pincer crashed upward from underneath, spearing the dome and wrenching it down into the sea.

02:11:10

Reyes and Cully set another fire, a large blaze this time that engulfed an entire residential dome within minutes. The Ice King gave it short shrift. In a show of contempt, it flattened the dome with a heavy stroke of one pincer.

"Let's tally up what we've achieved so far," said Sigursdottir as the Marines and Dev gathered outside Mazu's main central dome. There were almost exactly two hours left until the *Astounding* was due.

"We've lost about a quarter of the township," said Milgrom.

"We've had a fair few close shaves," said Blunt.

"But we're still alive, all of us," said Sigursdottir, "and Mazu's still afloat and the Ice King's still here. That's a win in my book."

"But we're only halfway to the *Astounding*'s ETA," said Fakhouri. "The Ice King could decide to wander off at any time."

"Or decide to trash the place completely," said Reyes, "and us with it."

"The trick is to make sure it stays curious but doesn't get bored or frustrated," said Dev. "A fine line, and so far you've walked it. But we need something more. Something else."

"Ideas?" said Sigursdottir.

"A vague one."

"You work on that, Harmer. Meanwhile, we'll carry on as we have been."

The syzygy storm began to abate. The rain was marginally less torrential, the winds now gale force only, screeching somewhat less deafeningly than before. The storm still seemed to have a few more hours left in it, but a peak had been reached and passed.

Dev hopped the rail of a footbridge and went looking for Ethel below.

He stayed in the shadow of Mazu, casting a watchful eye around him, making sure he knew where the Ice King was at all times. The township clanked and creaked and groaned overhead. He swam through clumps of wreckage and detritus, including a miasma of mucus-green sludge from the disintegrated algae farm.

The search seemed fruitless. He presumed Ethel had quit the area, and he wouldn't have blamed her if she had. Mazu was not a safe place to be, as long as the Ice King was loitering around.

It even crossed his mind that the Ice King might have caught and eaten the manta sub and its two occupants. The Marines had been keeping it busy with their diversions and their harrying attacks, but there'd been periods when the monster had submerged out of sight and its whereabouts had been unclear. Maybe during one of these intervals Ethel had unwarily strayed into its path.

He rejected the idea. She was too canny to allow that to happen.

He came across the manta sub almost without realising. It was using Mazu for cover, hiding right up under the base of one of the domes, next to an anchor column, dark amid darkness. Ethel spotted him and beamed a greeting, a flicker of warm welcome brightness like a lighthouse on a cloudy night.

You've stuck around, he said through the cockpit's corneal membrane.

I told you. I want to see the Ice King get its comeuppance.

Dev outlined the methods the Marines were using to ensure the Ice King stayed put.

Sounds dangerous, Ethel said. Can they manage it much longer?

If they don't, it won't be for lack of trying. I'm wondering if you'd be willing to draw the Ice King back here if it decides it's had enough and leaves. I know that's a lot to ask, but...

I can do my best. The manta's worn out. I'm not sure how much more I can ask from it today. Another sprint might kill it.

The kid chipped in. We could fetch help. Reinforcements.

Who? said Dev. Who do you have in mind?

People. Anyone in the region. Seems to me a single manta sub isn't much compared to the Ice King, but if there are dozens of subs, hundreds of them...

Ethel looked at the kid, and there was no hiding the surprise she was feeling, or how impressed she was.

How quickly could you gather these reinforcements? Dev asked. Where would you find them?

I don't know. Depends. Back where the drift cluster was destroyed would be a good place to start looking.

Then what are you waiting for?

Ethel turned back to Dev. It may not be enough. I can't guarantee we'll return with anyone at all.

Frankly I'd prefer it if you weren't here anyway, he said. In case things go belly up and the Ice King pummels the entire township to pieces. Don't want you getting caught up in that.

Noble of you, but I can take care of myself.

I know. It just had to be said.

Good luck, ungilled. Survive this if you can.

You too. Both of you.

The manta sub pivoted about and winged downward. Just when it was almost too deep to be seen, it levelled out and began swimming horizontally, on a course that would take it back towards Opochtli.

It was a slim hope that Ethel and the kid would find Tritonians willing and able to pitch in and help. Even the faint prospect of backup, though, beat the thought of having none whatsoever.

60

THE ICE KING whittled away at Mazu, responding to each and every provocation the Marines threw at it.

Soon the township was pitted with gaps where domes had stood, and dotted with charred, smouldering wreckage. It was like an organ that had turned cancerous, riddled and rotten.

The Marines ran, goaded, evaded, ran again, sometimes singly, sometimes in pairs. Sigursdottir orchestrated the sorties, reacting to airborne reconnaissance intel offered by either Milgrom or Blunt.

The Ice King didn't appear to tire, but the law of diminishing returns set in. More and more dramatic stunts were required from the Marines to spark retaliation from the gargantuan crab. It was growing wise to their ruses.

Then, perhaps inevitably, the Marines started taking casualties.

Fakhouri was the first.

No one could be quite sure what happened to her. No one saw. Fakhouri was on her own, hatching some new scheme for attracting the Ice King's attention. There were spurts of gunfire, followed by a scream that was cut short.

Fakhouri!

"Fakhouri!"

The other Marines called for her, both aloud and via commplant. She didn't answer.

"Fuck," said Milgrom eloquently. "Fuck the fucking fucker."

At Fakhouri's last known position they found a footbridge broken in two, and blood. Blood on the bridge. Blood in the water. Much too much blood.

Reyes was next. She and Cully had been dispatched to set up a perimeter around the largest remaining intact section of the township, a pair of medium-sized apartment domes. Sigursdottir intended to use this area as a last refuge, a redoubt they could retreat to if – more likely *when* – Mazu became dangerously unstable. Explosive charges could be remote detonated to sever the section's ties to the rest of the township and isolate it. That way, should Mazu sink, it wouldn't drag this makeshift life raft down with it.

Reyes was underwater, attaching one set of charges to the end of a footbridge. Cully was on lookout duty. Both she and Reyes had an amplified lung capacity and an enhanced oxygen capture efficiency rate. They could hold their breath for three minutes with little difficulty.

Reyes was due to come up for air when Cully noticed that the sea had taken on a strange, unnatural texture. It had developed a kind of turbid smoothness, like a saucepan of water on a rolling boil.

An immense shape passed below. Cully saw the reddish-brown of the Ice King's carapace. It was so close she could make out the bumps and craters that covered it, like the surface of some uncolonised desert planet.

Then it was gone, and she waited for Reyes to show her face. She gave her a full minute, knowing that, in emergency,

Reyes was just about capable of staying submerged for that extra length of time.

Then she dived in.

Reyes was easy to find.

At least, half of Reyes was.

She was clinging to the underside of the footbridge, arms hooked over the support braces.

From the waist down, however, she was gone. The Ice King had sliced her in two while she had been dangling there. Cully imagined Reyes holding herself as still as possible, hoping against hope that the Ice King would not spot her.

Already, fish were collecting around Reyes's entrails and wriggling up into her stomach cavity.

Cully scrambled back out onto the footbridge and vomited copiously. Then she announced the news of Reyes's death over the commplant link and described the grisly circumstances involved.

Sigursdottir had only cold comfort for everyone.

Ice King's getting wilier. Sneakier. We need to be even more vigilant than before. Can't let our guard down for a second.

She instructed Cully to continue laying the charges but not take any unnecessary risks while doing so. Cully assented, and Dev could only admire her bravery. Agreeing to carry on the work that had just cost her colleague her life...

With over an hour left before the *Astounding*'s scheduled arrival, Blunt became the Ice King's next victim.

She was struggling to keep control of her hoverdrone, concentrating on her commplant rather than on her surroundings.

That was how the Ice King was able to catch her unawares.

The gargantuan crab rose up under the esplanade she

was standing on. The impact fractured sheet steel and sent Blunt hurtling several metres into the air. She landed in the water, and as soon as she surfaced and orientated herself, she started swimming.

The Ice King reached for her with the very tip of one pincer and managed to snare her leg just above the knee. The act had a kind of delicacy, like taking hold of a single strand of hair with a pair of tweezers.

Blunt felt herself being pulled back, reeled in. She swung round and emptied an entire clip from her sidearm into the pincer.

When that had no appreciable effect – not that she had thought it would – she unclipped a Ninety-Nine Point Nine from her belt, just as Francis had done. She resolved to sell herself dearly to the Ice King, copying the example of her comrade and very close friend.

Perhaps the Ice King saw this coming. Perhaps it remembered all too clearly the pain Francis had inflicted on it.

Its solution was to release Blunt – by snipping clean through her leg.

Blunt clambered out of the water, shivering with shock, numbed. That was how Dev and Milgrom found her a minute later, after she had sent out a distress call.

Den tourniqueted the stump of Blunt's leg with a strip of fabric torn from his tunic, while Milgrom administered a shot of fentanyl citrate to anaesthetise her. They carried her to the plaza of the central dome, where Handler draped a polyimide thermal blanket over her which he had requisitioned from a nearby hardware store. She lay beside Jiang, who remained unconscious.

Sigursdottir removed her helmet to scrub a hand back and forth over her hair, which was plastered to her scalp by sweat and rain. She delivered a sour assessment of the situation.

"Four down, an hour to go, and the Ice King's messing with us. Bastard's figured out how to get to us. It's picking us off one by one, and it knows there's not a thing we can do to stop it."

"Putting a positive spin on that," said Dev, "the Holy Crabbiness isn't going anywhere in a hurry. It's having too much fun now. It's got into the game."

"In other words, we've succeeded."

"A bit too well. Hooray for us."

"You said your Tritonian pals are fetching reinforcements."

"I said they said they'd try."

"No sign of them so far."

Dev raised his hands and let them drop. "It wasn't a definite. Maybe they can't find anyone, or maybe Tritonians are a great deal smarter than us and can't see the attraction in making themselves bait for a vast murderous crustacean."

"The novelty's sure as shit wearing off for me," said Milgrom, with a sombre glance at the space where Blunt's leg ought to have been.

Sigursdottir was about to reply when the entire dome reverberated like a gong. Something had struck it from below.

"No prizes for guessing who that was," she said.

The dome resounded again, the plaza floor shuddering. A geodesic panel fell from the roof and shattered nearby into a thousand fragments of polycarbonate.

"Right. The Ice King's located us. We fall back to the redoubt."

Cully, those charges set yet?

Cully confirmed that she had just finished placing the final one.

We're on our way.

Milgrom scooped up Blunt, cradling her in her arms as though she were a child. Dev hoisted Jiang onto his back in a piggyback. She lay against him, head lolling on his shoulder, dead weight. Light enough to carry, though, even for someone without Milgrom's modified musculature.

The dome shook a third time, and the plaza floor erupted upwards. The tip of a pincer smashed through from below, accompanied by a liberal spray of seawater.

Sigursdottir took point, followed by Handler, then Dev and Milgrom with their respective loads.

"That exit ahead," she said. "Then the second dome along."

The Ice King widened the hole it had created, working its claw round, crumbling the edges. Water sluiced across the floor like combers rolling in over a beach. The humans found themselves suddenly wading shin-deep in ocean. They slogged on towards the exit, while the dome screeched around them as if in protest, objecting to the indignities being perpetrated on it by the Ice King.

The pincer enlarged the hole to the point where it could fit through unimpeded. The Ice King reached inside the dome, probing. Its claw crashed against street furniture, lampposts, a shopfront, café tables, as it groped blindly around.

When it failed to find any prey to latch onto, the Ice King withdrew its arm, then punched more holes in the base of the dome.

All at once the plaza was flooded from end to end. Water boiled up, engulfing the shattered remnants of what had been, until a couple of minutes ago, a tidy, well-ordered communal space.

The dome tipped at a sharp angle just as Dev, Handler and the Marines arrived at the doors that led outside. They began sliding backwards, downhill. They scrabbled for purchase, battling to stay upright.

Milgrom stuck out a leg to catch Sigursdottir as she

went slithering past. She booted her commanding officer unceremoniously back up to the door. Sigursdottir clutched on to the handle and swung the door open.

Handler hauled himself through. Dev went next, bent forward, knock-kneed, back flat in order to maintain his balance and stop Jiang tumbling off him.

The group scurried around the dome's perimeter walkway, leaning to compensate for the acute angle it now lay at. They veered off onto the first available footbridge, which was raised out of the water at one end. They slip-skidded down to the other side.

Behind them, the main dome sank ponderously thunderously under the waves. The footbridge they had just crossed snapped in two, as did all the other footbridges radiating off the dome.

Now Mazu had lost its core, its epicentre, its nucleus, and the township became an agglomeration of loosely connected components. These began to detach and drift apart, driven away from one another by the bludgeoning force of the storm.

> Cully, get ready. Soon as we reach you, blow
> all the charges.

Even as Sigursdottir gave the order, the group came within sight of the redoubt. They crossed an outdoor recreation area, a section of town that was flat as a lilypad, holding multiple-purpose games courts, a children's playground and a climbing wall. They didn't know whether the Ice King was chasing them. It didn't really matter. Mazu was succumbing, the entire structure in its death throes. They weren't running *from* anything, they were running towards the only place left to run to.

The instant they were across the footbridge to the nearer of the two apartment domes, Cully transmitted the detonation command. As one, the charges blew, disconnecting the two domes from everything around them.

Now this barbell-shaped remnant of Mazu was all they had left. It was where they would, if necessary, make their final stand against the Ice King.

61

SIGURSDOTTIR DIDN'T LET them rest even for a moment.

"We commandeer one of the higher apartments. Use that as our base."

An outside staircase provided access to the dome's narrowing tiers of residential accommodation. On the topmost level, they arrived at a locked door.

"I've got a size seven key," said Sigursdottir, kicking it down.

They piled into a two-bedroom penthouse apartment with a curved balcony.

Cully took up lookout position on the balcony. Dev dumped Jiang onto a bed. Milgrom did likewise with Blunt.

Outside, everything was cacophony. The howl of the storm was interspersed with ear-splitting wails and shrieks as Mazu was torn asunder by the driving wind and waves. Inside, crockery and glassware rattled on shelves, furniture legs drummed on the floor, windows shook in their frames.

Sigursdottir cast a solemn, appraising eye over the two injured Marines.

"Jiang's probably got a cerebral oedema," she said. "Only reason anyone'd be out for so long. Blunt looks stable but the blood loss will have been severe. These two need proper medical attention, not whatever we can rustle up from our first aid kits. If the *Astounding* doesn't get here soon..."

"If the *Astounding* doesn't get here soon," Handler said, "we're all dead anyway, so it won't make a difference."

"It'll come. Captain Maddox won't let us down."

"I'm not one for speeches –" Dev began.

"Could've fooled me," Milgrom butted in. "I don't think I've met anyone who finds it as hard to keep their trap shut as you do."

"Conceded. I just want to say, though, that you've done everything you can, all of you, and you've done it well. I've been part of teams before. I served with some of the best and brightest during the war. Some real dunderheads as well, but that's another story. You guys have been outstanding. If we die today –"

"Seriously, give it a rest, Harmer. Save the schmaltz for some other time. We're not going to die today."

"All evidence to the contrary," Handler muttered.

"I'm with Milgrom," said Sigursdottir. "If you want a group hug moment, you're shit out of luck. We've still got a job to do, and it isn't over until it's over."

Dev shrugged. "Well, that's me shot down in flames. All I was trying to do was boost morale. From now on I'll keep my *proud-to-have-known-you* sentiments to myself."

"When you're around Marines, that would be advisable. Milgrom? Hoverdrone up, please."

"On it, lieutenant. Juice is running low, though. Flying in the storm."

"I don't suppose I'm included in that 'well done, all of you,' am I?" said Handler as the two Marine officers departed from the room.

"Don't suppose you are, Mishandler."

Handler's lip curled. "A new nickname."

"I give them to people I dislike sometimes, as well as people I like."

"For the umpteenth time, I haven't done anything wrong. I was only following ISS protocol. I contacted central office for instructions as soon as the growth vat flagged up problems with your host form. They pointed me in the direction of the nucleotide serum."

"And you applied the first dose before I was even was installed?"

"Yes. I'll admit to that. But again, it was protocol. Maddox was quite clear that the serum needed to be put to work as soon as possible. The cellular breakdown had already begun while the host form was still in the vat. The sooner we started retarding it, the better."

"Wait, what did you just say?"

"I said, the sooner we started retarding it…"

"No. Before that. Did you say *Maddox* was quite clear?"

Handler looked flustered, but realised he couldn't deny it. He'd uttered the name loud and clear. "Yes."

"Captain Arkady Maddox?"

"Who else?"

"What was he doing giving you advice about the serum?"

"Well," said Handler, "he's the one I got it from."

"Whoa, whoa, whoa," said Dev. "It wasn't supplied by ISS? It wasn't something you had handy at the outpost?"

"No. Nothing of the sort. Central office told me the outpost wasn't equipped to deal with the problem with your host form, but they knew through back channels that there was a potential solution locally. The serum. It just so happened Maddox had some."

"It just so happened," Dev echoed.

"Yes. It's… It's something the military have been trialling, apparently. A battlefield remedy for fatigue and injury. A way of repairing troops and keeping them going longer, extending their usefulness in combat situations."

"So they can fight on even when riddled with bullet holes."

"Something like that. Central office instructed me to approach Maddox about it. He had a batch of the serum at Station Ares, and he shipped it over by delivery drone within an hour of my requesting it, pretty much."

"Why didn't you mention this before?" Dev said, voice hollow with exasperation.

"It didn't seem relevant," Handler replied lamely.

"Didn't seem – ! You were pumping me full of some crap the military are *trialling*, and you didn't think to tell me that at any point? You didn't think to tell me that you'd got it from Maddox, either. All of this just somehow slipped your mind?"

"No, not exactly."

"What, then?"

"Well... Maddox suggested I shouldn't."

"Shouldn't...?"

"Tell you where the serum originated. He assured me it would work, but he felt you wouldn't take kindly to the idea that it came from a source other than ISS. Your psych evaluation seemed to back him up, in that respect. Given that you're a war veteran and that you were severely wounded in combat, your trust in the military infrastructure might be... coloured by experience."

"And you went along with that?"

"We've already established that Captain Maddox is a hard man to say no to," said Handler.

"This is the absolute truth?" Dev insisted. "You're not bullshitting me?"

"Why would I lie? Now of all times?"

"Repeat it in Tritonese." Dev switched to the other language. You have been giving me an experimental medicine obtained from those whose concern is defeating others.

I have, said Handler.

And you had no reason to suspect it wasn't exactly what you were told it was?

Why would I? Orders are orders. I obeyed them to the letter.

"Shit," Dev said, as the revelation sank in. "All along I've been a lab rat."

"I'm afraid so. And I've been the scientist in the white coat. It simply never occurred to me that the serum could be anything but beneficial. I honestly believed I was helping you. Perhaps I should have had my doubts, but I'm not by nature a suspicious person."

No, thought Dev. *No. You're a good little employee, that's all. A trusting drone. Mindlessly following your directives. The perfect pawn.*

"I think," he said, "that I may owe you an apology."

"I think," said Handler, "that we're both owed one. The question is, by whom? ISS or the Marine Corps?"

"Either. Both. I wouldn't hold my breath waiting for it, though."

"You've convinced the serum was causing the symptoms you had? The bleeding, the hives, and so forth?"

"I am, but there's only one way to find out for sure."

"Which is?"

"Confront Maddox."

"Rather you than me." Handler gave a shudder that was almost completely mimed, but only almost.

A shout came from Milgrom in the living room. "People, we have company. Big, shelly company."

"The Ice King cometh," said Handler. "Oh, joy."

Dev half laughed. "A wisecrack. Not bad. You're starting to get the hang of gallows humour. Before now you'd just have been blubbering."

"If the past couple of days have taught me anything, it's how to cope with threats to my life. For that I have you to thank."

"All part of the service."

The ISS liaison's mouth turned down at the corners. "There's a part of me that wishes I'd never had this experience. But on balance I'm glad I have."

Dev clapped him on the back. "Join the club. Now let's go and face our certain doom."

62

THE THREE MARINES were out on the balcony.

The Ice King was forging a path through the disintegrating township. It shouldered aside wrecked modules and pontoons with its carapace, swimming with monstrous, implacable grace towards the redoubt.

"This is it," said Cully. "We have bullets, knives, grenades and a bad attitude, and none of them are going to stop that son of a bitch."

"I've got an idea," Dev said. "Something we can try. A last-ditch effort. But Milgrom, you're not going to like it."

"Does it involve you going down there and getting torn apart by pincers?"

"Nope."

"Then I don't like it. But let's hear it anyway."

"How much weight could your hoverdrone carry?"

"Don't know. It's built for flight, not freight. Maybe a kilo or so."

"Cully, any of those high-ex charges left?"

"A couple. Why? Ohhh. I get it."

"Nice," said Milgrom, nodding approval.

She summoned her hoverdrone down until it was within

arm's reach. Its spinning rotor fans whirred almost silently, blurry like a hummingbird's wings.

"Attach the charges here," she told Cully, pointing to the machine's underside.

Cully complied. The cuboid charges adhered automatically, a surface layer of covalent smart-bond material fusing with the hoverdrone's graphene-nickel composite casing.

The hoverdrone arose once more, less agile and more cumbersome in the air now that it was weighed down with a cargo of explosive.

"Detonators are primed," Cully said. "Just say when."

"Bye-bye, birdie," said Milgrom as the hoverdrone swooped towards the Ice King.

"Aim for the mouth," Dev said.

"Dunno about 'aim,' right now, but sure. Not an eye?"

"It's got a spare of those. The mouth's harder to penetrate, but it's got to be soft and vulnerable inside, hasn't it? We're not going to be able to kill the Ice King this way, but we're definitely going to be able to show it who's boss."

"Or just piss it off even more," said Sigursdottir.

"So we're off its birthday party list. Who cares? As long as we buy ourselves a little more time."

Under Milgrom's mental guidance, the hoverdrone matched its pace to the Ice King's.

"Wait..." said Dev. "Wait 'til it pokes its face out of the water."

"What if it doesn't?" said Cully.

"Oh, it will," Dev said, unholstering the hypervelocity pistol.

He took aim and fired several sabot rounds at the front of the approaching Ice King.

The monster reared up, as if offended. It raised its pincers aloft, great segmented towers of chitin and muscle.

Dev fired further rounds directly at its mouth until the HVP's magazine ran dry.

Mandibles flared in outrage.

"Now, Milgrom! Go!"

The hoverdrone dived clumsily for the exposed opening and bumped into one of the mouth parts. Quick as a flash, the Ice King caught hold of it.

"Motherfucker!" Milgrom growled.

"Never mind," said Dev. "That's close enough. Cully, do it."

Cully narrowed her eyes, and the hoverdrone erupted in a blazing ball of flame.

The explosion evaporated the whole of one mandible, reduced another to shreds, and put cracks in a couple more.

The Ice King let out that earthquake scream again. It recoiled, lumbering backwards. It pawed at its mouth with a pincer, like a dog with a thorn in its muzzle.

"Yeah!" Milgrom whooped. "That's what you get when you mess with the Marines!" She slapped Dev on the back so hard he was briefly winded. "Nice work, fishface. I like your style."

"And I like my ribcage all in one piece," Dev replied, choking.

"So we've delayed the inevitable by a few minutes," Handler said as the Ice King sank back into the sea. "What now?"

"A couple of hundred years ago," Cully said, "this is when people would have started praying, begging God for a miracle."

Sigursdottir scanned the horizon. "The *Astounding*'s the nearest we're going to get to one – and there's still no sign of it."

"Come on, Ethel," Dev murmured under his breath. "If you're going to come through for us, now would be the time."

The Ice King didn't stay under for long. It returned to the redoubt in fury, launching itself headlong at the apartment dome where the humans were holed up – the humans who had caused it so much frustration and suffering. Its mutilated mandibles waved in ghastly, spidery semaphore as it propelled itself out of the water and began clambering up the side of the dome.

Under its weight the dome began to tilt steeply and sink. Dev, Handler and the Marines fell against the balcony's parapet. Windows shattered, glass spraying outwards. Items of furniture tumbled through the shard-fringed frames.

All they could see was the Ice King's loathsome, disfigured face, rising towards them. Those eyes, burning with hungry malevolence. Those mouth parts, the remaining mandibles now reaching for them...

63

AND THEN THE Ice King halted.

It had them at its mercy; it could have plucked them off the balcony one by one like chocolates from a selection box.

But it seemed to be having second thoughts.

As if something had distracted it.

It shrank back a few metres.

Then, abruptly, it spun sideways, plunging with purpose towards the sea.

The dome righted itself, screeching and shuddering, sending Dev and the others rolling backwards across the balcony over a carpet of window fragments. All of them picked up cuts, scrapes and bruises. All of them, nonetheless, were glad – and surprised – to be alive.

"What just happened?" said Cully.

Dev hauled himself to his knees and shuffled to the parapet to peer over.

At first, all he could see was the Ice King thrashing about in the raging sea. The gargantuan crab was turning this way and that and lashing out, as though it had gone mad and was trying to fight the syzygy storm itself.

Then he spied movement in the water around the monster.

There were large shapes flitting to and fro, darting in and out of range, besieging the Ice King.

"Submarines," he said. "Tritonian subs."

Twenty – thirty – no, fifty or more – he couldn't keep a count of them – scores of craft – were beleaguering the behemoth from all sides. A host of the living vessels were executing a loosely coordinated campaign of attack.

They went for the Ice King's legs, its rear, its underside. Wherever it wasn't facing, wherever it couldn't see them, that was where they zipped in.

They pummelled, stung, bit, rammed, slashed, butted, barged, slapped, each sub using whatever offensive attributes nature had kitted it out with. None made so much as a dent in the Ice King's thickly armour-plated hide, but it felt them. It felt every blow and nip and thump, and it swivelled, desperate to catch its assailants and punish them.

The subs retreated every time it spun their way, however, and others seized the opportunity to zoom in and harass the Ice King on its blind side. The Ice King shook its claws and waggled its legs, like it was trying to fend off a swarm of wasps.

Some it swatted. Its pincer arms, more by luck than judgement, struck several of the subs. Here, there, a fatally injured vessel rolled over and over in agony near the surface, or spiralled limply down out of sight.

Dev looked for Ethel's manta. There were a number of ray-like creatures among the attacking horde, and they were too distant and moving too swiftly for him to spot which, if any, had a ruptured cockpit cornea.

There was a manta, however, which appeared to be bolder and more determined than any of the others. It was setting an example, hammering the Ice King persistently with its wings and withdrawing to safety only at the very last possible moment.

He decided, with a certainty that was based on gut feeling as much as the evidence of his eyes, that it was Ethel. It had to be – could only be – her.

"Well, spank me with a paddle and call me Maurice," said Milgrom, shaking her head in incredulity. "It's the sea monkey navy, sailing to the rescue. Right in the nick of time."

"The *what* navy?" Dev said.

"All right, Tritonian. Happy?"

"Ecstatic."

"And that wasn't an offer, by the way. The spanking-with-a-paddle thing. Don't be getting ideas."

"It never occurred to me that it was, until now. Now I can't *stop* getting ideas."

"You'd never be so lucky."

"'Lucky' isn't the word I'd –"

> – you receiving me? I repeat, this is the *Astounding*. We've patched our comms into an open-channel frequency in this area. We believe it is being used by a team of Marines under the command of Lieutenant Eydís Sigursdottir. If so, please respond.

"It's them," Cully declared. "I don't believe it. It's them!" Sigursdottir responded:

> Reading you loud and clear. This is Lieutenant Sigursdottir. State your position.

The voice from the *Astounding* came back with the news none of them had thought they would live to hear.

> Estimating your location by signal strength, we're ten minutes out. What is your status?

Sigursdottir gave a succinct précis of the situation, emphasising that immediate retrieval would be welcome.

> Understood, lieutenant.

She added:

> We also have your mission objective, right in
> front of us. Do you have payload prepped and
> ready to deliver?

The *Astounding* replied in the affirmative.
Sigursdottir said:

> You're already within range. We can attempt
> evac unaided, but we have injured. Please
> advise.

Silence from the Marine hydrofoil, a silence that spoke of option-weighing and decision-making.

"Are you really asking them to lob a Sunbaker right at us?" Dev said.

Sigursdottir shrugged. "It may be their best and only chance. The Ice King's here, cornered, corralled. Targeting'll be simple. All they have to do is program the *Astounding*'s gun to lock in on our signal source and calculate the appropriate firing solution."

"Giving us fuck-all time to get to minimum safe distance?"

"Nobody said soldiering was easy."

"And what about the Tritonians? The ones who've, let's not forget, just pulled our fat from the fire? You're not going to leave them to get incinerated along with the Ice King, surely."

"It's out of my hands."

The next voice that came over their commplants was a familiar one.

> Lieutenant Sigursdottir, this is Captain
> Maddox. I understand you have a visual on
> this so-called Ice King.

Sigursdottir confirmed it:

> It's a couple of hundred metres from our
> current position. We've kept it here as long as
> we could, in anticipation of your arrival.

Maddox sounded satisfied:

> Excellent work. Commendable. You realise
> I'm faced with a difficult choice, of course.
> The creature cannot be allowed to continue to
> roam unchecked. By your own admission, you
> lost track of it once already. Who's to say that
> might not happen again?

Sigursdottir glanced round at her fellow Marines. Neither Milgrom nor Cully would meet her gaze.

> That's an affirmative, sir. We realise what
> you're saying. We appreciate the candour.

Again, Maddox sounded satisfied.

> I knew you would. I'm registering Harmer's
> commplant ID on this channel.
>
> I'm here, Maddox. Alive and kicking.
>
> Delighted to hear it. Sigursdottir's last report had

you missing, whereabouts unknown. Tell me, in
your professional opinion as an ISS operative,
has there been Polis Plus activity on Triton?

That's not really important right now. What's
important is —

For the record, Harmer. I need to know. Are
Polis Plus behind the insurgency? Do you have
conclusive proof that the digimentalists have
been carrying out covert operations on this
planet?

I wouldn't call it conclusive, but the balance of
probabilities suggests so. The Ice King itself is,
I reckon, a Plusser construct, animated by an
installed Plusser sentience.

Would you swear to that?

I don't see how it matters. At the moment, the
priority is killing the fucking thing.

I'm going to have to push you. Yes or no?

All right. Yes. It's the Plussers. Now listen.
Before you let the Sunbaker fly, you have to
give me, Handler and your Marines time to
clear the area. All I'm asking is five minutes'
grace.

"How do we get far enough away in five minutes?" said
Sigursdottir. "Maybe if we had a boat. But we don't."

"Same way we got away from the Ice King after it downed
the *Admiral Winterbrook*," Dev said. "Hitch a ride on the
back of a Tritonian sub. I can arrange that. I just have to
persuade Maddox to hold off from firing long enough."

Five minutes would give the Ice King the
chance to get away too, Harmer. I'm afraid I
can't allow that. Can't take the risk.

This is crazy. You're not only going to kill us,
you're going to kill about a hundred Tritonians
as well.

Indigene casualties I can live with. Collateral
damage. The rest… is a matter of regret, to be
sure. But you were a soldier once, Harmer. You'll
know about sacrifice and the greater good.

That's bullshit, Maddox. You're signing a death
warrant for a hundred-plus people. It's too
high a price to pay just to eliminate the Ice
King. There's another way. We both know that.
There must be.

It's the burden of rank to have to make tough
calls. I want it to be known, Harmer, that you
have done a sterling job. And you, Lieutenant
Sigursdottir – Eydís – you and your team
have served with distinction. I'm committing
this conversation to commplant memory,
for posterity's sake. A transcript will go on
your service records, and you will all gain
posthumous citations for your actions here
today, I promise you that.

Maddox, you fucking lunatic! Don't do this!

Let's not besmirch the moment with name-
calling, Harmer. I'm signing off now. In a
minute or so, the Sunbaker will be on its way.
Kindly make your peace with that fact.

No!

But Dev was hurling the word into the void. Maddox had
disconnected. He was gone.

Dev looked round at Sigursdottir.

"A shell travels at five hundred metres per second," he
said. "If the *Astounding* is ten minutes away, that's, what,

fifteen kilometres. Meaning thirty seconds from launch to impact. Add another thirty seconds, say, to deliver and confirm the go command, and approximately a minute for the artillery officer to input the firing solution and elevate and rotate the cannon."

"Two minutes max," said Sigursdottir. "Even on a Tritonian sub, we'd still be within blast radius. But," she added, "*you* won't."

"Huh?"

"You and Handler. And the Tritonians. Anyone with gills. You can dive. Dive deep. The water will protect you, cushion you. It'll absorb the force of the explosion better than air does. On the surface none of us stands a chance, but under, you just might."

"Who'll keep the Ice King on the spot, if the Tritonians all go? Who's to say it won't chase after us as we dive?"

"That'll be our business," said Milgrom. "Face it, we're fucked whatever. You and Handler, get to the Tritonians and tell them to skedaddle. We'll take care of the rest."

"And Jiang? Blunt?"

"They're lucky," said Sigursdottir. "They'll never know what hit them."

Dev flicked his gaze from Sigursdottir to Cully, then to Milgrom.

Their minds were made up. They were resigned, stoical.

Good soldiers.

In that instant, he despised Captain Maddox. More than he had ever despised anyone.

"Guys…"

"Go!" Milgrom barked. "Get your bony backsides into the water! Now!"

64

DEV AND HANDLER dashed-stumbled-leapt down the stairs.

Reflexively, Dev reset his countdown timer yet again. Another rough estimate. Another lethal deadline.

00:01:30

Out from the foot of the staircase.

Diving into the water, into the thick of the battle between the Tritonians and the Ice King.

00:01:17

Spread the word, Dev told Handler. Make it clear to them that if they don't get out of here this instant, they're ashes.

Handler went one way, Dev the other. Over and over they beamed the message. To every Tritonian in every eye socket cockpit they saw, they delivered the warning and told them to pass it on.

Gradually, but picking up pace, the Tritonians spread the word, flickering from one to the next like signal fires.

00:01:02

Dev swam round the ring of subs, battling through turmoil of cross-currents and vortexes, thanks to the frantically gyrating bulk of the Ice King.

There!

00:00:59

Ethel's manta. He kicked hard, digging deep, finding every last erg of energy he had.

Descend! he flared at her. Descend or die!

She picked up on the fear, the sheer burning urgency of the statement.

00:00:52

Dev crawled to the surface for one last look.

He was just in time to see Milgrom leap from the penthouse balcony onto the Ice King's back, a thirty-metre drop.

The huge Marine broke her leg as she landed, but didn't let it stop her. She staggered upright, pulled a gun and emptied it into the Ice King's carapace. She was singing, howling, screaming, swearing, all at once, a barely coherent berserker caterwaul of defiance and hate.

More bullets rained down onto the Ice King from Sigursdottir and Cully on the balcony.

00:00:47

Dev took it all in at a glance. His last abiding image of Milgrom was her hobbling across the Ice King, dragging a leg with a shattered tibia, like a wounded Amazon warrior queen making her final, fatal stand against some mythical monster.

He ducked back under, to find Ethel's manta waiting for him.

Don't just float there, she said. Grab on!

Dev seized hold of the nearer of the manta's cephalic lobes, and the sub flipped up its tail, and down they went.

00:00:39

Down, with a motley school of other subs beside them.

Down, like a storm, like hail.

00:00:27

Down from light to thickening darkness, and Dev had no idea how far they would have to go to escape the Sunbaker's blistering, multimillion-degree incandescence, how much water they needed to put behind them so as not to get flash-fried...

00:00:15

The manta beat its wings. Dev felt pressure mounting in his ears.

00:00:08

From photic zone to aphotic. From bathyal realm to abyssal.

00:00:03

He pictured the fusion warhead shell in flight, and Sigursdottir, Cully and Milgrom now able to hear it coming, the projectile hurtling through the air with a noise like reality being ripped in two. Inside, the seed of a miniature star, waiting to be born.

00:00:02

He pictured the three Marines looking up, knowing their lives were measured in a handful of seconds, and all the while Jiang and Blunt lay indoors, unconscious, cocooned in blissful ignorance.

00:00:01

Everything was black around him now, apart from the lights of Tritonian faces, near and far, photophores ablaze with unrestrained panic.

00:00:00

Nothing.

No explosion.

No glare of brilliance from above.

Maybe he had underestimated the length of time it would take to launch the Sunbaker.

Maybe Maddox had thought better of it, rescinded the order.

Maybe –

Then it came.

The undersea world turned magnesium white.

Every sub was limned with silver, given a glowing halo.

Every detail of every one of the giant sea creatures' bodies was picked out in sharp, pristine relief. The sucker on a tentacle, the fluted ribbing on a fin, the join between shell plates.

It was as though Dev was seeing it all in freeze frame, a snapshot of a terrified downward stampede.

Then came the pressure wave.

Appalling.

Deafening.

Cataclysmic.

65

LATER – DAZED BUT recovering – they felt able to speak again.

Is it dead? said Ethel.

Has to be, said Dev. Nothing could have survived that.

They were cruising along at a subdued, fragile pace, the manta rising through the ocean at a shallow incline. Other subs accompanied them. They had no particular destination. They were heading just anywhere, anywhere that took them away from ground zero and the spreading cloud of lightly irradiated seawater left behind by the Sunbaker.

Good riddance, said the kid. Fuck the Ice King and fuck everything it stood for.

I think there are plenty of Ice King worshippers who'd agree with that, said Ethel. Some of them are out there right now, beside us.

She indicated the flotilla of subs.

You brought insurgents to help you fight it? said Dev. You managed to turn them against their own god? Wonders will never cease.

It wasn't hard, said the kid. Dozens of them were there when the Ice King attacked the drift cluster. It was a turning point for them, as it was for me. They felt baffled and betrayed, and that feeling transformed into anger quickly enough.

The Ice King's error of judgement had cost it dearly, Dev thought. A single act of random divine cruelty had made apostates out of acolytes. Veneration had become vengeance.

Disgruntled, disillusioned, the insurgents had realised they'd been following a false idol, and had all too happily agreed to tear it down.

I'm just amazed you found so many willing bodies in so little time, he said.

We were fortunate, said Ethel. Another drift cluster passed nearby the spot where the Ice King had struck. Refugees from the ruined drift cluster were taken in by the inhabitants of the other one. The insurgents who'd witnessed the event were there too.

They were only too eager to tell everyone how the Ice King had gone mad, the kid said. They were already trying to distance themselves from it. They had no way of justifying what it had done.

The god they'd been waiting for so long, Dev said, the god whose return was supposed to usher in an age of freedom for your people... is actually a bit of a dick.

Dark blue laughter from both Ethel and the kid.

And now that it's an ex-god, Dev said, what next? What happens to the insurgency?

I don't know, said Ethel. The same issues remain, the same complaints and grudges. You ungilled are still here and you don't look like you're leaving any time soon. It could all boil up again.

Don't forget we fought side by side with you against the Ice King, Dev said. Seven good people — ungilled — died up there to make sure that monster got what it deserved.

Ethel shone lilac-white sympathy at him. So, too, did the kid.

That will count in your favour, she said. Definitely.

As will the fact that it was ungilled who provided the means to kill the Ice King, the kid said.

We'll make sure all of that becomes public knowledge, said Ethel. We'll broadcast it far and wide. Everyone in the Nautilus Movement will know and will tell others.

Everyone in the insurgency too, said the kid.

No guarantees, but we'll do what we can on our side to smooth relations out.

I'll do what I can as well on our side, Dev said. So will our ambassador — assuming he was able to get away from the explosion unscathed.

You did.

Yes, but I have previous form with this sort of thing. I'm more used to life-and-death situations than he is. Also, I had help from you.

Perhaps he, like you, managed to get taken aboard a sub at the last minute.

I hope so.

You don't dislike him anymore, I see.

I made a mistake. He was keeping secrets from me, but he was cowed into doing it. It'd be wrong to hold that against him. There are other people who've got a lot more to answer for. One person in particular.

Who?

Someone you've no wish to meet, Dev said. But someone I myself would very much like to see again. Soon.

The manta swam on, upward into lightening, life-filled waters.

Dev turned to the kid.

Tell me something, he said. How's that name of yours coming along?

I think I have it.

The kid sent out a display of colours. As before, it was a blend of frustration, regret, and guilt, but the optimism in it was stronger and the mixture as a whole was different, richer, more resonant. More fitting. It was a name that had been hard-won, a lesson learned through bitter experience.

Yeah, Dev said. That's you.

Ethel, likewise, felt the kid had earned it. We each get the name we deserve, she said. The name that life gives us. I wish I knew what yours was, ungilled.

It's impossible to translate, Dev said. Ungilled names don't tend to have any meaning. They only say who you are, not what. They're just convenient labels.

Because I don't have anything to call you, you feel slightly empty to me.

Perhaps that's what I am. A hollow space. An absence. It seems like that sometimes.

Self-pity? From you?

If you only knew what my life was like...

A perpetual traveller. A wisp of binary data dancing from one host form to the next. Never resting, never alighting anywhere for long. Swept from world to world with no say over the where or the why. Lured along by the dim, distant promise of one day being fully himself again, master of his own existence.

But no, you're right, he said. Self-pity. Doesn't suit me.

It shouldn't, Ethel said. You make a difference. Know that.

The kid agreed. I don't understand everything about you. I don't understand why you do what you do. I do understand, though, that you do it with conviction, with your heart.

The sea teemed around them. The manta was up near the surface, and the sky above the waves was no longer a single expanse of tormented grey. Shafts of sunlight were poking through.

Where can we take you? Ethel asked. The least we can do is drop you off at one of your ungilled settlements.

We.

He looked from her to the kid and back again.

He saw, in them, the hope for an undivided future for Triton. Animosities would have to be buried, and that wouldn't be easy.

But here – here was proof that it was possible.

You, he said, can take me to...

66

STATION ARES. NIGHT.

Dev glided out of the oil-black water, close to the axis of the snowflake-shaped Marine base. He loitered on a walkway, shivering slightly in the breeze. Someone was bound to wander by soon.

Someone did. A lone private, plodding along on watch detail.

The instant he caught sight of Dev, he whipped his rifle from patrol ready to on guard.

"Who's that? State your name!"

"Relax," Dev said. "I'm an unarmed civilian." He put his hands up and rotated through a full turn on the spot. The expended HVP and its holster belt had long since been consigned to the ocean. "See?"

"Don't move. I asked you your name."

"I'm here to see Captain Maddox. I would have told him I was coming, but he might not have agreed to make time for me if I had. This way's better."

"The captain is very busy right now."

"I'll bet he is. I'd be obliged if you'd message him anyway. Tell him it's Dev Harmer. Tell him I can wait all night if I have to. Tell him we have things to discuss and we might as well do it now, man to man. Clear the air, as it were."

The private wavered.

"Go on," Dev said. "What do you think your senior CO would say if you failed to report an intruder on the base requesting audience with him? Do you think the fearsome Captain Arkady Maddox would be pleased about that?"

"No. No, I suppose not."

"Just a quick commplant call. Don't forget the name: Dev Harmer."

The private's face blanked for a few seconds. Then he said, "Captain Maddox has asked me to escort you to his quarters. It's this way."

"I know."

A couple of minutes later, Dev was in Maddox's office, across the desk from him.

"You should have called first, Harmer," Maddox said genially. He dismissed the private with a cursory flap of the hand. "Not that I mind you showing up unannounced. I'm concerned, that's all. You could have got yourself shot."

"Lovely that you care. I just thought I'd surprise you. A formal visit might have been harder to arrange. You might have said no."

"Now why would I do that?"

Dev shrugged. "Anything's possible."

"I must say, I *am* surprised, though. I assumed you were..."

"Dead?"

"Well, yes. It did seem likely. Why didn't you report in immediately afterward? Let me know as soon as you could that you were okay?"

"Felt it was a good idea to wait," Dev said. "To break the news in person."

"Not that I'm not pleased. Relieved, too."

"But you'd probably have preferred it if the Sunbaker had got me, like it did your seven Marines."

Maddox's brow creased. "Why do you say that?"

"Because I'm an inconvenience. A loose end. Or rather, I could be."

"What *are* you talking about?" The Marine captain shut off the floatscreen in front of him and rose from his chair. "Let me fix you a drink. I'm sure you could do with one. The past few days have been pretty stressful, eh? They certainly have for me. You wouldn't believe the amount of paperwork I'm having to wade through."

"Poor you."

"Damn straight, poor me. Reports. Letters of condolence. There are about twenty forms I have to fill in, accounting for the use of a Sunbaker. You can't chuck one of those things about and not have to explain in excruciating, mind-numbing detail why. Bureaucracy is the bane of the peacetime warrior. If we were at war, no none would even ask twice whether it had been necessary. Mind you..."

Maddox uncorked the bottle of local rotgut that had knocked Dev sideways the last time he'd been here.

"Military high command back on Earth is fairly excited about the Ice King and all that it implies," he said. "Word is, the top brass and TerCon are treating this as the most serious Border Wall incident since, well, since the Border Wall was drawn up on the map at the Tezuma Conference. The most overt piece of Polis+ aggression yet. Using a bogus incarnation of the indigenes' god in order to foment a rebellion... Sneaky, yet at the same time blatant. As if they thought we wouldn't cotton on."

He half-filled two tumblers with the greasy, greenish liquor.

"But we did, didn't we?" he said. "All thanks to you, Harmer. You with your ISS expertise. You saw through it."

He offered one of the tumblers to Dev, who refused.

"Once bitten," Dev said.

"Sure?"

"Positive."

"Shame. Your loss." Maddox downed both helpings of booze in quick succession. "Ahhh. Just what the doctor ordered."

"It wasn't nucleotides," Dev said.

"Hmmm? What's that?"

"In the serum."

"What are you talking about?"

"Earlier today I stopped off at the ISS outpost on Tangaroa and used the mediplinth to run a full-spec analysis on my host form. It picked up traces of excess lysosome enzymes in my system. Those are enzymes – in case you don't know, although I'm betting you do – that are released by dead and dying cells and cause autolysis. Autolysis literally means self-eating. Cells digesting themselves."

"How fascinating."

"Isn't it? And the net result of an excess of these enzymes is known as sub-lethal damage. Now, it would be possible that these enzymes were a by-product of my host form falling apart – except that according to the mediplinth their DNA isn't a match for my host form's. It's generic-template DNA, the kind that's designed to map onto existing DNA, the kind that forms the basis for every gene-based therapy going. Which suggests that the enzymes were introduced artificially. Externally."

"Via the serum, you mean."

"Simply put, the serum you supplied Handler with was a non-deadly toxin. It wasn't some military wonder drug after all, as you'd had him believe. It wasn't keeping my supposedly compromised host form alive. It was the serum that was compromising me."

"I'm not sure what, if anything, you're hoping to achieve with these accusations," said Maddox. "These, I might add, baseless accusations."

"Somehow," Dev went on, "you managed to tamper with the growth vat so that it registered host form sustainability issues that weren't actually there. It worries me that you were able to do that, but I guess no system is impregnable. You gambled on ISS then instructing Handler to ask for your serum. You poisoned me with that so that I was off my stroke, not thinking straight. Suggestible. Biddable."

Maddox said nothing.

"Knowing that you'd tried to hobble my mission from the outset," Dev said, "got me thinking. What else might you have done? What other little tricks might you have been pulling?"

Maddox sauntered back to his desk, casual as you please.

"For instance," Dev said, "it occurred to me that you'd deliberately selected a team of Marines to go with me who were perhaps not the best at their jobs. A bunch of duds."

"Sigursdottir was an excellent soldier," Maddox snapped. "Milgrom too. All of them. How dare you suggest they weren't."

"Oh, no, absolutely. I couldn't agree more. Ballsy as anything. I rejected the idea immediately. Then I got to thinking bigger. The bigger picture. A grander scheme."

Maddox sat down and began twirling one of the empty tumblers on the desktop with his forefinger.

"Go on," he said. "You're clearly itching to tell me about this 'grander scheme' – some nonsense you've fabricated."

"You had a good war, didn't you, Maddox? I remember you telling me that. Said you loved every minute of it. So what a comedown, to be stationed here, out in the back-end of beyond. Nothing to do all day but keep a watch on the Plussers' comings and goings. No excitement. No challenge. Precious little likelihood of the combat you miss so much."

"You're saying I concocted everything – the insurgency, the Ice King – because I was bored? Is that it? Do you have any idea how preposterous that sounds?"

"Nothing to do with boredom. Love of war. That's the motive. The desire to see hostilities between the Diaspora and Polis Plus reopened. An end to the truce so that we can start all that lovely fighting again."

Maddox's eyes widened briefly, almost imperceptibly. There was something hungry in the micro-expression, a yearning.

"I won't deny that I find the present state of peace... uncomfortable," he said. "The Frontier War was not settled conclusively. We didn't lose, but neither did we win. The Plussers ought to have been annihilated. They were, and remain, an existential threat. What we have now – this uneasy détente – is neither fish nor fowl. A bit like you in that host form."

"'Fish' I'll take, but 'fowl'? That's below the belt." Dev chuckled, mostly because Maddox didn't. "Look, captain, I'll lay it on the line. I don't reckon the Ice King was a Plusser construct after all."

"But you said it was. That's a matter of record. It's gone into my reports. In the informed opinion of an ISS operative, as stated in a commplant dialogue transcript, the huge sea beast was under the control of a Polis Plus sentience. Fact."

"You put me on the spot. I was saying that to keep you sweet, as much as anything."

"You still said it."

"And it wasn't only what you wanted to hear, it was what you needed, so that you could confirm to your superiors that the Plussers had been killing humans and attempting to drive us off Triton. You were using me, like you used Handler. You got me to supply you with a piece of evidence, not much but just enough to make the case that Polis Plus have committed an act that contravenes the peace accord. There's now a – what's the Latin phrase? A *casus belli*. A legitimate reason to start a war, if anyone in TerCon wants to."

Maddox's mouth creased into a slim smile. "This is an awfully complicated web you're saying I've spun. Above all else, it implies that I could somehow, singlehandedly, stir up an insurgency."

"No. That was ongoing already. What you did was exploit it and bolster it, by introducing the Ice King. You gave the insurgents what they craved: a god to put the divine seal of approval on their actions."

"*I* made the Ice King? How?"

"I admit, I was hoping you'd be able to answer that one for me. My best guess is you arranged to have an ordinary, innocent crab transformed by genetic manipulation, boosted to jumbo size."

"Easy to say, but do you know how one would go about doing that? Because I don't. Do I look like a master scientist to you? These ribbon bars on my chest are medals, not PhDs."

"No," said Dev. "Which leads me to an unwelcome conclusion. You're not working alone. You're not the prime mover, just a cog in a much larger machine."

"Hmmph."

Maddox stopped twirling the tumbler. His other hand, Dev noted, was out of sight. Down by one of the desk drawers, if he didn't miss his guess.

Dev tensed. The encounter was playing out as he'd expected, though not as he might have liked.

"Well, I think I've heard enough," Maddox said.

"Enough as in I'm a crank and I'm spouting utter garbage and you want me to leave and never darken your door again?"

"No," said Maddox with a touch of world-weariness. "Enough as in you've figured out just the right amount to pose a danger."

A pistol appeared above the desk.

"You come across as a smartmouthed dimwit, Harmer," he said, cocking the gun, "but beneath the goofy exterior you're shrewd. That's a fairly neat piece of misdirection."

"As was your tumbler-twirling."

"Distracting you with one hand so you won't observe what the other hand is up to. Cunning, eh? The question now is do I shoot you on the spot, or do I think of something cleverer?"

"Shooting me on the spot isn't your best option."

"You would say that."

"No. Think of the mess. The paperwork. You'd have to account to a lot of people for why you put a bullet in me."

"I could say you attacked me. I was defending myself."

"But why would I attack you? Why would I turn up at this base unarmed, let myself be brought to your quarters, all meek and obliging, and then just go nuts and launch myself at you? Also, why shoot me when you're big enough and well-trained enough to incapacitate me bare-handed? It doesn't hold up. It isn't consistent."

"Which is the reason you're not dead already. I mean, you're a loose cannon, but not *that* loose. I'd have too much explaining to do."

"Yeah, the last thing you want right now is to look suspicious. You need to keep your nose super clean. If you killed me for no good reason after this whole Ice King business, someone might come sniffing around, asking awkward questions."

"Oh, I'm going to kill you all right, Harmer. Be under no illusion about that. You don't get to walk away. It's a case of where and when, that's all."

"If you want a suggestion, there's always –"

"Outside, I think," Maddox said. "That would be best."

"Outside. Just what I was going to say."

"By the water's edge."

"Yes, because then you can dispose of the body easily. The sea will swallow the evidence."

"The sea, and what's in the sea."

WORLD OF WATER

"Maybe I was trying to escape from you. You warned me you'd shoot if I ran, and I ignored you and ran, so you shot."

Maddox nodded approvingly. "Excellent. I like it. I was escorting you off the premises. You bolted – I don't know why, you just did. It surprised me. I told you to come back or I'd shoot. You didn't comply."

"*Bang*, and I plop into the water, never to be seen again."

"Much neater that way. Thanks for chipping in. I appreciate the input."

"I never thought I'd be collaborating in covering up my own murder."

"Peace makes strange bedfellows," Maddox said. "Stranger even than war." He gestured at the door with the gun. "Let's go, shall we? Get this over with."

67

THEY WALKED OUT into a brisk breeze and double moonlight. Captain Maddox kept the muzzle of the pistol snugged into Dev's back, staying close to him to keep the gun out of sight. Witnesses would assume Maddox and Dev were simply out for a stroll.

Not that there was anyone. It was late. The great majority of Station Ares's Marines were in bed. And Maddox was familiar with the timing of patrols and their routes, and so was able to avoid them.

"You can spill now, if you like," Dev said. "About the Ice King. Where it came from. How it was made."

"Why should I? What difference will it make?"

"To you? Not much. But to me, to satisfy my own personal curiosity…"

Maddox deliberated. "Well, I can't see that it'd do any harm. Given that five minutes from now you're going to be fish food. The technology is remarkably compact. The starter pack, if you can call it that, is an oval thing not much bigger than a football. A manmade egg."

"Containing a crab embryo and a growth medium."

"Pretty much. I believe the design incorporates elements

reverse-engineered from Plusser tech."

"But to turn an ordinary unborn crab into something of the Ice King's proportions, you'd require a massive energy source. It would have to feed on *something*. A whole lot of something. And where would you hide it while it was growing to maturity?"

"The answer to both questions is Triton's core. It has an energy source in abundance: all that methane clathrate trapped in the ice."

"I see. You dump the 'egg' in the ocean, it sinks to the bottom, then it taps into the methane clathrate to power an accelerated exponential growth."

"Hey presto, in just a few weeks a giant crab is roaming the oceans. The moment the creature is large enough to fend for itself, the 'egg' untethers it, and off it goes, looking for food."

"The pressures on the ocean floor would crush almost any other species, but not a crustacean."

"Especially not one that's been tweaked for extra hardiness."

"And you dropped this so-called starter pack in the sea yourself?"

"I personally supervised an expedition to the Tropics of Lei Gong not long ago. We were on exercises. Routine stuff. All I had to do was slip out on deck one night, make sure no one was around, switch the device on and hoick it overboard."

"Who supplied it?" Dev asked. "That's what enquiring minds really need to know."

"And that's the one thing I cannot – will not – reveal. It's more than my life's worth."

"Oh, come on. Condemned man's request. You can't refuse."

"Seriously," Maddox said. "It's not going to happen."

"Spoilsport."

"All I'm going to say is that there are bigger forces at work than you realise, Harmer. You're right, I'm just a cog in a machine. But what a machine! Powerful interests, some of them much closer to home than you might think. Honestly, you have no idea."

It wasn't just the night air that gave Dev goosebumps then.

"You're saying there's some wider conspiracy at work," he said. "This goes high up."

"You may infer that. I couldn't possibly confirm or deny it."

"Someone important wants the peace accord to collapse. Someone wants us to go to war with the Plussers all over again."

"Is that so hard to believe?" said Maddox. "I'm not the only person who thinks that an enemy that hasn't been totally eradicated is an enemy that hasn't been defeated. Look at it the other way round. Do you imagine that Polis Plus doesn't want the Diaspora gone? Do you think they're not plotting our downfall even as we speak? Shouldn't we be doing the same? That would be prudent at least."

"The war was as huge a drain on the Plussers' resources as it was on ours. They suffered just as much as we did."

"Harmer, Harmer, Harmer. You're not naïve. All these covert shenanigans, all this espionage – you assume it maintains balance, keeps order."

"It does."

"No, it doesn't. It's dress rehearsal, is what it is. Probing. Testing. Intelligence gathering. Preparation for the moment, the *inevitable* moment, when conflict is triggered again."

"Inevitable?"

"Oh, yes. All these potential flashpoints you ISS people visit, these cloak-and-dagger schemes you foil... Don't you see? Surely you do. They're sparks from a flint, and sooner or later one of them is going to ignite the tinder-dry underbrush, and then..."

"Then people like you are going to get the hit you're jonesing for. Frontier War Two, the sequel. 'This time it's for keeps.'"

Maddox snorted, half in amusement, half in contempt. "Joking to the end. I kind of admire you, Harmer. It's almost as though you don't appreciate how hopeless your position is."

They had arrived at the tip of one of the snowflake's arms, beside the field gun emplacement. Waves lapped loudly at Station Ares's structure. Triton's two moons cast double shadows. Twin silhouettes stretched from Dev's feet in a long V, one slightly less dark than the other.

"Hopeless?" he said. "I've got a warmongering maniac with a gun in my back, just about to blow a hole in me and send me to a watery grave. I suppose that is more or less the definition of hopeless. If only I had some cunning get-out plan. An ace up my sleeve."

"But you don't," said Maddox, and then, a fraction less certainly: "Do you?"

"I don't appear to."

"Well then. The Ice King is now just an unhappy memory, a casualty of a phoney war, and you're about to be next. Possibly, if nobody hears the gunshot, I won't even have to make up an excuse about why I killed you. I'll just tell anyone who asks that you came, we chatted, you left, I never saw or heard from you again. That'd be simpler, more conveni –"

He broke off, his last word becoming a guttural huff of air, an involuntary exhalation. It was accompanied by a muffled crackling, the sound of a discharge of electricity.

Maddox slumped to his knees, the pistol dropping from his hand with a clatter. Dev whirled round and scooped up the gun.

There was a whiff of singed uniform fabric, and the scent of burning flesh. Maddox mouthed words at him silently, a look of incomprehension contorting his features.

Behind him stood Xavier Handler, water sheeting off him, a Tritonian shock lance in his hands. Handler's face was contorted too, in pure hatred.

"You played me, you bastard," he hissed. "Lied to me, made me your bitch. How does it feel, now that the tables have been turned? What's it like to have someone stab *you* in the back?"

"Technically that wasn't a stab," Dev pointed out. "That was a jolt."

"Oh, what*ever*," said Handler. "Don't ruin the moment for me."

Maddox tried to turn his head to look round, but his muscles wouldn't function properly.

"A second burst should do it," Handler said. "The lance has recharged. I just want you to know, captain, that you screwed with the wrong person. You tried to kill me with that Sunbaker, kill all of us, as though we were just... just flies. A trivial annoyance. I – we – had done everything you wanted. Then we were surplus to requirements, and *whoosh*. Vaporisation. That's how little other people's lives matter to you, isn't it? We're only here for you to –"

"Handler," Dev cut in. "Xavier. Enough grandstanding. We can't hang about. Someone might come. If you're going to do it, do it."

Handler's brow knitted. He wasn't a natural born killer, or a soldier. He didn't have the instinct or the training to take a life.

What he did have was a grudge so powerful, it was overwhelming.

The shock lance crackled again.

Maddox juddered spastically, then keeled forward, flat on his face.

Dead.

Dev bent down, levered his arms under the corpse like the prongs of a forklift truck, and rolled Maddox into the sea.

He went in with barely a splash, and swiftly sank.

Dev tossed the pistol in after him.

Handler was breathing hard, almost hyper-ventilating. His eyes were starkly wide, his legs trembling.

"Good work," Dev reassured him. "Maddox was a scumbag. You've done us all a favour."

"I know, but..."

"Don't even think about it. It's over. Great timing, too. I swear he was seconds away from pulling the trigger. I was beginning to worry you weren't going to make it."

"No, I was shadowing the pair of you underwater, just like you said. Keeping you in sight. The only problem came when I was climbing out. I was terrified he'd hear me."

"You were the king of stealth."

With a sudden horrified shudder Handler tossed the shock lance aside, into the water.

"I never want to do that again."

"With luck, you'll never have to."

"What was it all about, Harmer? The Ice King, Maddox, everything. What have we been up against? What's it all been in aid of?"

"You're better off not knowing," Dev replied, with feeling. "Even I'm not sure what to put in my final report to ISS – what to include, what to leave out. There's a lot more going on here than meets the eye. I think I'm going to have to be pretty careful what I say to who. As are you."

Maddox: *Powerful interests, some of them much closer to home than you might think.*

"If you insist," Handler said.

"I do. I believe, now, that it wasn't Maddox who tampered with the growth vat at all. Or if it was, he had inside help."

"You don't mean me?"

"Of course not."

"Someone else in ISS?"

"That's what I'm afraid of. That's why we need to watch our step."

"You don't have to worry about me on that score," Handler said with finality. "I'm out. I've had enough." He looked at the patch of water where Dev had consigned Maddox's body. "There's no coming back from what I've just done. I don't belong in the Diaspora anymore."

"That's pretty extreme. What are you going to do? Where are you going to go?"

"After I've helped you data 'port out, I'm going to try my luck with the Tritonians. Join one of their communities. If they'll take me."

"Really?"

I prefer their honesty, Handler said in Tritonese. *Duplicity doesn't suit me.*

You know what? Dev replied. *I don't think that's the worst decision you could make. And if I can help keep ungilled–Tritonian relations sweet from their side rather than ours, so much the better.*

You've found your calling. Good luck with that.

"Meanwhile," Dev added in normal speech, "we'd better scram, before someone starts wondering where Maddox has got to and comes looking for him."

Handler nodded, and they both dived.

Ethel was waiting a kilometre away in her manta sub. Then it would be back to Tangaroa and time to data 'port out to wherever Dev was next assigned to visit.

Somewhere dry, he hoped. He'd had enough of being drenched and sodden to last a lifetime.

68

1000000101001001111010 NINTH EXTRASOLAR Engineers 11
11100101001100010100100110010100011100101001011
  01010111000010101010101111110111100010101011011
11010111110101111011100111111 Leather Hill 110010
10101000101

101001 the war against the digimentalists is not over 1110
00010010111110000111111101111001010 a little closer to
your thousand 1000101001011100110110111000110111
11100101010001101010111111001011 Robinson D in the
Ophiuchus constellation, also known as Triton 111011111
10111111110100101001001010001100

 you make a difference 0010001110111011010001010000001
110001110101010101110000000000011101000101011100
1011 powerful interests 1101011100010100011

"And where the fuck am I now?" were the first words out
of Dev's mouth, even before the ache of the data 'porting
hangover could set in. "If there's so much as a puddle on this
planet, I am out."

The response was crisp laughter. Female laughter.

"You couldn't be anywhere much drier," the woman said.
"PearlTwo."

"PearlTwo?"

"Gas giant. Owned and run by –"

"The Orb Consortium." Dev sat up on the mediplinth. Absently, he touched his neck, checking with his fingertips. No gills. Just the solid, unfissured flesh of a Terratypical neck. No webbing between his fingers, either.

Small mercies.

"That's right. I'm Belinda Tell. Your liaison."

"Of course you are."

She was tall, thin, with a face so chiselled and angular it was almost a polygon.

"This is a holiday resort," Dev said. "I know that much. Playground for the rich and famous, and the wannabe rich and famous. What am I needed here for? We're nowhere *near* the Border Wall. The Plussers can't have a presence. There's got to have been some mistake. Maybe I got diverted somewhere in ultraspace. I've been installed in the wrong host form."

Belinda Tell shrugged. "You are Dev Harmer, is that correct?"

"As far as I can remember. I feel like I've been dozens of different people, dozens of different models, but yes, that's the chassis number."

"Then there hasn't been any mistake. You're where you're scheduled to be."

There was a window. Dev saw clouds – long sunlit streaks of them, in layers both above and below, with a pocket of clear air in between. He detected a faint vibration all around him. He was aboard an airborne vessel, not quite in motion. Hovering. At altitude.

Outside, a man in a wingsuit glided by, fabric stretched taut between his arms and legs, like the wings on a flying squirrel. A third panel between the man's calves acted as an airfoil, providing extra stabilisation.

A half-dozen other wingsuited people arrowed past, all with broad, exhilarated grins curving beneath their eye goggles.

PearlTwo.

A pleasure planet. Adventure and luxury, in one expensive bundle. Safe thrills galore.

Nothing bad happened in a place like this.

Did it?

Acknowledgements

Many thanks to the Facebook brains trust of Marc Francis, Paul Simpson, Jonathan Morgantini and Adam Baker for helping me out with a couple of weapons-tech ideas when I was stumped. On that same score, no thanks at all to Julian Beck, Debbie McMahon, Kit Reed and Stephanie Thorne, who did their best to derail the highly cerebral hive-mind thinking process with frivolous suggestions...

Thanks, too, to Jake Murray for another storming book cover, turning an almost impossible brief into a thing of beauty.

Look out for Book 3, *World Of Air*,
coming soon...

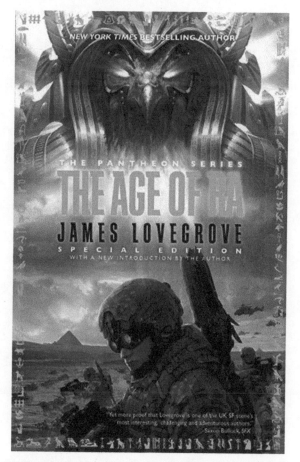

UK ISBN: 978-1-78108-410-6 • US ISBN: 978-1-78108-409-0 • £8.99/$9.99

"However you label it, it's great stuff. Mr. Lovegrove is one of the best writers out there... Highly, highly recommended." The Fantasy Book Critic

The Ancient Egyptian gods have defeated all the other pantheons and claimed dominion over the earth, dividing it into warring factions. Lt. David Westwynter, a British soldier, stumbles into Freegypt, the only place to have remained independent of the gods' influence.

There, he encounters the followers of a humanist leader known as the Lightbringer, who has vowed to rid mankind of the shackles of divine oppression. As the world heads towards an apocalyptic battle, there is far more to this freedom fighter than it seems...

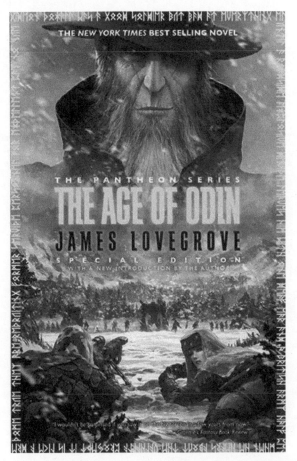

UK ISBN: 978-1-78108-422-9 • US ISBN: 978-1-78108-408-3 • £8.99/$9.99

"Intelligent and provocative, it's yet more proof that Lovegrove is one of the UK SF scene's most interesting, challenging and adventurous authors."
Saxon Bullock, *SFX* on *Age of Ra*

Gideon Coxall was a good soldier but bad at everything else, until a roadside explosive device leaves him with one deaf ear and a British Army half-pension. So when he hears about the Valhalla Project, it's like a dream come true. They're recruiting former service personnel for excellent pay, no questions asked, to take part in unspecified combat operations.

The last thing Gid expects is to find himself fighting alongside ancient Viking gods. The world is in the grip of one of the worst winters it has ever known, and Ragnarök – the fabled final conflict of the Sagas – is looming

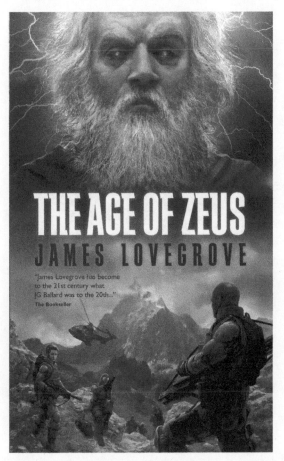

UK ISBN: 978-1-906735-68-5 • US ISBN: 978-1-906735-69-2 • £7.99/$8.99

"This is the kind of complex, action-oriented SF Dan Brown would write if Dan Brown could write." *The Guardian*

The Olympians appeared a decade ago, living incarnations of the Ancient Greek gods on a mission to bring permanent order and stability to the world. Resistance has proved futile, and now humankind is under the jackboot of divine oppression.

Until former London police officer Sam Akehurst receives an invitation too tempting to turn down: the chance to join a small band of guerrilla rebels armed with high-tech weapons and battlesuits.

Calling themselves the Titans, they square off against the Olympians and their ferocious mythological monsters in a war of attrition which some will not survive.

WWW.SOLARISBOOKS.COM

Follow us on Twitter! www.twitter.com/solarisbooks